Phoebe and Her Unicorn

Phoebe and Her Unicorn

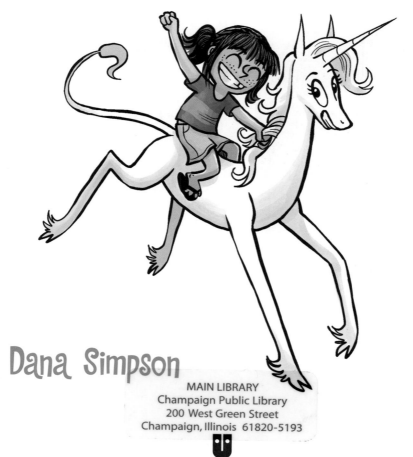

Dana Simpson

Andrews McMeel
PUBLISHING®

INTRODUCTION

I would dearly love to claim at least some connection to the origins of Marigold Heavenly Nostrils, the innocently arrogant unicorn who preens so charmingly through Dana Simpson's delightful comic strip bearing her name. And perhaps I can. Scholarly articles have been written, after all, about the fact that prior to my 1968 novel *The Last Unicorn* there were no female unicorns to be found in any of the world's varied mythologies. And in the early pages of that book I did write "Unicorns are immortal. It is their nature to live alone in one place: usually a forest where there is a pool clear enough for them to see themselves—for they are a little vain, knowing themselves to be the most beautiful creatures in all the world, and magic besides . . ."

A little vain . . . Marigold would be an appalling monster of ego, utterly self-concerned and completely unlikable, if it weren't for her sense of humor and her occasional surprising capacity for compassion—both crucial attributes when bound by a wish granted to a nine-year-old girl in need of a Best Friend to play invented superhero games with, to introduce to slumber parties and girl-talk gossip and to ride through the wind after being called nerd and Princess Stupidbutt one time too many. For Phoebe is a remarkably real little girl, as bright and imaginative as Bill Watterson's Calvin, as touchingly vulnerable as Charles Schulz's Charlie Brown. And if these strike you as big names to conjure with, I'll go further and state for the record that in my opinion *Phoebe and Her Unicorn* is nothing less than the best comic strip to come along since *Calvin and Hobbes*. Simpson is that good, and that original.

Part of the charm of *Phoebe and Her Unicorn* is the way in which Simpson plays her two characters' opposed world views—immortal and contemporary— against each other, along with their egos: for Phoebe's determination to be recognized as Awesome quite matches Marigold's impregnable superiority to the entire human species. Consequently, both delight in sticking the needle in where they can, and on this ground they are equals. There is real affection between them, but it grows by degrees. Simpson takes her time with this, always remaining in full control of her material, including artful cultural references and the gradual development of additional characters and themes.

The temptation is to quote at least every gag and panel, but that would be wrong. Enchantment doesn't retail well at secondhand; like Robert Frost's definition of poetry, it gets lost in translation. I'll simply suggest that you go read *Phoebe and Her Unicorn* in a serious hurry.

Like now!

— Peter S. Beagle
Oakland, California
September 2013

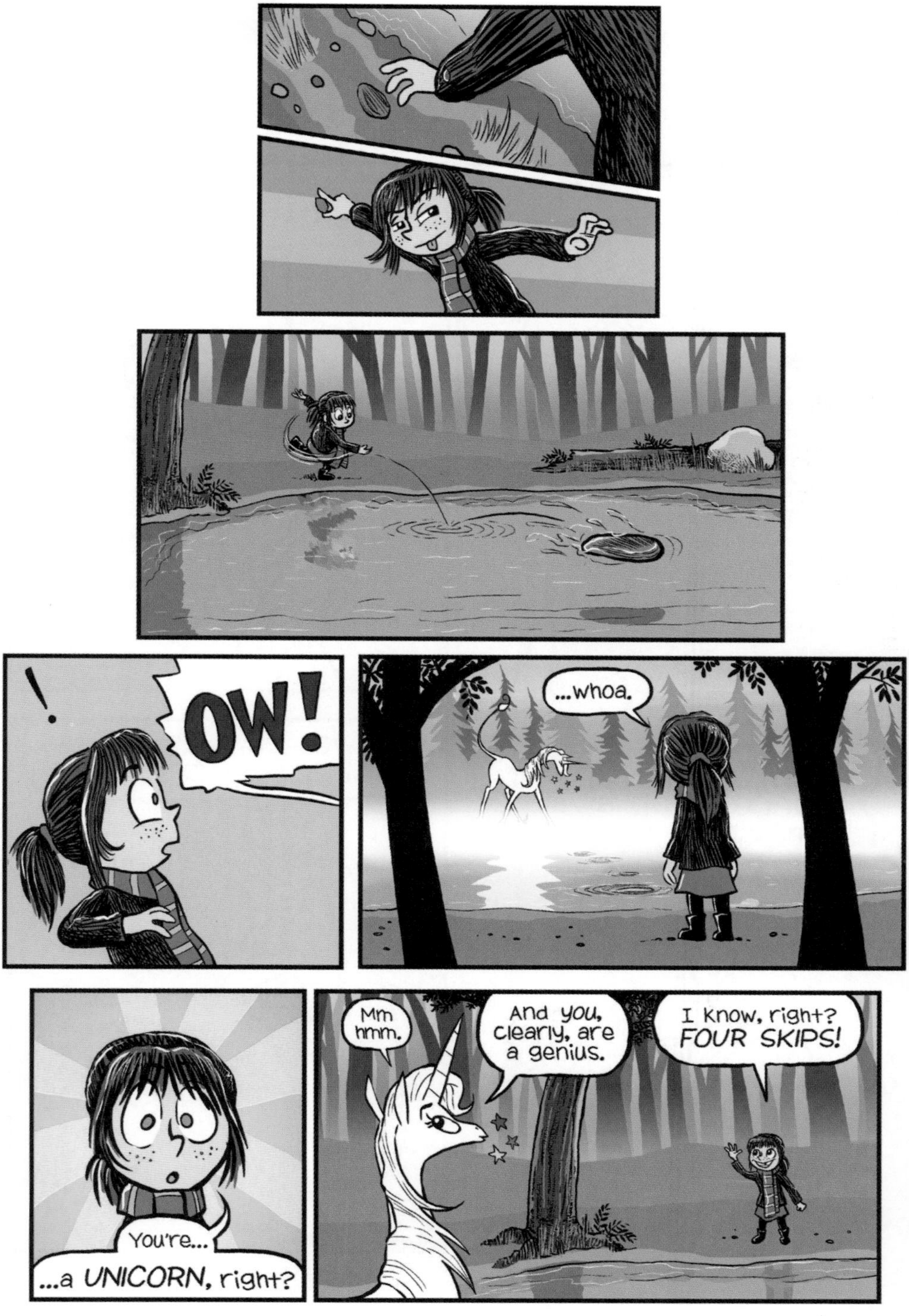
!
OW!
...whoa.
You're...
...a UNICORN, right?
Mm hmm.
And you, clearly, are a genius.
I know, right? FOUR SKIPS!

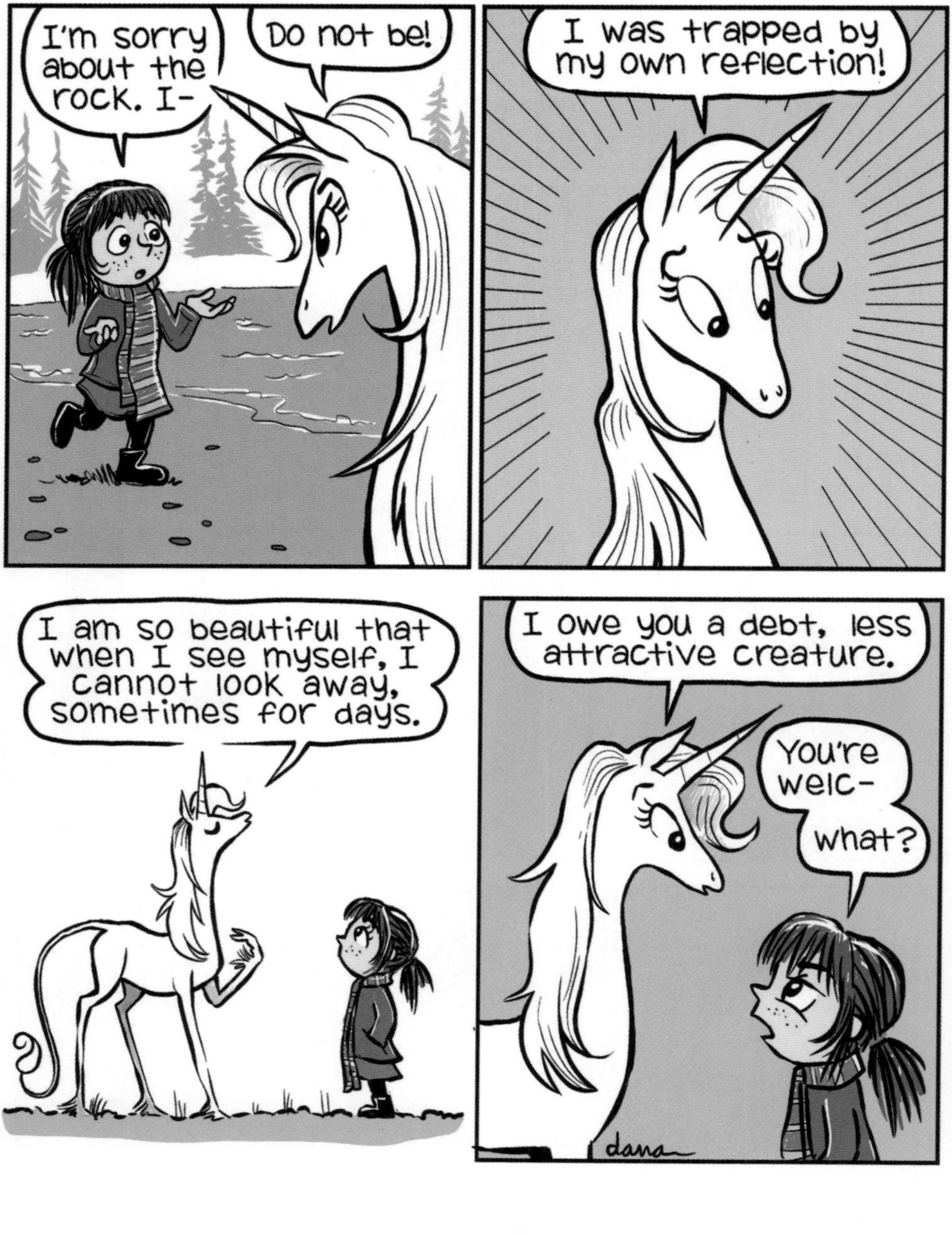

I'm sorry about the rock. I-
Do not be!
I was trapped by my own reflection!
I am so beautiful that when I see myself, I cannot look away, sometimes for days.
I owe you a debt, less attractive creature.
You're welc-
what?
dana

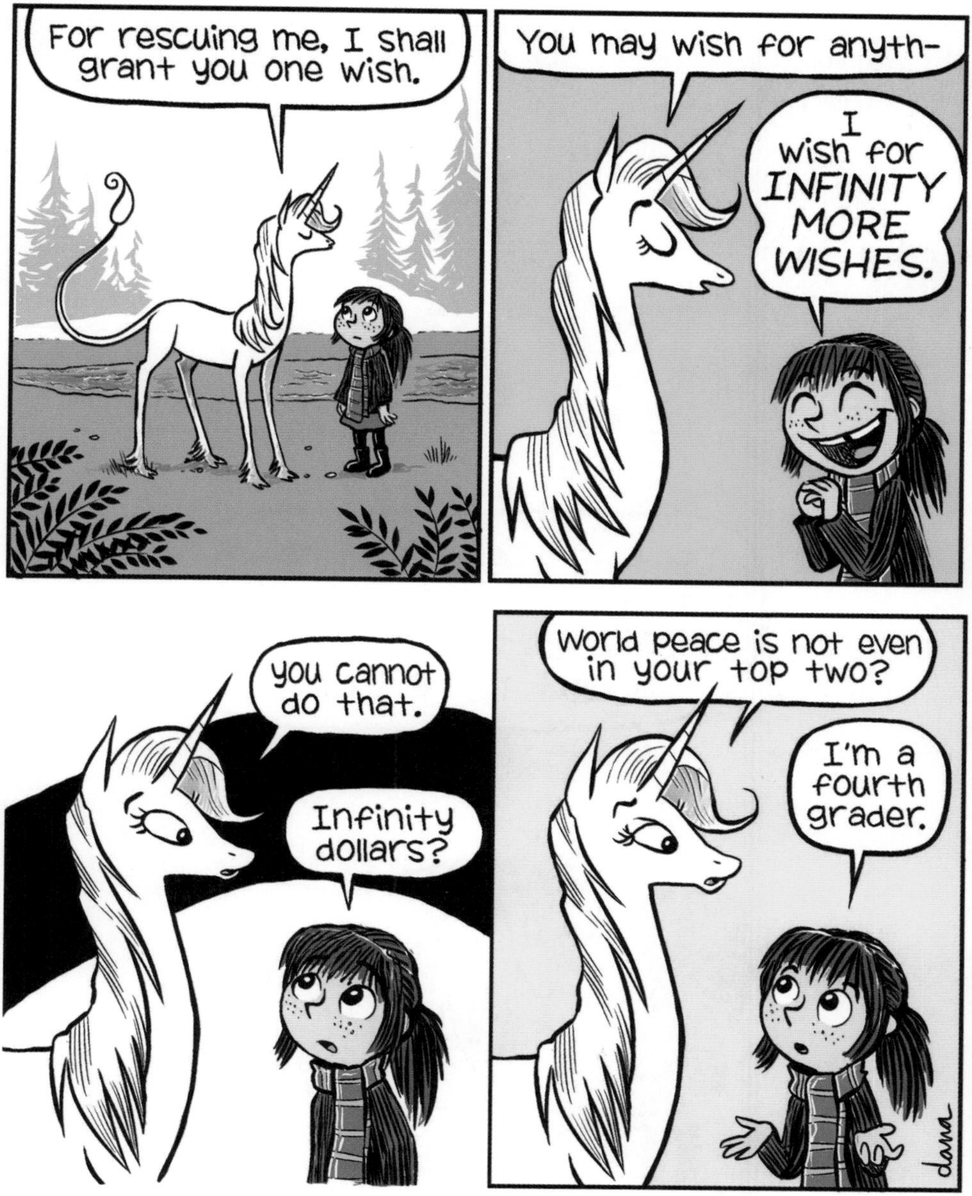
For rescuing me, I shall grant you one wish.
You may wish for anyth-
I wish for INFINITY MORE WISHES.
You cannot do that.
Infinity dollars?
World peace is not even in your top two?
I'm a fourth grader.
dana

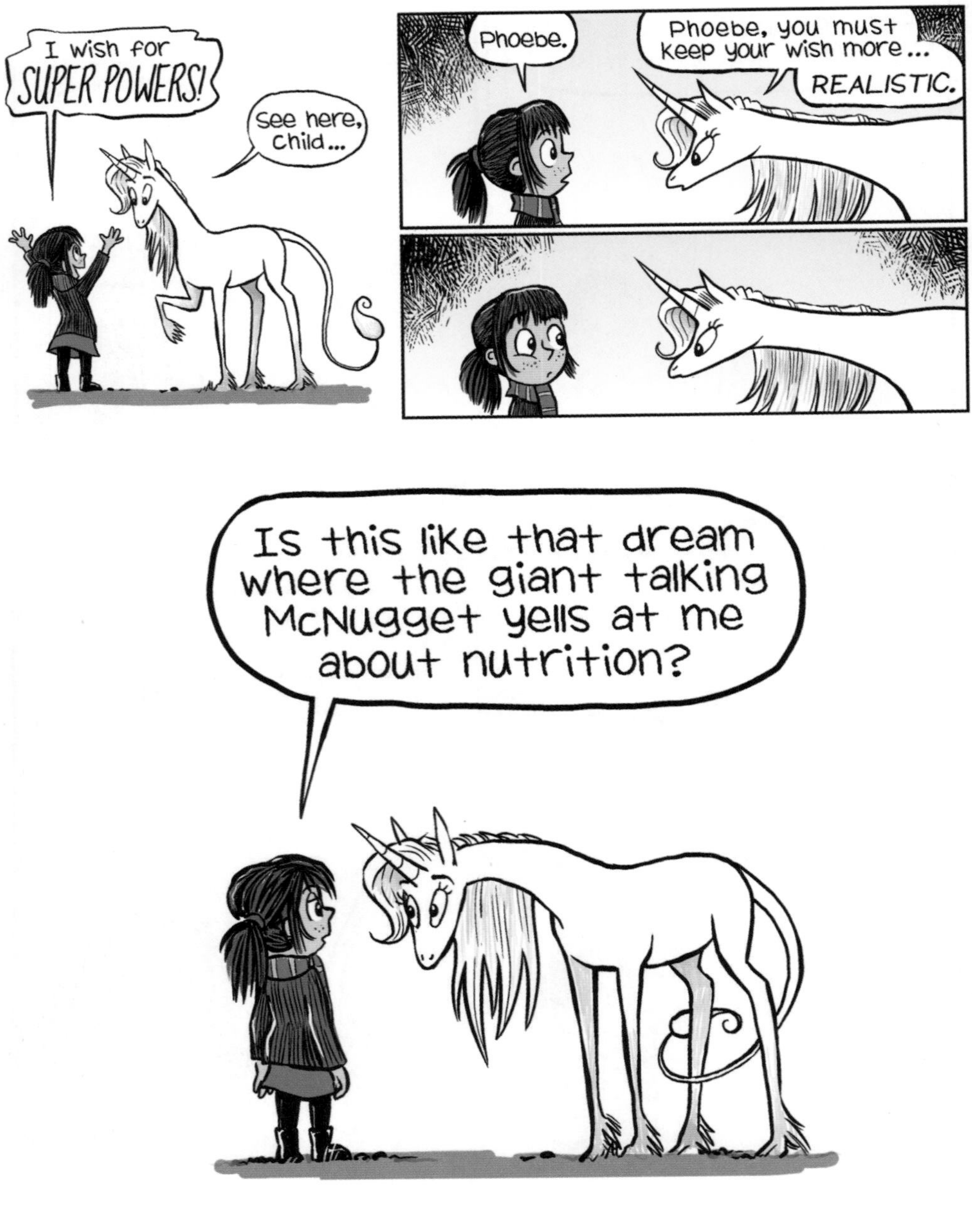
I wish for SUPER POWERS!
See here, child...
Phoebe.
Phoebe, you must keep your wish more... REALISTIC.
Is this like that dream where the giant talking McNugget yells at me about nutrition?

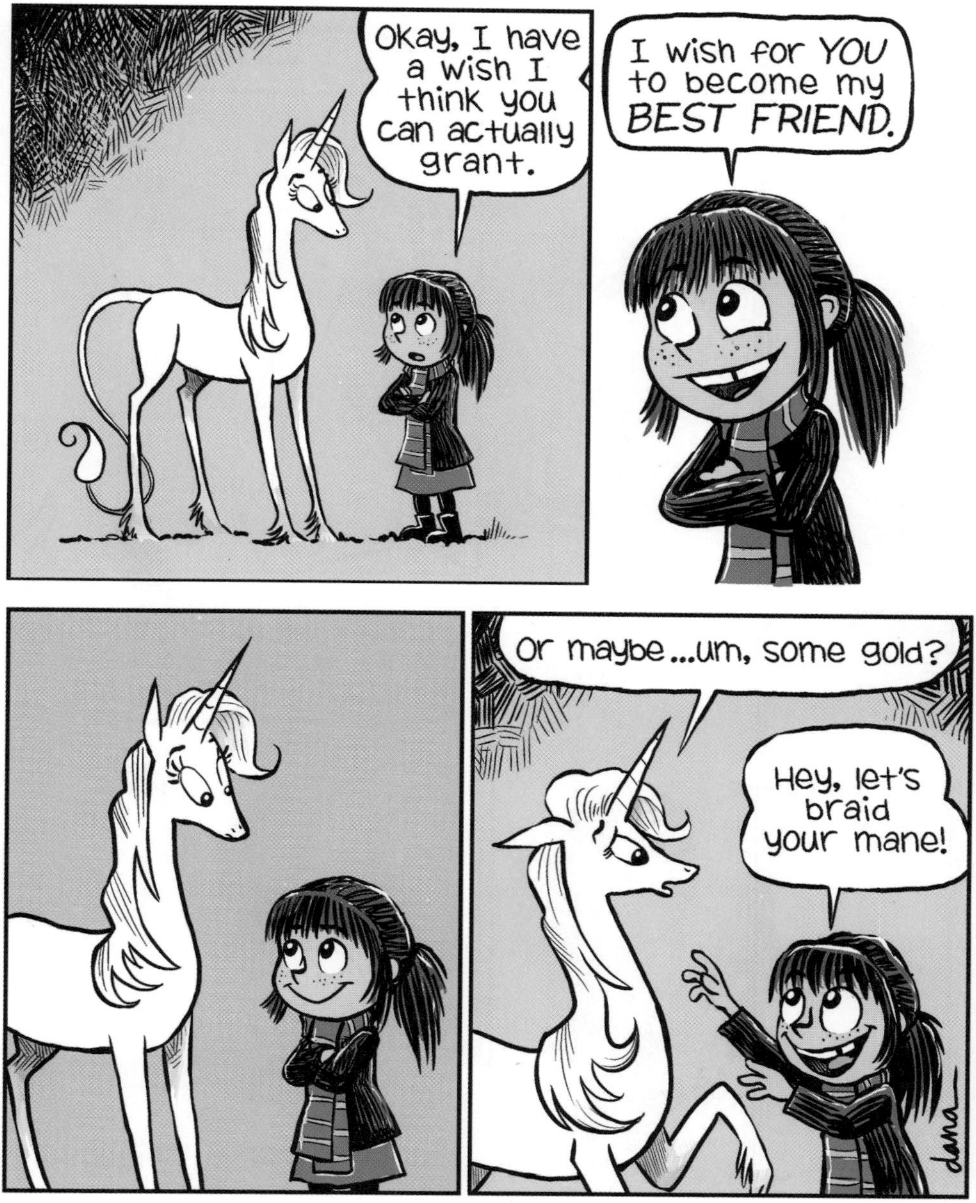
Okay, I have a wish I think you can actually grant.
I wish for YOU to become my BEST FRIEND.
Or maybe...um, some gold?
Hey, let's braid your mane!
dana

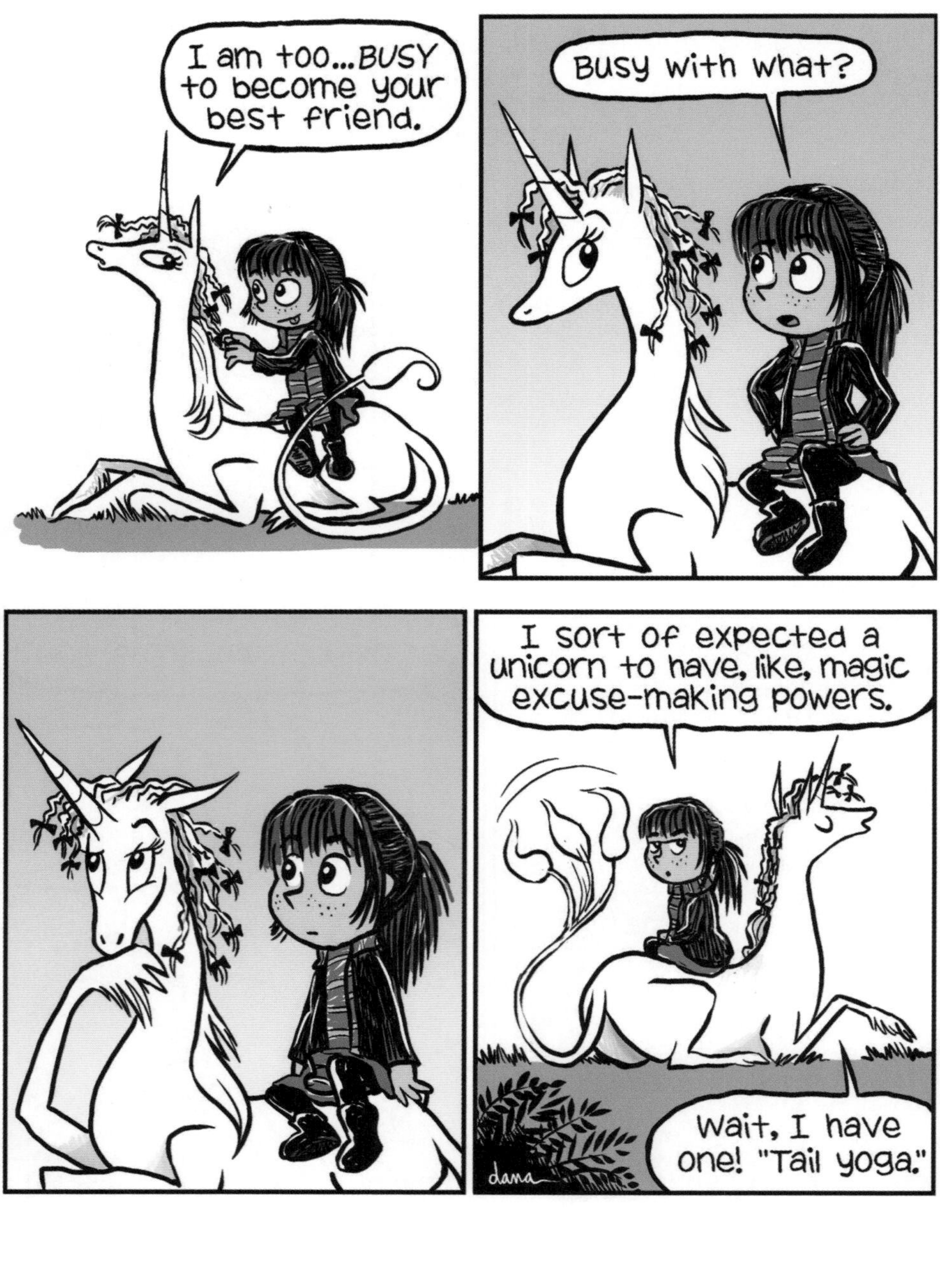
I am too...BUSY to become your best friend.
Busy with what?
I sort of expected a unicorn to have, like, magic excuse-making powers.
Wait, I have one! "Tail yoga."
dana

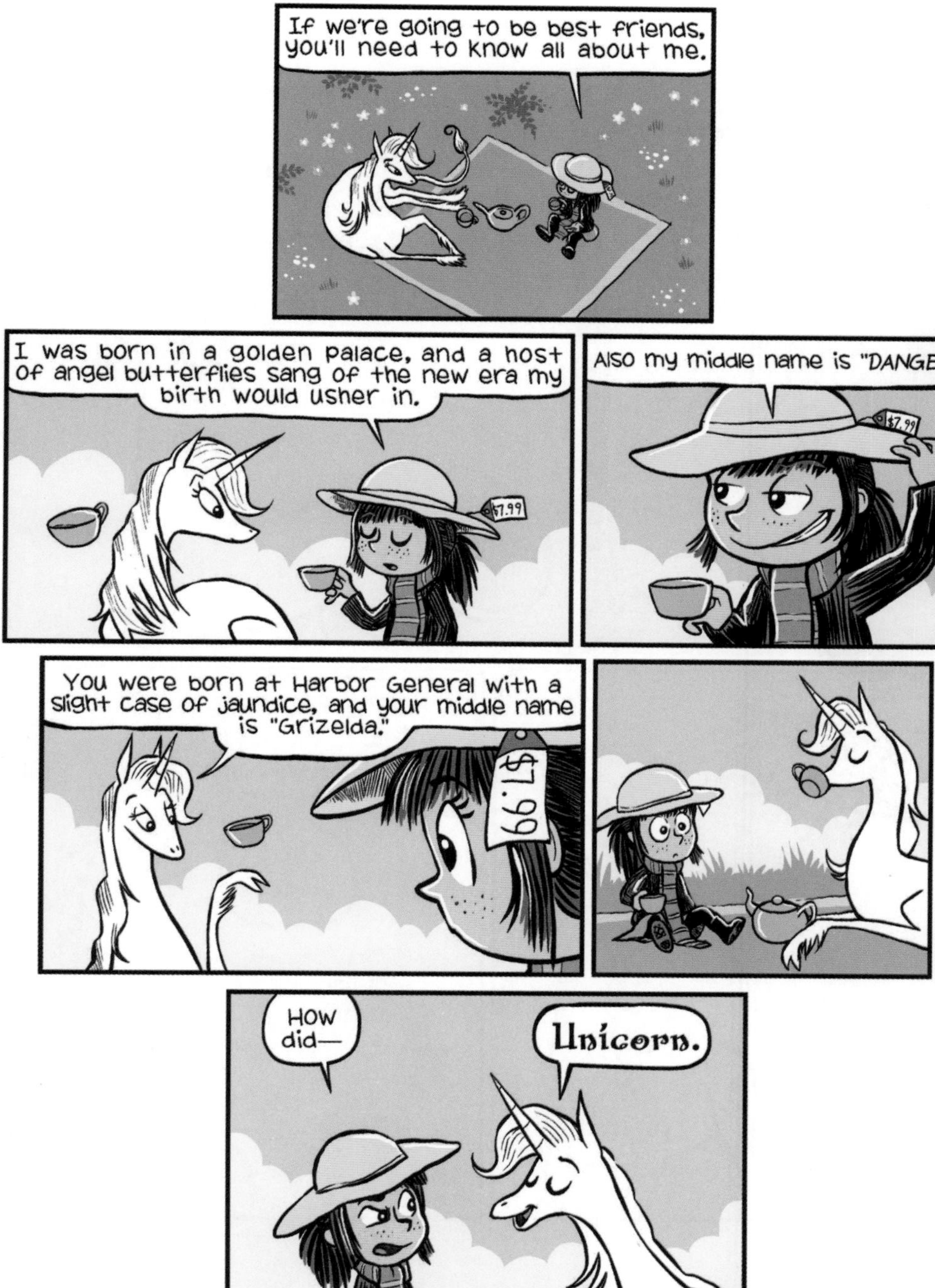
If we're going to be best friends, you'll need to know all about me.
I was born in a golden palace, and a host of angel butterflies sang of the new era my birth would usher in.
$7.99
Also my middle name is "DANGER."
$7.99
You were born at Harbor General with a slight case of jaundice, and your middle name is "Grizelda."
$7.99
HOW did—
Unicorn.

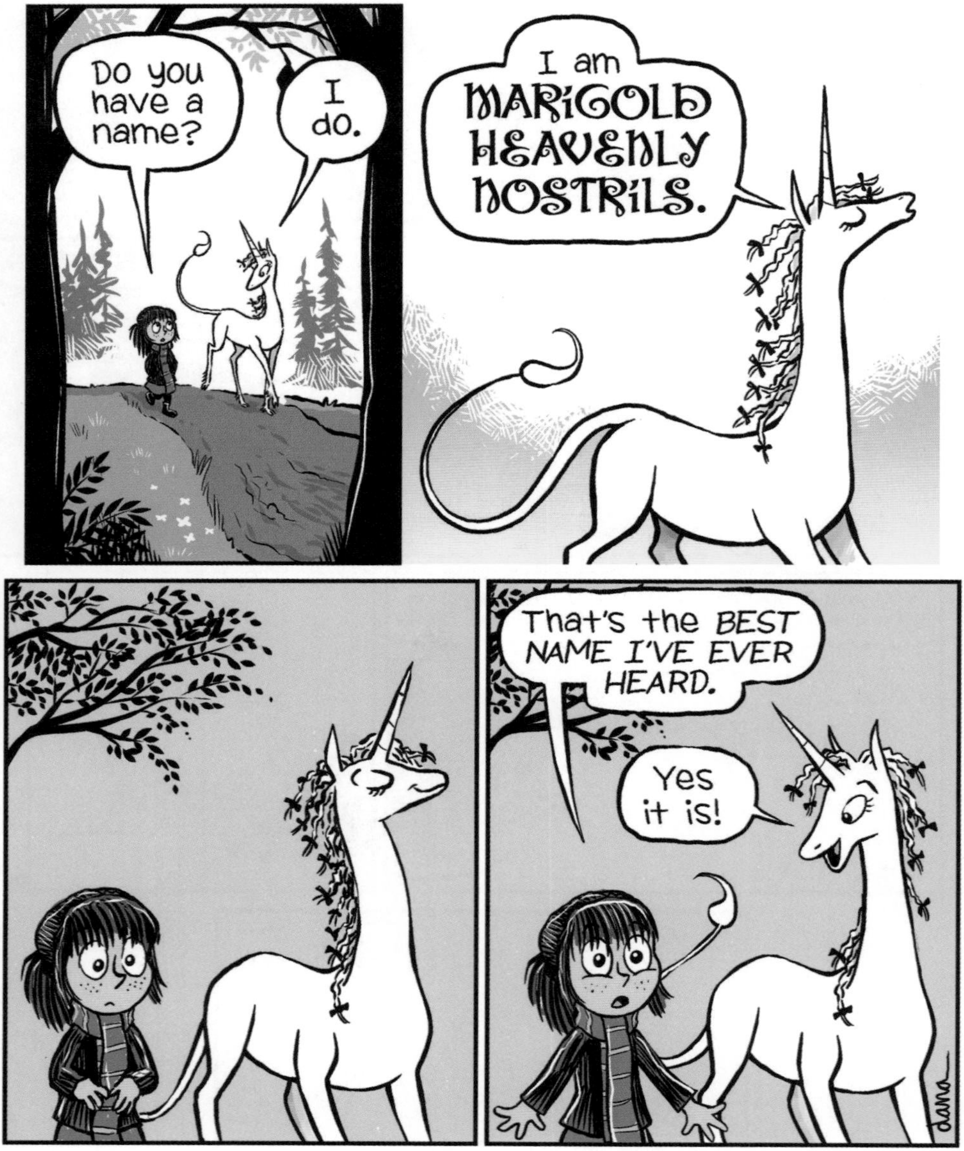
Do you have a name?
I do.
I am MARIGOLD HEAVENLY NOSTRILS.
That's the *BEST NAME I'VE EVER HEARD.*
Yes it is!
dana

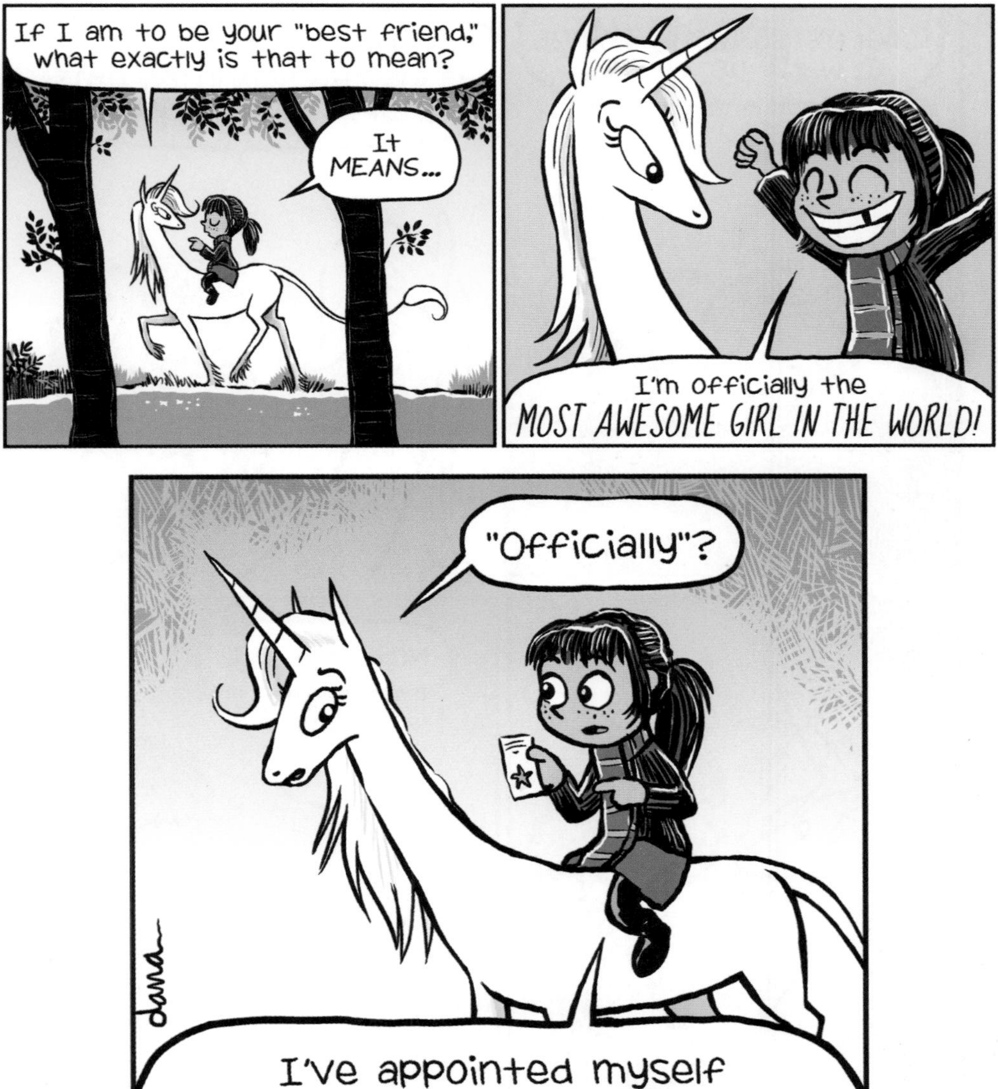
If I am to be your "best friend," what exactly is that to mean?
It MEANS...
I'm officially the MOST AWESOME GIRL IN THE WORLD!
"Officially"?
I've appointed myself Federal Awesomeness Inspector.
dana

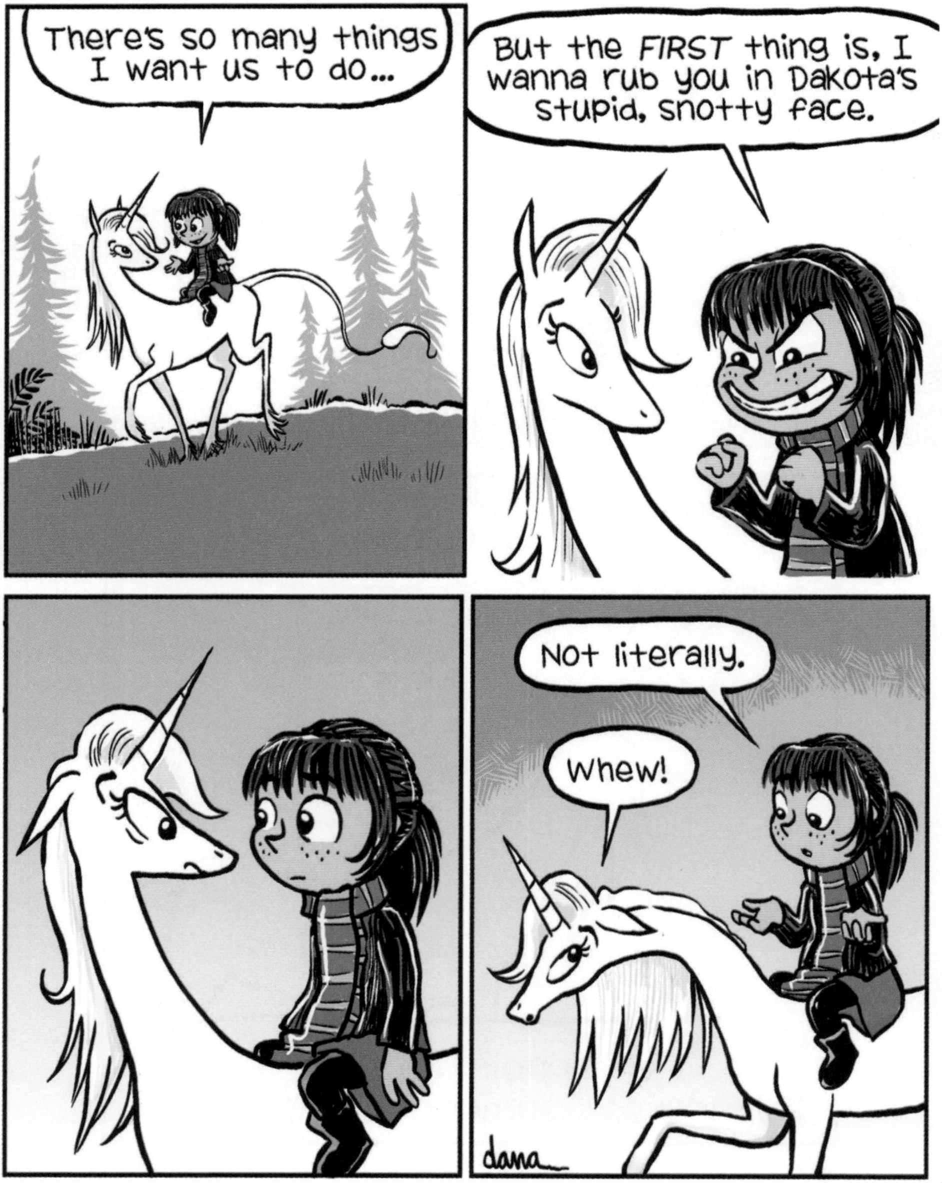
There's so many things I want us to do...
But the FIRST thing is, I wanna rub you in Dakota's stupid, snotty face.
Not literally.
Whew!
dana

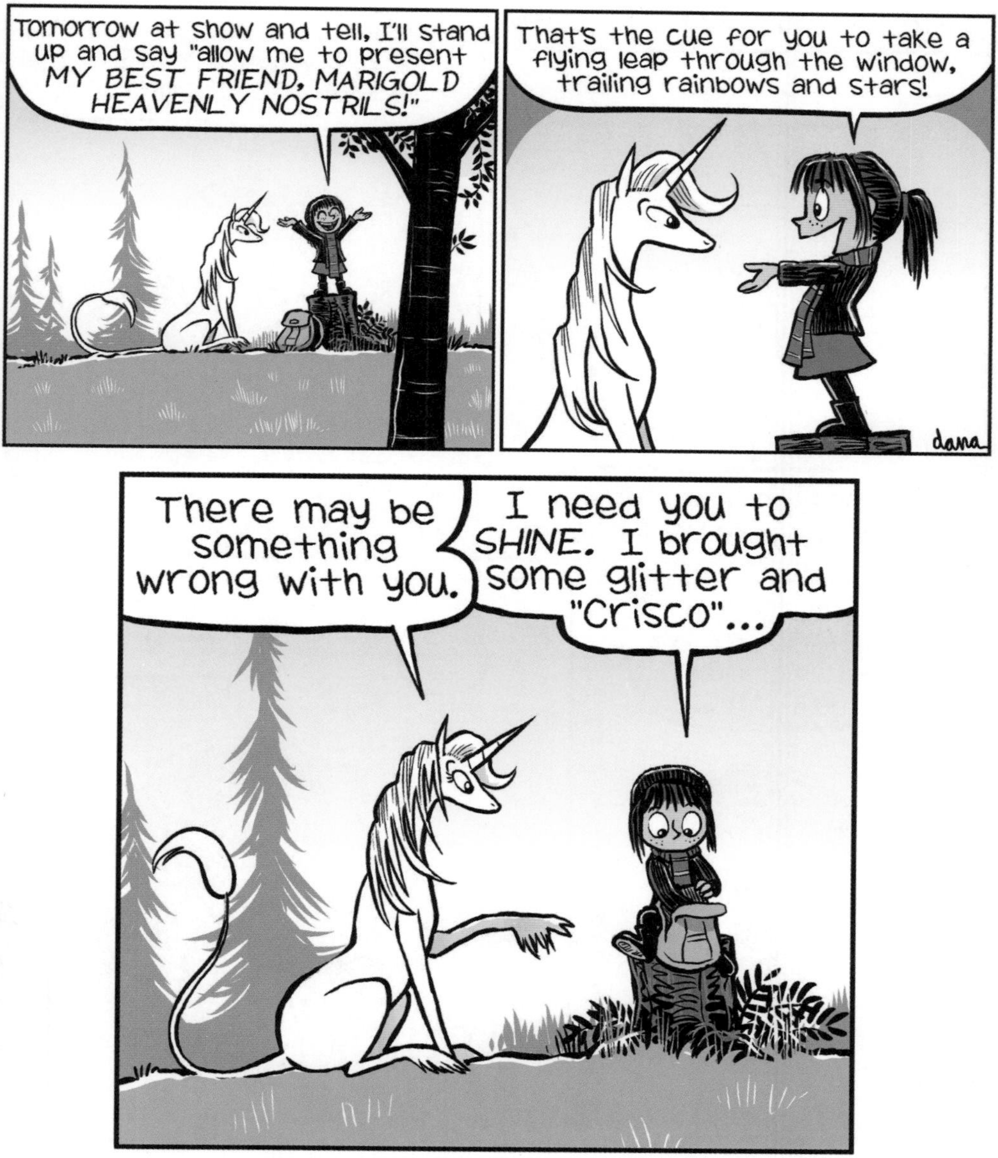
Tomorrow at show and tell, I'll stand up and say "allow me to present MY BEST FRIEND, MARIGOLD HEAVENLY NOSTRILS!"
That's the cue for you to take a flying leap through the window, trailing rainbows and stars!
dana
There may be something wrong with you.
I need you to SHINE. I brought some glitter and "Crisco"...

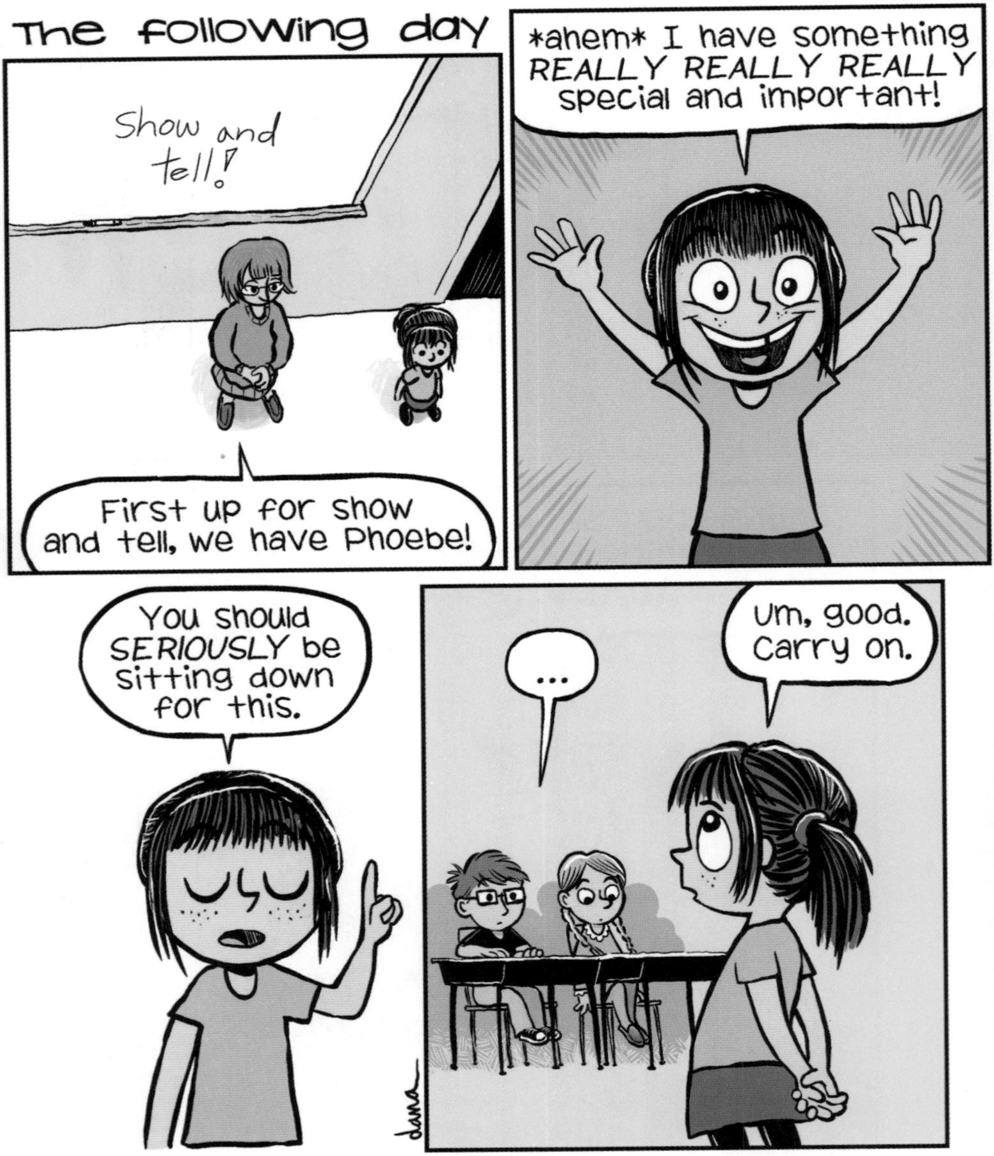
The following day
Show and tell!
First up for show and tell, we have Phoebe!
ahem I have something REALLY REALLY REALLY special and important!
You should SERIOUSLY be sitting down for this.
...
Um, good. Carry on.
dana

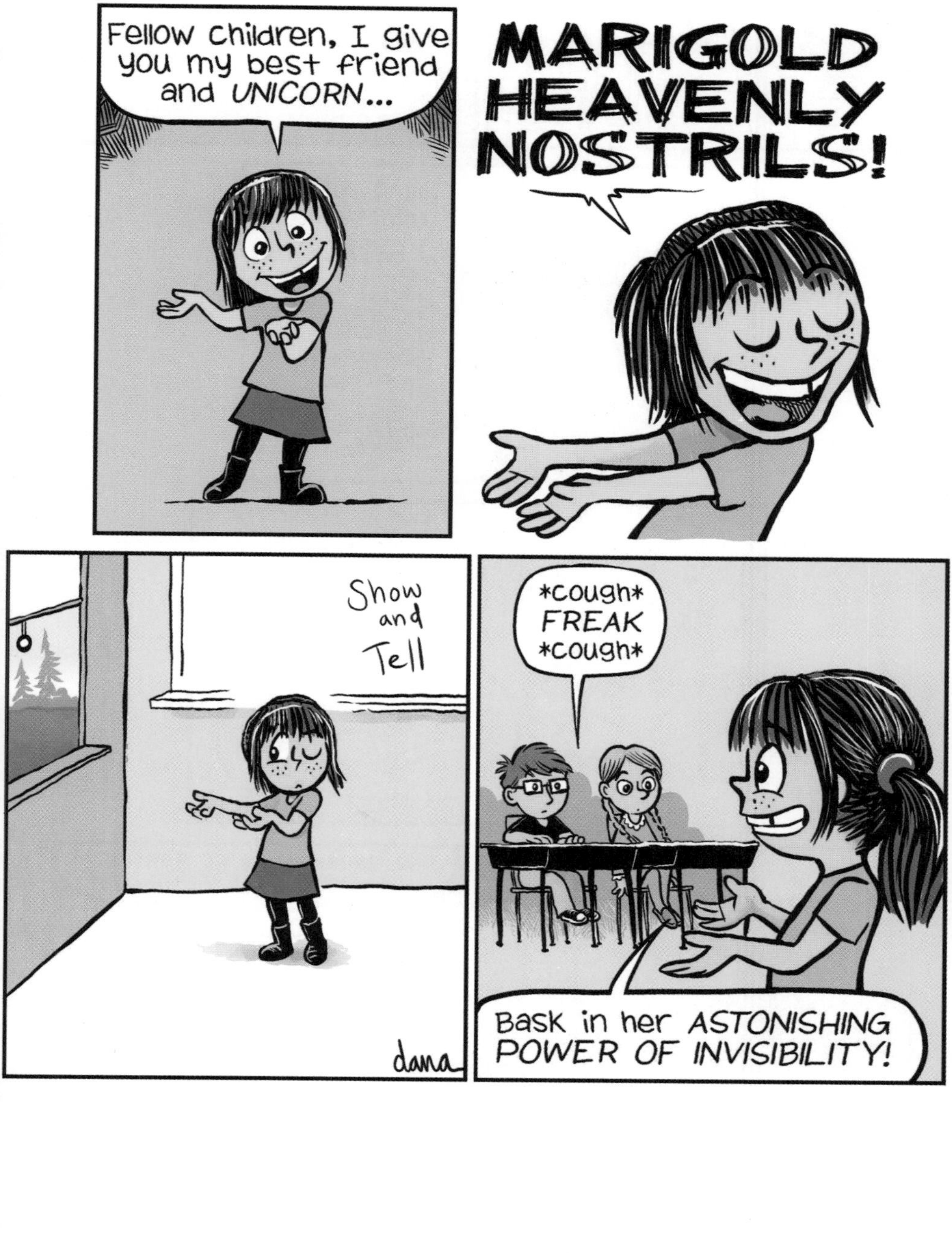
Fellow children, I give you my best friend and UNICORN...
MARIGOLD HEAVENLY NOSTRILS!
Show and Tell
cough FREAK *cough*
Bask in her ASTONISHING POWER OF INVISIBILITY!
dana

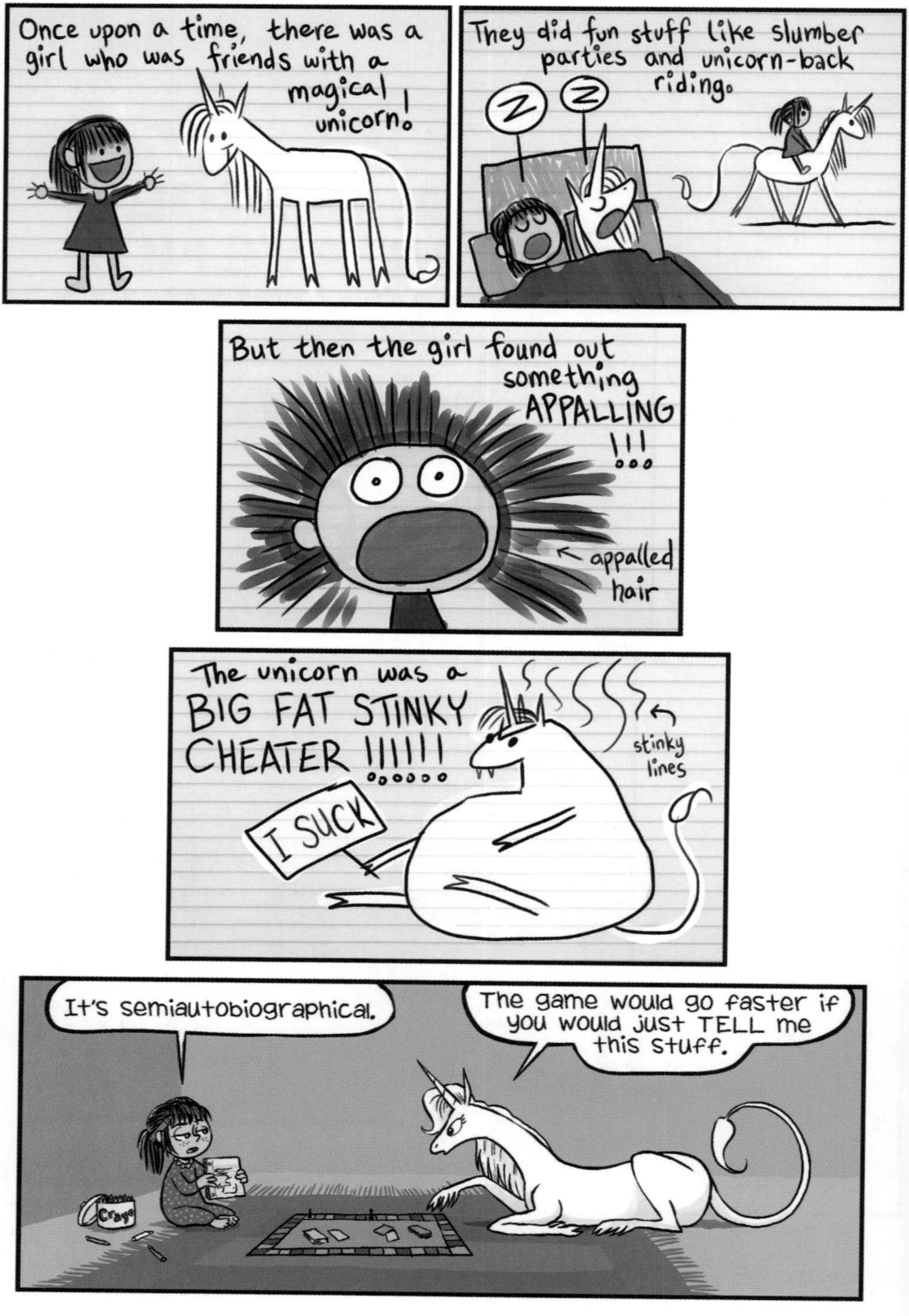
Once upon a time, there was a girl who was friends with a magical unicorn!
They did fun stuff like slumber parties and unicorn-back riding.
Z
Z
But then the girl found out something APPALLING !!!
appalled hair
The unicorn was a BIG FAT STINKY CHEATER !!!!!!
stinky lines
I SUCK
It's semiautobiographical.
The game would go faster if you would just TELL me this stuff.

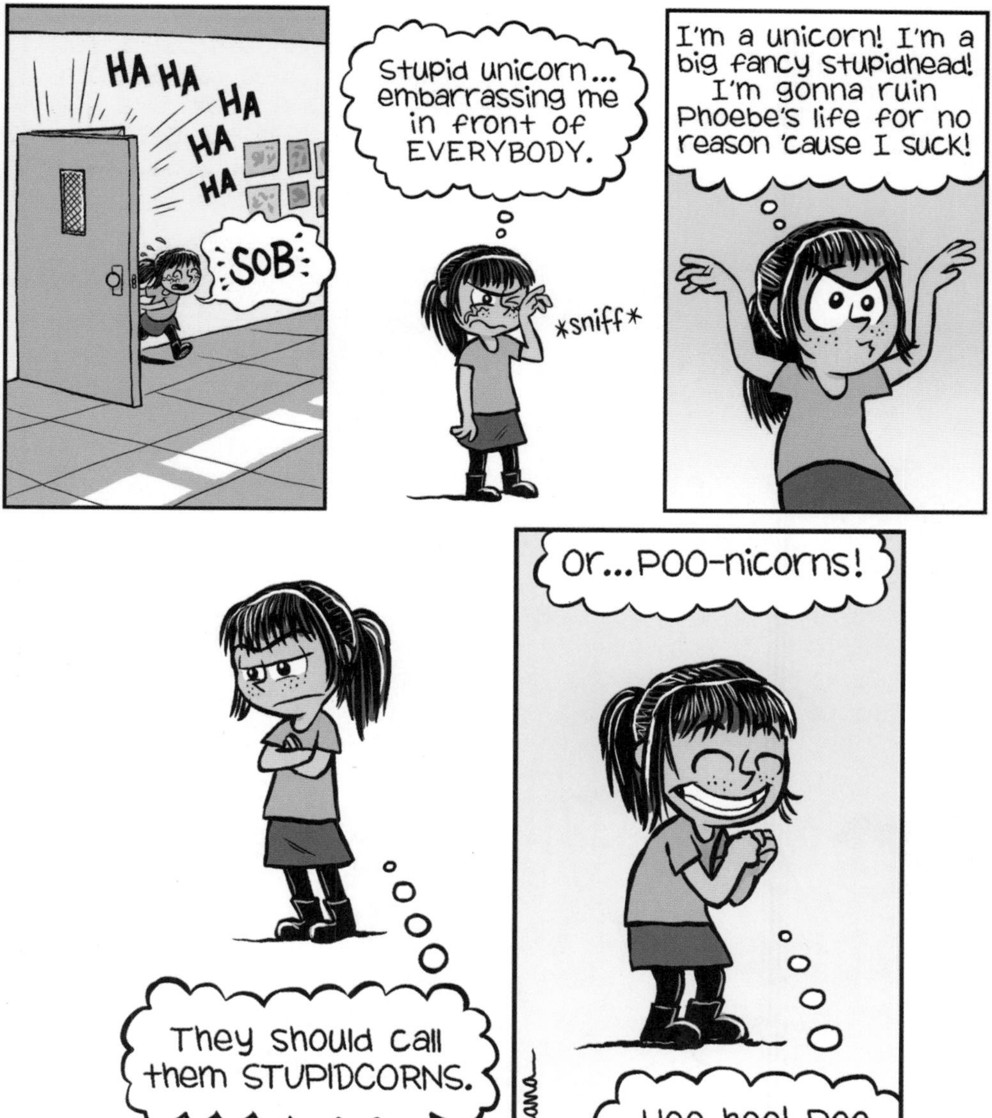
HA HA HA HA HA
SOB
Stupid unicorn... embarrassing me in front of EVERYBODY.
sniff
I'm a unicorn! I'm a big fancy stupidhead! I'm gonna ruin Phoebe's life for no reason 'cause I suck!
They should call them STUPIDCORNS.
Or...POO-nicorns!
Hee hee! Poo.
dana

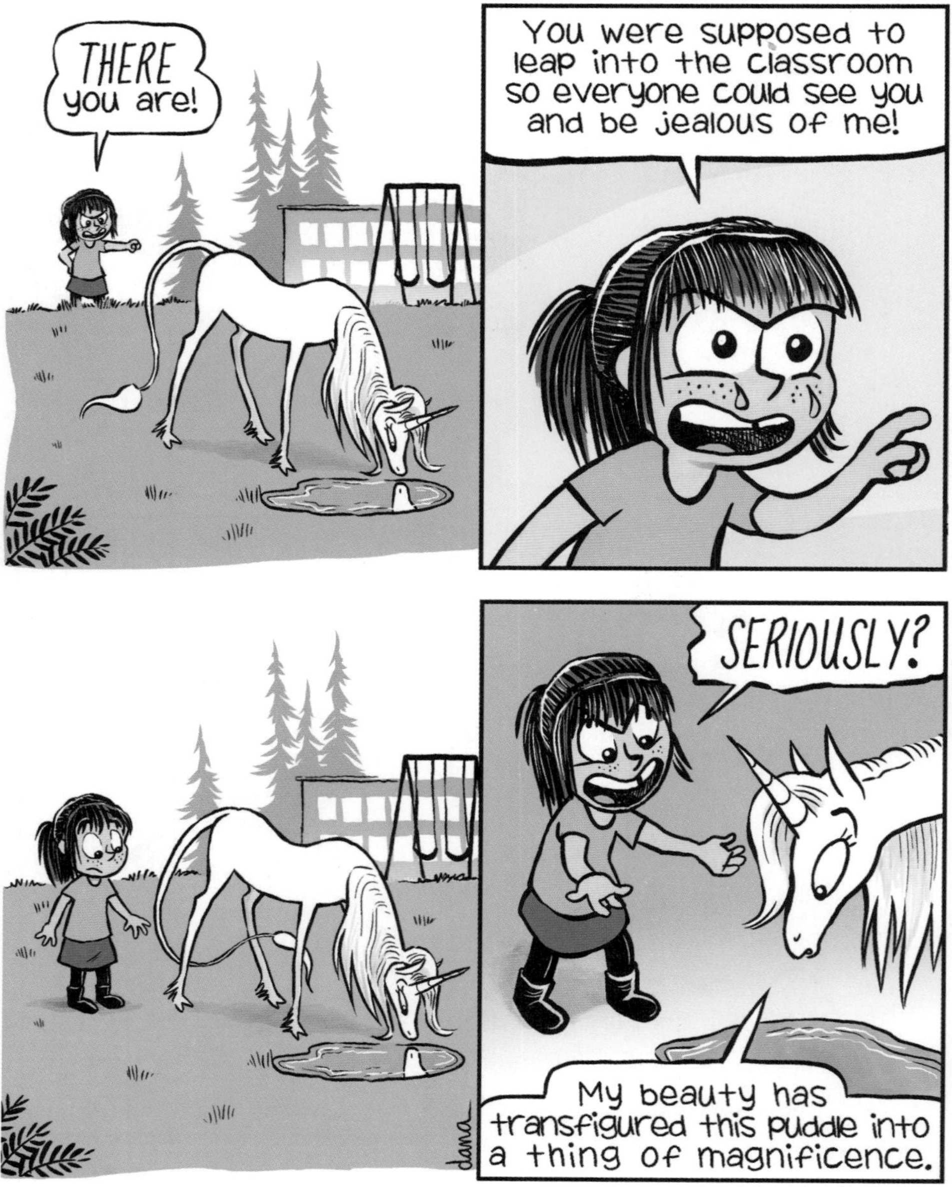
THERE you are!
You were supposed to leap into the classroom so everyone could see you and be jealous of me!
SERIOUSLY?
My beauty has transfigured this puddle into a thing of magnificence.
dana

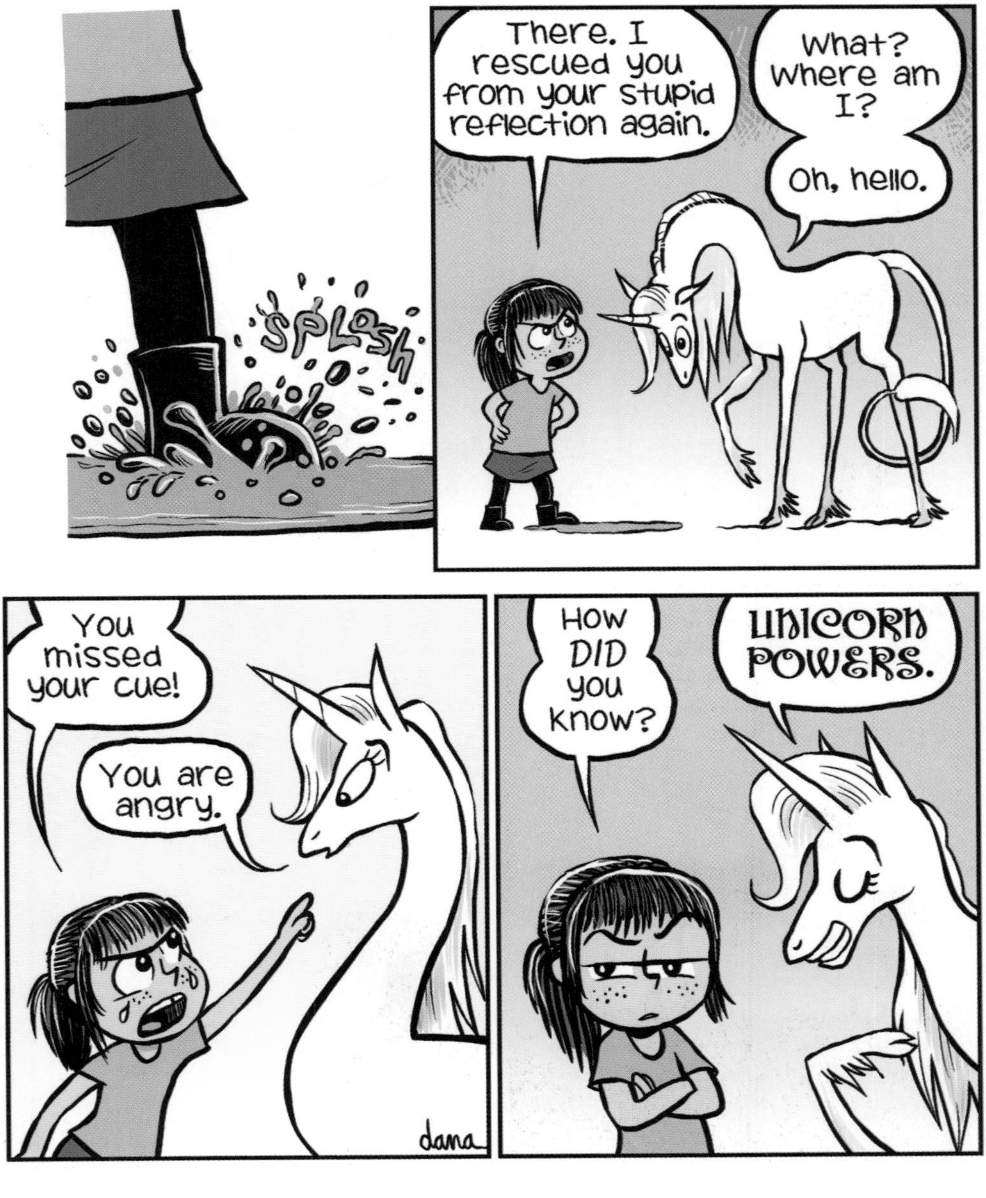
SPLASH
There. I rescued you from your stupid reflection again.
What? Where am I?
Oh, hello.
You missed your cue!
You are angry.
How DID you know?
UNICORN POWERS.
dana

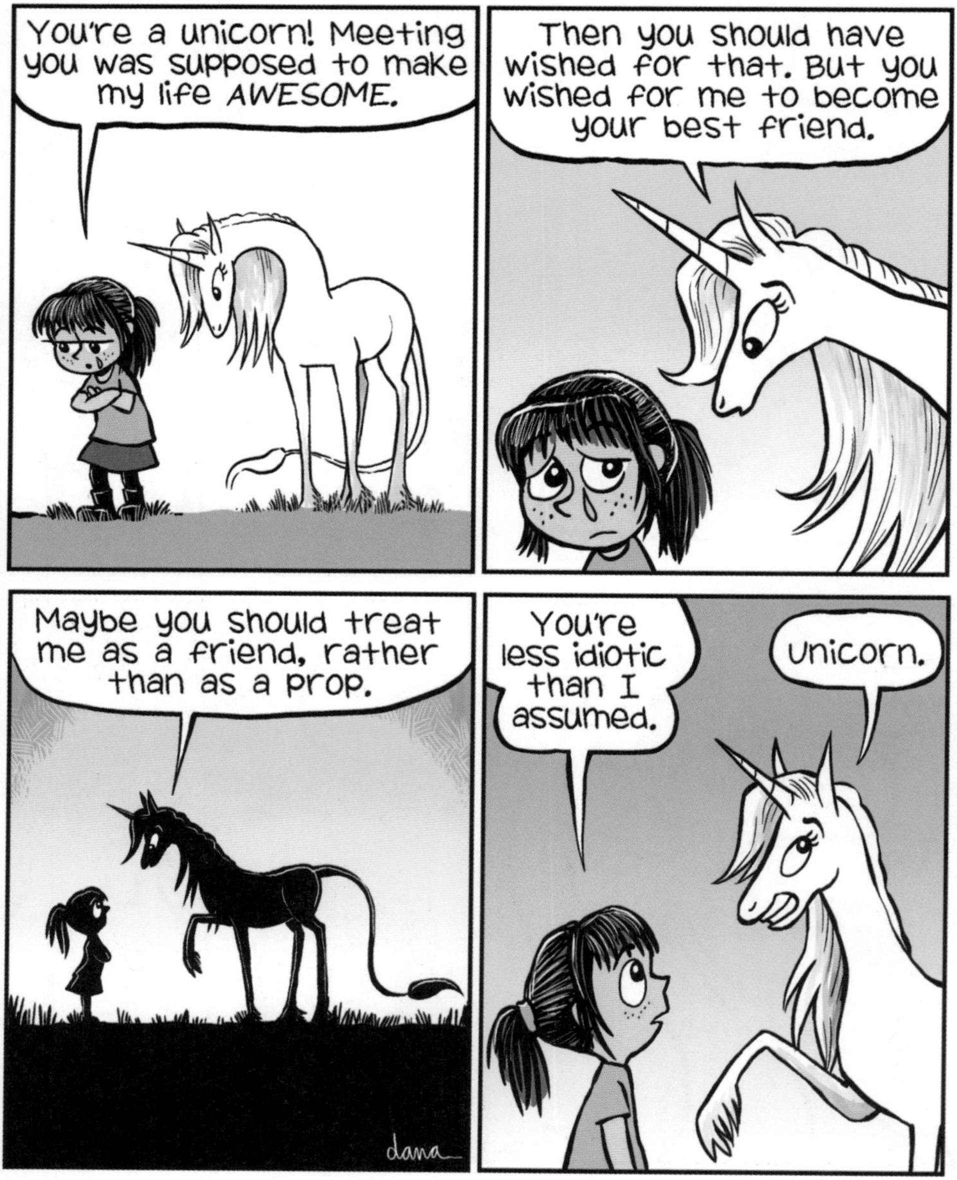
You're a unicorn! Meeting you was supposed to make my life AWESOME.
Then you should have wished for that. But you wished for me to become your best friend.
Maybe you should treat me as a friend, rather than as a prop.
dana
You're less idiotic than I assumed.
Unicorn.

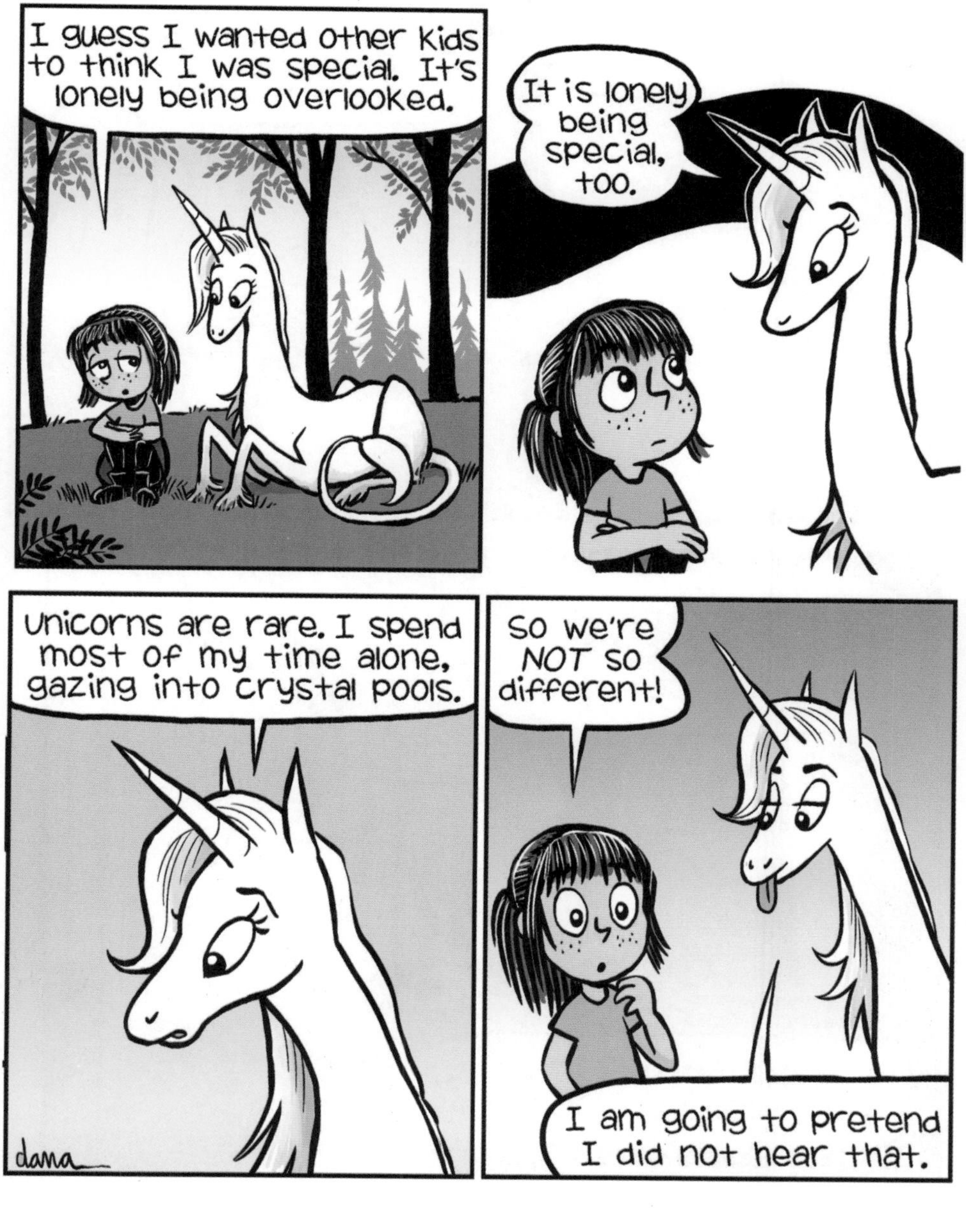
I guess I wanted other kids to think I was special. It's lonely being overlooked.
It is lonely being special, too.
Unicorns are rare. I spend most of my time alone, gazing into crystal pools.
So we're *NOT* so different!
I am going to pretend I did not hear that.
dana

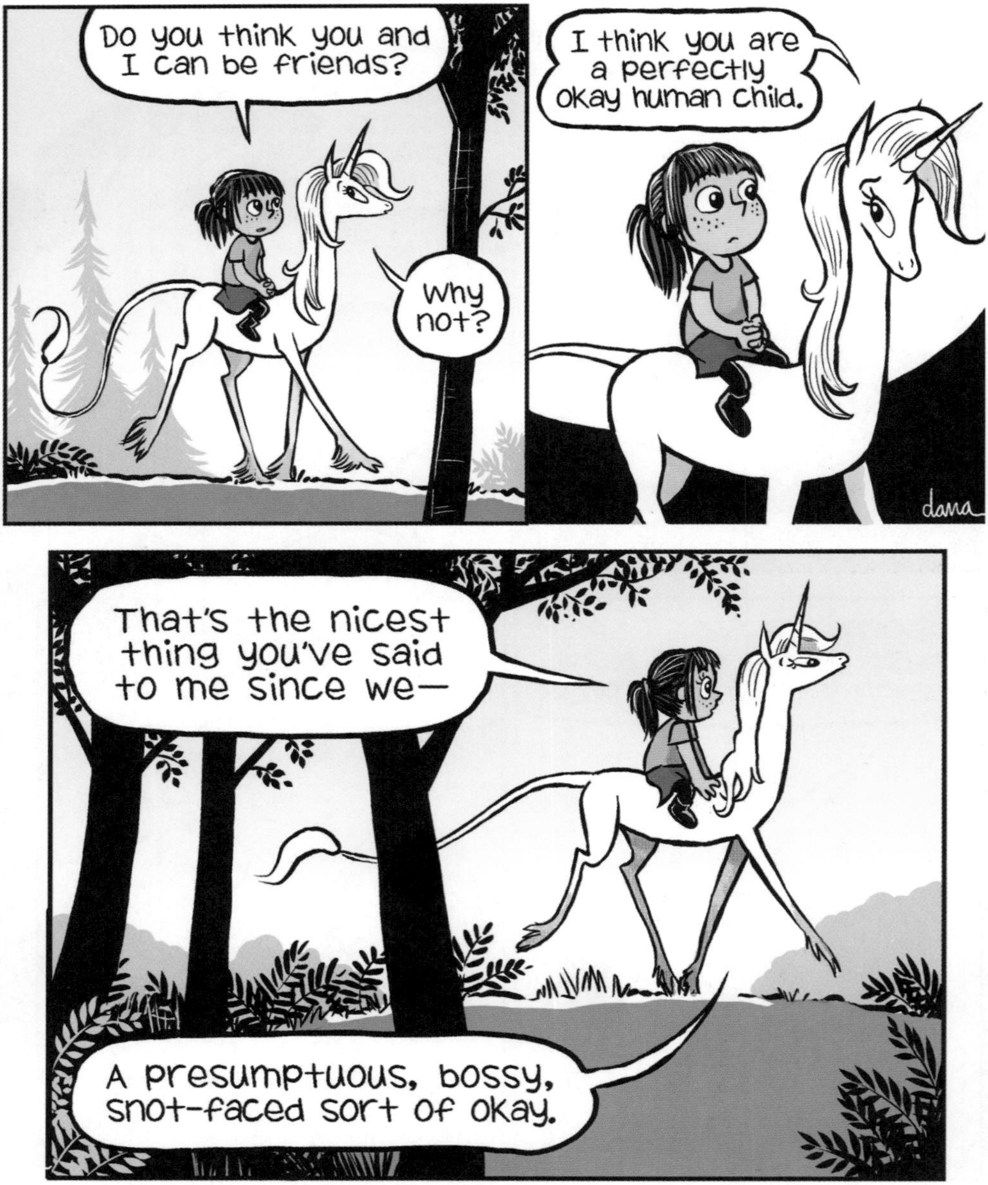
Do you think you and I can be friends?
Why not?
I think you are a perfectly okay human child.
dana
That's the nicest thing you've said to me since we—
A presumptuous, bossy, snot-faced sort of okay.

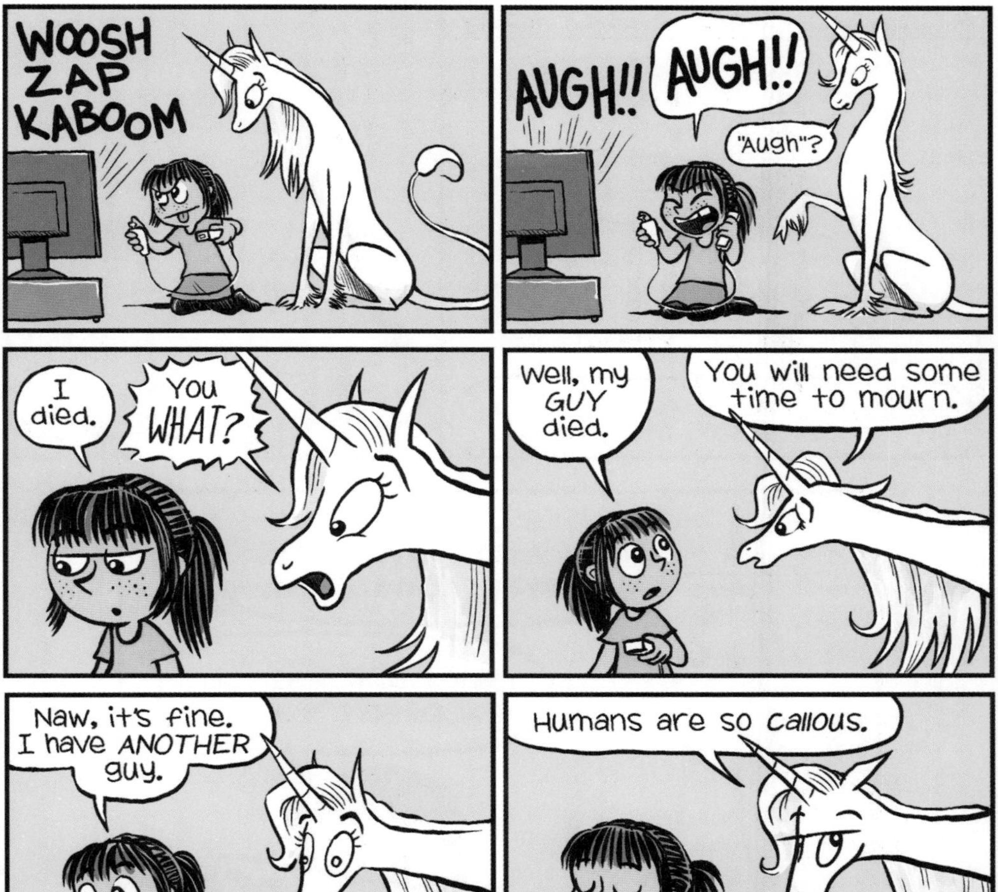
WOOSH
ZAP
KABOOM
AUGH!!
AUGH!!
"Augh"?
I died.
You WHAT?
Well, my GUY died.
You will need some time to mourn.
Naw, it's fine. I have ANOTHER guy.
Humans are so callous.
He knew the risks.

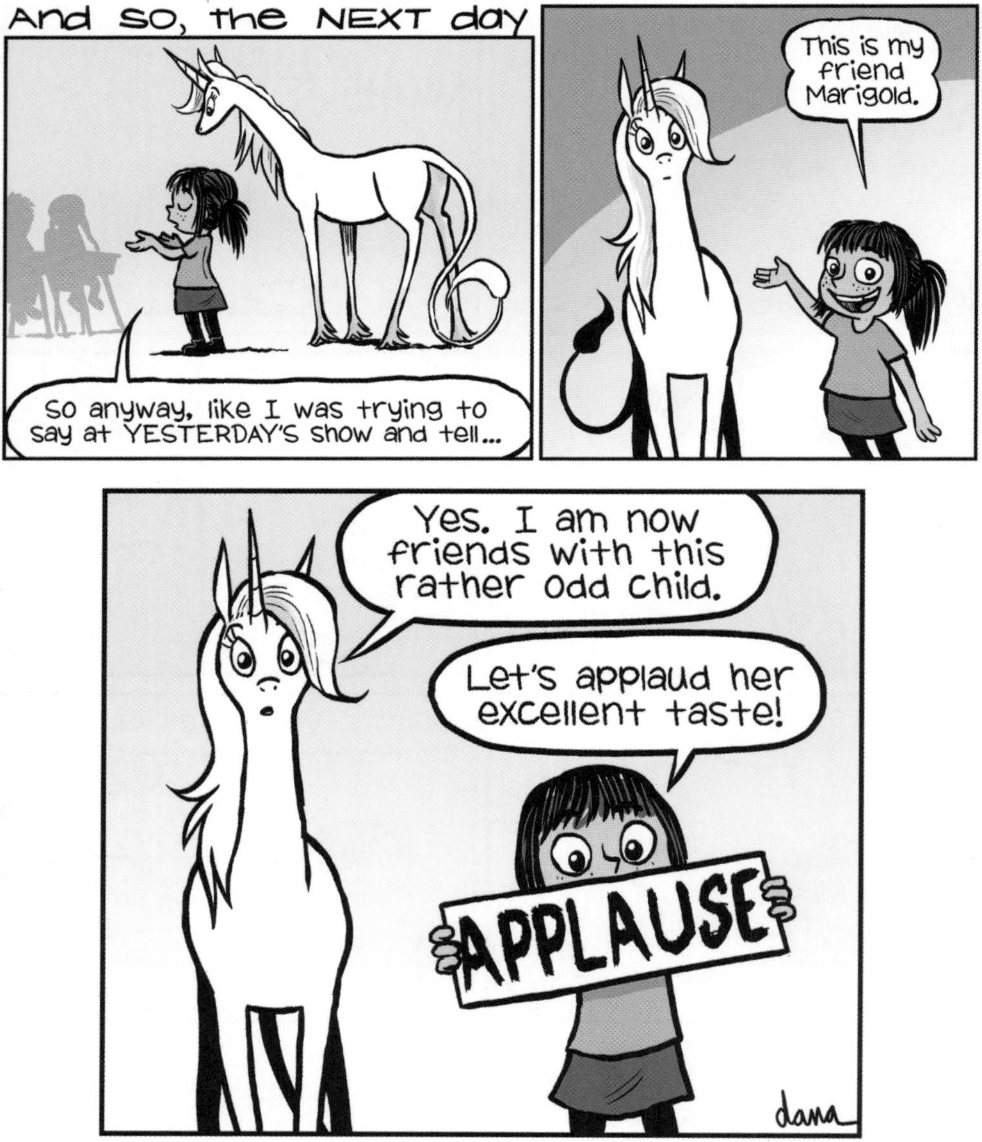
And so, the NEXT day
So anyway, like I was trying to say at YESTERDAY'S show and tell...
This is my friend Marigold.
Yes. I am now friends with this rather odd child.
Let's applaud her excellent taste!
APPLAUSE
dana

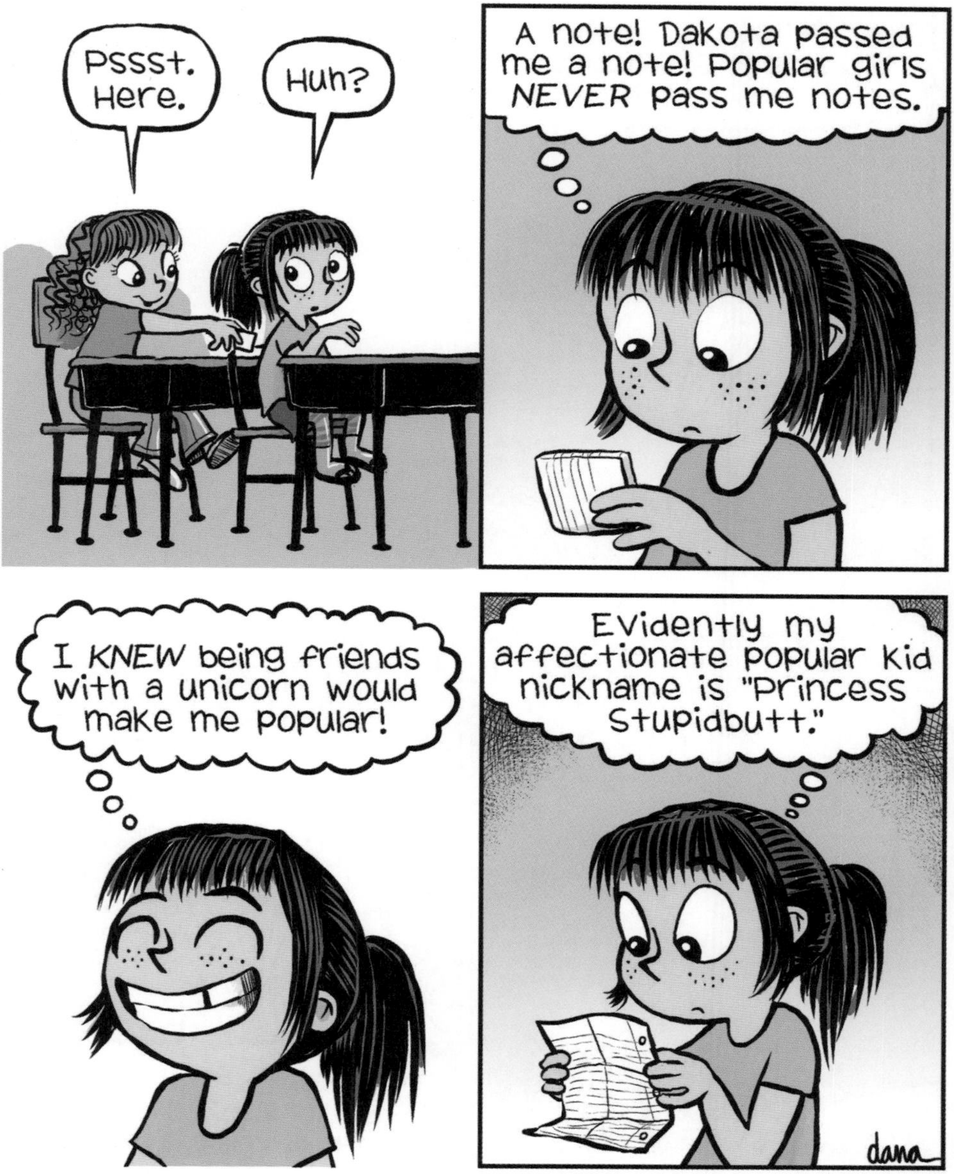
Pssst. Here.
Huh?
A note! Dakota passed me a note! Popular girls *NEVER* pass me notes.
I *KNEW* being friends with a unicorn would make me popular!
Evidently my affectionate popular kid nickname is "Princess Stupidbutt."
dana

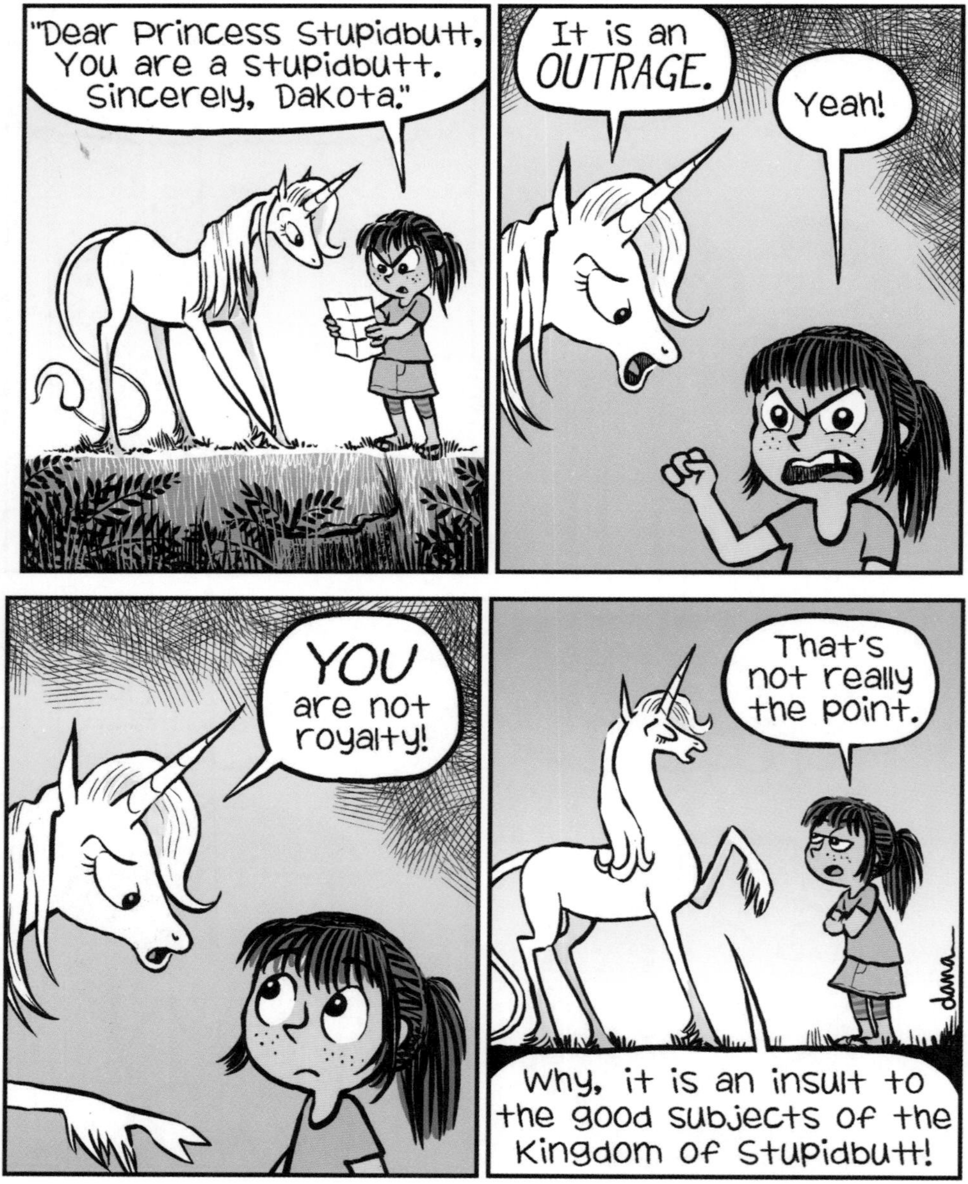
"Dear Princess Stupidbutt, You are a stupidbutt. Sincerely, Dakota."
It is an *OUTRAGE*.
Yeah!
YOU are not royalty!
That's not really the point.
Why, it is an insult to the good subjects of the Kingdom of Stupidbutt!
dana

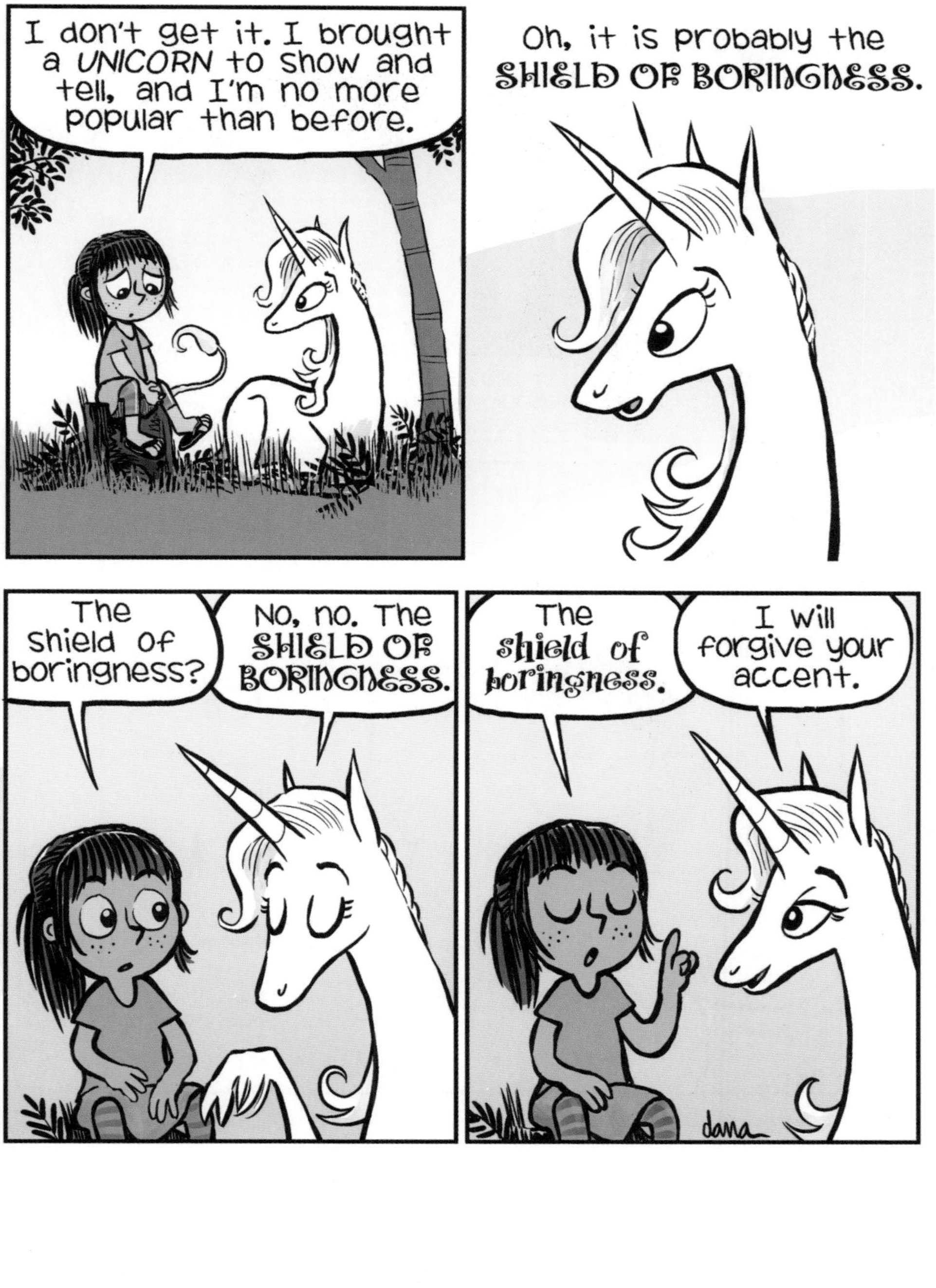
I don't get it. I brought a UNICORN to show and tell, and I'm no more popular than before.
Oh, it is probably the SHIELD OF BORINGNESS.
The shield of boringness?
No, no. The SHIELD OF BORINGNESS.
The shield of boringness.
I will forgive your accent.
dana

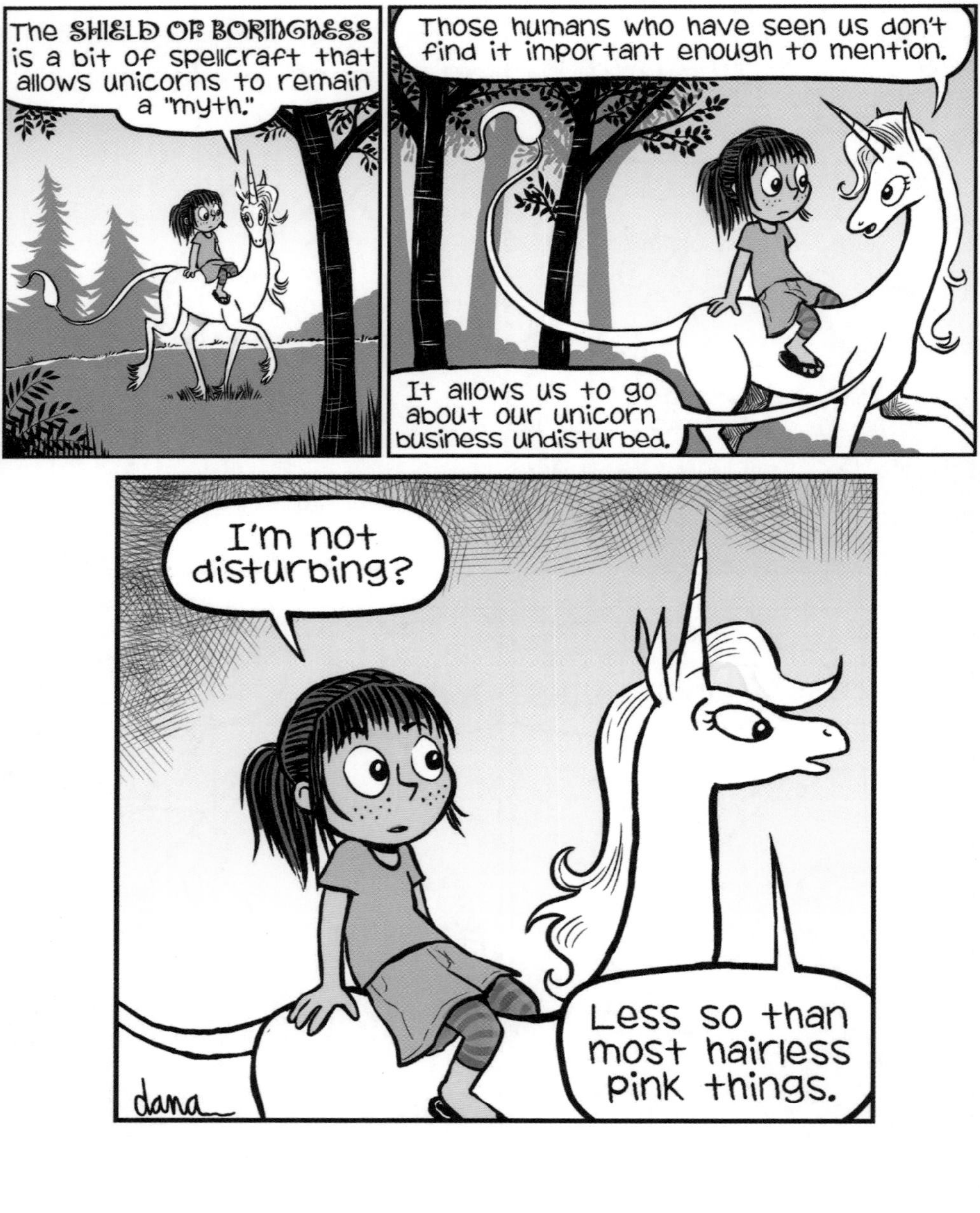
The SHIELD OF BORINGNESS is a bit of spellcraft that allows unicorns to remain a "myth."
Those humans who have seen us don't find it important enough to mention.
It allows us to go about our unicorn business undisturbed.
I'm not disturbing?
Less so than most hairless pink things.
dana

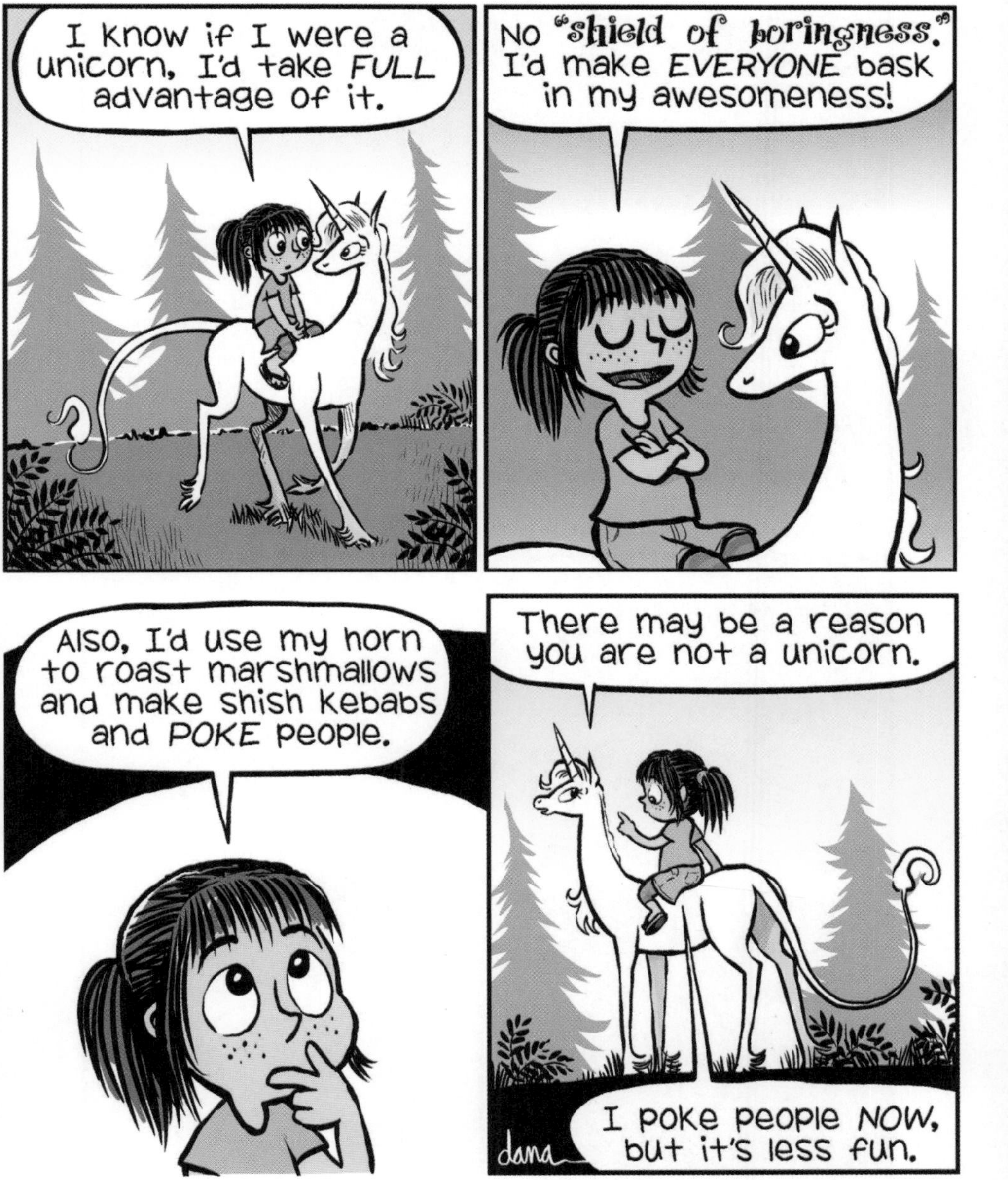
I know if I were a unicorn, I'd take FULL advantage of it.
No "shield of boringness." I'd make EVERYONE bask in my awesomeness!
Also, I'd use my horn to roast marshmallows and make shish kebabs and POKE people.
There may be a reason you are not a unicorn.
I poke people NOW, but it's less fun.
dana

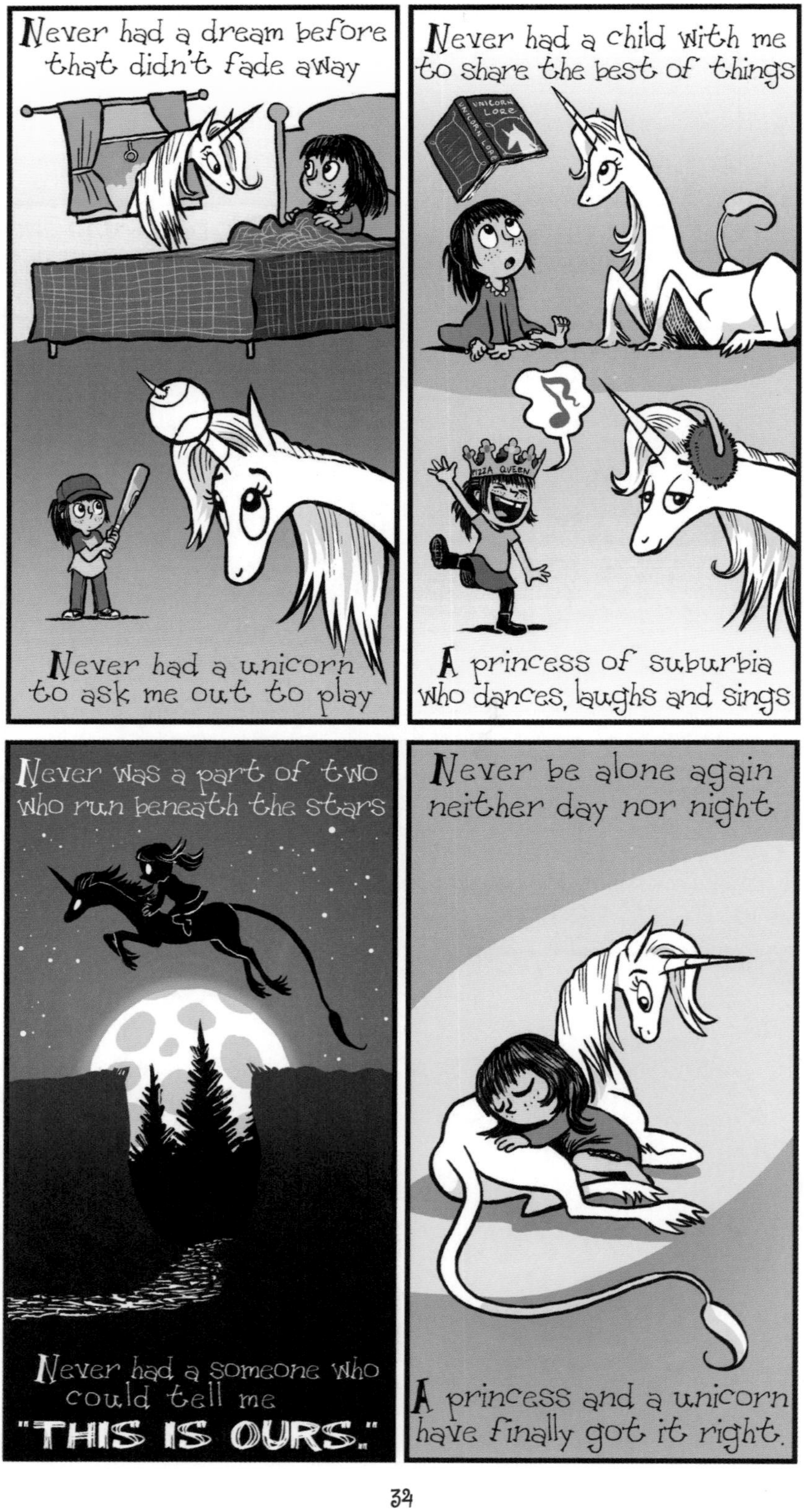
Never had a dream before that didn't fade away
Never had a unicorn to ask me out to play
Never had a child with me to share the best of things
UNICORN LORE
UNICORN LORE
PIZZA QUEEN
A princess of suburbia who dances, laughs and sings
Never was a part of two who run beneath the stars
Never had a someone who could tell me
"THIS IS OURS."
Never be alone again neither day nor night
A princess and a unicorn have finally got it right.

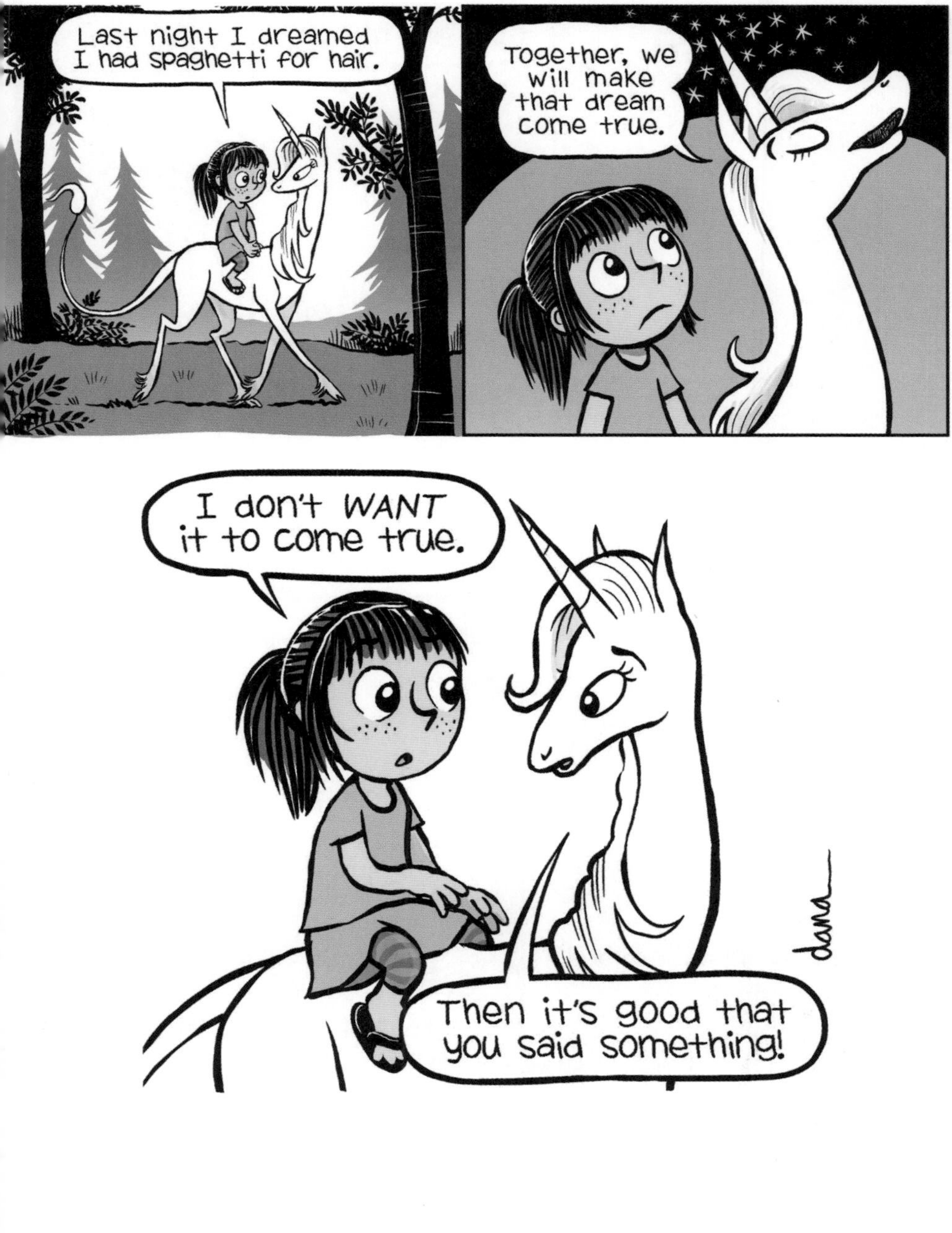
Last night I dreamed I had spaghetti for hair.
Together, we will make that dream come true.
I don't WANT it to come true.
Then it's good that you said something!
dana

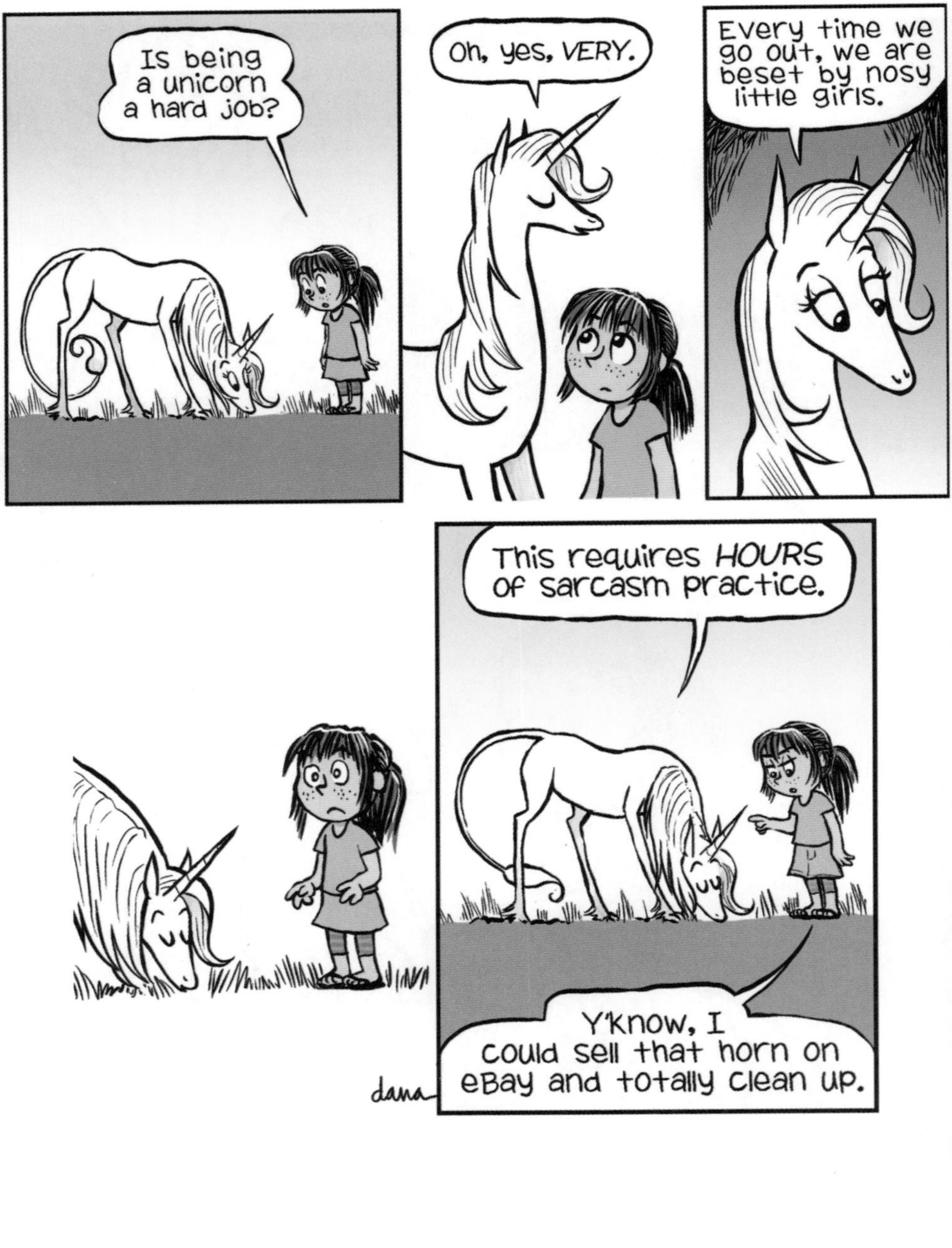
Is being a unicorn a hard job?
Oh, yes, VERY.
Every time we go out, we are beset by nosy little girls.
This requires HOURS of sarcasm practice.
Y'know, I could sell that horn on eBay and totally clean up.
dana

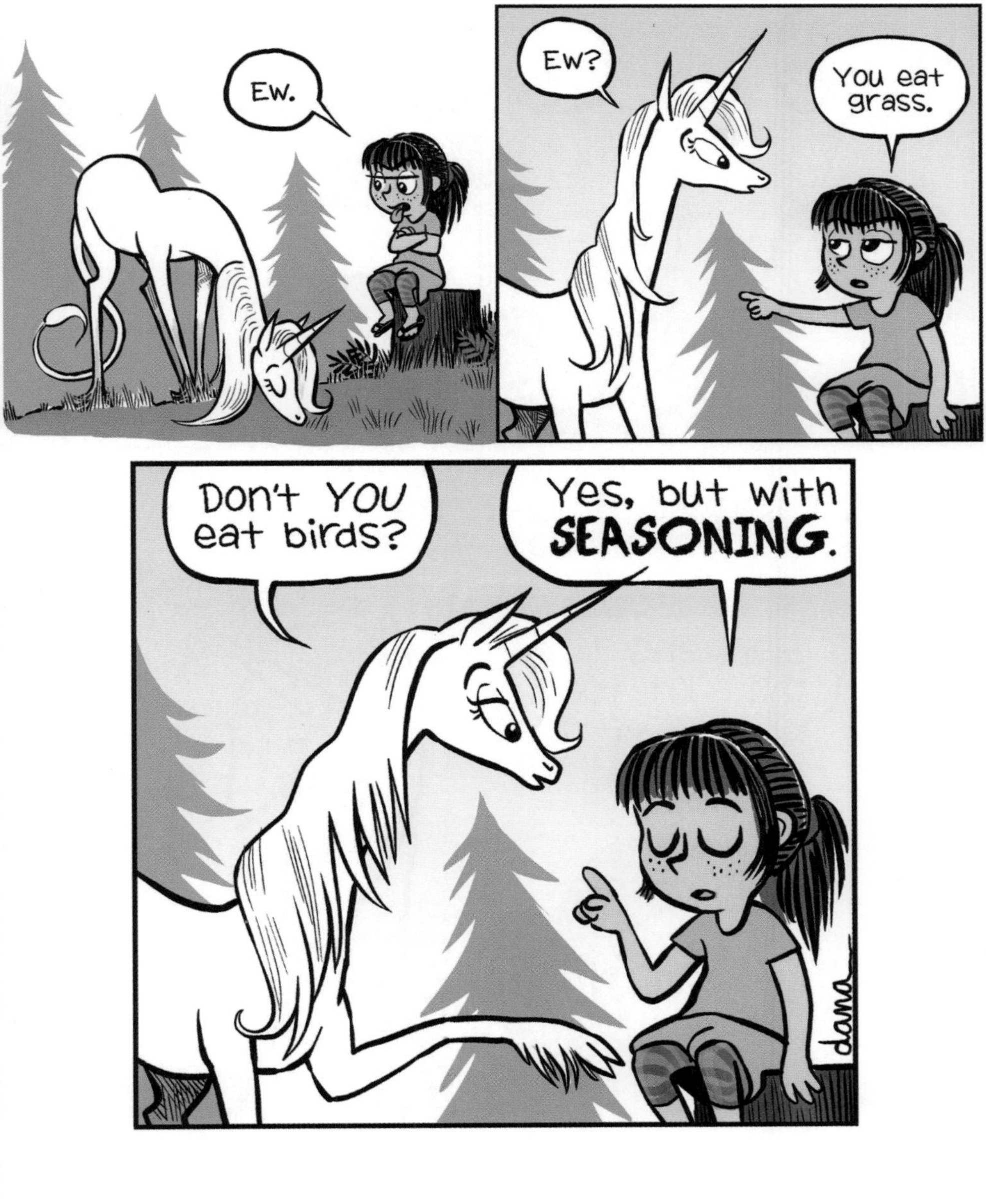
Ew.
Ew?
You eat grass.
Don't YOU eat birds?
Yes, but with SEASONING.
dana

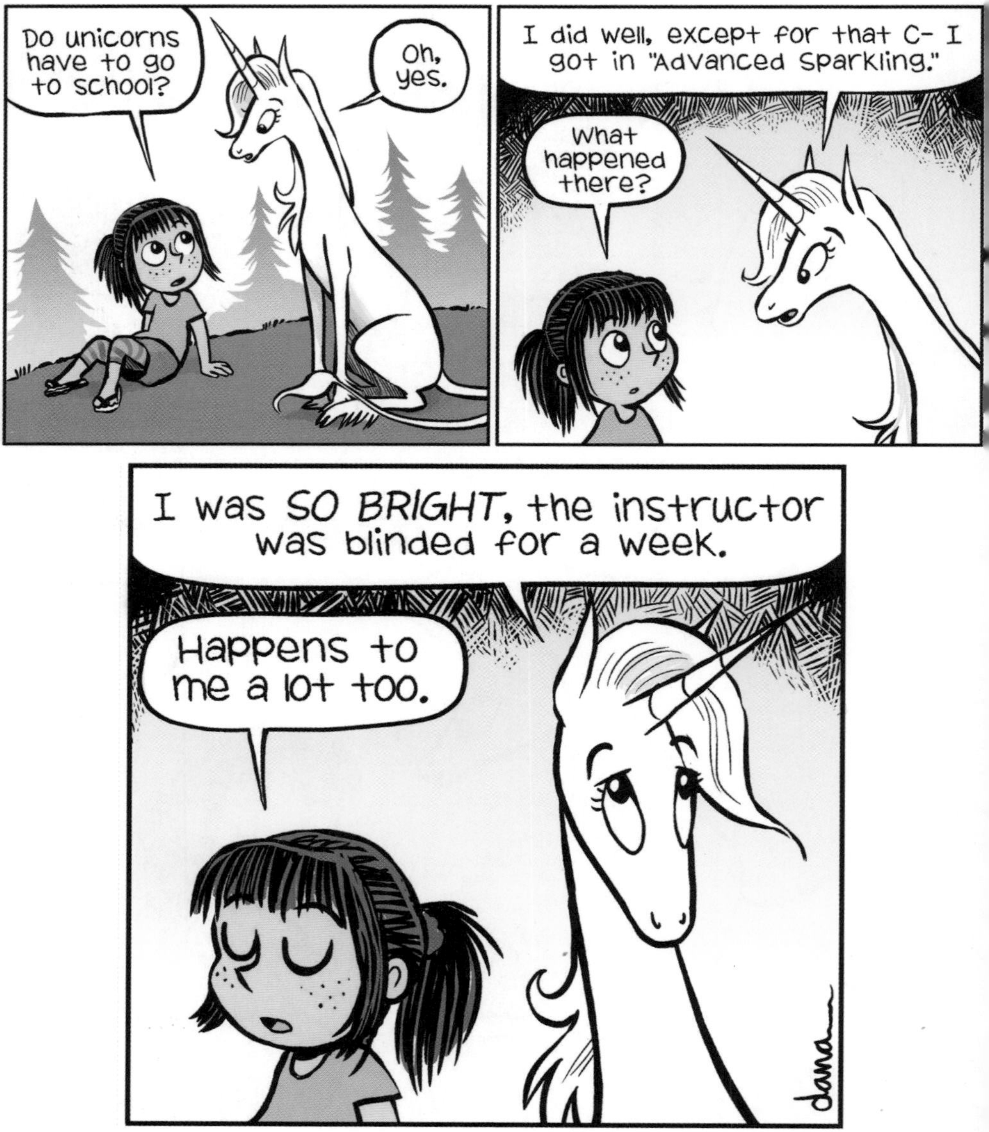
Do unicorns have to go to school?
Oh, yes.
I did well, except for that C- I got in "Advanced Sparkling."
What happened there?
I was *SO BRIGHT*, the instructor was blinded for a week.
Happens to me a lot too.
dana

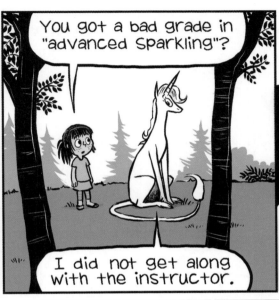

You got a bad grade in "advanced sparkling"?

I did not get along with the instructor.

She was literally a **POINTY-HEADED INTELLECTUAL.**

That's unicorn humor, is it?

Yes, it is pretty much all variations on that joke.

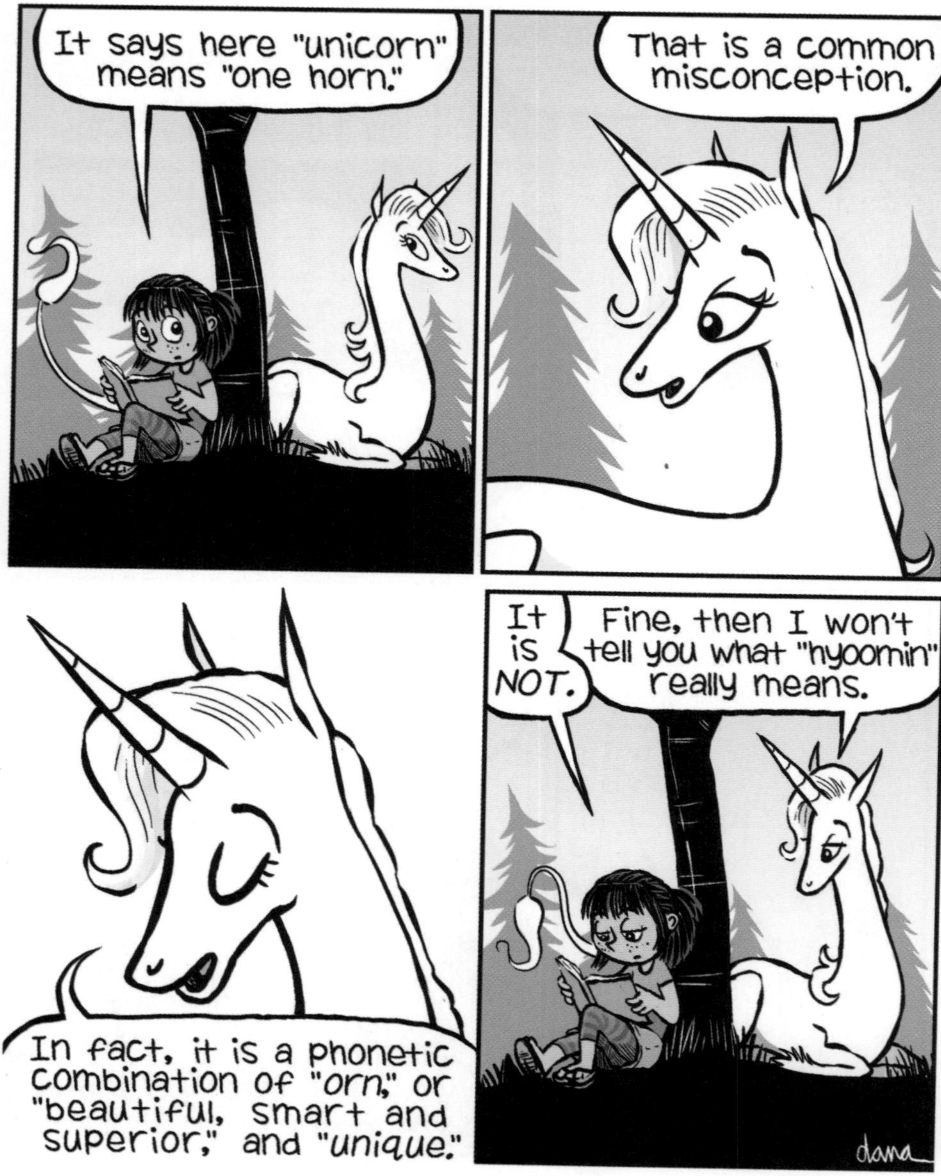

It says here "unicorn" means "one horn."
That is a common misconception.
In fact, it is a phonetic combination of "orn," or "beautiful, smart and superior," and "unique."
It is NOT.
Fine, then I won't tell you what "hyoomin" really means.
dana

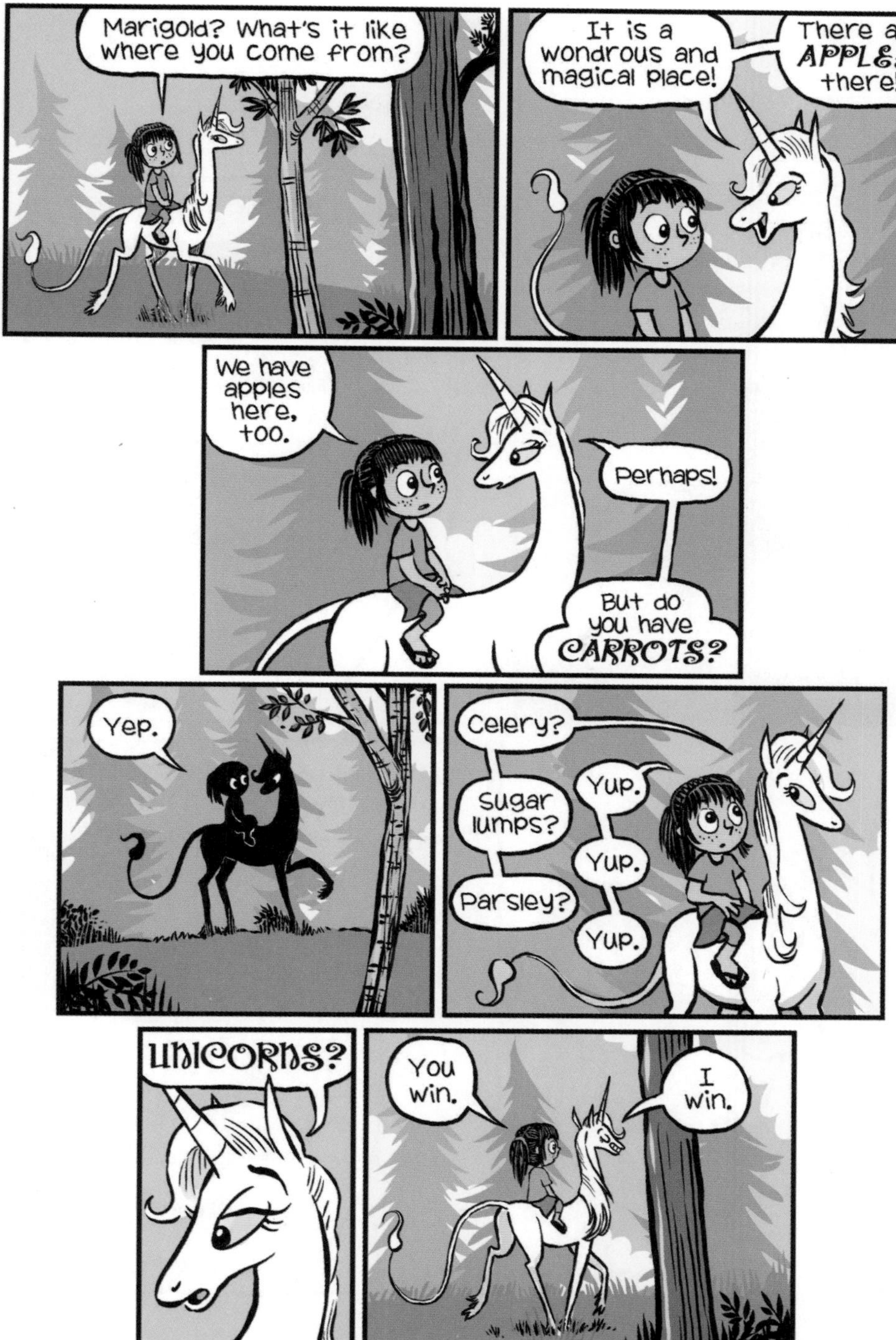
Marigold? What's it like where you come from?
It is a wondrous and magical place!
There are APPLES there!
We have apples here, too.
Perhaps!
But do you have CARROTS?
Yep.
Celery?
Yup.
Sugar lumps?
Yup.
Parsley?
Yup.
UNICORNS?
You win.
I win.

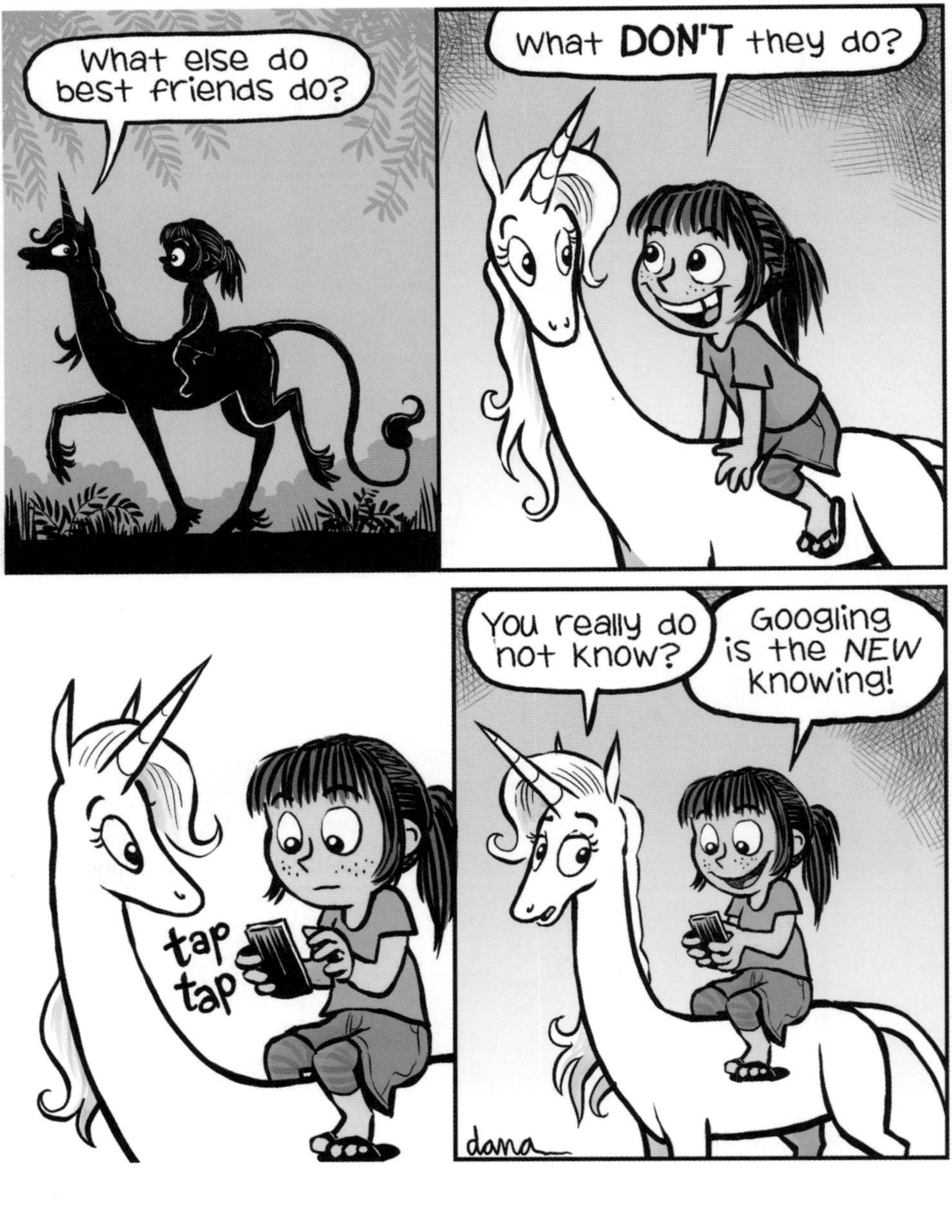
What else do best friends do?
What DON'T they do?
tap tap
You really do not know?
Googling is the NEW knowing!
dana

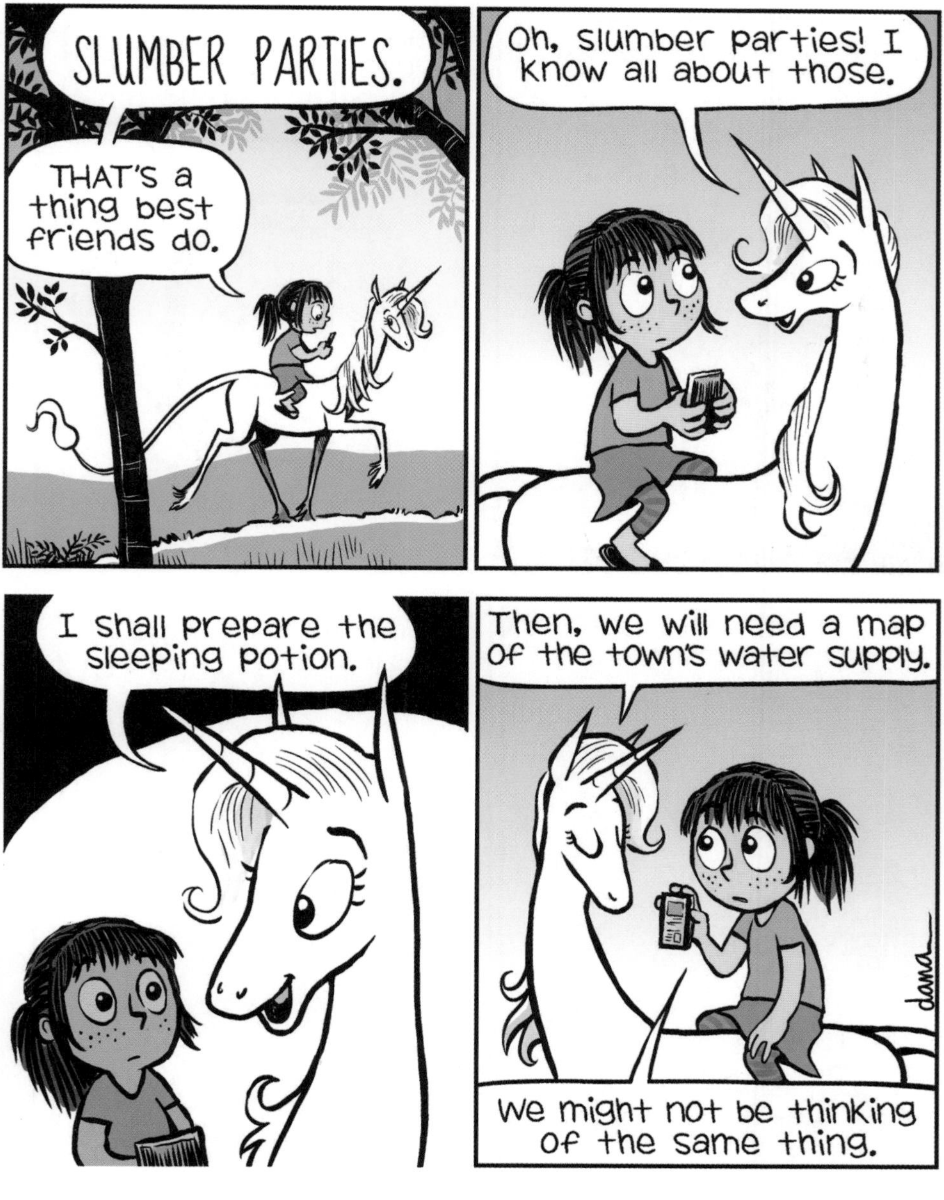
SLUMBER PARTIES.
THAT'S a thing best friends do.
Oh, slumber parties! I know all about those.
I shall prepare the sleeping potion.
Then, we will need a map of the town's water supply.
We might not be thinking of the same thing.
dana

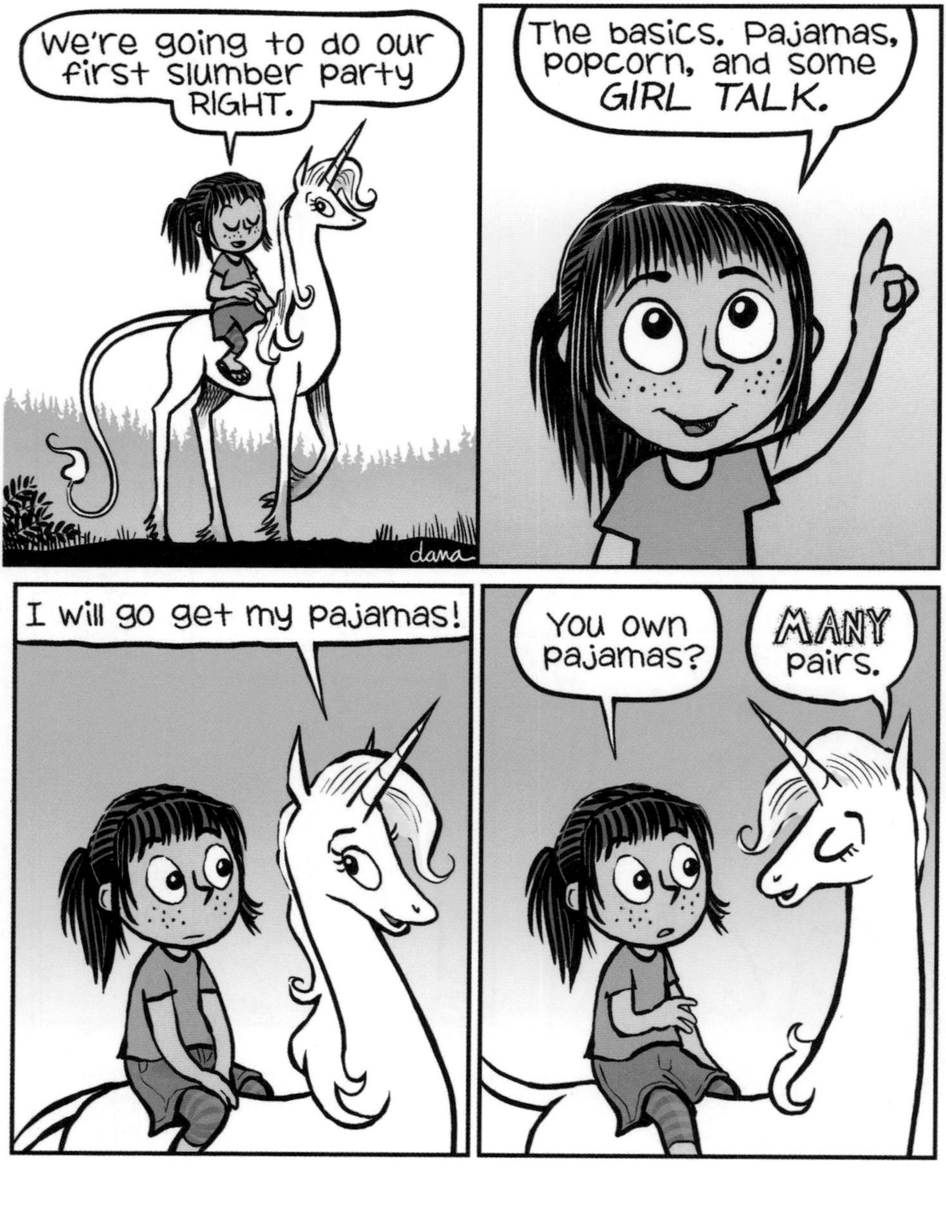
We're going to do our first slumber party RIGHT.
dana
The basics. Pajamas, popcorn, and some GIRL TALK.
I will go get my pajamas!
You own pajamas?
MANY pairs.

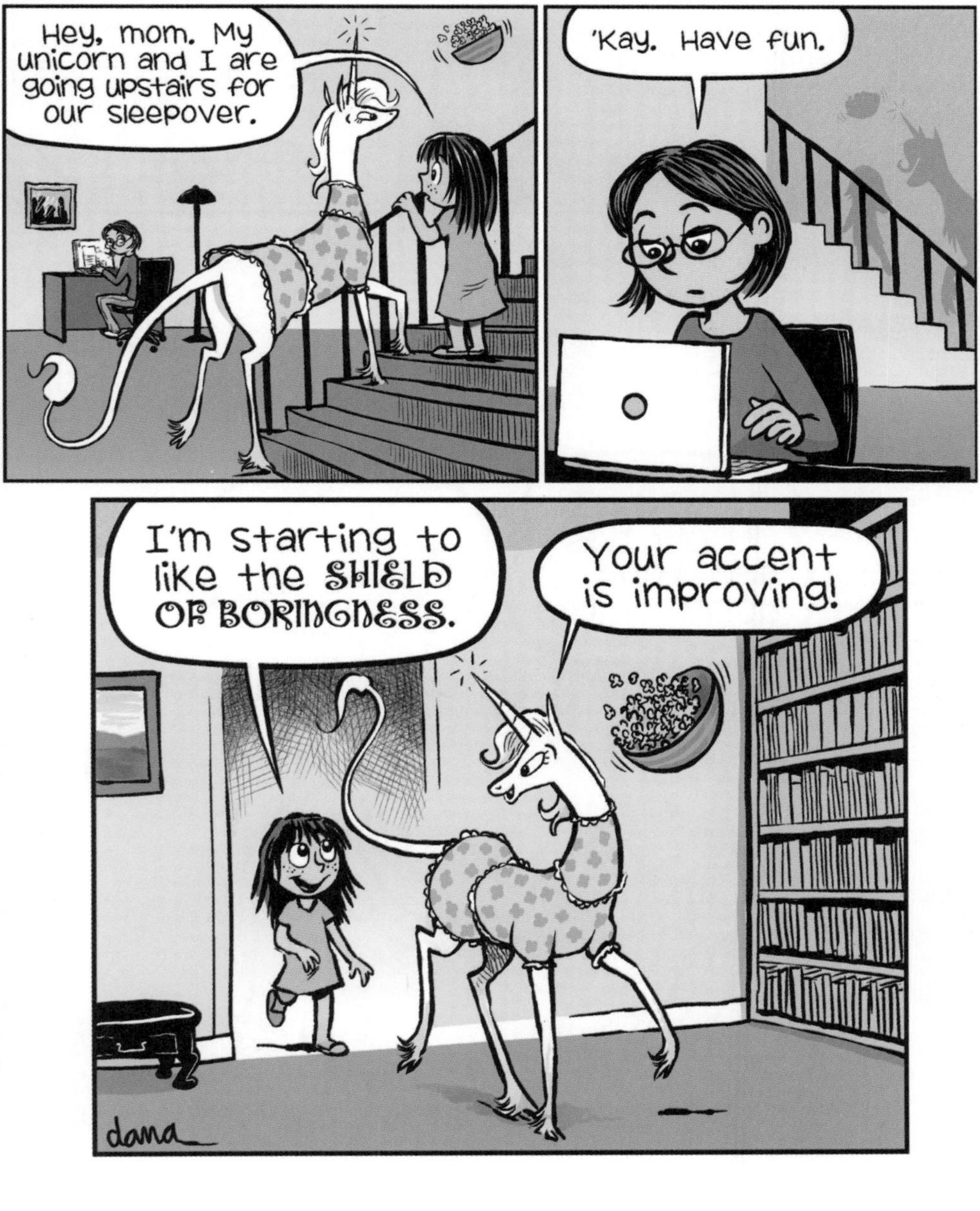

Hey, mom. My unicorn and I are going upstairs for our sleepover.
'Kay. Have fun.
I'm starting to like the SHIELD OF BORINGNESS.
Your accent is improving!
dana

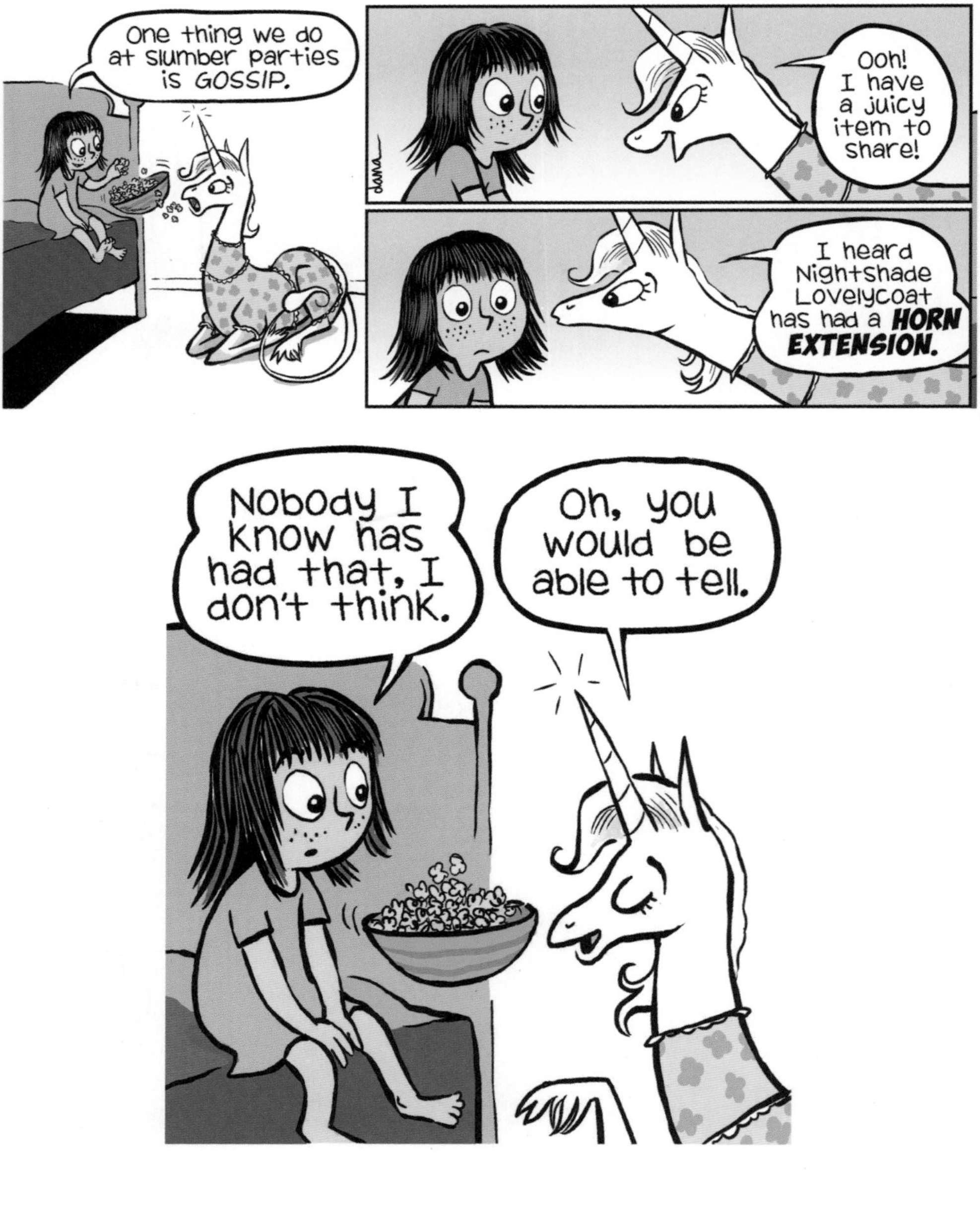
One thing we do at slumber parties is *GOSSIP.*
Ooh! I have a juicy item to share!
I heard Nightshade Lovelycoat has had a **HORN EXTENSION.**
Nobody I know has had that, I don't think.
Oh, you would be able to tell.

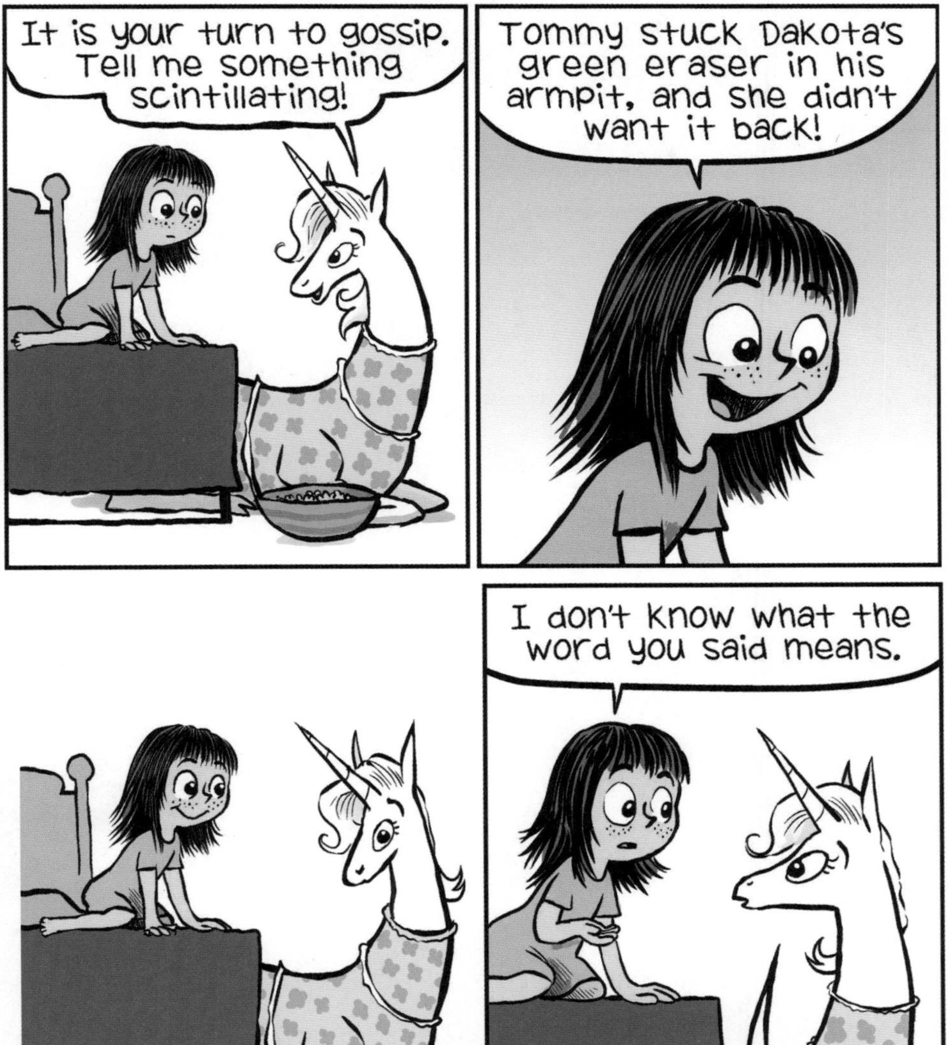
It is your turn to gossip. Tell me something scintillating!
Tommy stuck Dakota's green eraser in his armpit, and she didn't want it back!
I don't know what the word you said means.
That may only be one of many problems.
dana

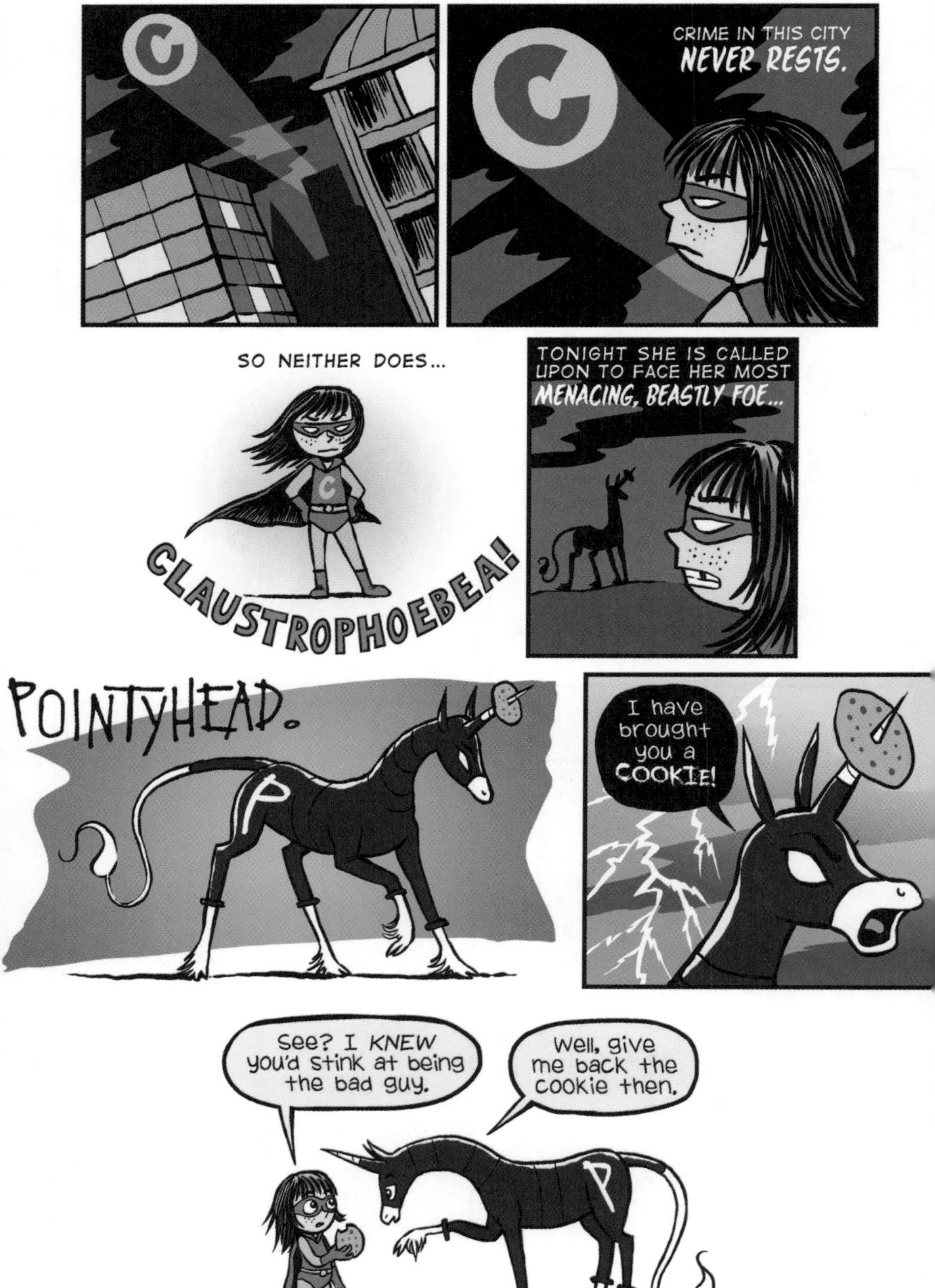
CRIME IN THIS CITY
NEVER RESTS.
SO NEITHER DOES...
CLAUSTROPHOEBEA!
TONIGHT SHE IS CALLED UPON TO FACE HER MOST
MENACING, BEASTLY FOE...
POINTYHEAD.
I have brought you a COOKIE!
See? I KNEW you'd stink at being the bad guy.
Well, give me back the cookie then.

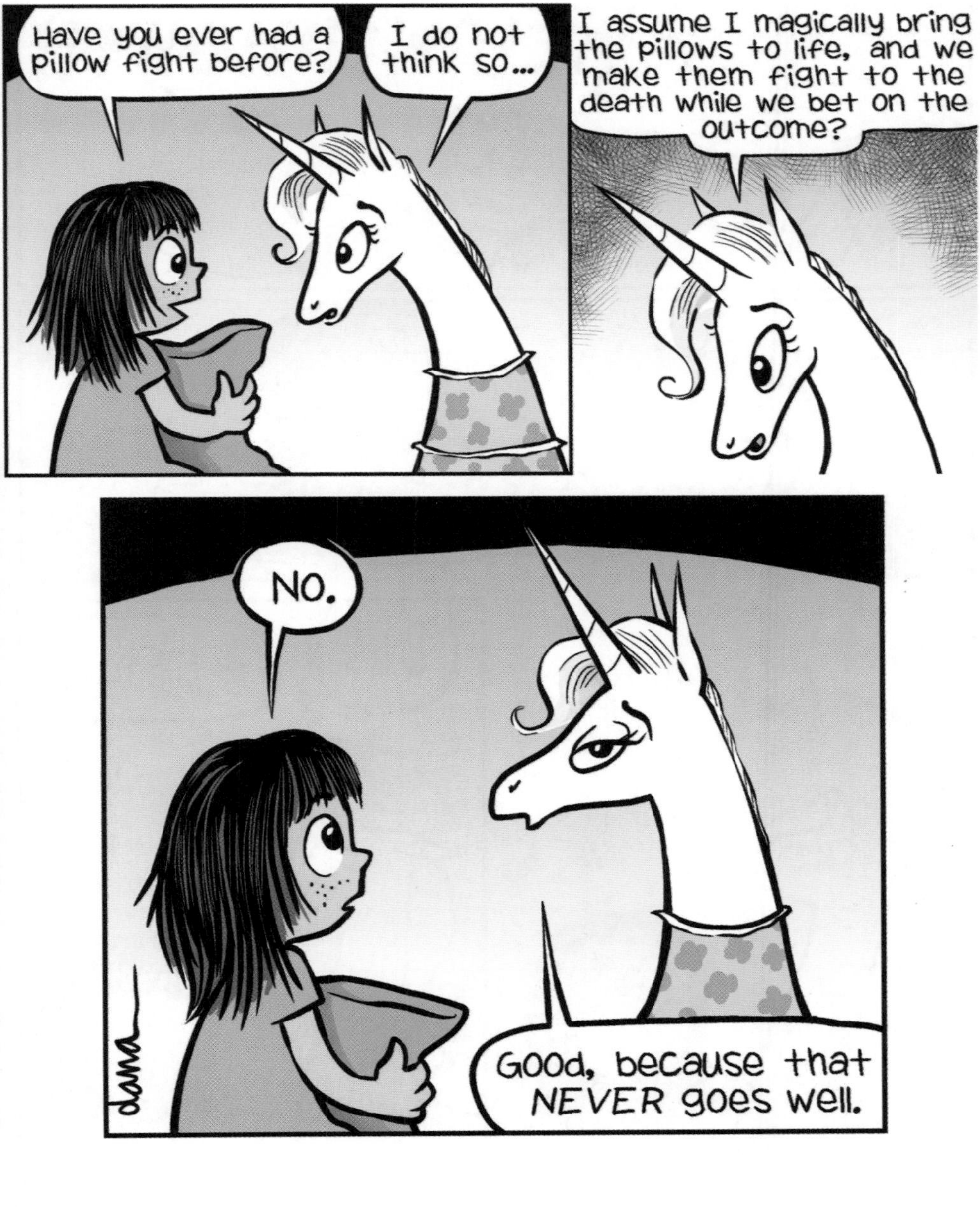
Have you ever had a pillow fight before?
I do not think so...
I assume I magically bring the pillows to life, and we make them fight to the death while we bet on the outcome?
NO.
Good, because that NEVER goes well.
dana

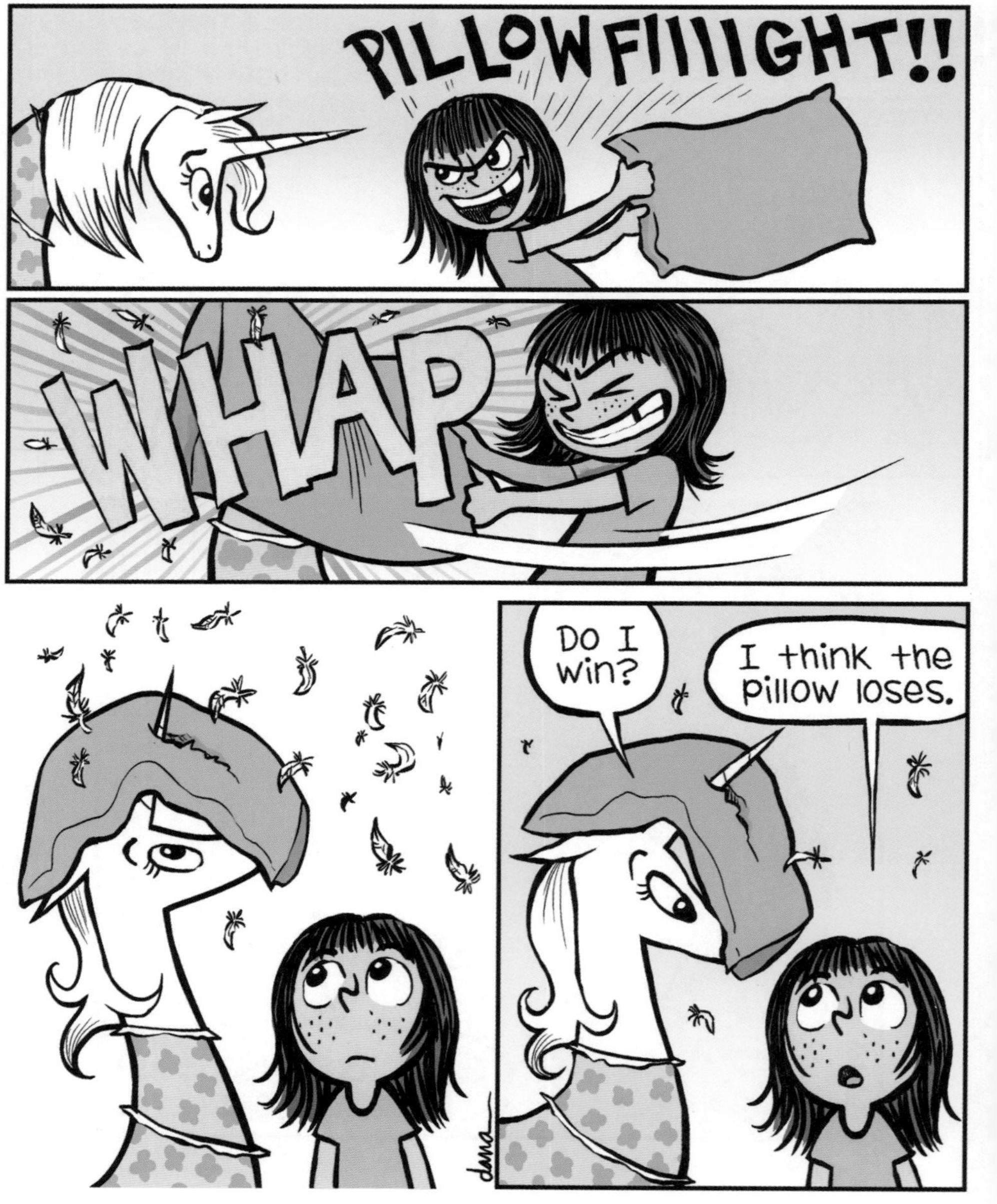
PILLOW FIIIIGHT!!
WHAP
Do I win?
I think the pillow loses.
dana

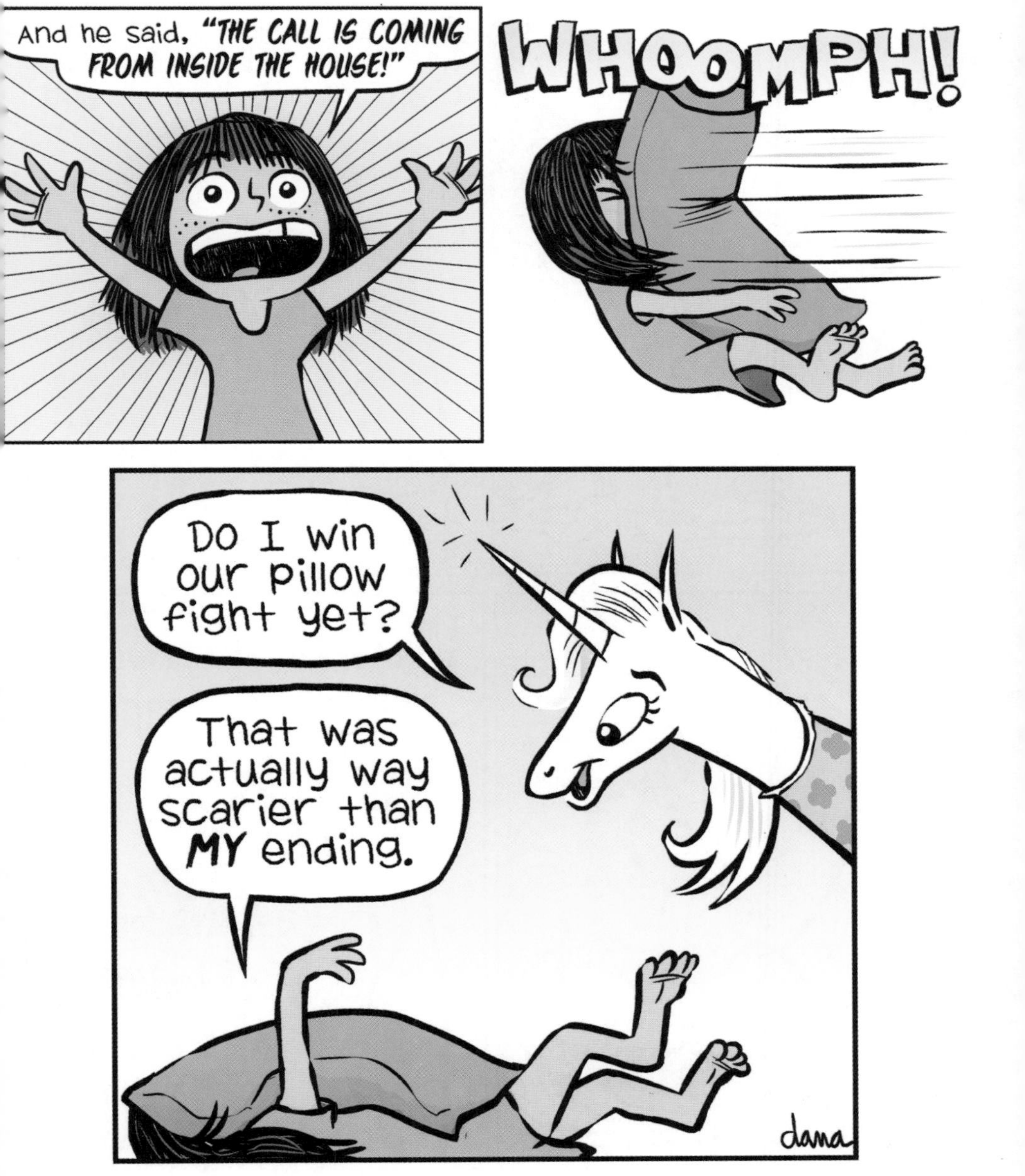
And he said, "THE CALL IS COMING FROM INSIDE THE HOUSE!"
WHOOMPH!
Do I win our pillow fight yet?
That was actually way scarier than MY ending.
dana

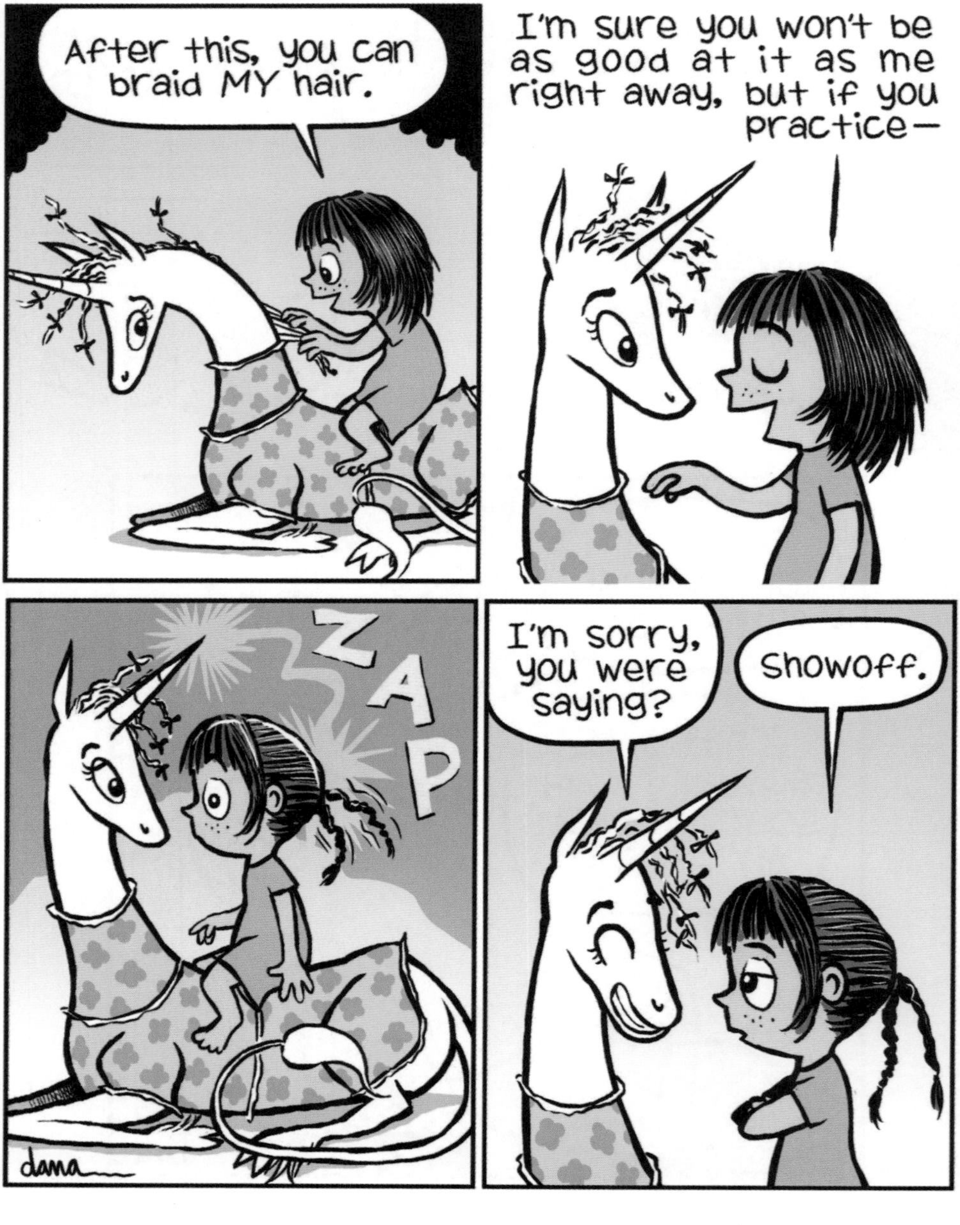
After this, you can braid MY hair.
I'm sure you won't be as good at it as me right away, but if you practice—
ZAP
dana
I'm sorry, you were saying?
Showoff.

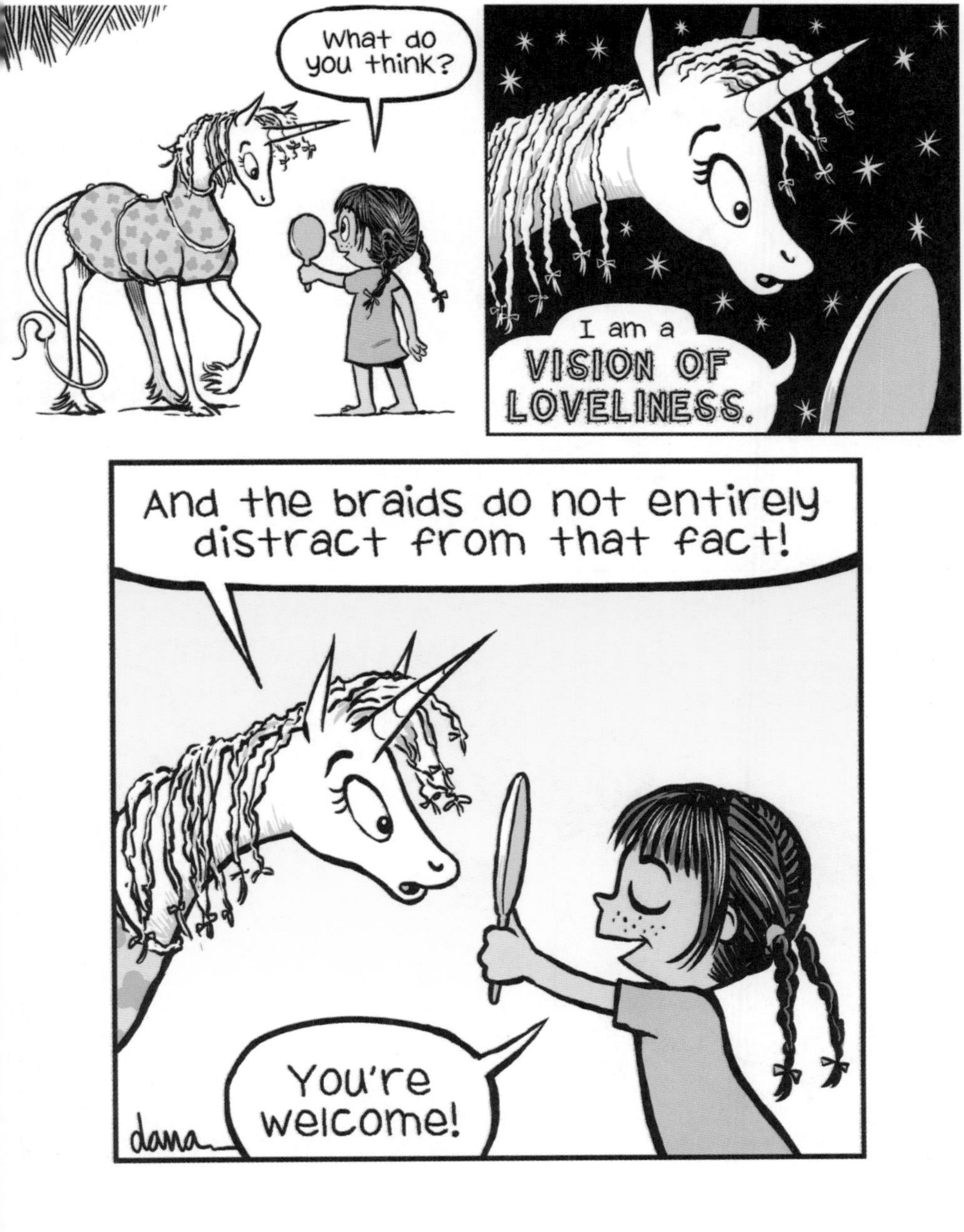
What do you think?
I am a VISION OF LOVELINESS.
And the braids do not entirely distract from that fact!
You're welcome!
dana

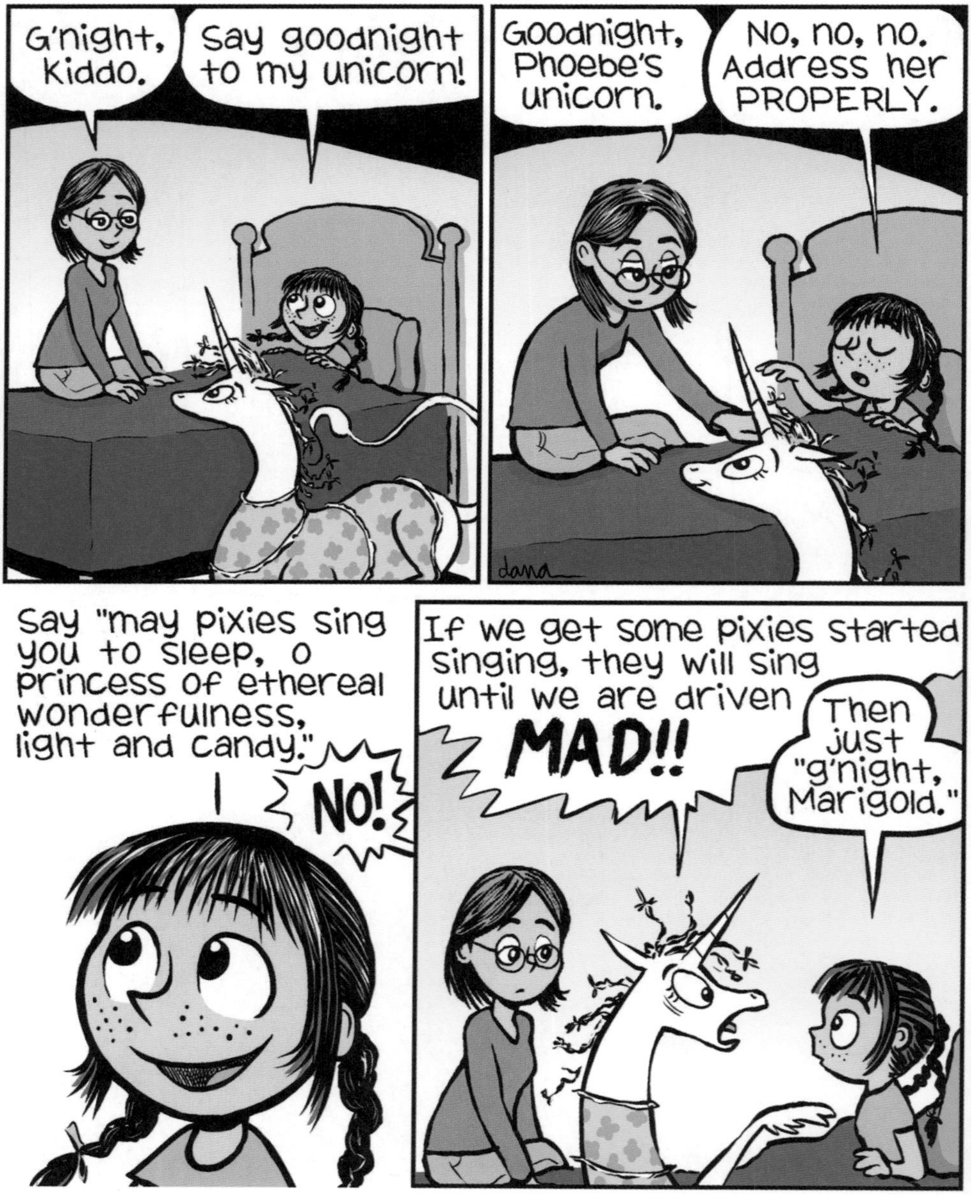
G'night, Kiddo.
Say goodnight to my unicorn!
Goodnight, Phoebe's unicorn.
No, no, no. Address her PROPERLY.
dana
Say "may pixies sing you to sleep, o princess of ethereal wonderfulness, light and candy."
NO!
If we get some pixies started singing, they will sing until we are driven MAD!!
Then just "g'night, Marigold."

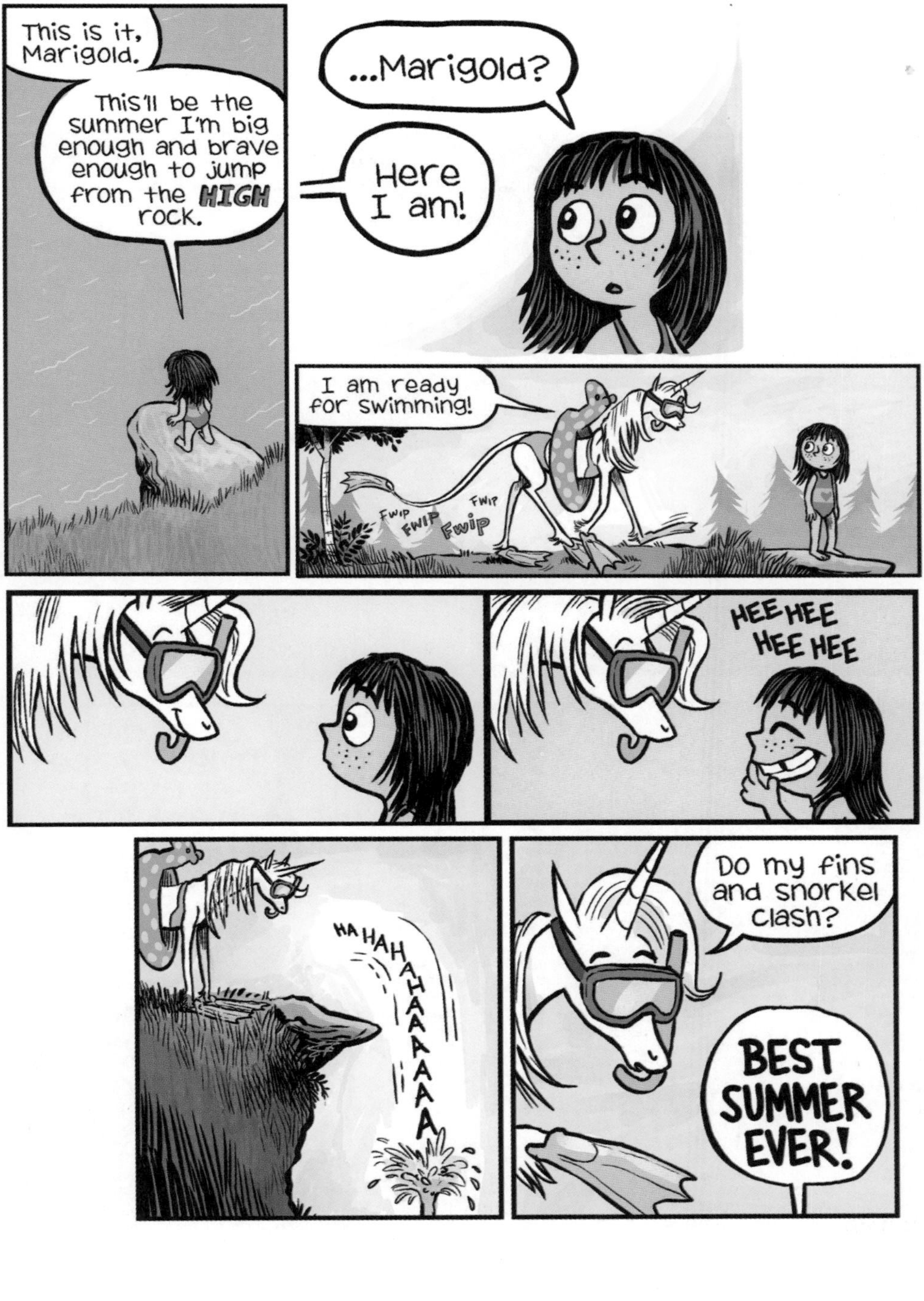
This is it, Marigold.
This'll be the summer I'm big enough and brave enough to jump from the HIGH rock.
...Marigold?
Here I am!
I am ready for swimming!
FWIP FWIP FWIP Fwip
HEE HEE HEE HEE
HA HA HA HAAAAAAAAA
Do my fins and snorkel clash?
BEST SUMMER EVER!

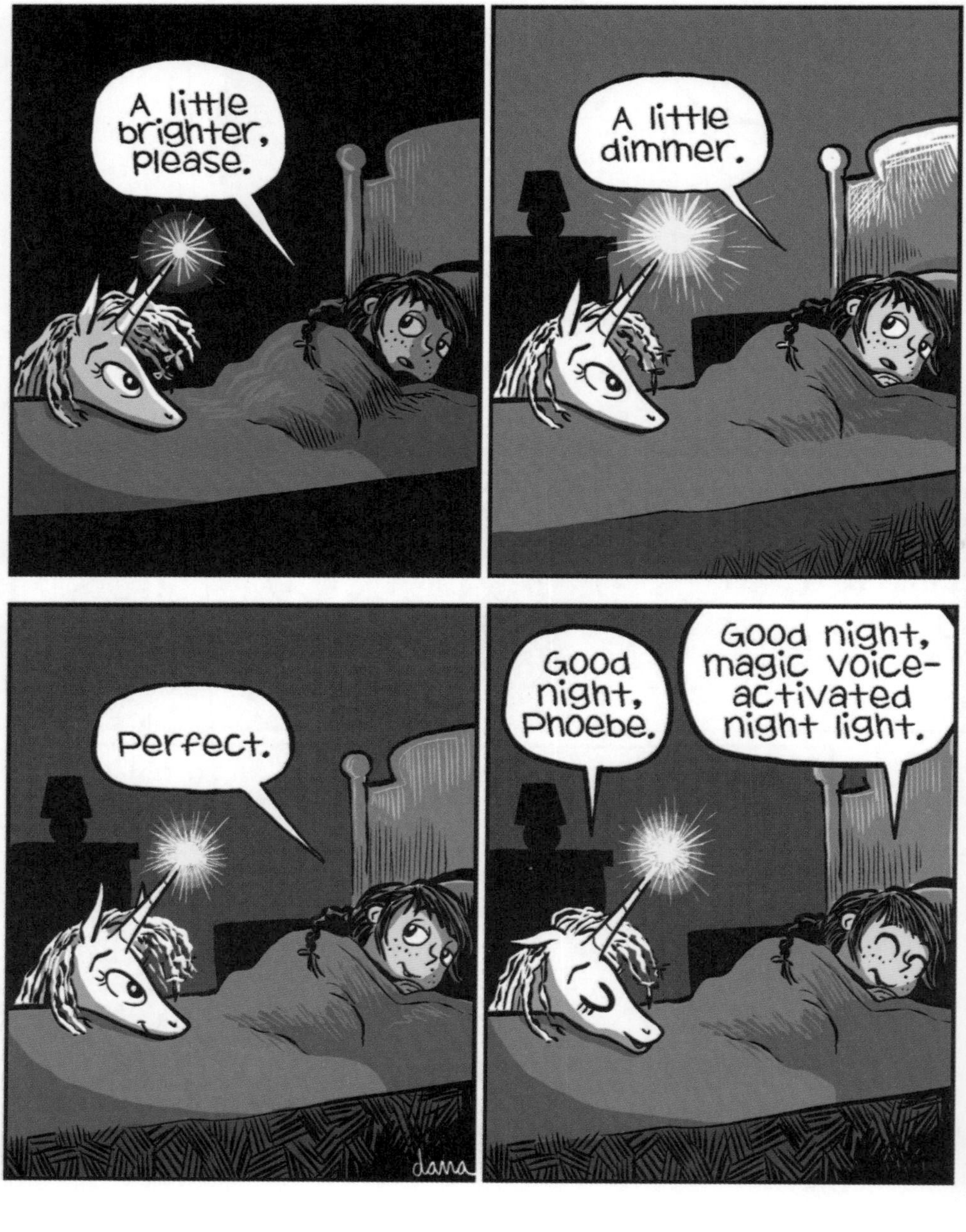
A little brighter, please.
A little dimmer.
Perfect.
Good night, Phoebe.
Good night, magic voice-activated night light.
dana

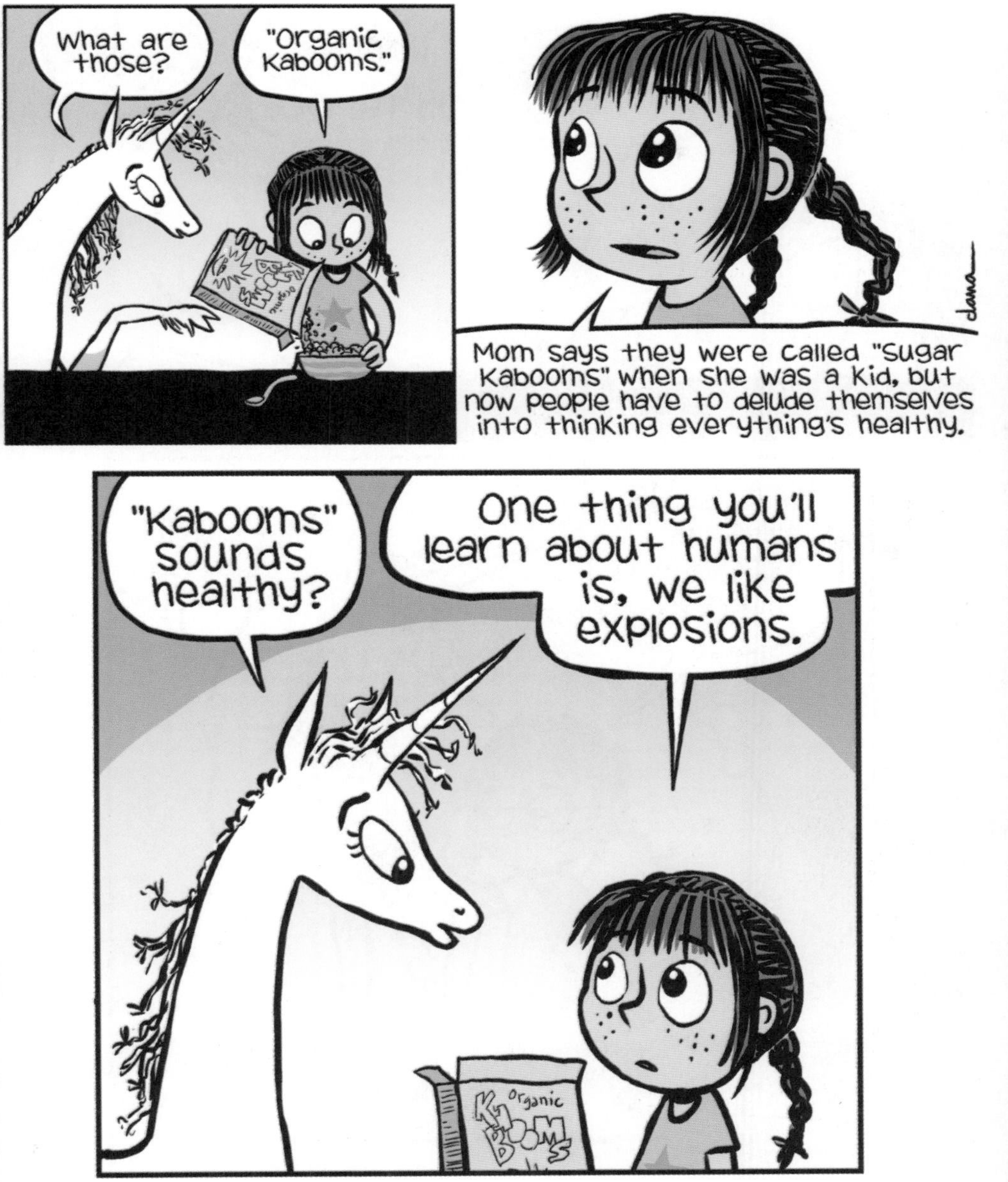
What are those?
"Organic Kabooms."
Mom says they were called "Sugar Kabooms" when she was a kid, but now people have to delude themselves into thinking everything's healthy.
"Kabooms" sounds healthy?
One thing you'll learn about humans is, we like explosions.
Organic
KaBOOMS

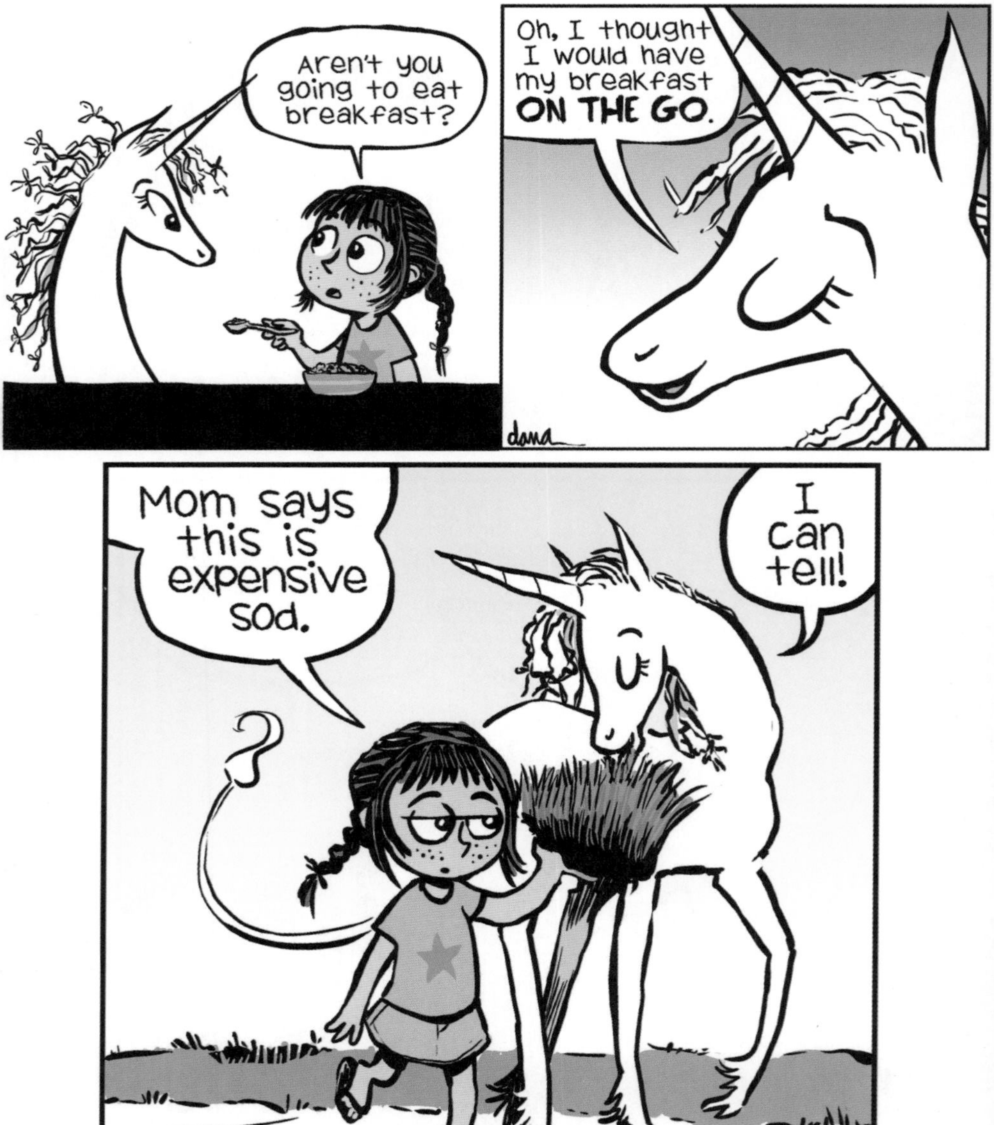
Aren't you going to eat breakfast?
Oh, I thought I would have my breakfast **ON THE GO**.
dana
Mom says this is expensive sod.
I can tell!

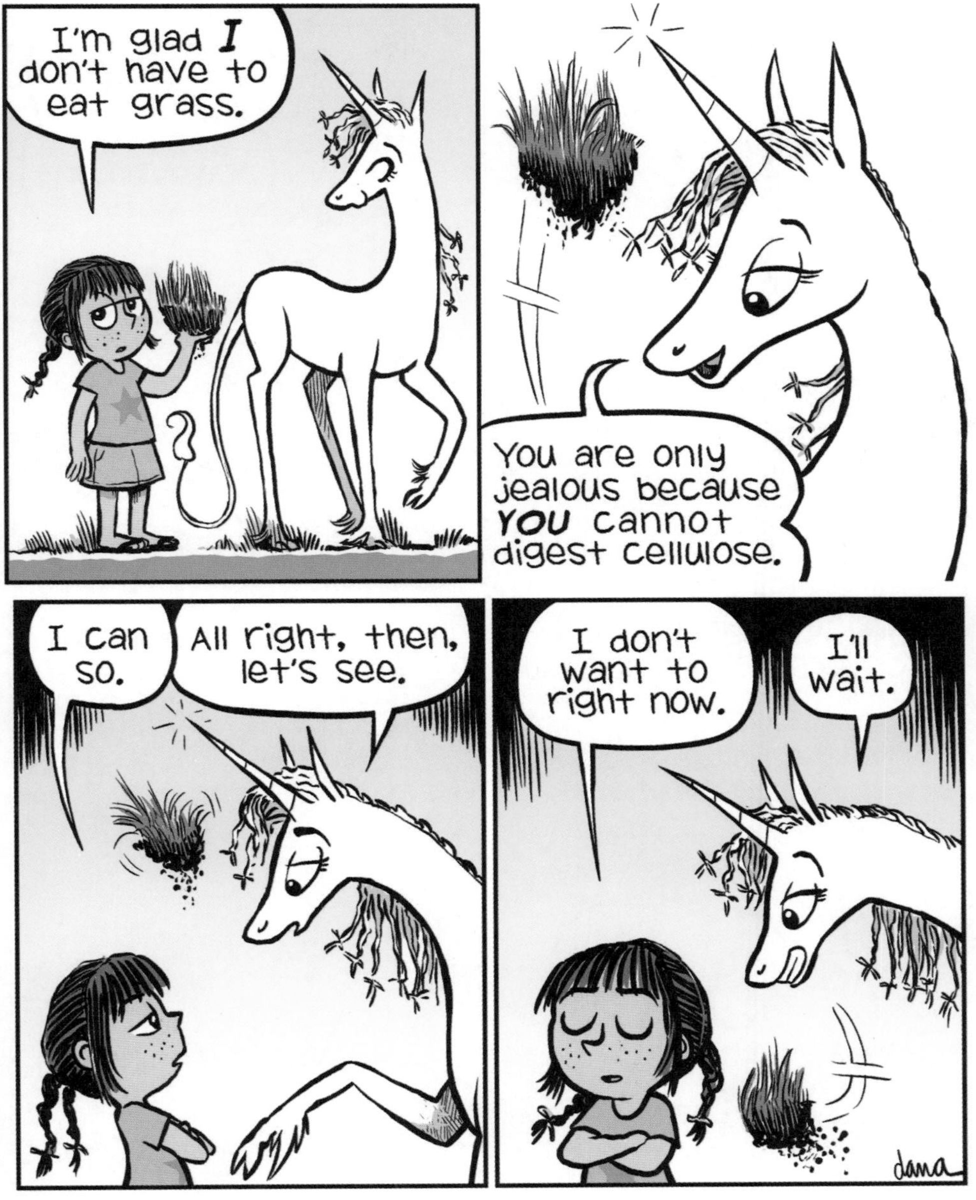
I'm glad *I* don't have to eat grass.
You are only jealous because *YOU* cannot digest cellulose.
I can so.
All right, then, let's see.
I don't want to right now.
I'll wait.
dana

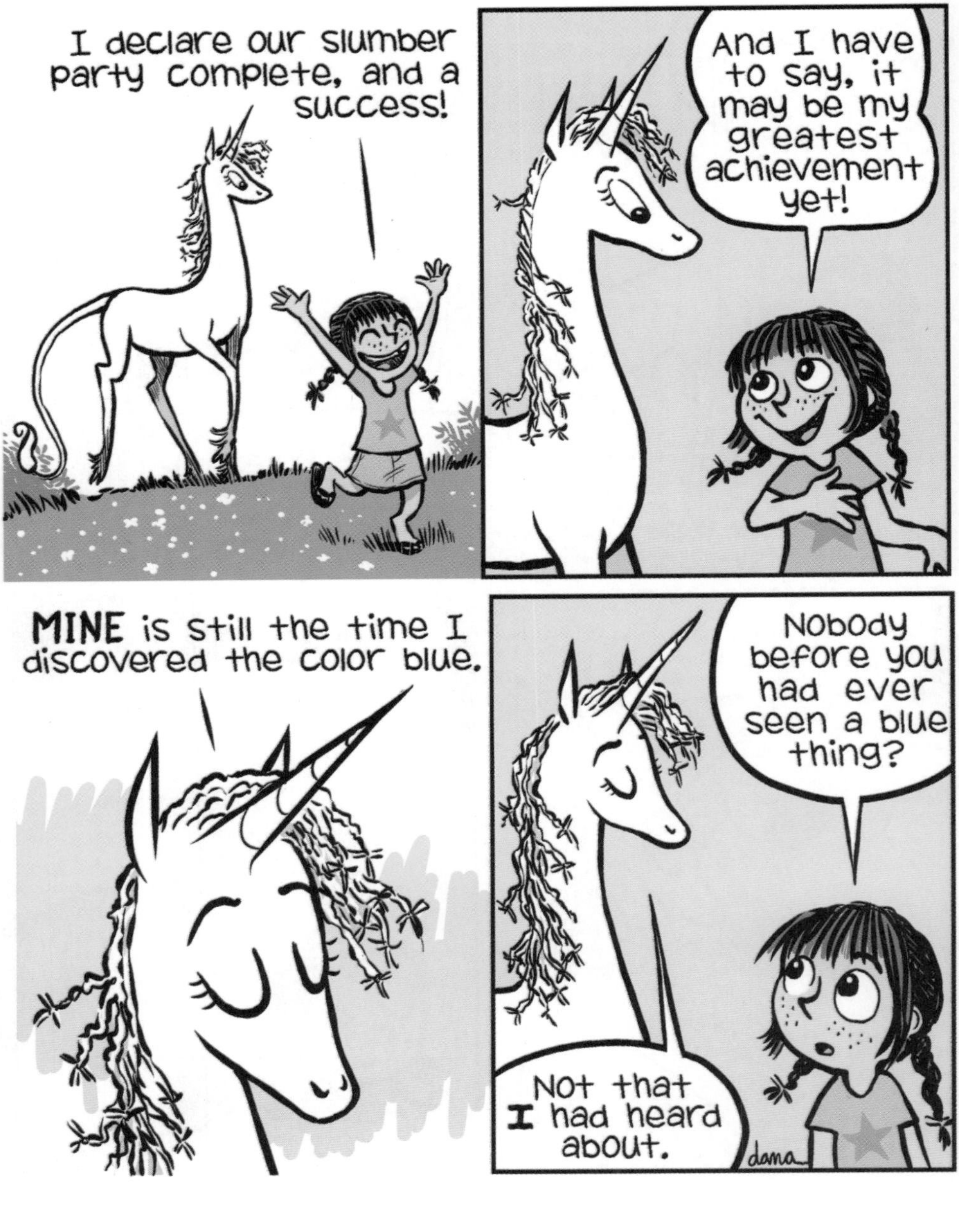
I declare our slumber party complete, and a success!
And I have to say, it may be my greatest achievement yet!
MINE is still the time I discovered the color blue.
Nobody before you had ever seen a blue thing?
Not that I had heard about.
dana

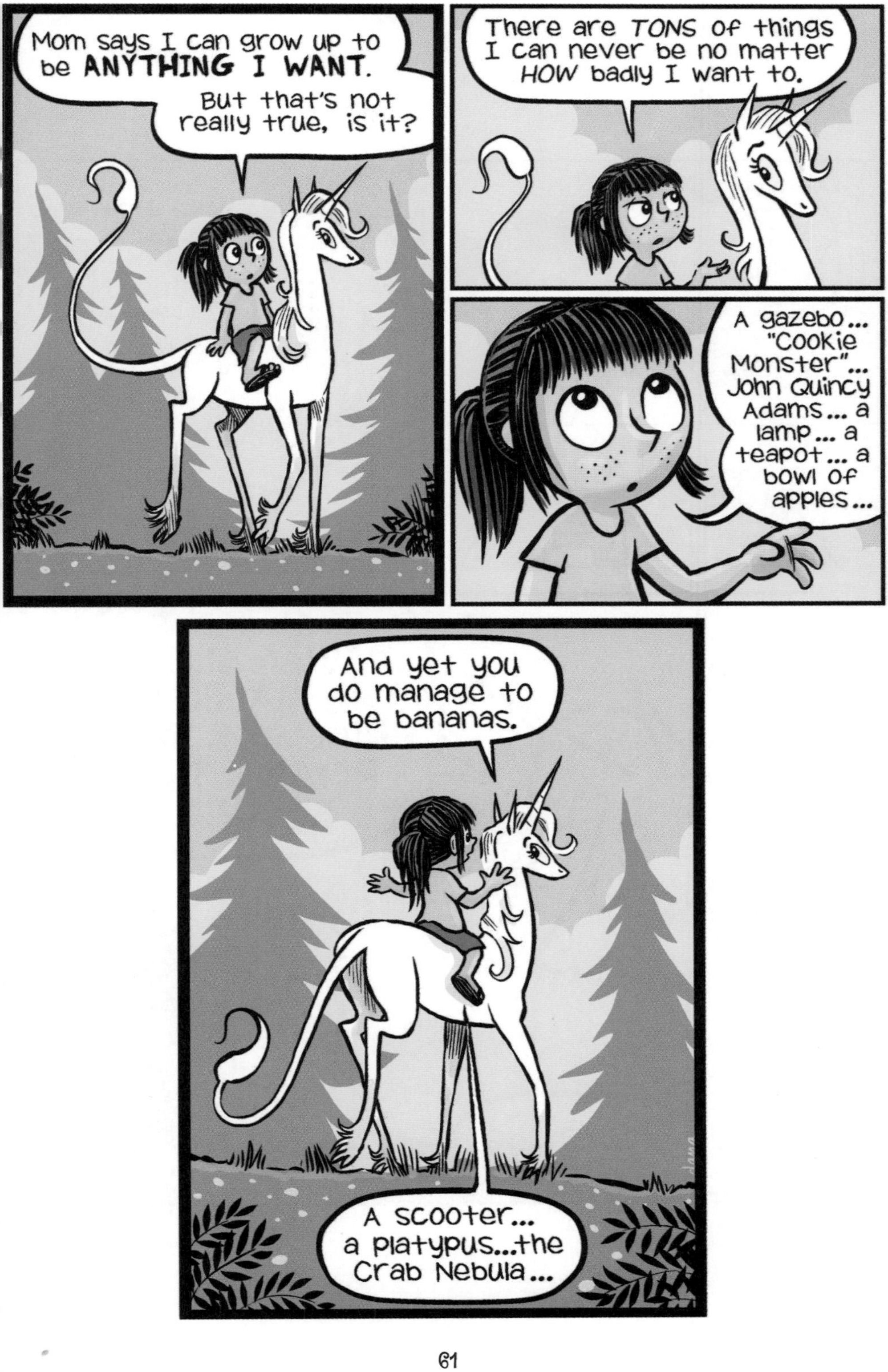
Mom says I can grow up to be **ANYTHING I WANT**.
But that's not really true, is it?
There are *TONS* of things I can never be no matter *HOW* badly I want to.
A gazebo... "Cookie Monster"... John Quincy Adams... a lamp... a teapot... a bowl of apples...
And yet you do manage to be bananas.
A scooter... a platypus...the Crab Nebula...

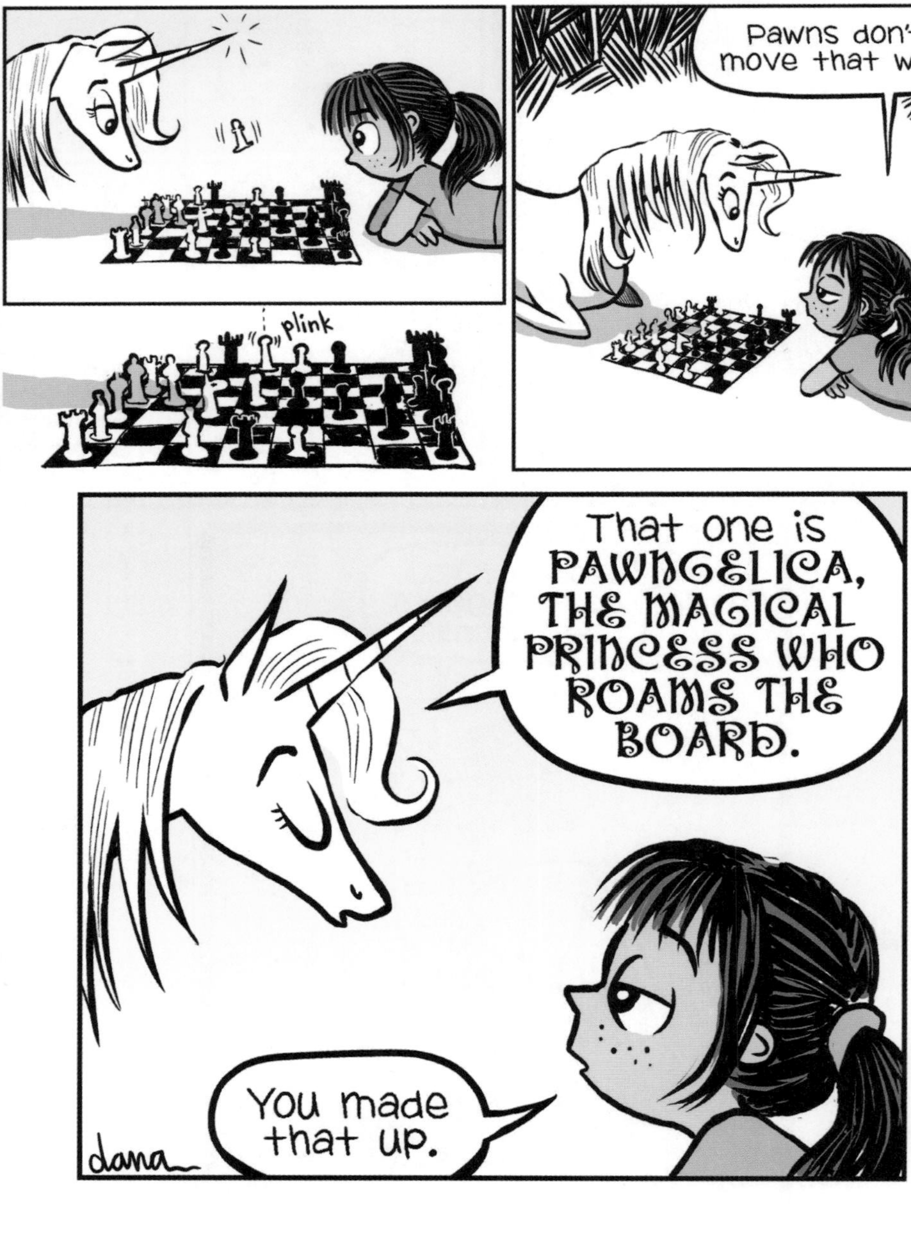
plink
Pawns don't move that way.
That one is PAWNGELICA, THE MAGICAL PRINCESS WHO ROAMS THE BOARD.
You made that up.
dana

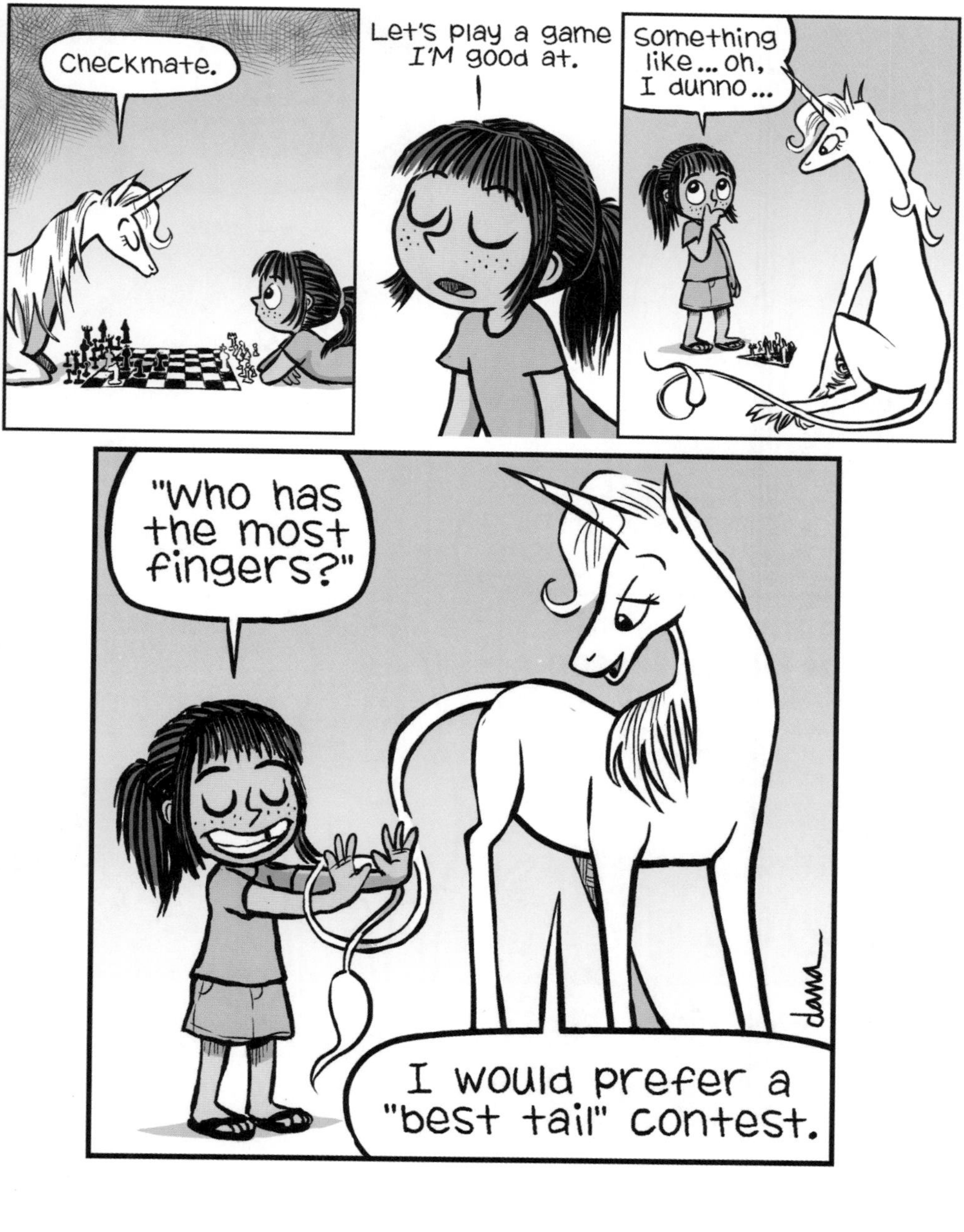
Checkmate.
Let's play a game I'M good at.
Something like... oh, I dunno...
"Who has the most fingers?"
I would prefer a "best tail" contest.
dana

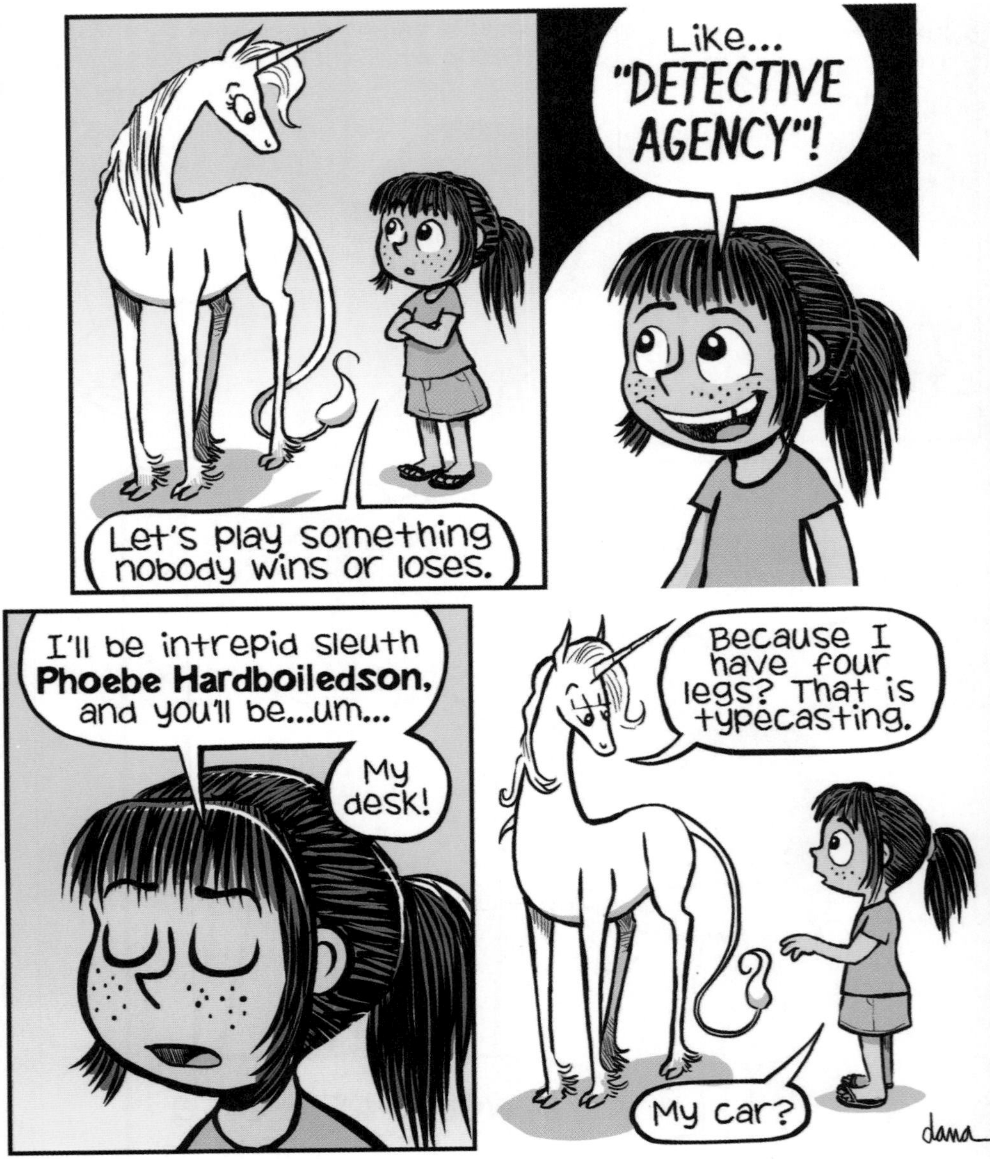
Let's play something nobody wins or loses.
Like... "DETECTIVE AGENCY"!
I'll be intrepid sleuth **Phoebe Hardboiledson,** and you'll be...um...
My desk!
Because I have four legs? That is typecasting.
My car?
dana

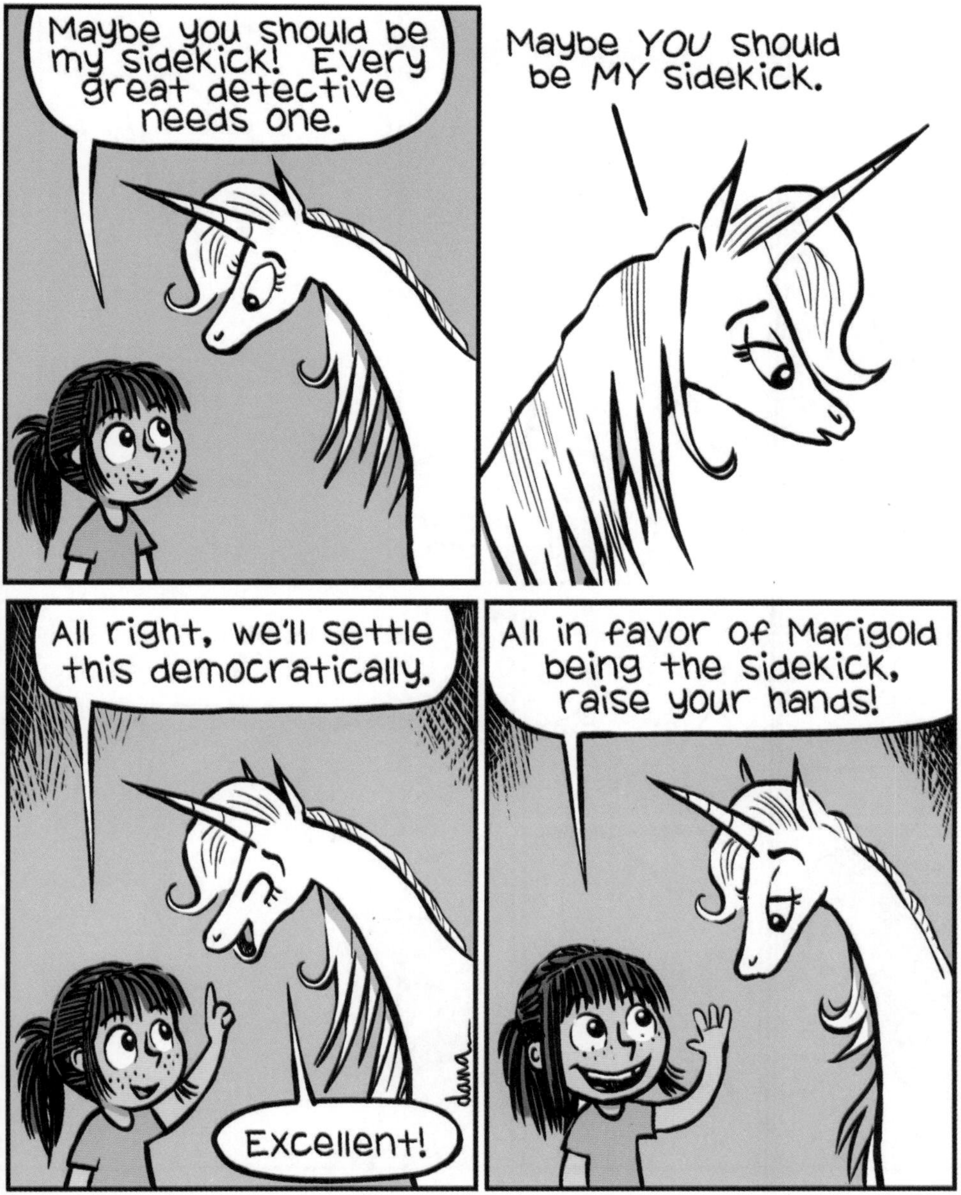
Maybe you should be my sidekick! Every great detective needs one.
Maybe YOU should be MY sidekick.
All right, we'll settle this democratically.
Excellent!
dana
All in favor of Marigold being the sidekick, raise your hands!

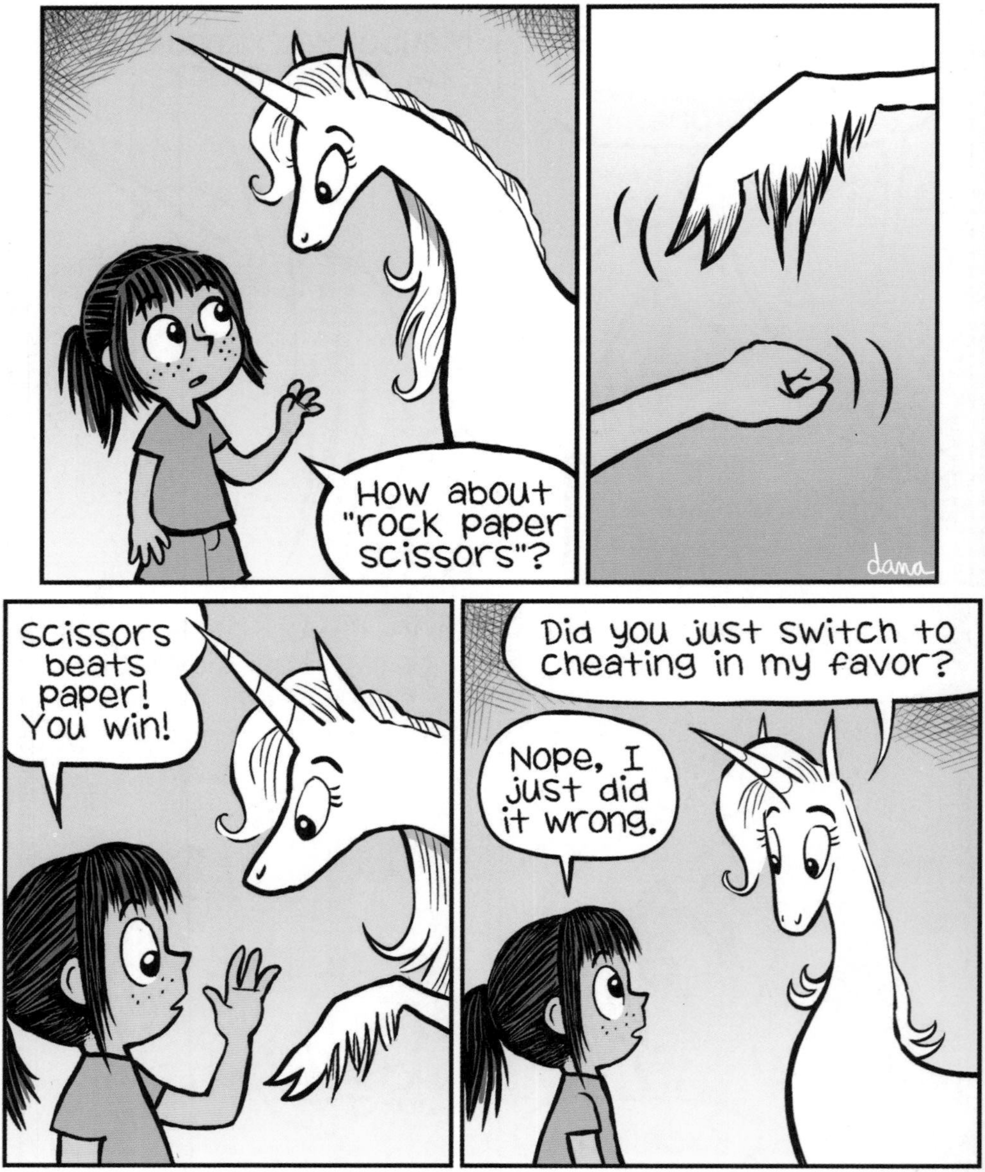
How about "rock paper scissors"?
dana
Scissors beats paper! You win!
Did you just switch to cheating in my favor?
Nope, I just did it wrong.

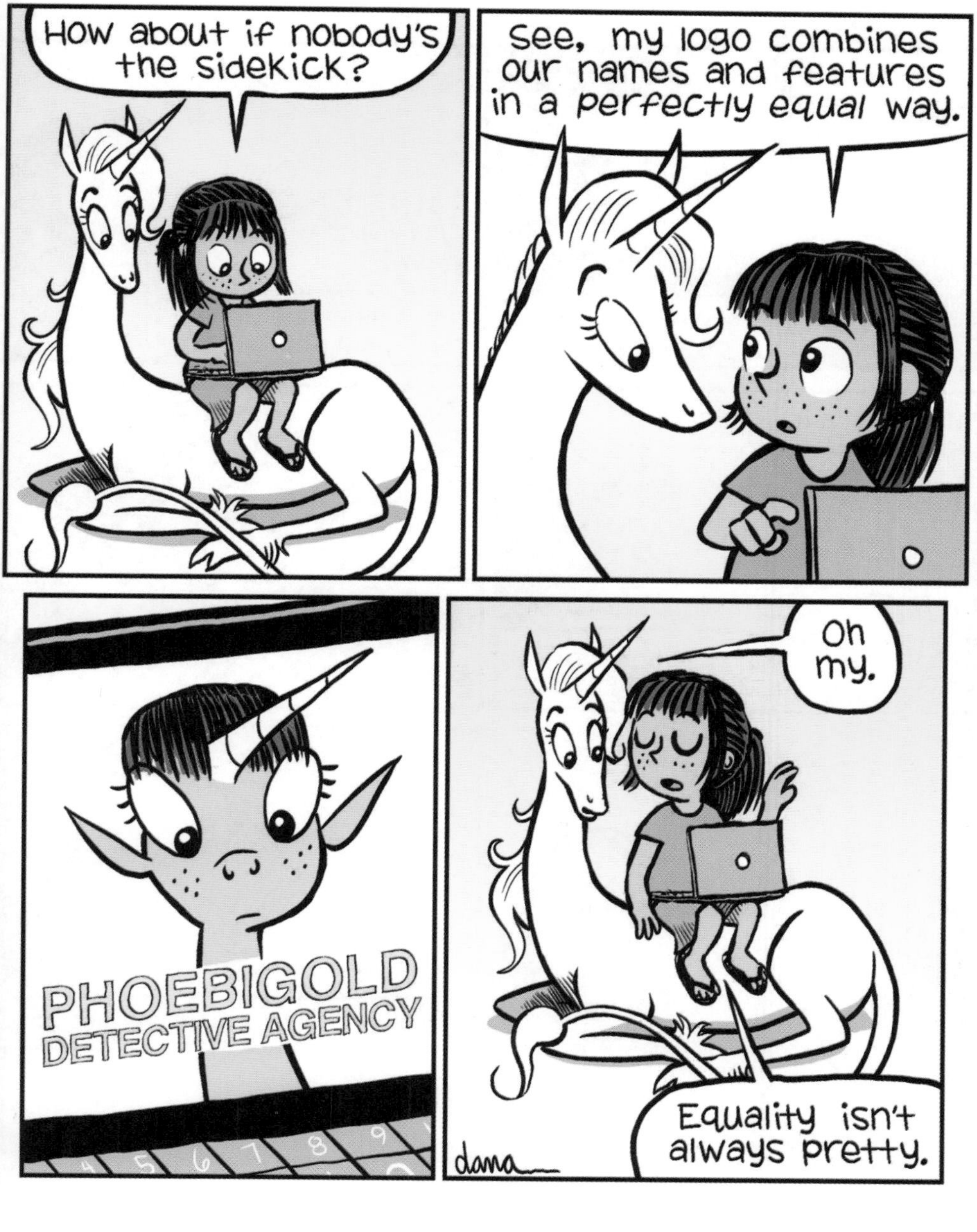
How about if nobody's the sidekick?
See, my logo combines our names and features in a *perfectly equal* way.
PHOEBIGOLD DETECTIVE AGENCY
Oh my.
Equality isn't always pretty.
dana

What is up?

I'm trying to create a comic strip!

It's called "Bickle the Fickle Pickle."

Does it have a story?

No, it's more of a SLICE OF LIFE thing.

Get it? SLICE? PICKLE?

HAHAHAHAHA

Too subtle?

Now I am hungry for pickles.

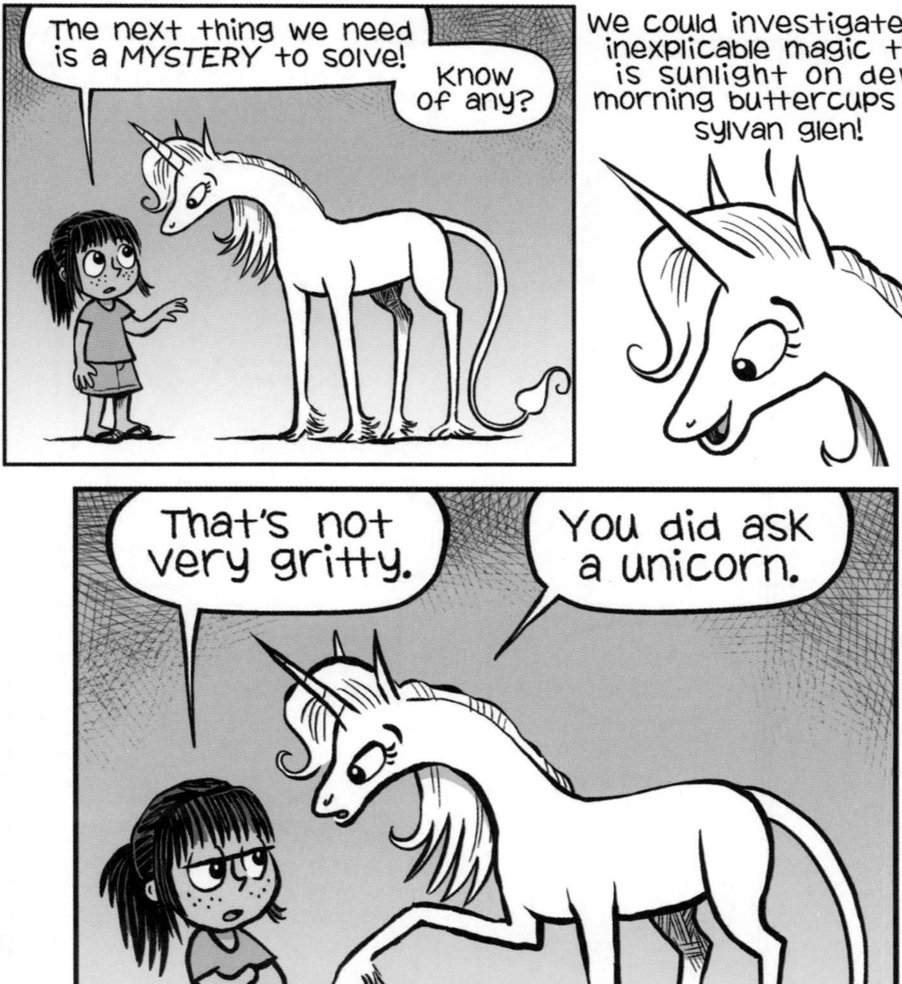
The next thing we need is a *MYSTERY* to solve!
Know of any?
We could investigate the inexplicable magic that is sunlight on dewy morning buttercups in a sylvan glen!
That's not very gritty.
You did ask a unicorn.
dana

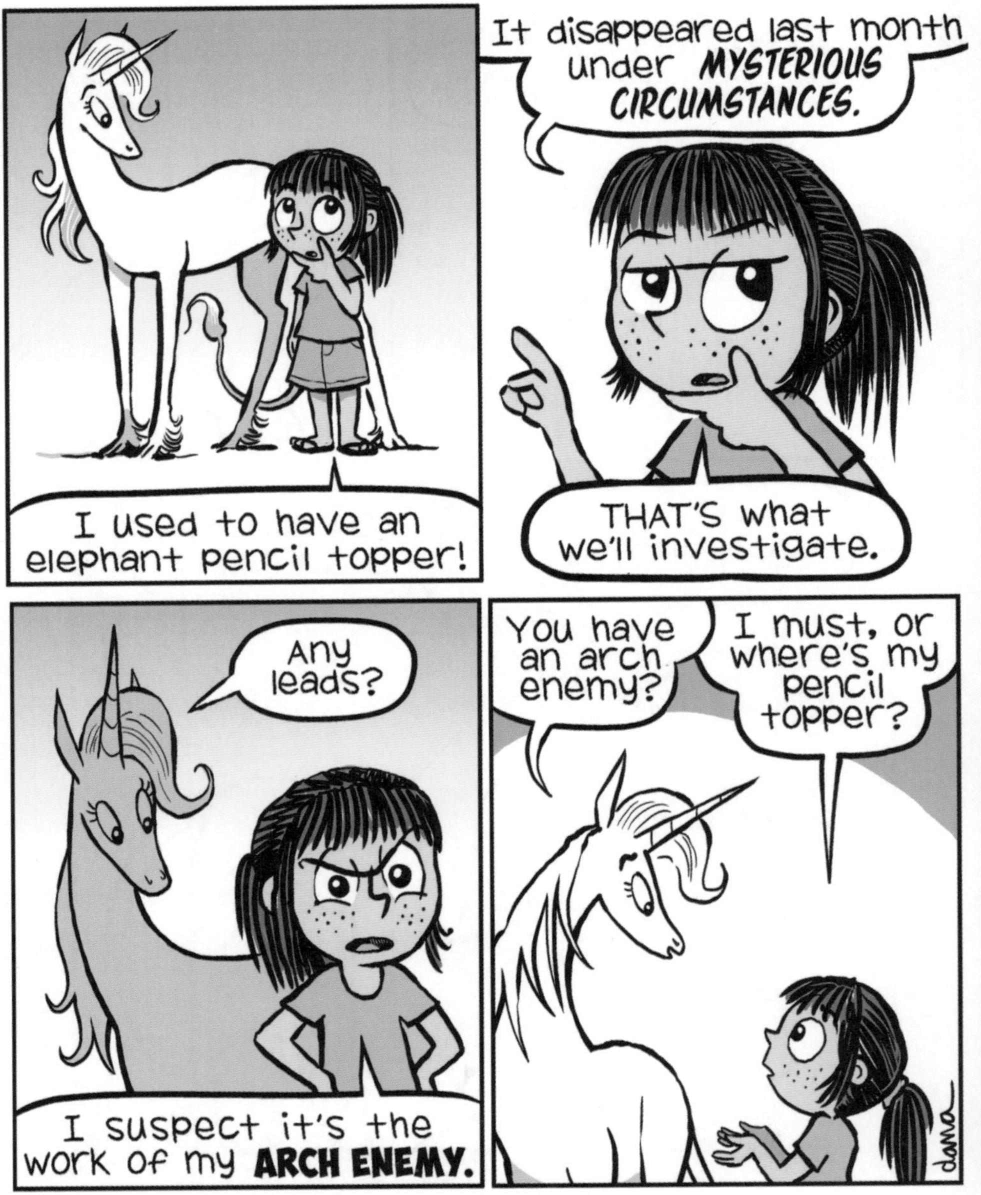
I used to have an elephant pencil topper!
It disappeared last month under MYSTERIOUS CIRCUMSTANCES.
THAT'S what we'll investigate.
Any leads?
I suspect it's the work of my ARCH ENEMY.
You have an arch enemy?
I must, or where's my pencil topper?
dana

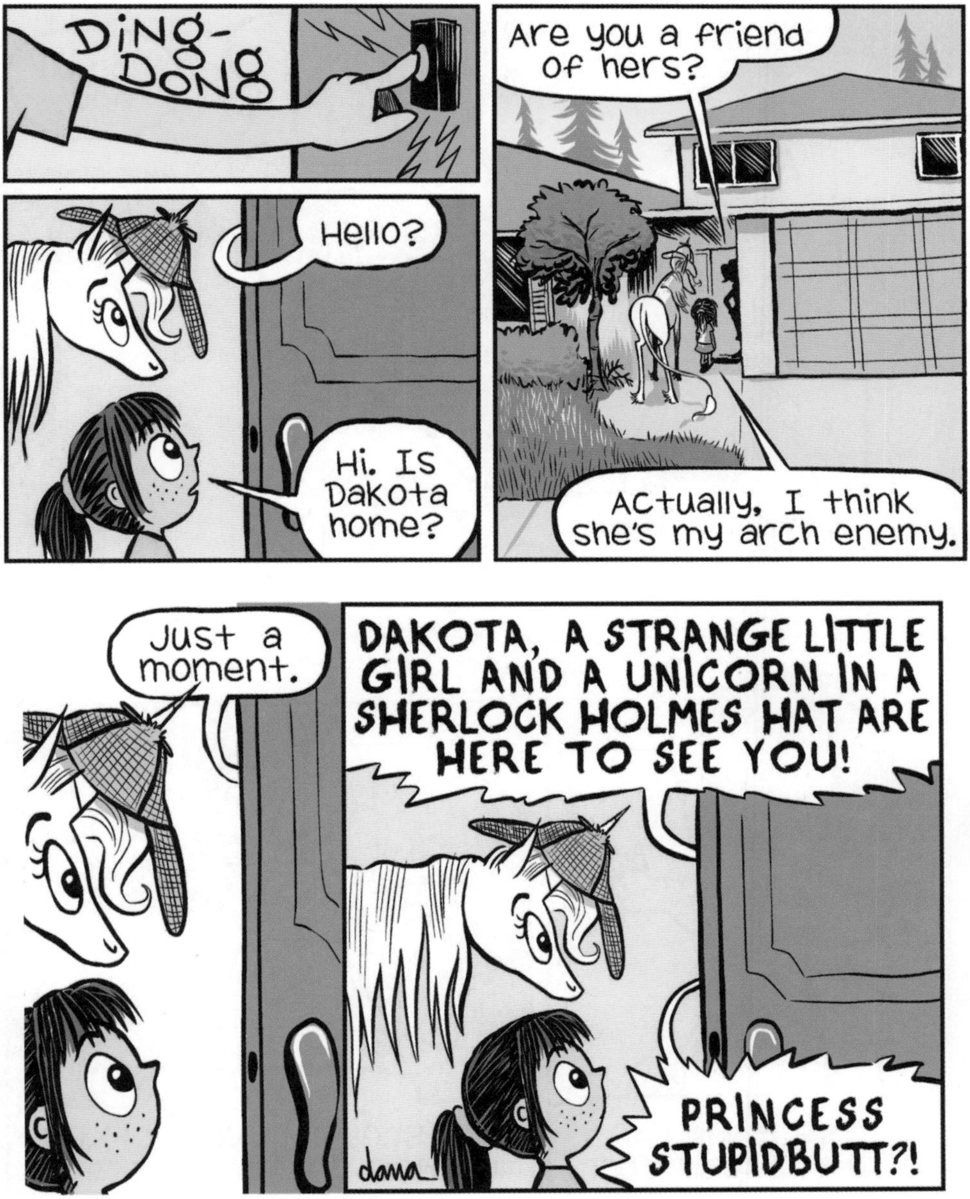
DING-DONG
Are you a friend of hers?
Hello?
Hi. Is Dakota home?
Actually, I think she's my arch enemy.
Just a moment.
DAKOTA, A STRANGE LITTLE GIRL AND A UNICORN IN A SHERLOCK HOLMES HAT ARE HERE TO SEE YOU!
PRINCESS STUPIDBUTT?!
dana

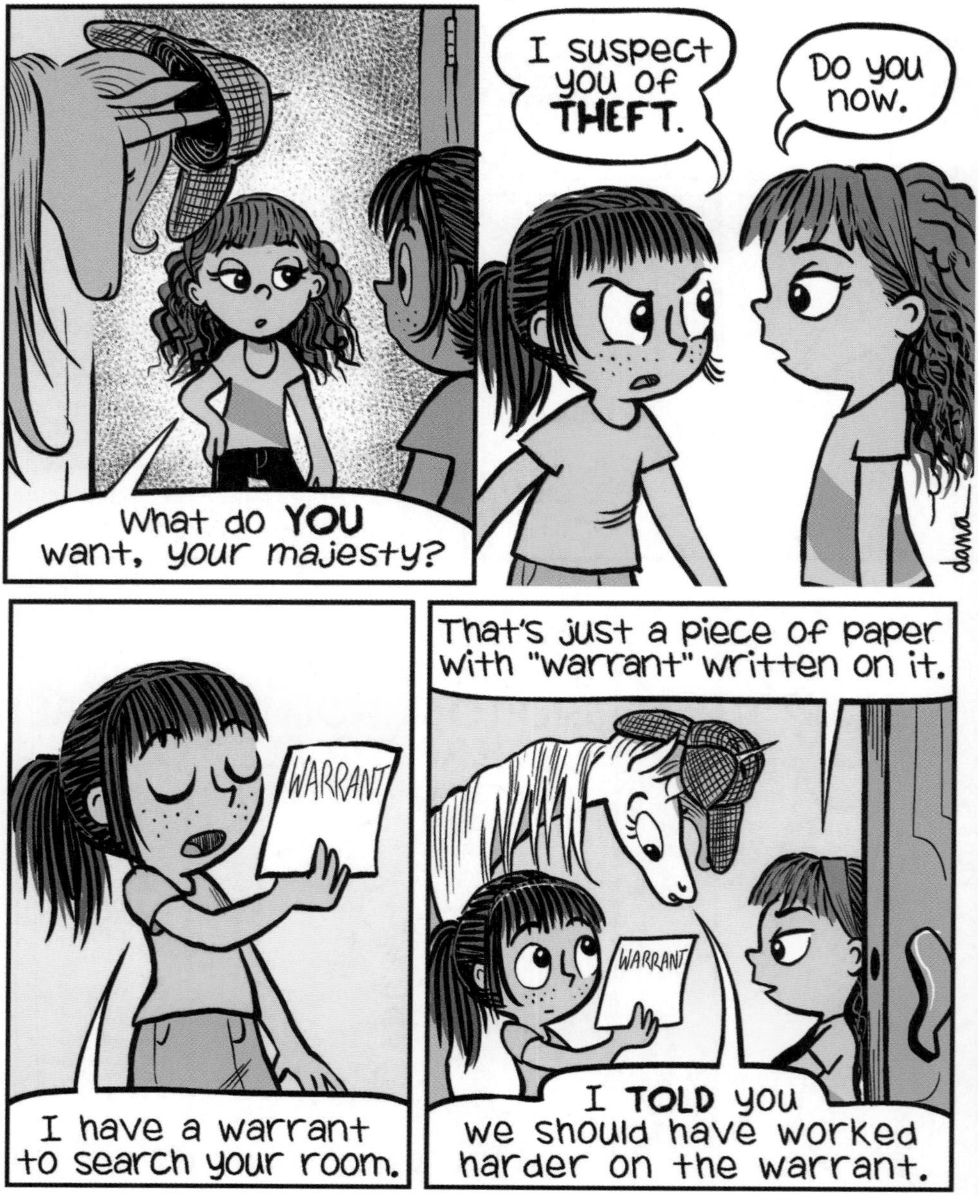
What do YOU want, your majesty?
I suspect you of THEFT.
Do you now.
dana
WARRANT
I have a warrant to search your room.
That's just a piece of paper with "warrant" written on it.
WARRANT
I TOLD you we should have worked harder on the warrant.

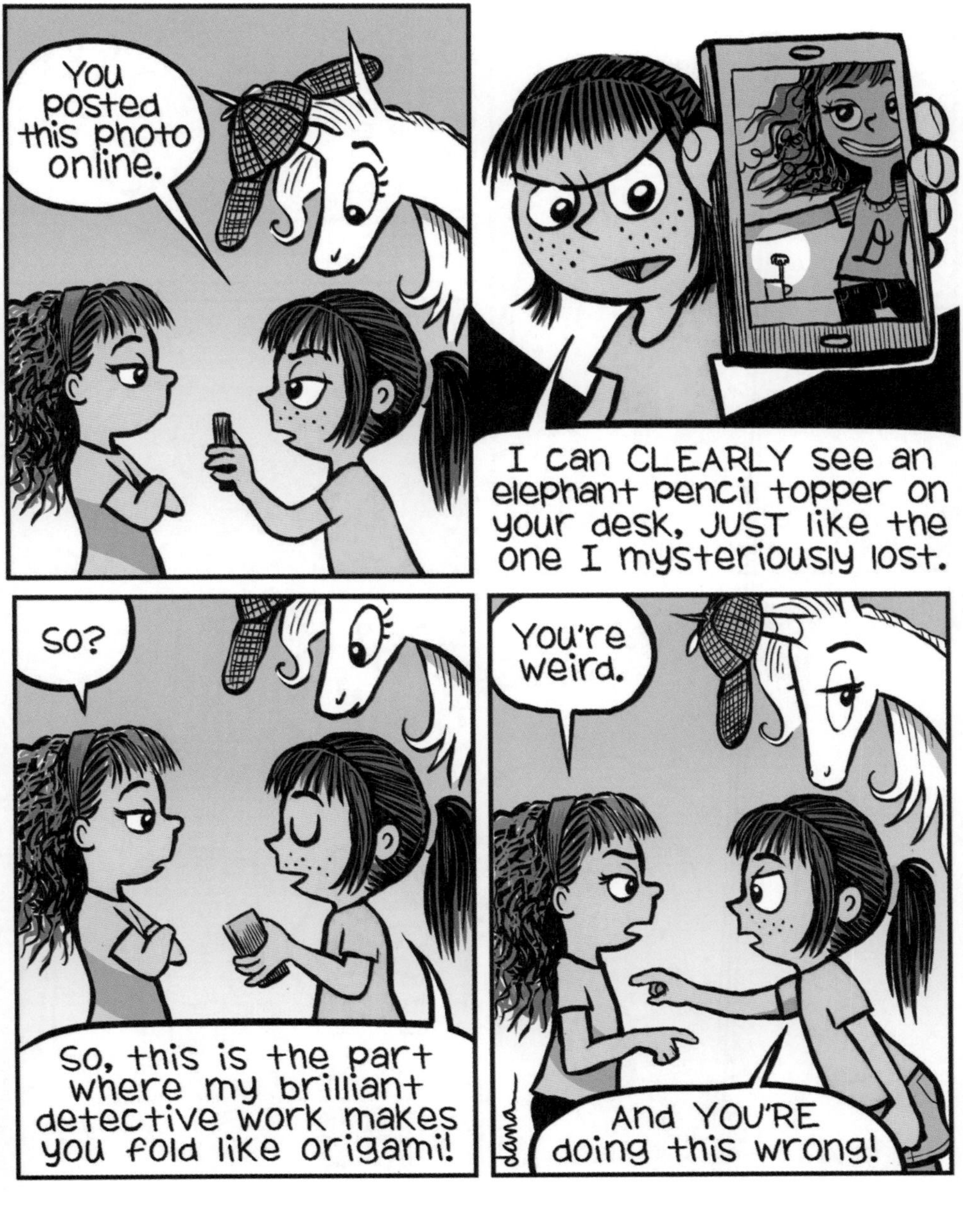
You posted this photo online.
I can CLEARLY see an elephant pencil topper on your desk, JUST like the one I mysteriously lost.
So?
So, this is the part where my brilliant detective work makes you fold like origami!
You're weird.
And YOU'RE doing this wrong!
dana

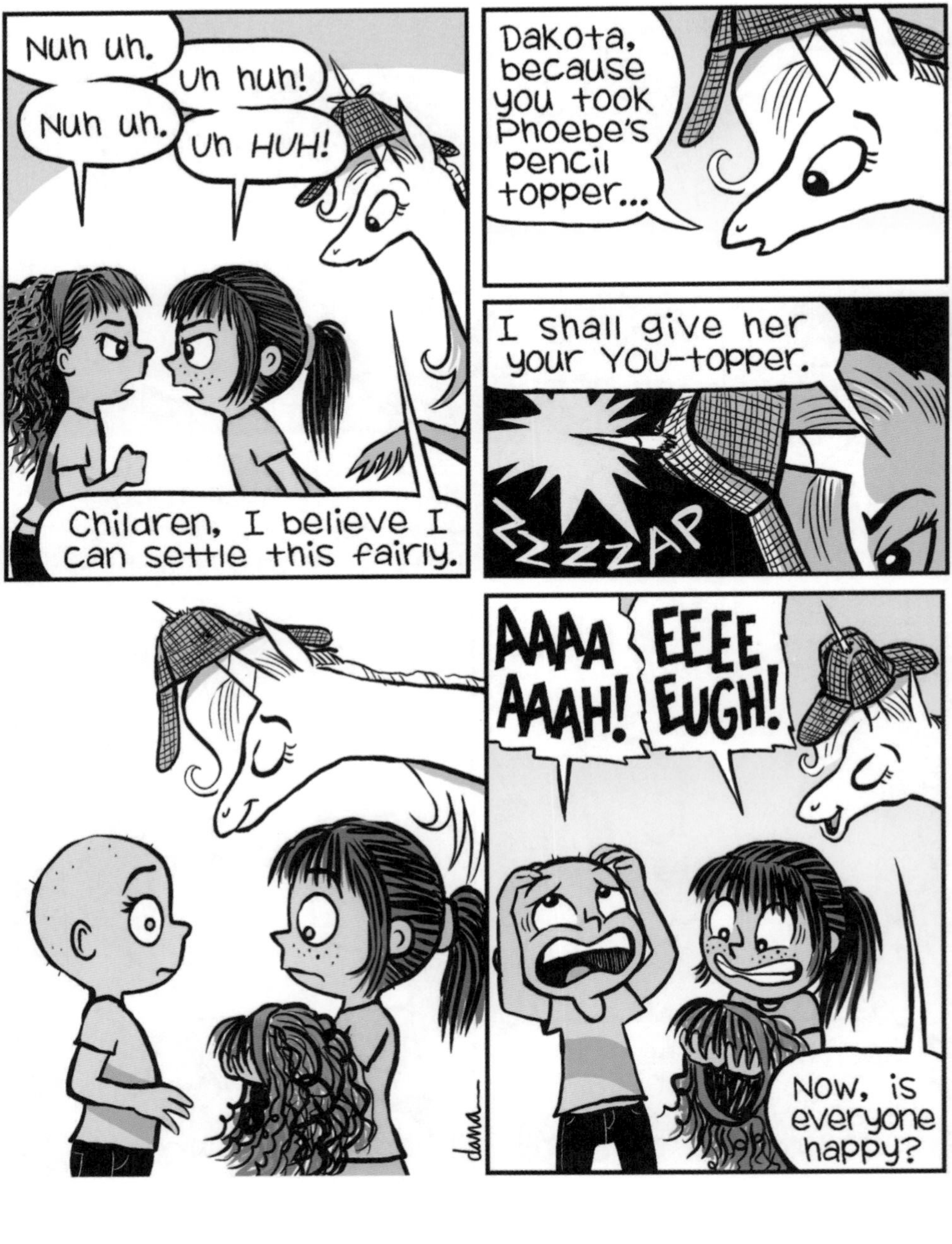
Nuh uh.
Uh huh!
Nuh uh.
Uh HUH!
Children, I believe I can settle this fairly.
Dakota, because you took Phoebe's pencil topper...
I shall give her your YOU-topper.
ZZZZZAP
AAAA AAAH!
EEEE EUGH!
Now, is everyone happy?
dana

AAAAA AAAAA!

AAAAAAAAAAAAAAAAAAAAAAA!

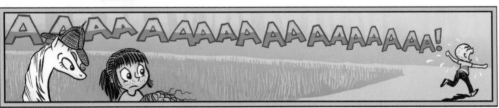

She is upset!

YOU **ZAPPED HER HAIR OFF.**

That is a big deal?

YES!

You humans are *MOSTLY* bald anyhow. I did not know you cared so much for what little hair you have.

I...can actually kinda see your logic, but...

what is a tiny bit of extra pink in a sea of fleshy human disgustingness?

Remember what I said about knowing when to stop talking?

75

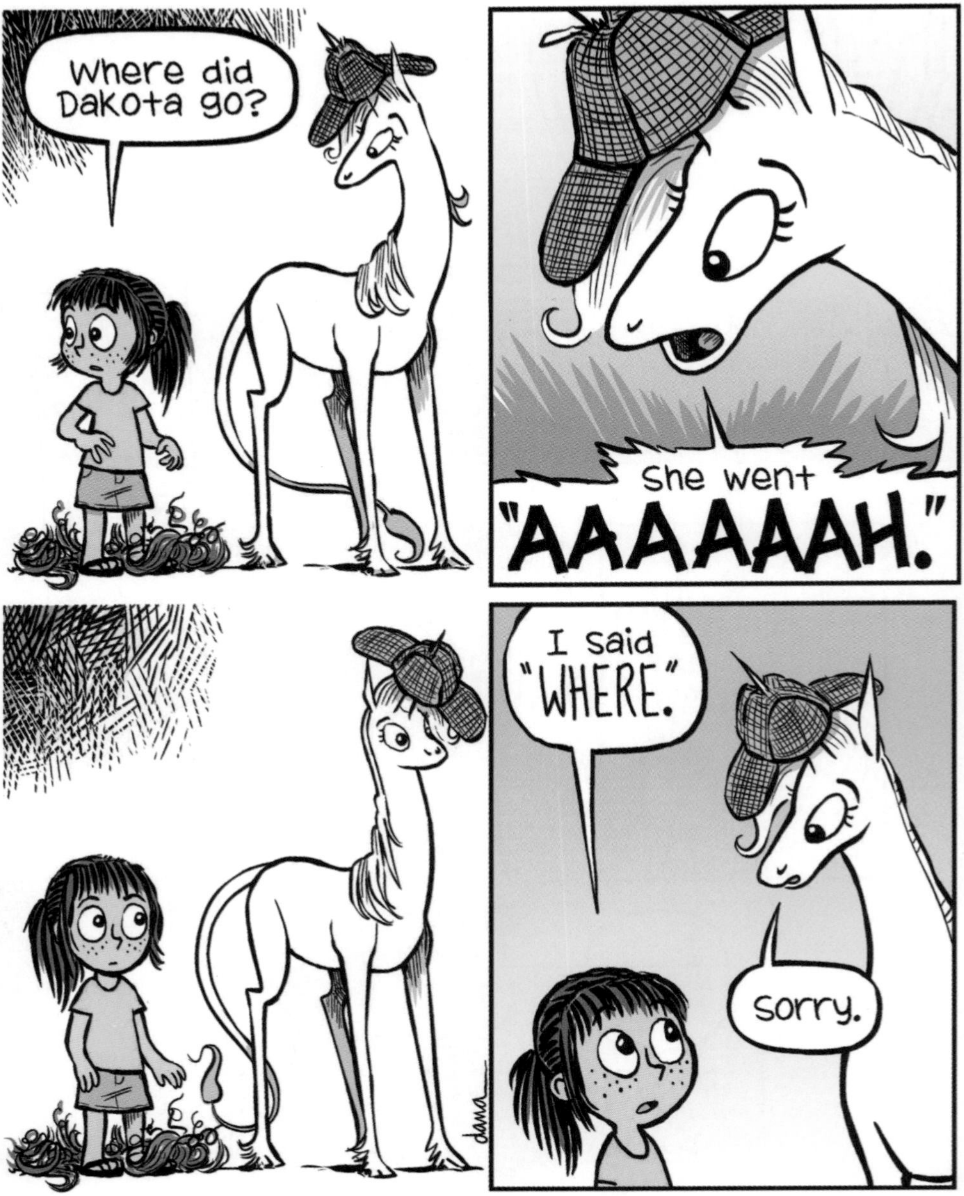
Where did Dakota go?
She went "AAAAAAH."
I said "WHERE."
Sorry.
dana

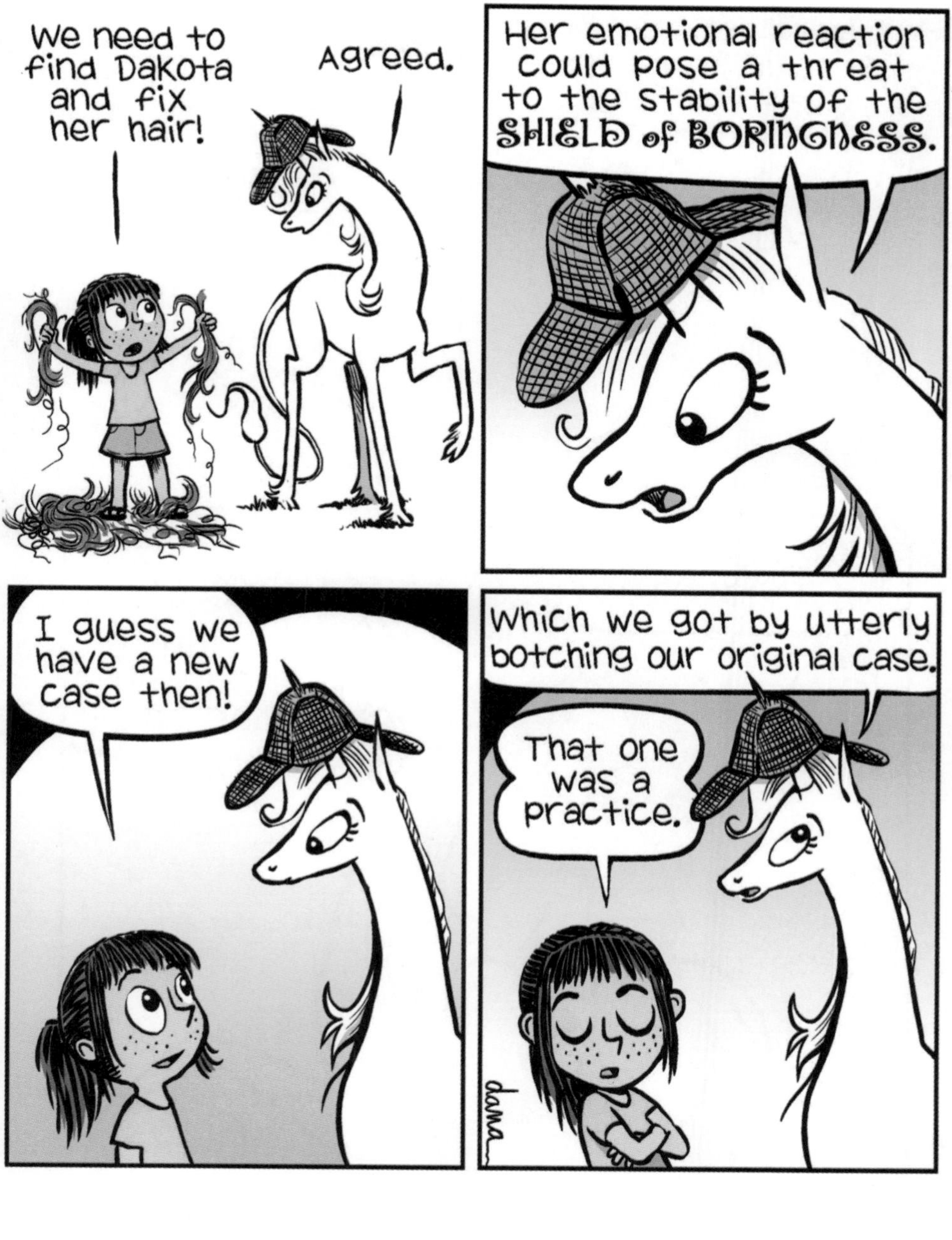
We need to find Dakota and fix her hair!
Agreed.
Her emotional reaction could pose a threat to the stability of the SHIELD of BORINGNESS.
I guess we have a new case then!
Which we got by utterly botching our original case.
That one was a practice.
dana

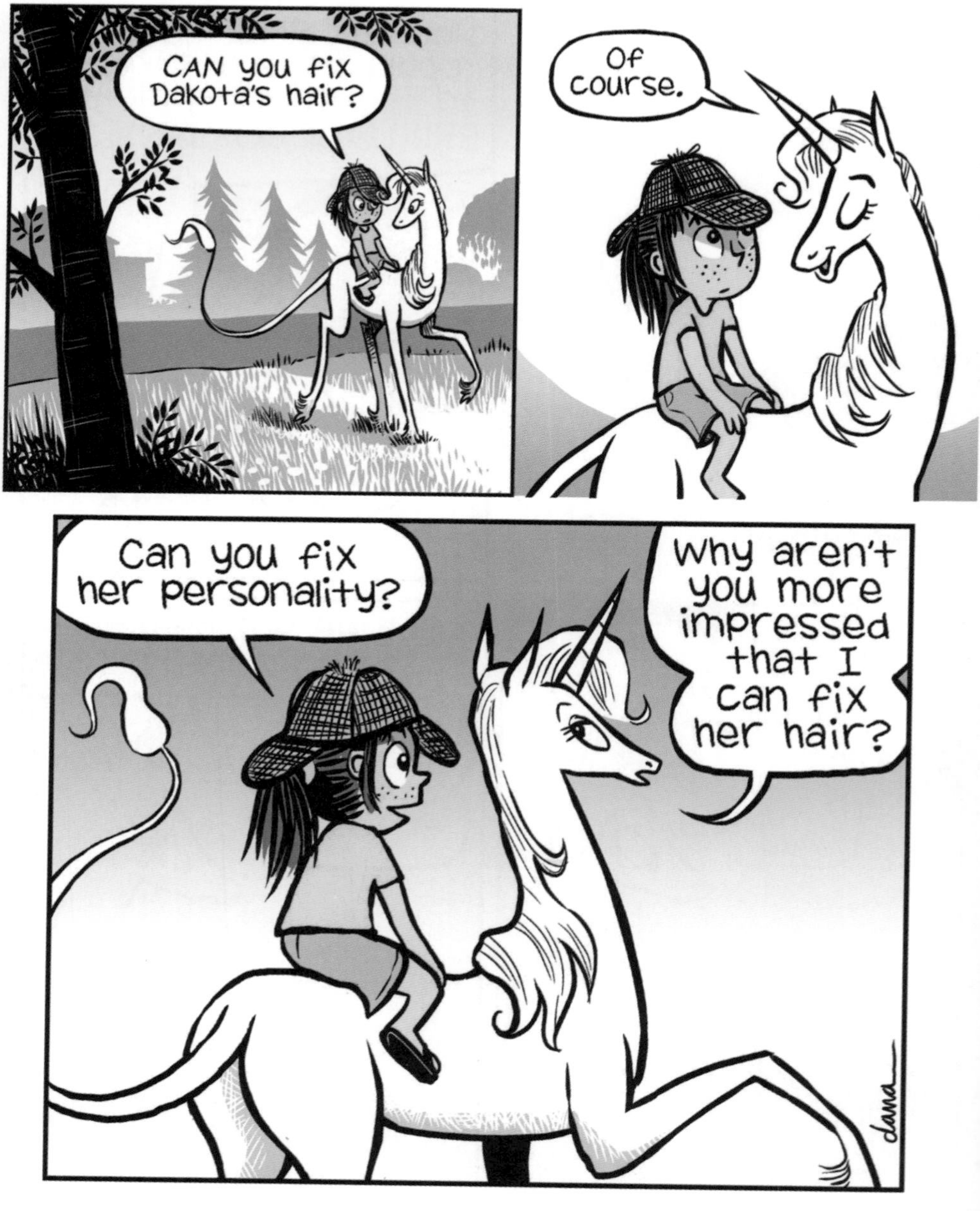
CAN you fix Dakota's hair?
Of course.
Can you fix her personality?
Why aren't you more impressed that I can fix her hair?
dana

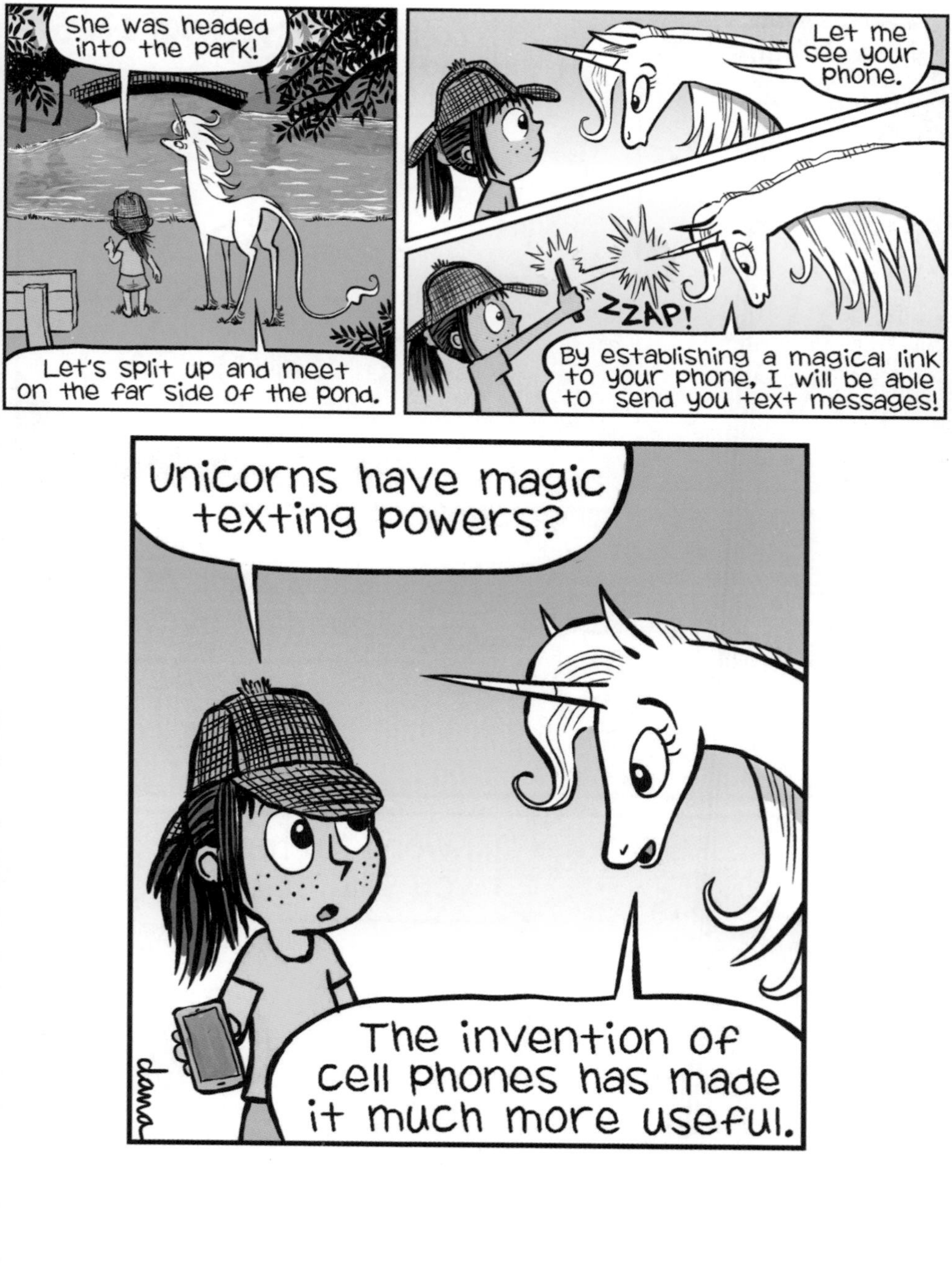
She was headed into the park!
Let's split up and meet on the far side of the pond.
Let me see your phone.
ZZAP!
By establishing a magical link to your phone, I will be able to send you text messages!
Unicorns have magic texting powers?
The invention of cell phones has made it much more useful.
dana

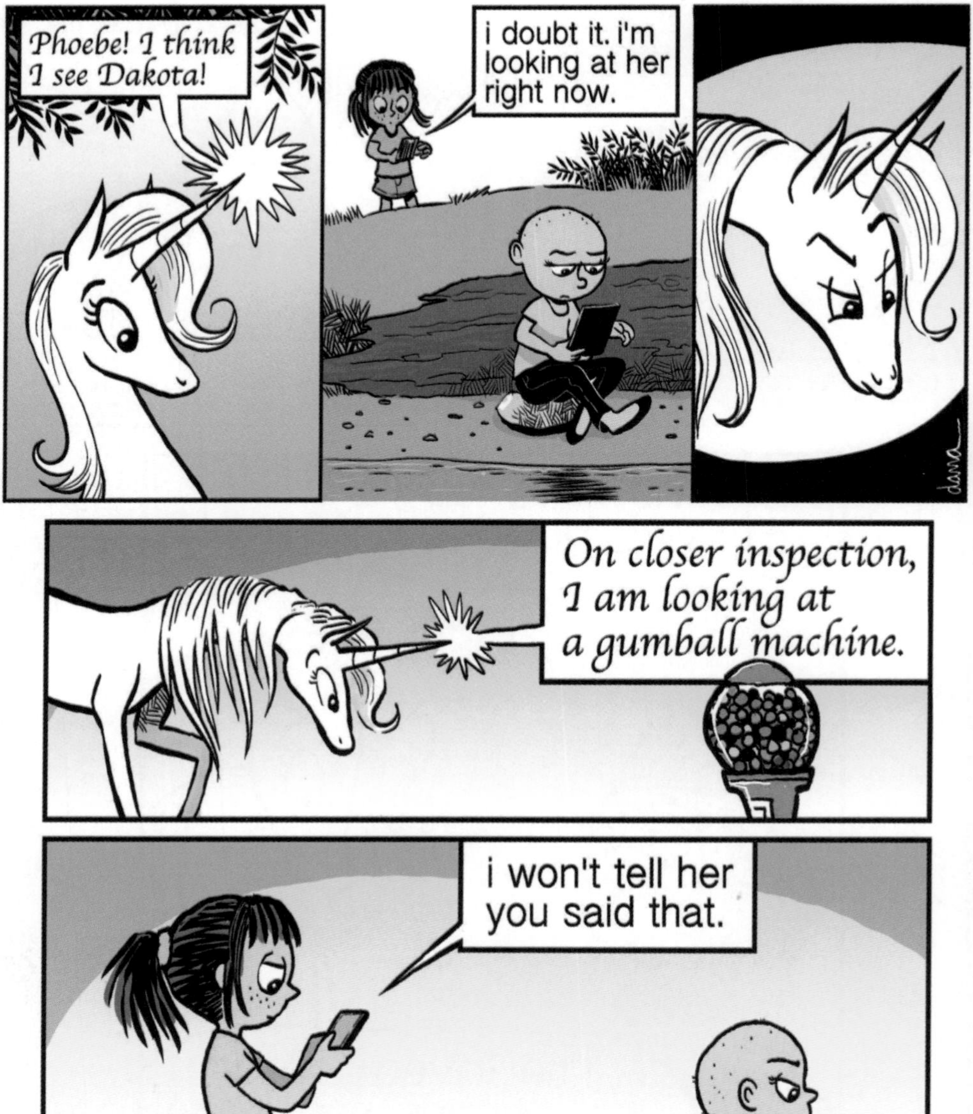
Phoebe! I think I see Dakota!
i doubt it. i'm looking at her right now.
On closer inspection, I am looking at a gumball machine.
i won't tell her you said that.
dana

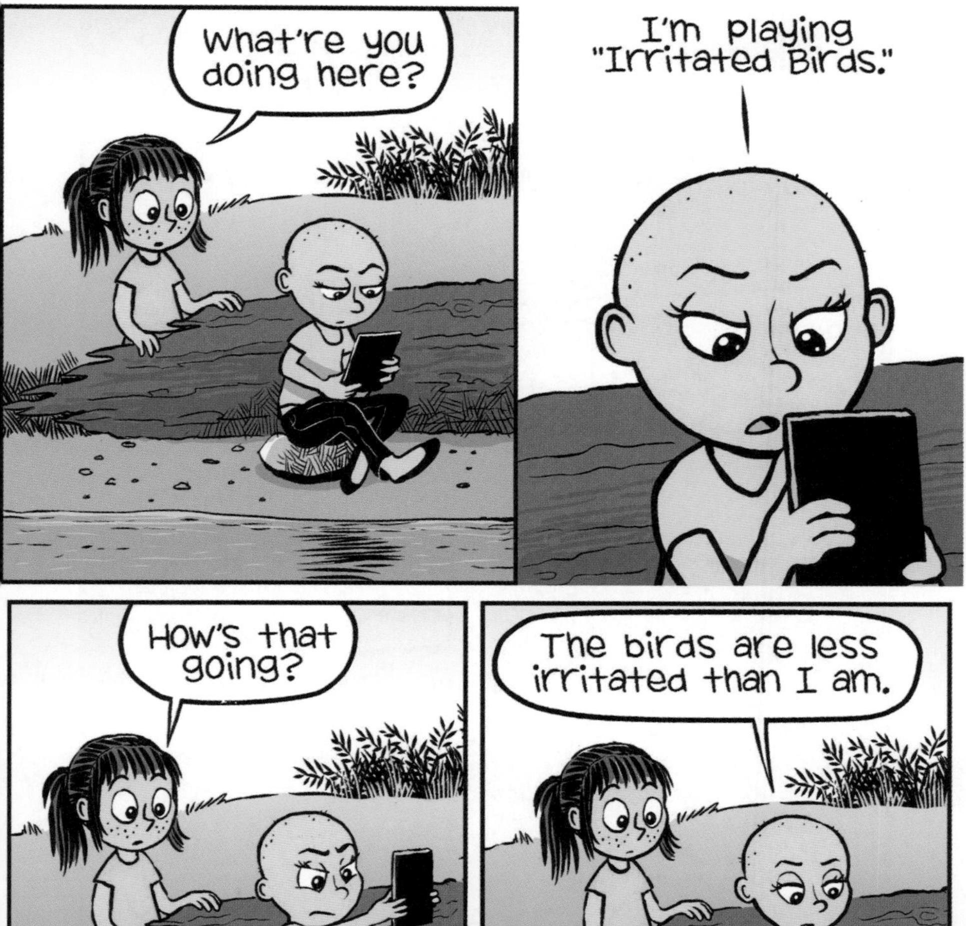
What're you doing here?
I'm playing "Irritated Birds."
How's that going?
The birds are less irritated than I am.
dana

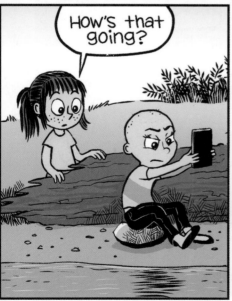

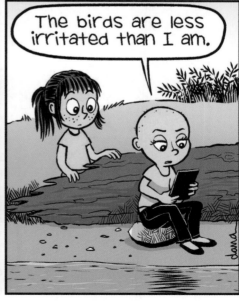

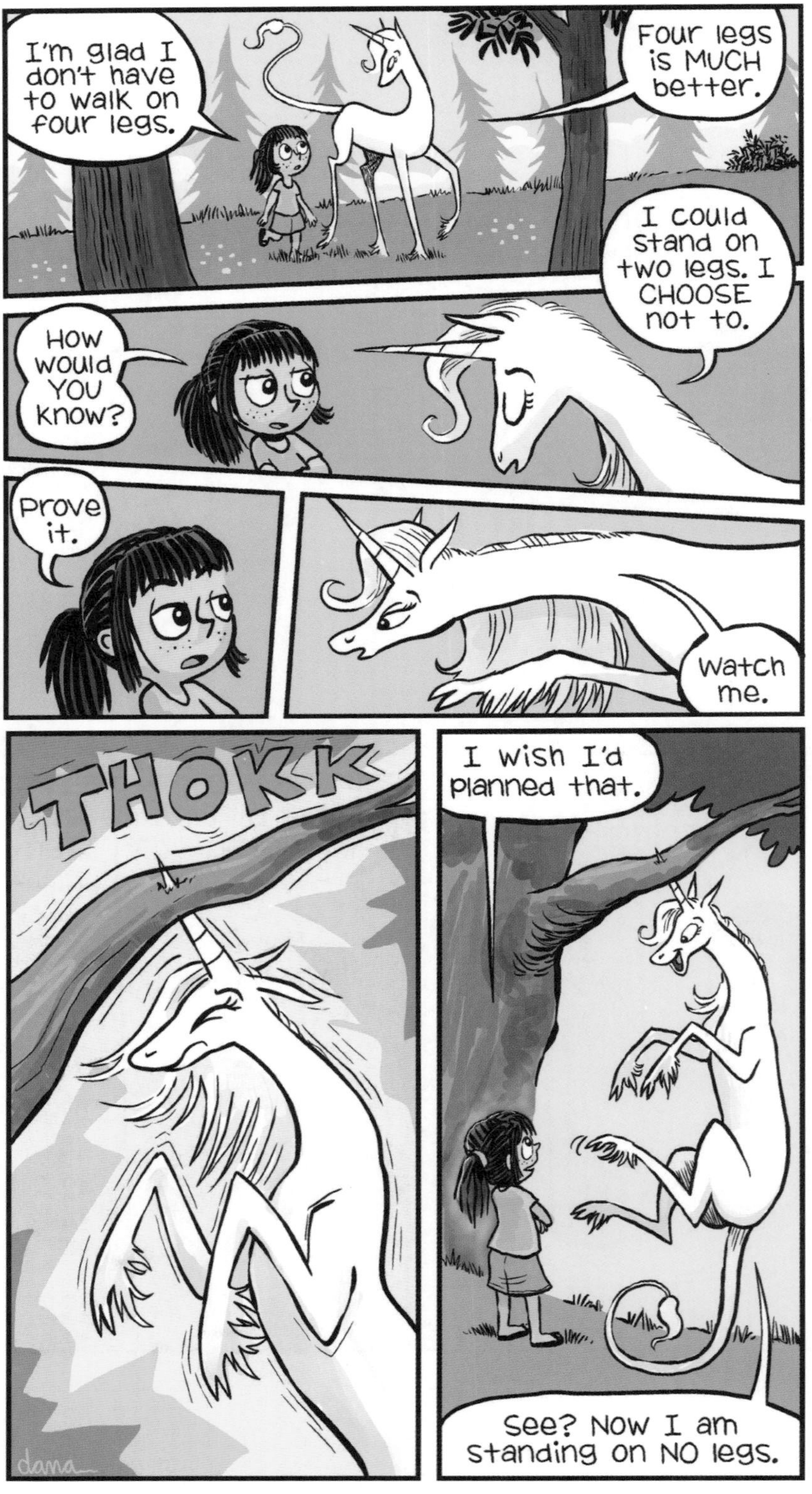
I'm glad I don't have to walk on four legs.
Four legs is MUCH better.
I could stand on two legs. I CHOOSE not to.
How would YOU know?
Prove it.
Watch me.
THOKK
I wish I'd planned that.
See? Now I am standing on NO legs.
dana

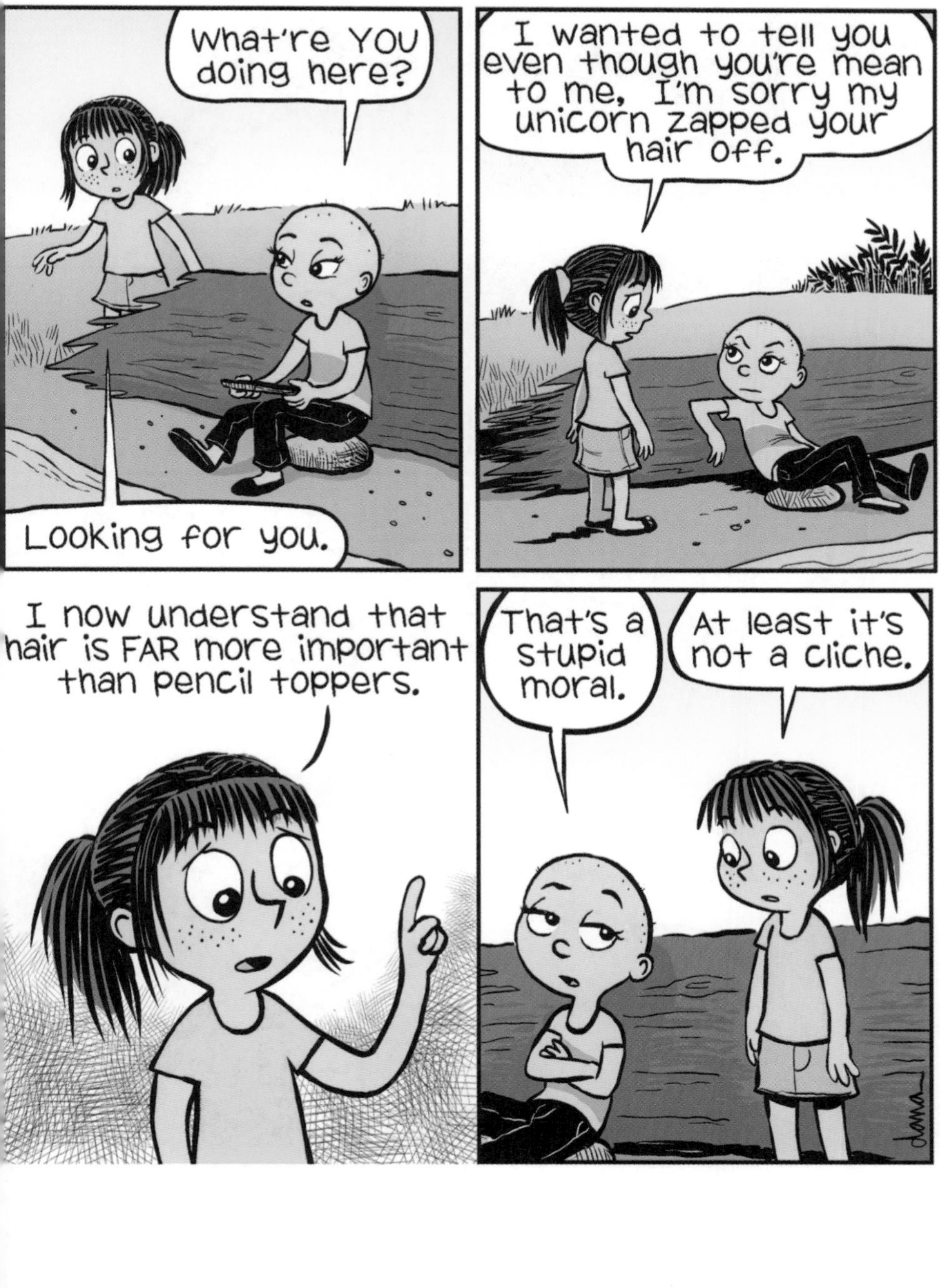
What're YOU doing here?
Looking for you.
I wanted to tell you even though you're mean to me, I'm sorry my unicorn zapped your hair off.
I now understand that hair is FAR more important than pencil toppers.
That's a stupid moral.
At least it's not a cliche.
dana

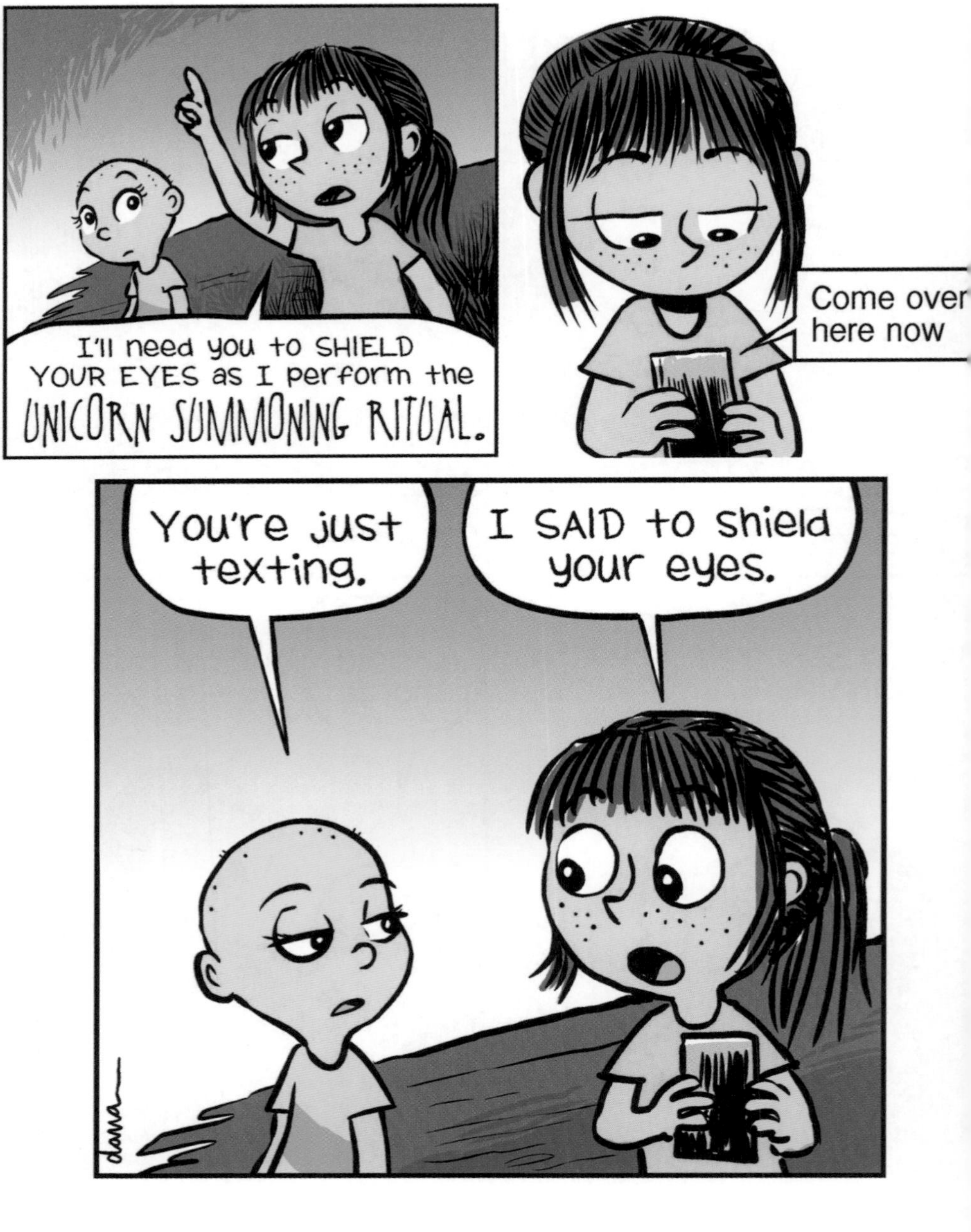
I'll need you to SHIELD YOUR EYES as I perform the UNICORN SUMMONING RITUAL.
Come over here now
You're just texting.
I SAID to shield your eyes.
dana

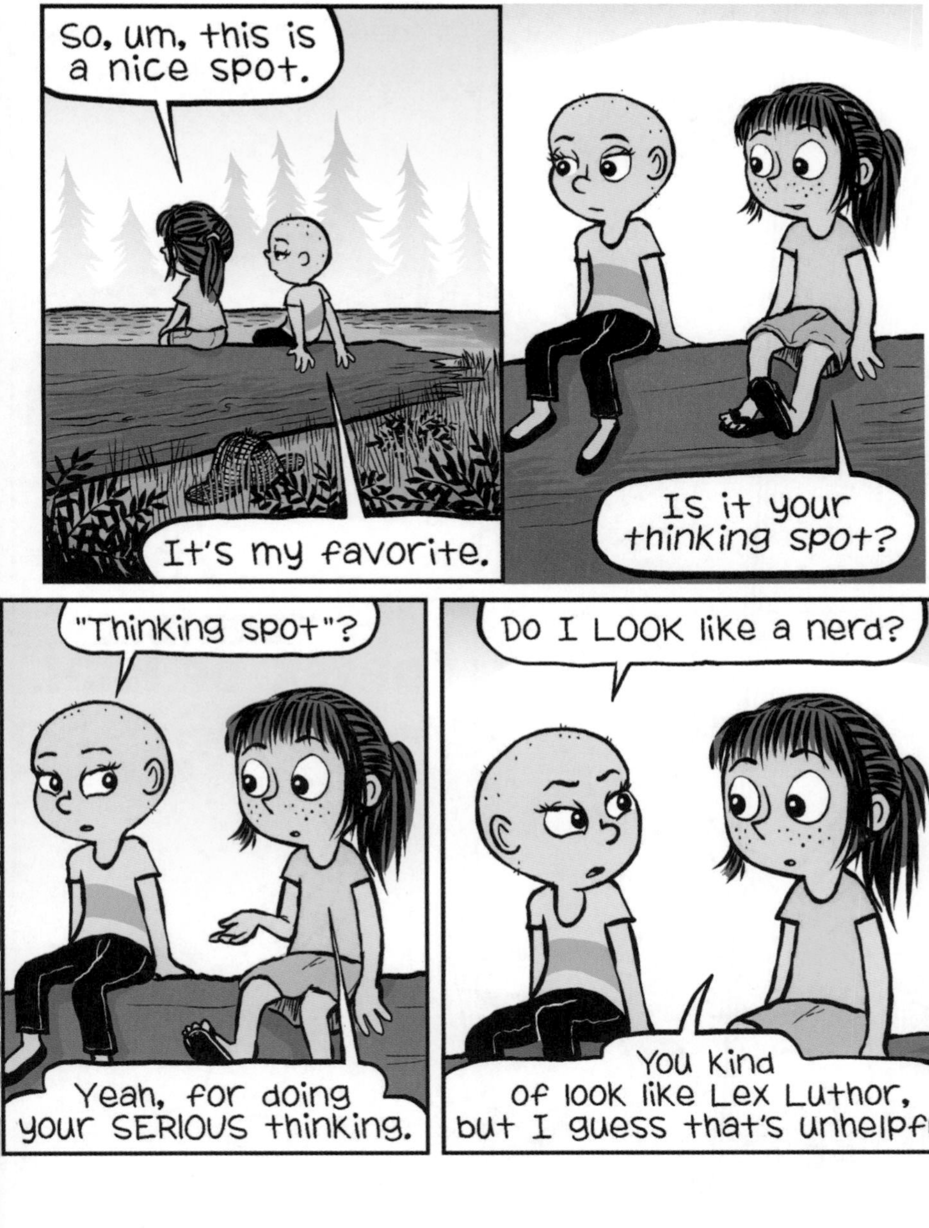
So, um, this is a nice spot.
It's my favorite.
Is it your thinking spot?
"Thinking spot"?
Yeah, for doing your SERIOUS thinking.
Do I LOOK like a nerd?
You kind of look like Lex Luthor, but I guess that's unhelpful.
dana

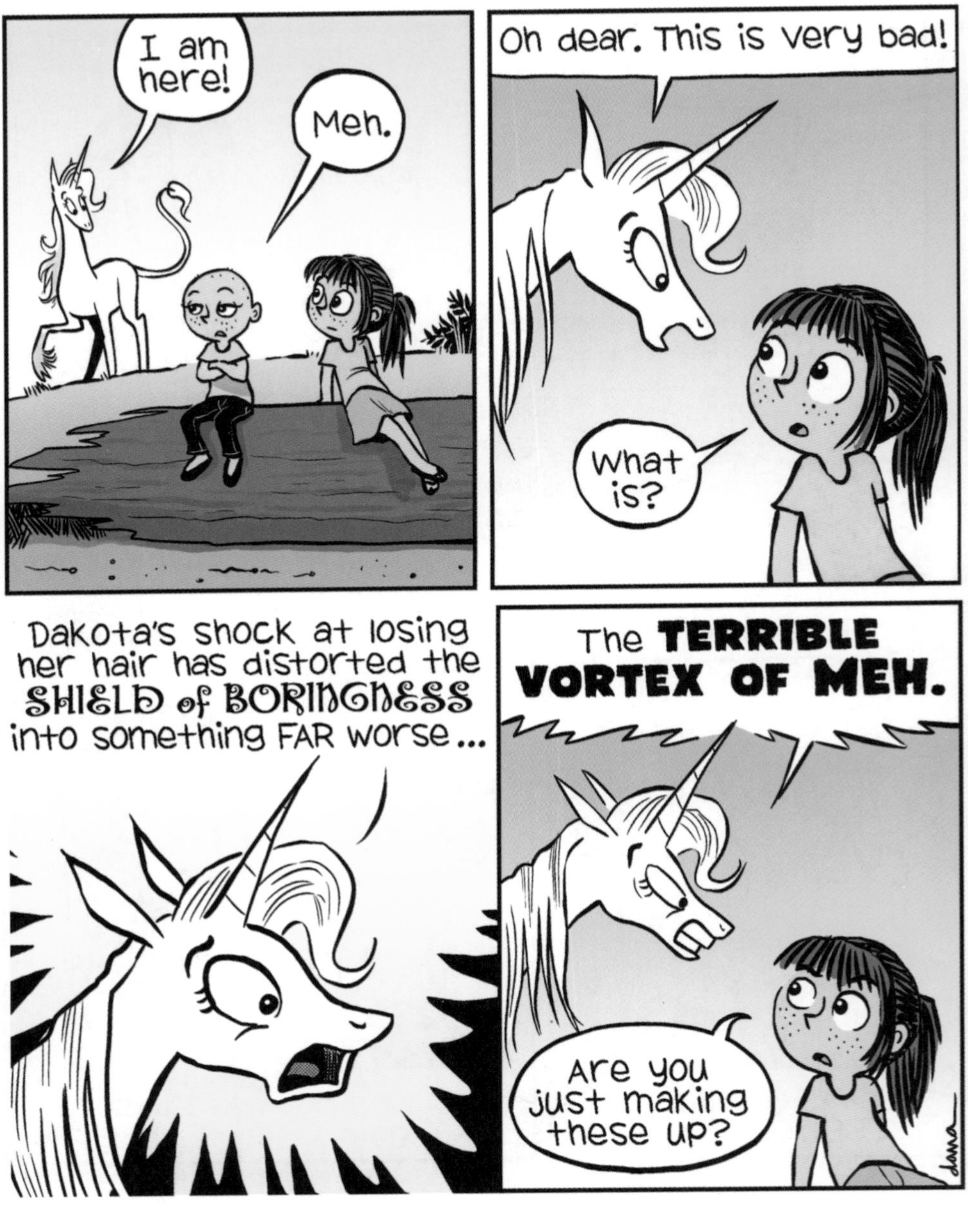
I am here!
Meh.
Oh dear. This is very bad!
What is?
Dakota's shock at losing her hair has distorted the SHIELD of BORINGNESS into something FAR worse...
The TERRIBLE VORTEX OF MEH.
Are you just making these up?
dana

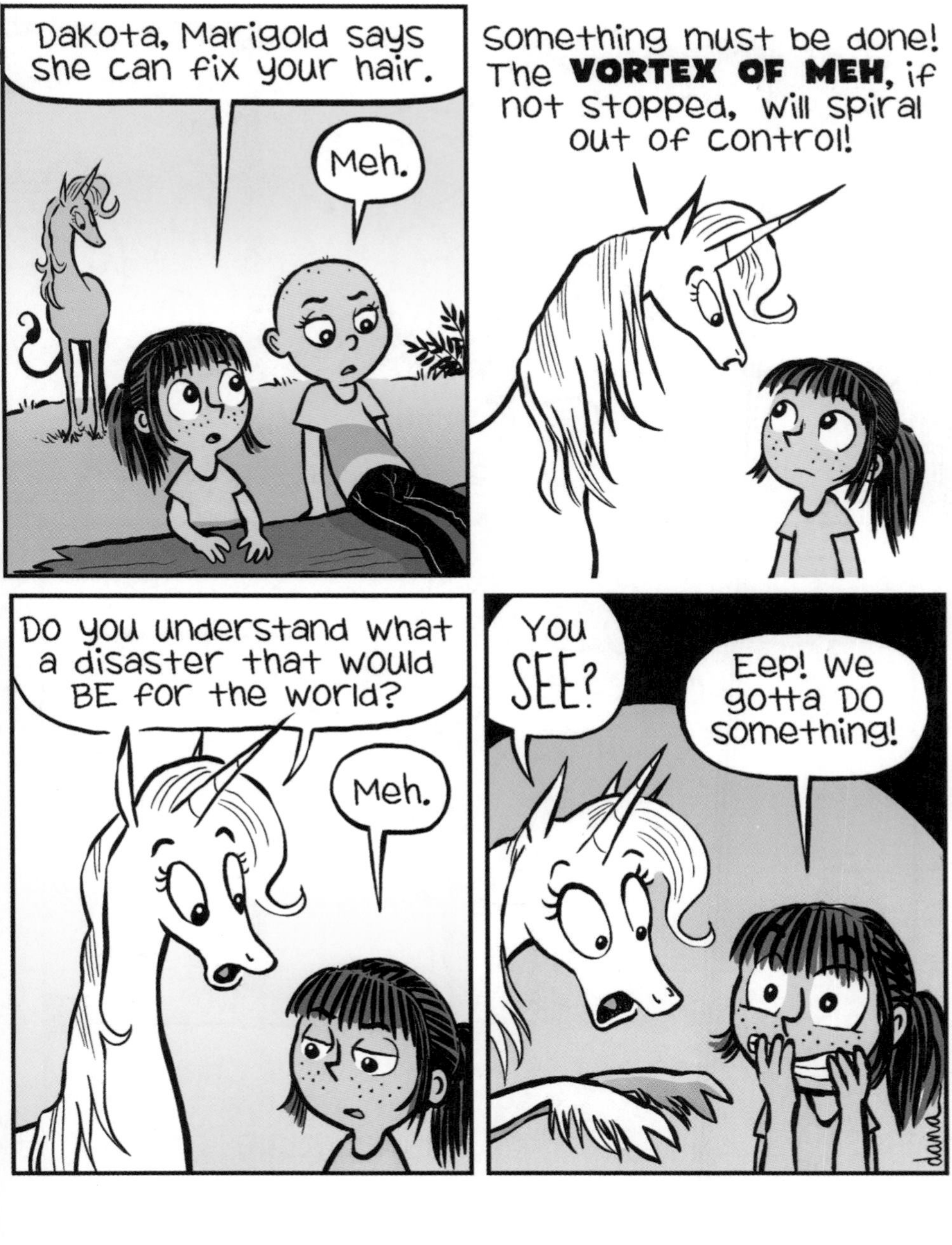

Dakota, Marigold says she can fix your hair.
Meh.
Something must be done! The VORTEX OF MEH, if not stopped, will spiral out of control!
Do you understand what a disaster that would BE for the world?
Meh.
You SEE?
Eep! We gotta DO something!
dana

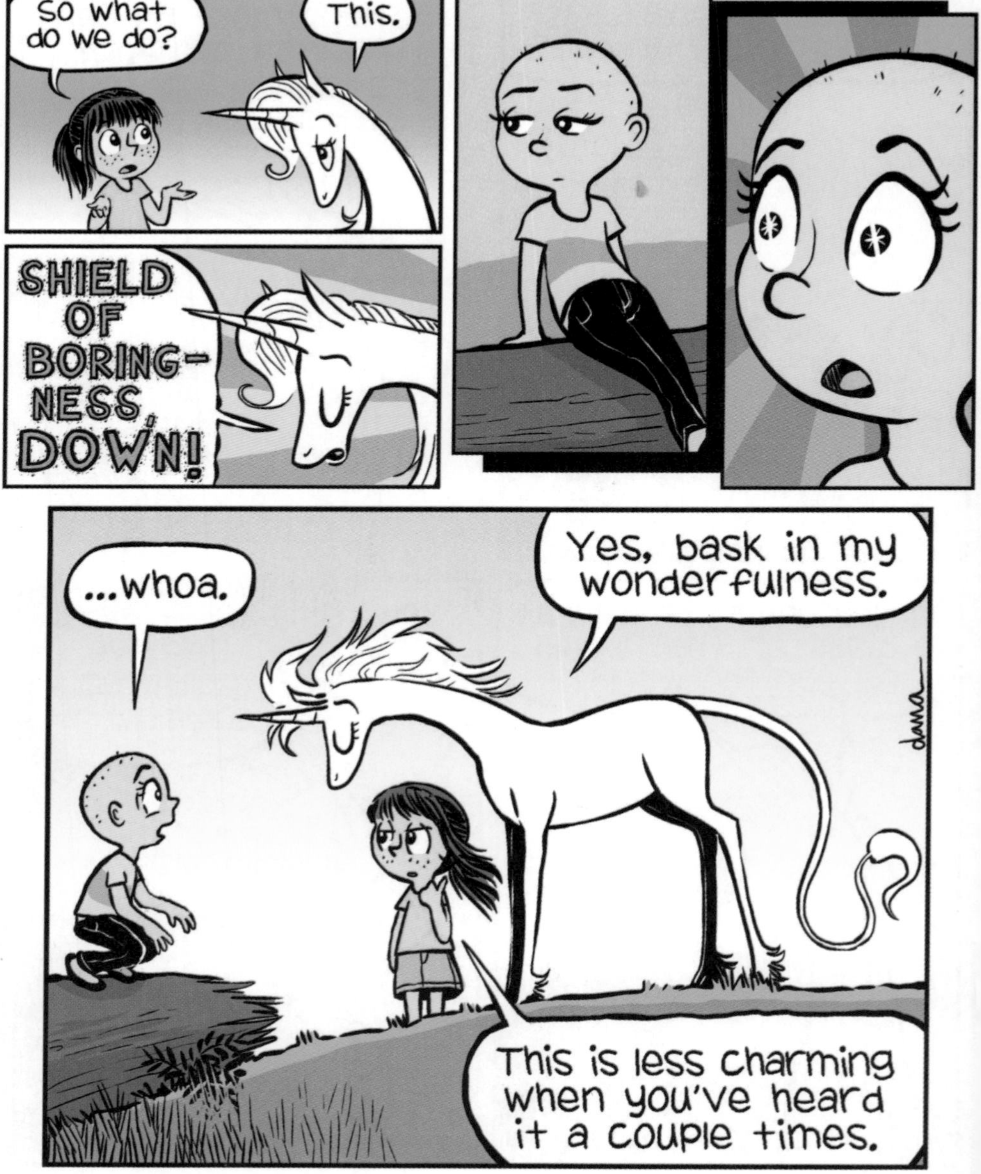
So what do we do?
This.
SHIELD OF BORING-NESS, DOWN!
...whoa.
Yes, bask in my wonderfulness.
This is less charming when you've heard it a couple times.
dana

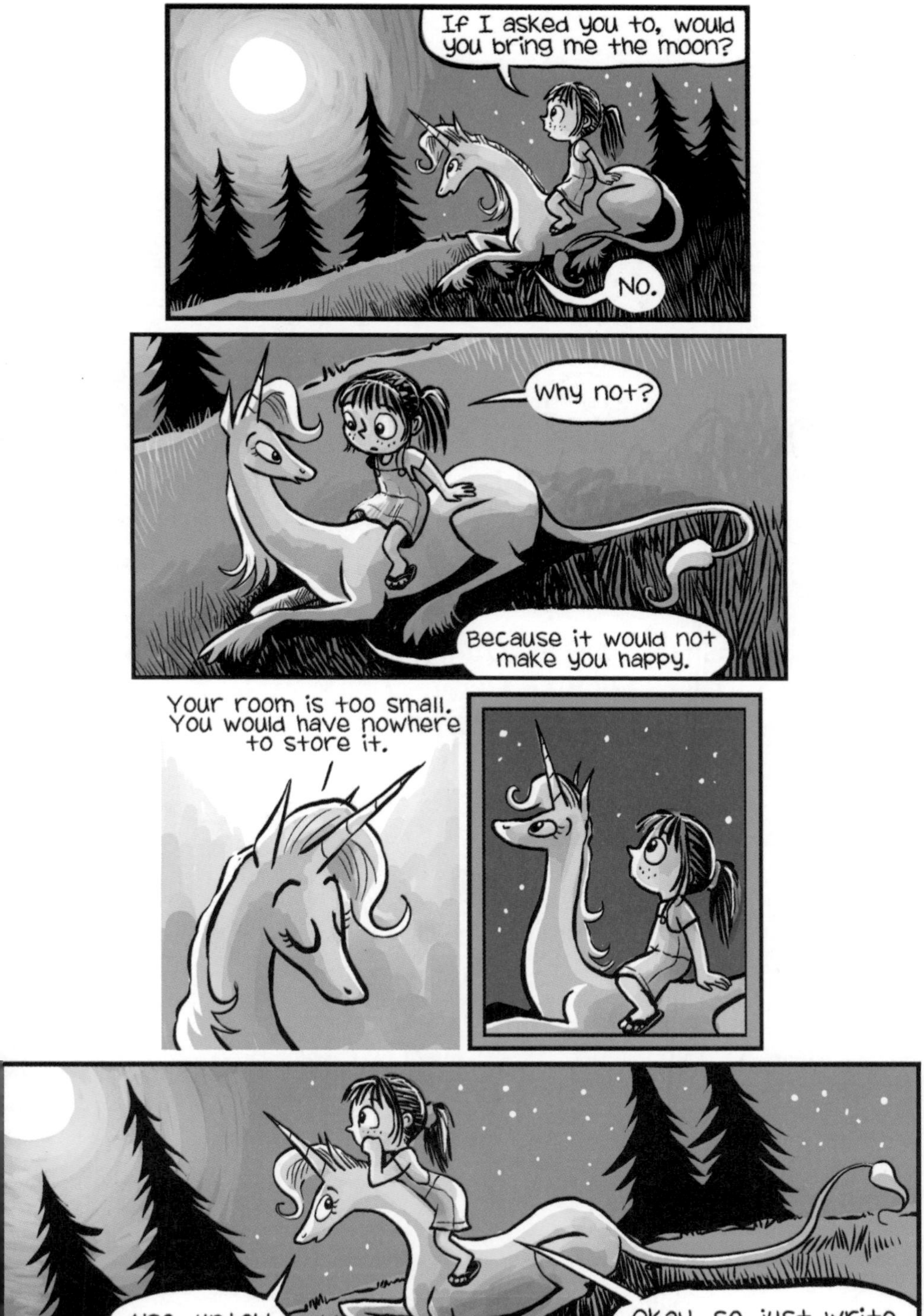
If I asked you to, would you bring me the moon?
No.
Why not?
Because it would not make you happy.
Your room is too small. You would have nowhere to store it.
Also, untold millions would perish.
Okay, so just write "PHOEBE RULES" on it in giant letters.

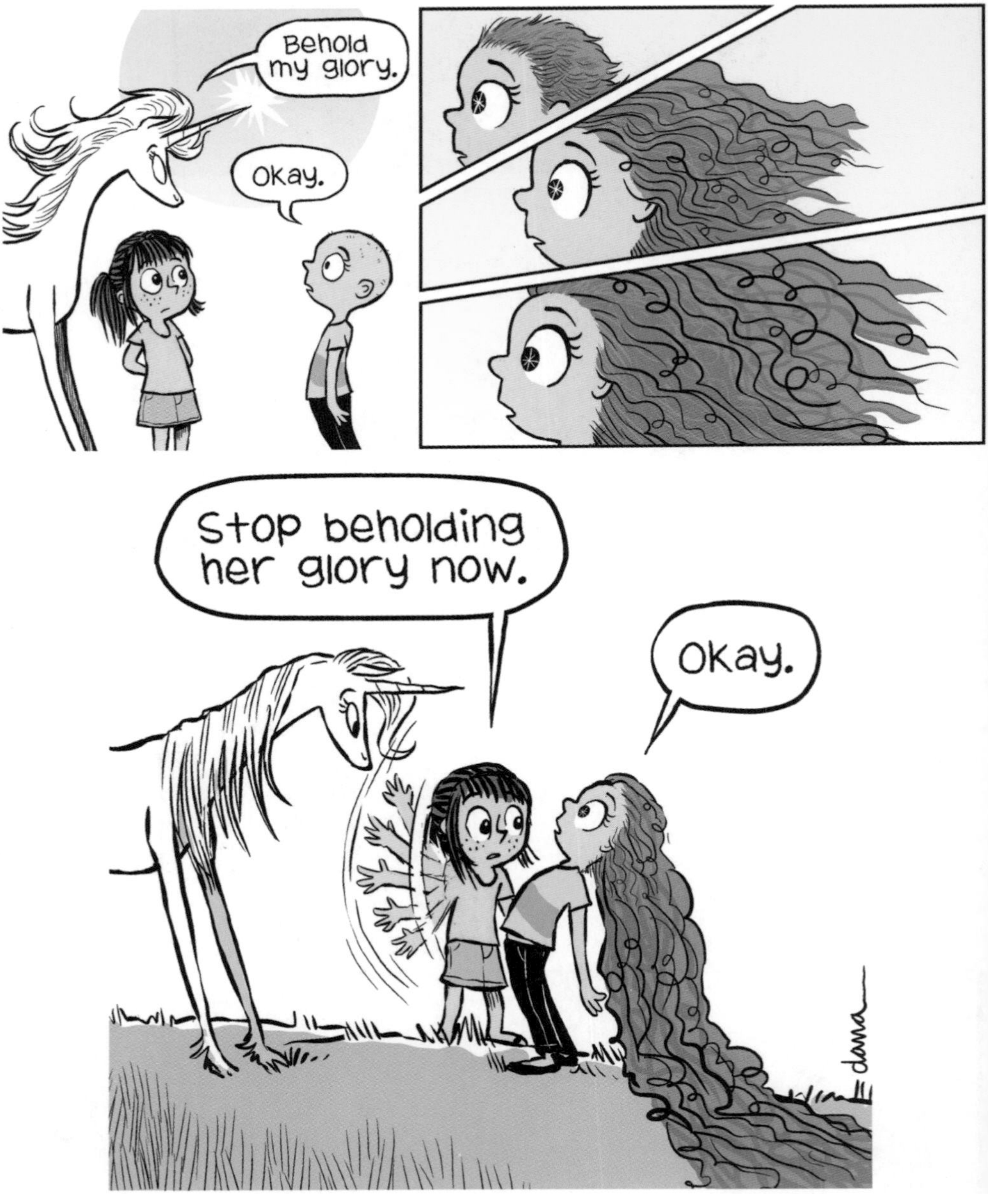
Behold my glory.
Okay.
Stop beholding her glory now.
Okay.
dana

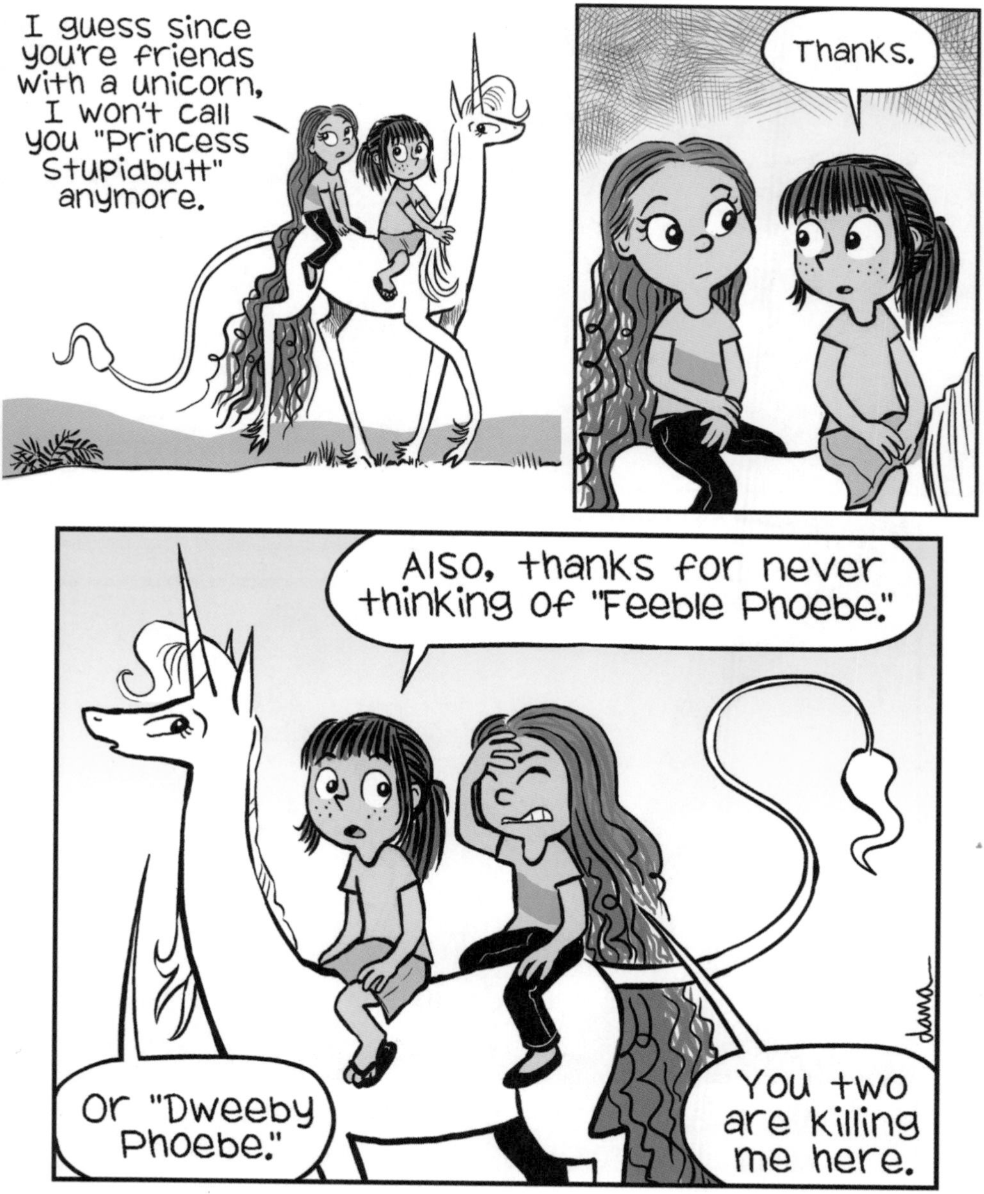
I guess since you're friends with a unicorn, I won't call you "Princess Stupidbutt" anymore.
Thanks.
Also, thanks for never thinking of "Feeble Phoebe."
Or "Dweeby Phoebe."
You two are killing me here.
dana

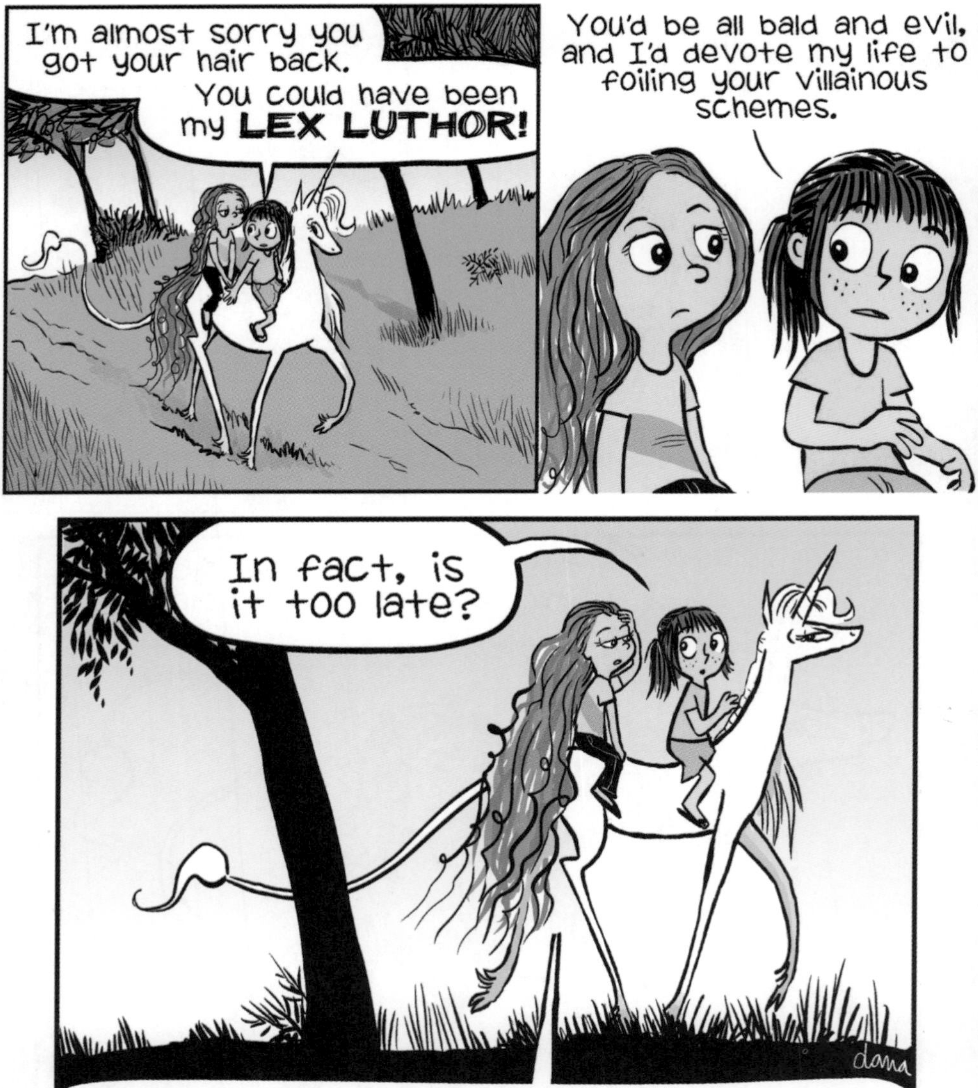
I'm almost sorry you got your hair back.
You could have been my LEX LUTHOR!
You'd be all bald and evil, and I'd devote my life to foiling your villainous schemes.
In fact, is it too late?
dana
I have about 50 pounds of hair, or I'd walk the rest of the way home now.

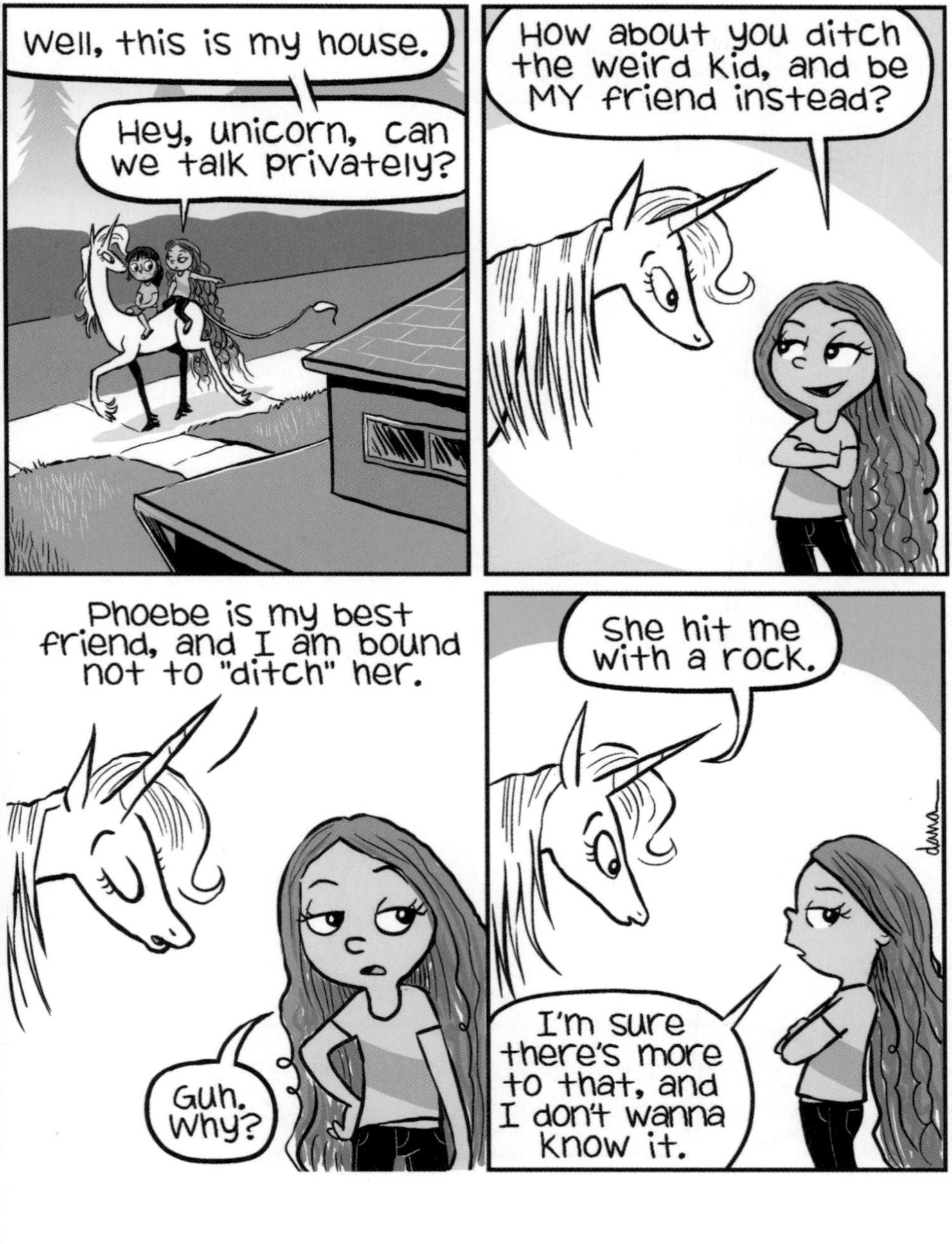
Well, this is my house.
Hey, unicorn, can we talk privately?
How about you ditch the weird kid, and be MY friend instead?
Phoebe is my best friend, and I am bound not to "ditch" her.
Guh. Why?
She hit me with a rock.
I'm sure there's more to that, and I don't wanna know it.
dana

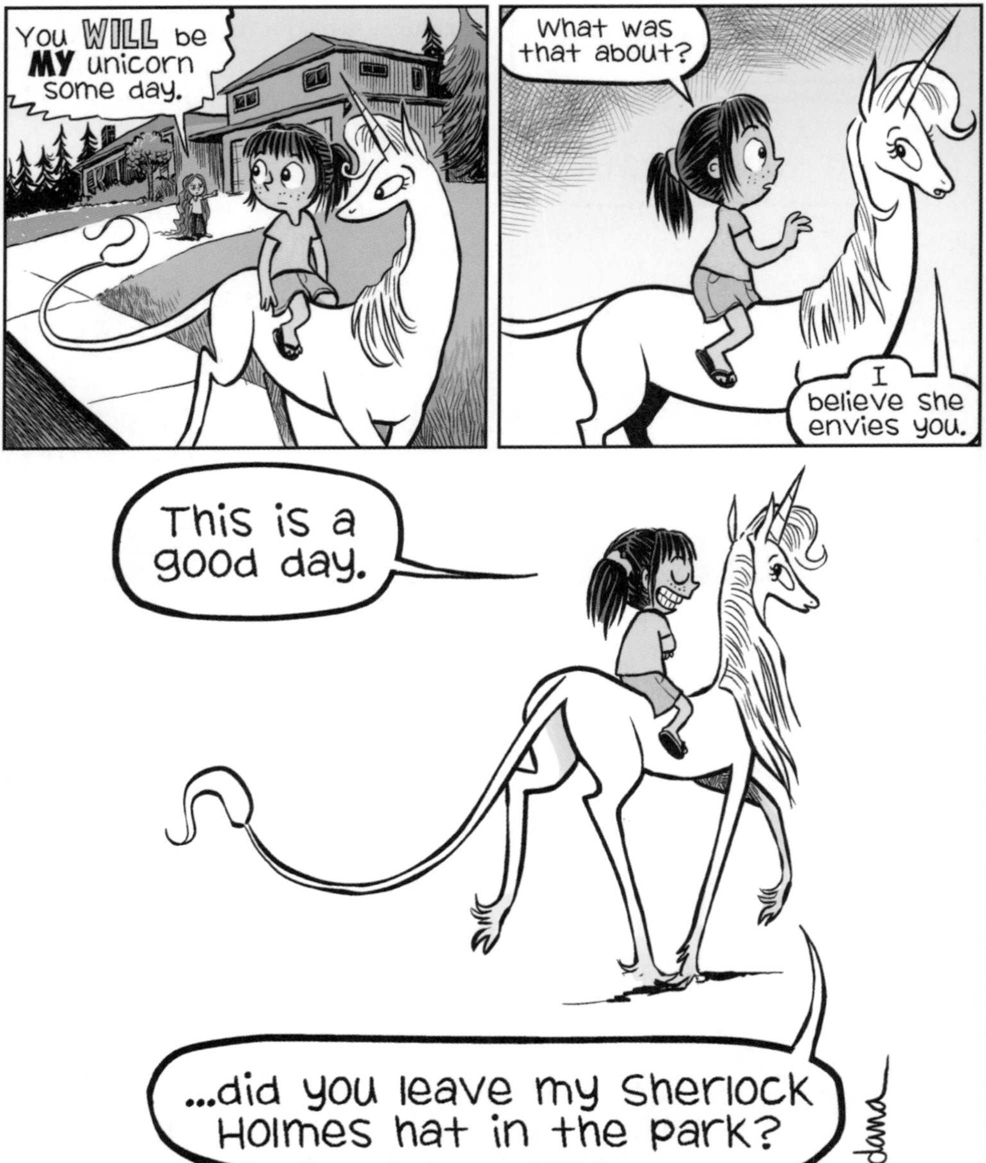
You WILL be MY unicorn some day.
What was that about?
I believe she envies you.
This is a good day.
...did you leave my Sherlock Holmes hat in the park?
dana

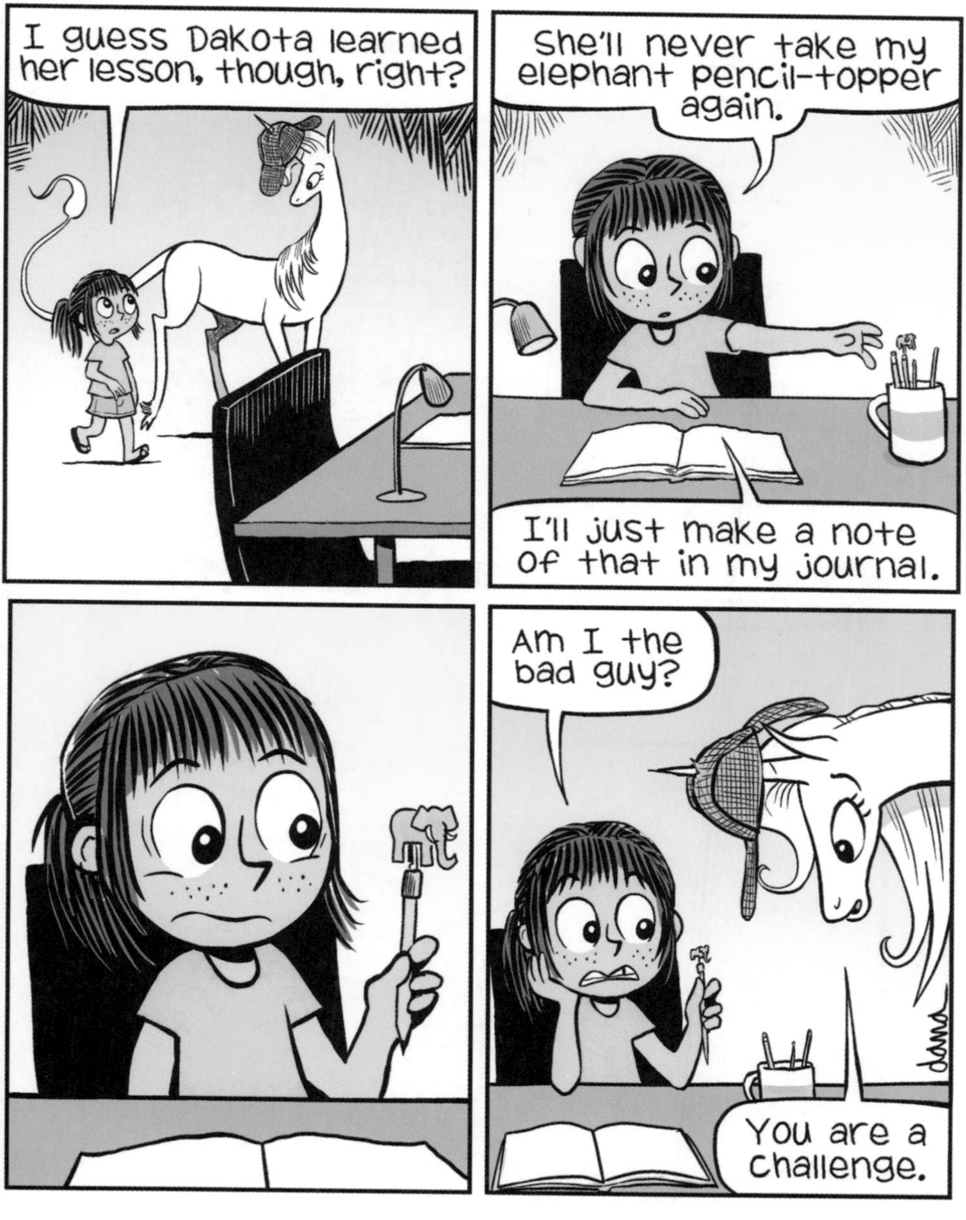
I guess Dakota learned her lesson, though, right?
She'll never take my elephant pencil-topper again.
I'll just make a note of that in my journal.
Am I the bad guy?
You are a challenge.

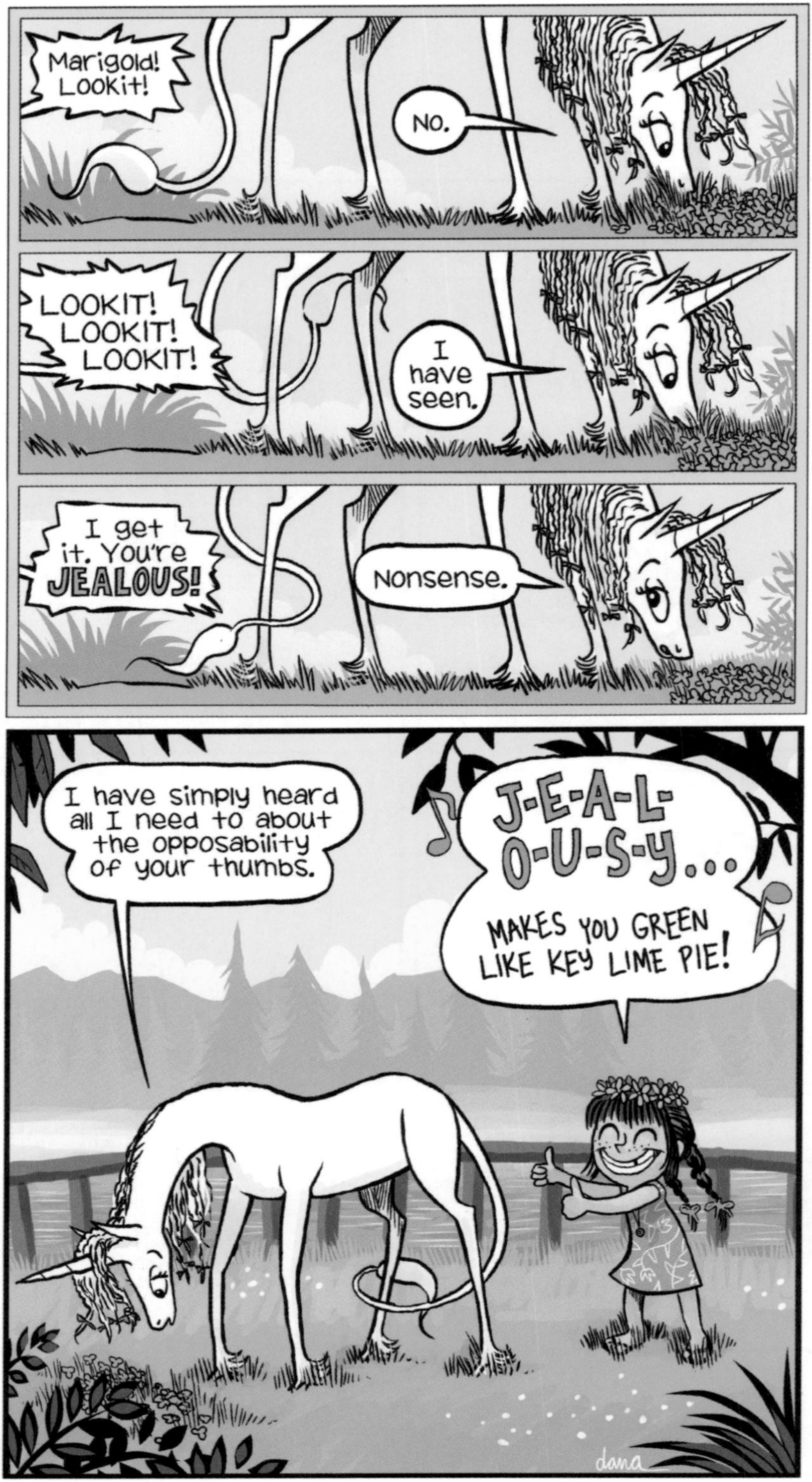
Marigold! Lookit!
No.
LOOKIT! LOOKIT! LOOKIT!
I have seen.
I get it. You're JEALOUS!
Nonsense.
I have simply heard all I need to about the opposability of your thumbs.
J-E-A-L-O-U-S-Y...
MAKES YOU GREEN LIKE KEY LIME PIE!
dana

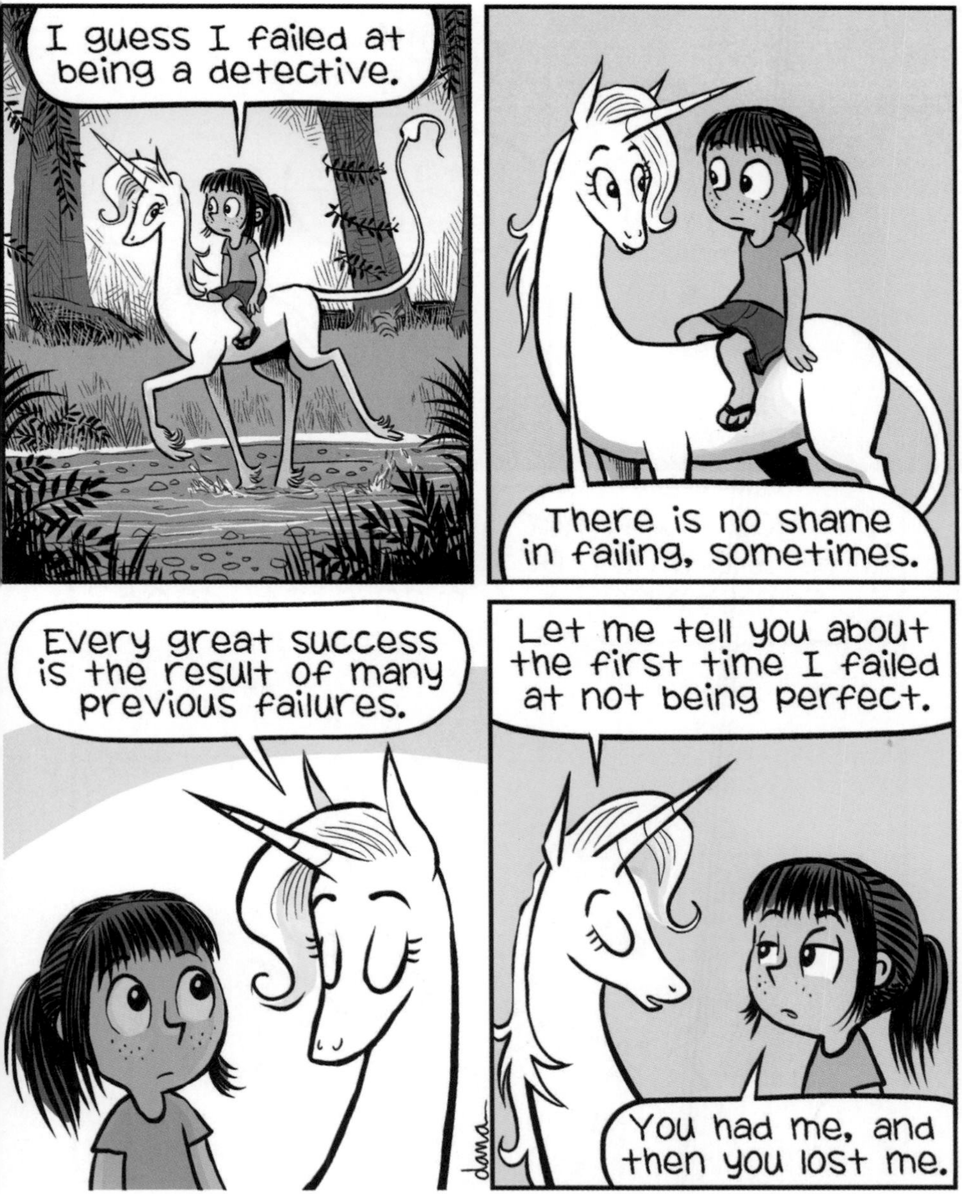
I guess I failed at being a detective.
There is no shame in failing, sometimes.
Every great success is the result of many previous failures.
Let me tell you about the first time I failed at not being perfect.
You had me, and then you lost me.
dana

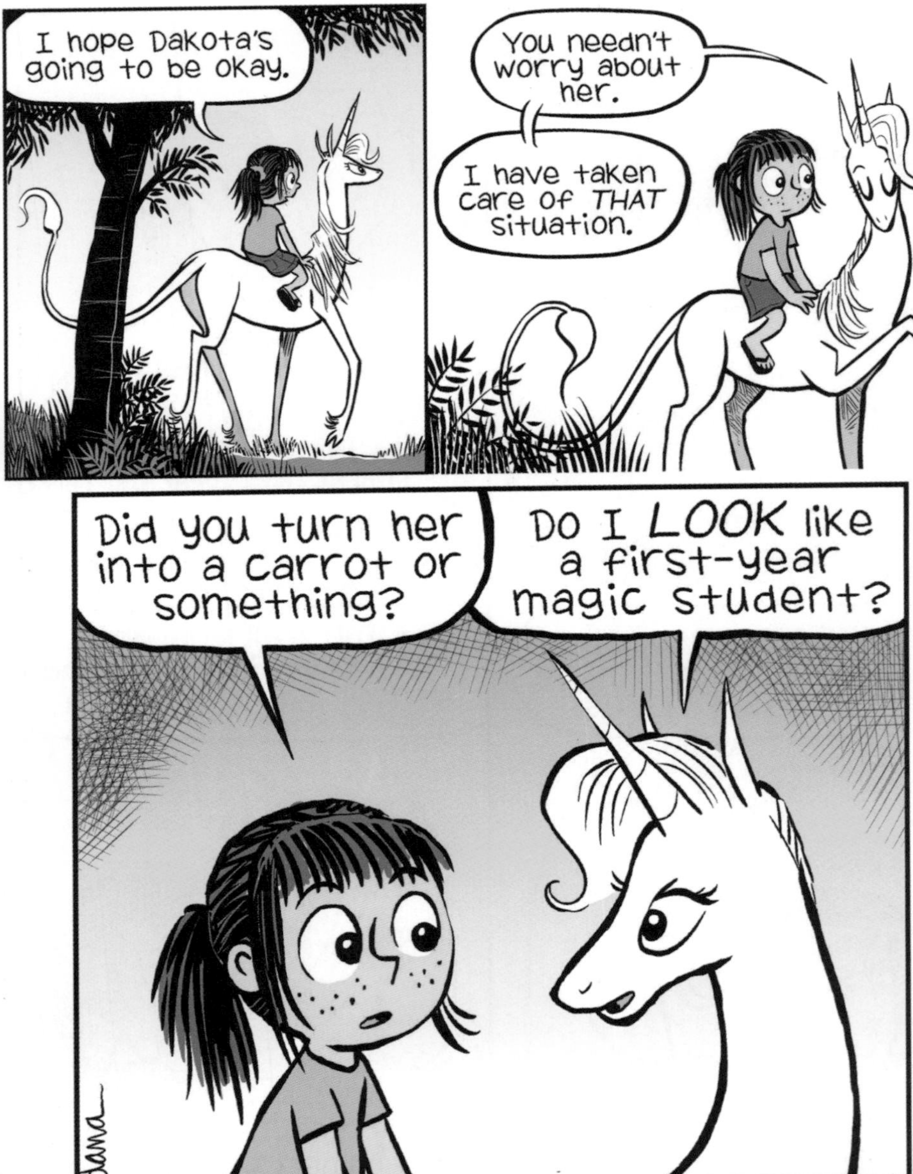
I hope Dakota's going to be okay.
You needn't worry about her.
I have taken care of THAT situation.
Did you turn her into a carrot or something?
Do I LOOK like a first-year magic student?
dana

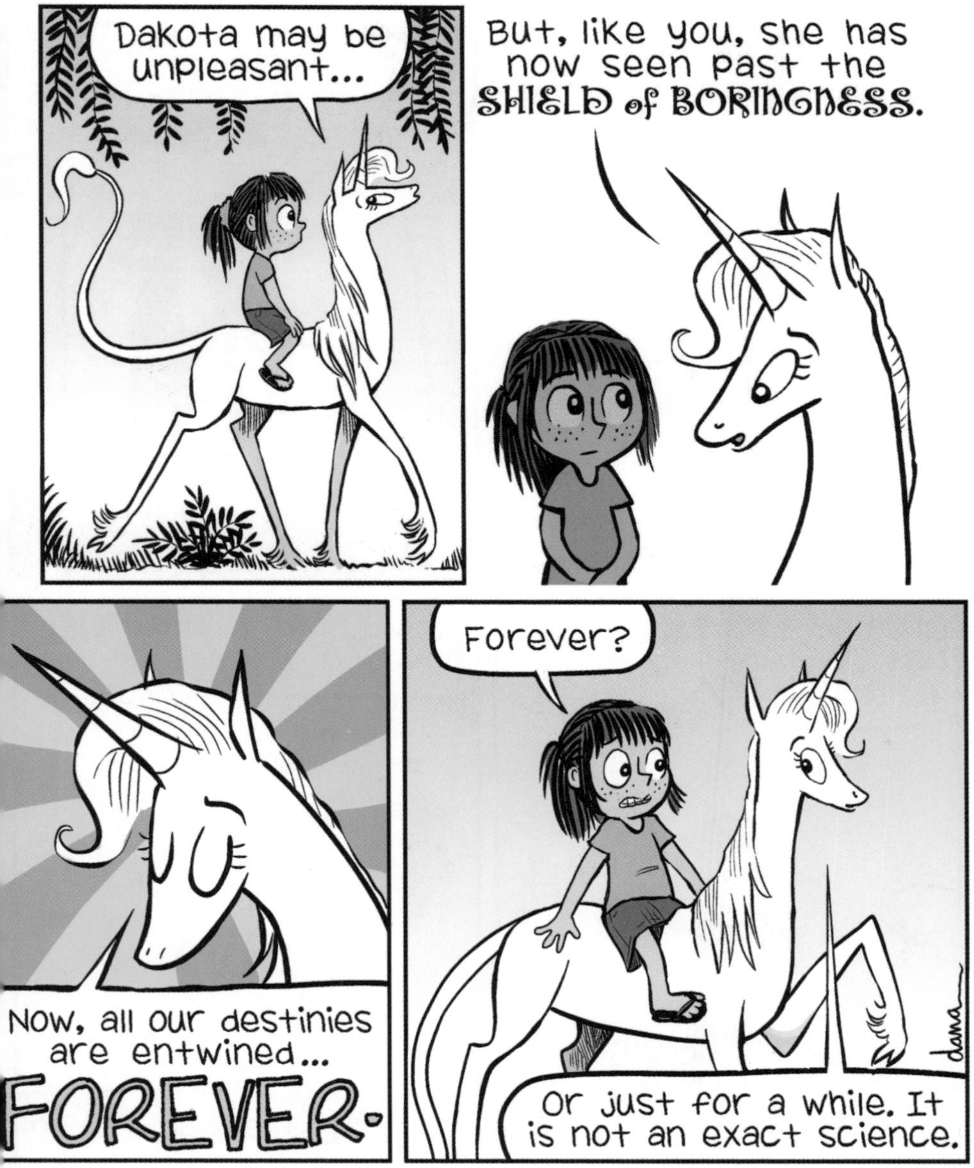

Dakota may be unpleasant...
But, like you, she has now seen past the SHIELD of BORINGNESS.
Now, all our destinies are entwined... FOREVER.
Forever?
Or just for a while. It is not an exact science.
dana

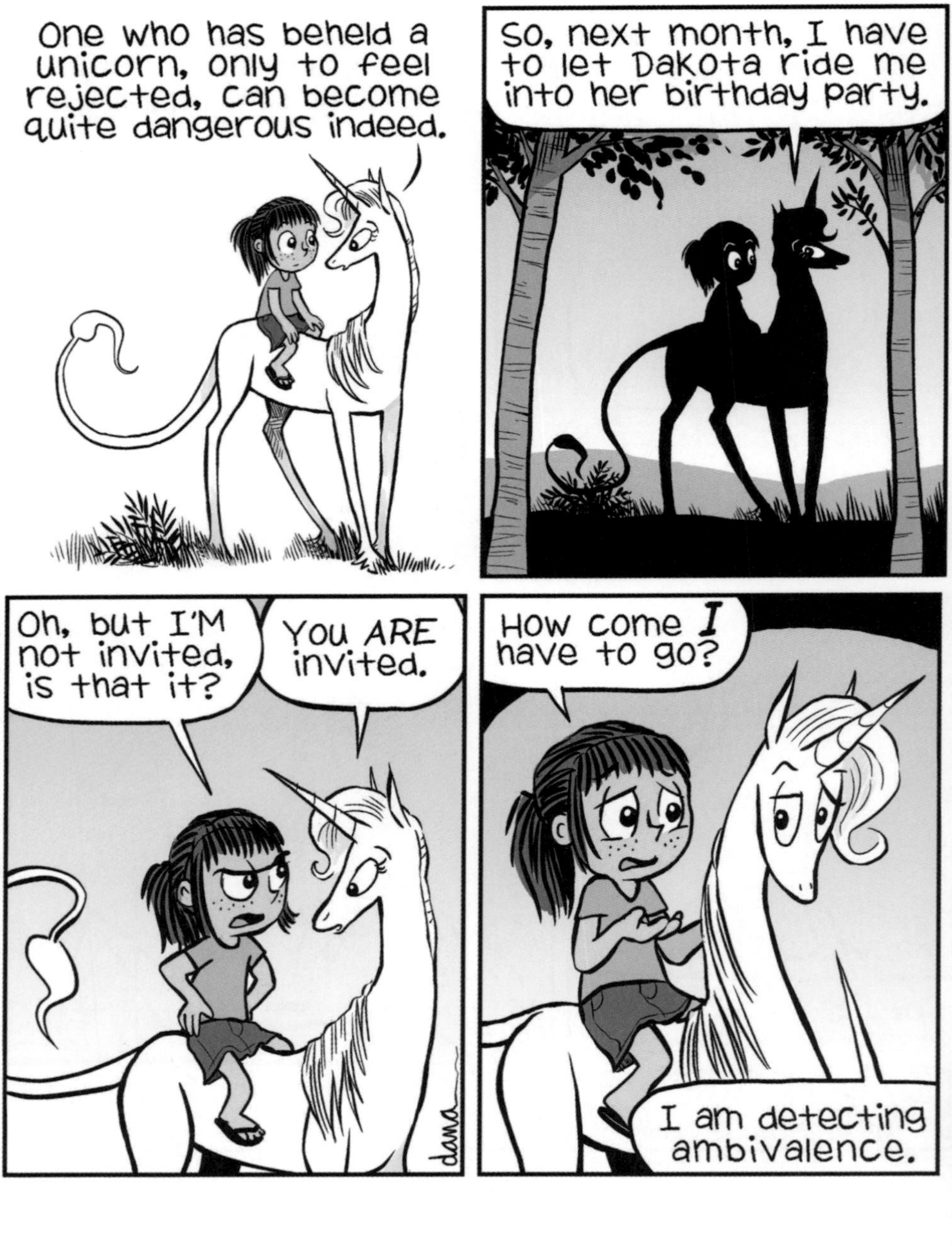
One who has beheld a unicorn, only to feel rejected, can become quite dangerous indeed.
So, next month, I have to let Dakota ride me into her birthday party.
Oh, but I'M not invited, is that it?
You ARE invited.
dana
How come I have to go?
I am detecting ambivalence.

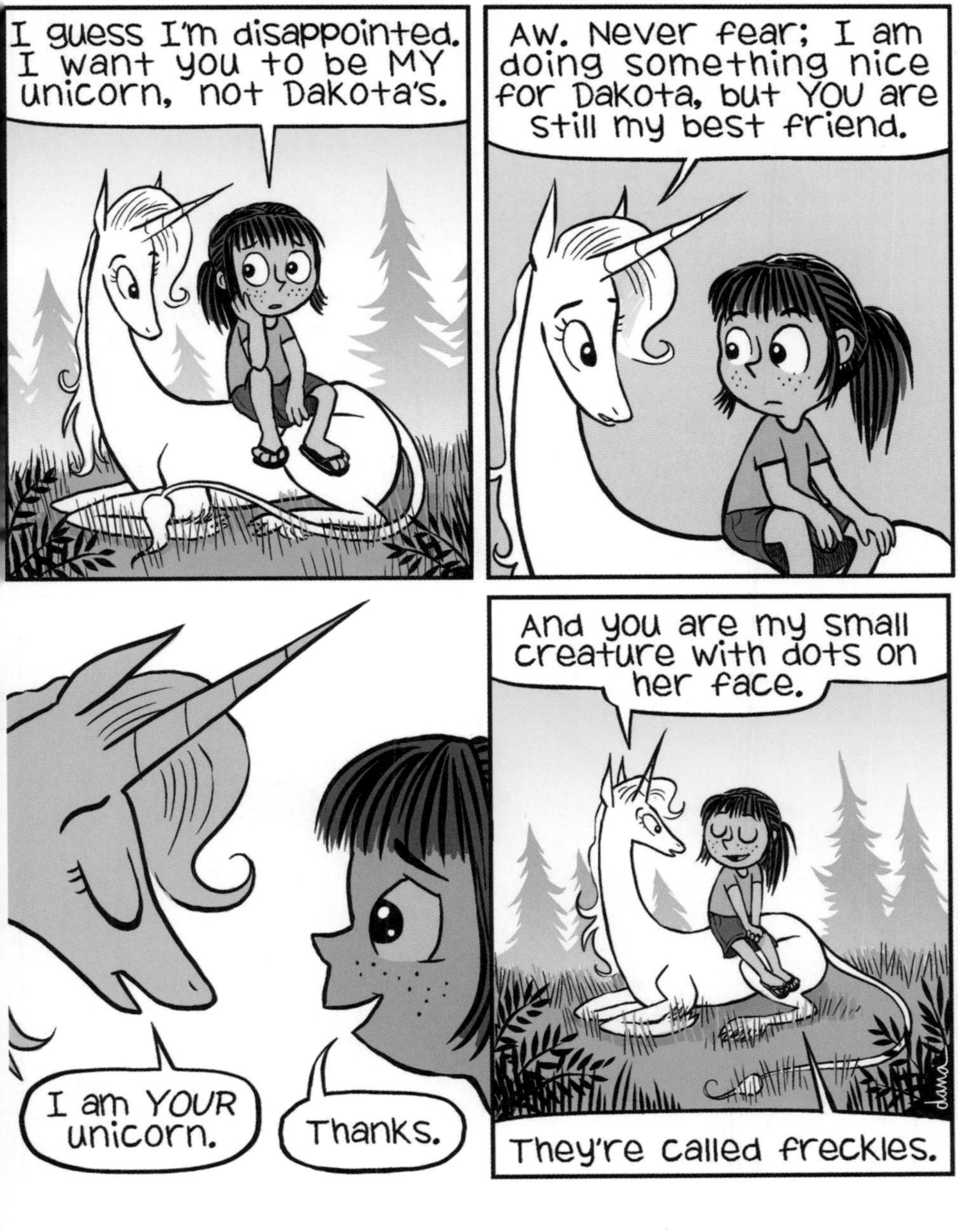
I guess I'm disappointed. I want you to be MY unicorn, not Dakota's.
Aw. Never fear; I am doing something nice for Dakota, but YOU are still my best friend.
I am YOUR unicorn.
Thanks.
And you are my small creature with dots on her face.
They're called freckles.

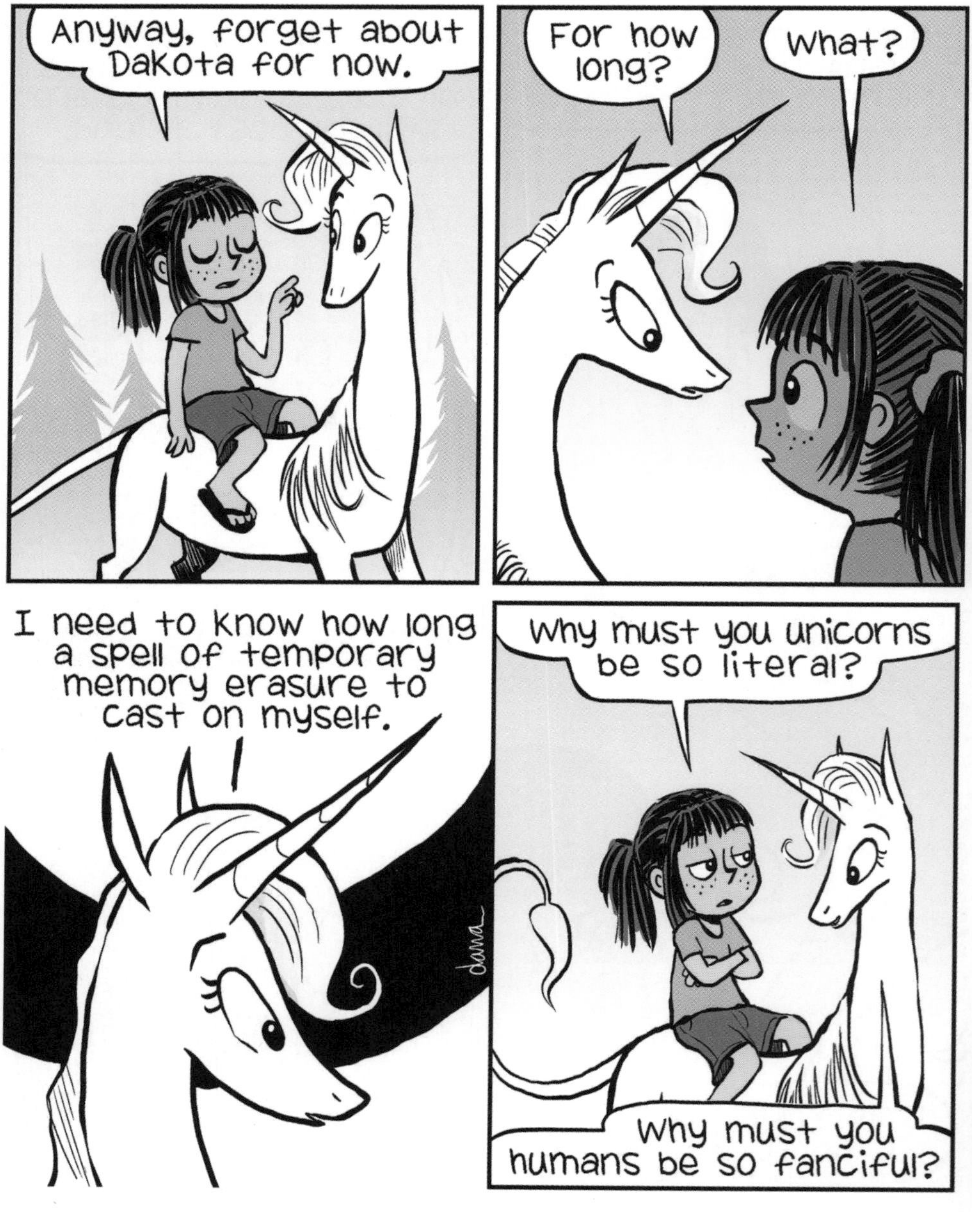
Anyway, forget about Dakota for now.
For how long?
What?
I need to know how long a spell of temporary memory erasure to cast on myself.
dana
Why must you unicorns be so literal?
Why must you humans be so fanciful?

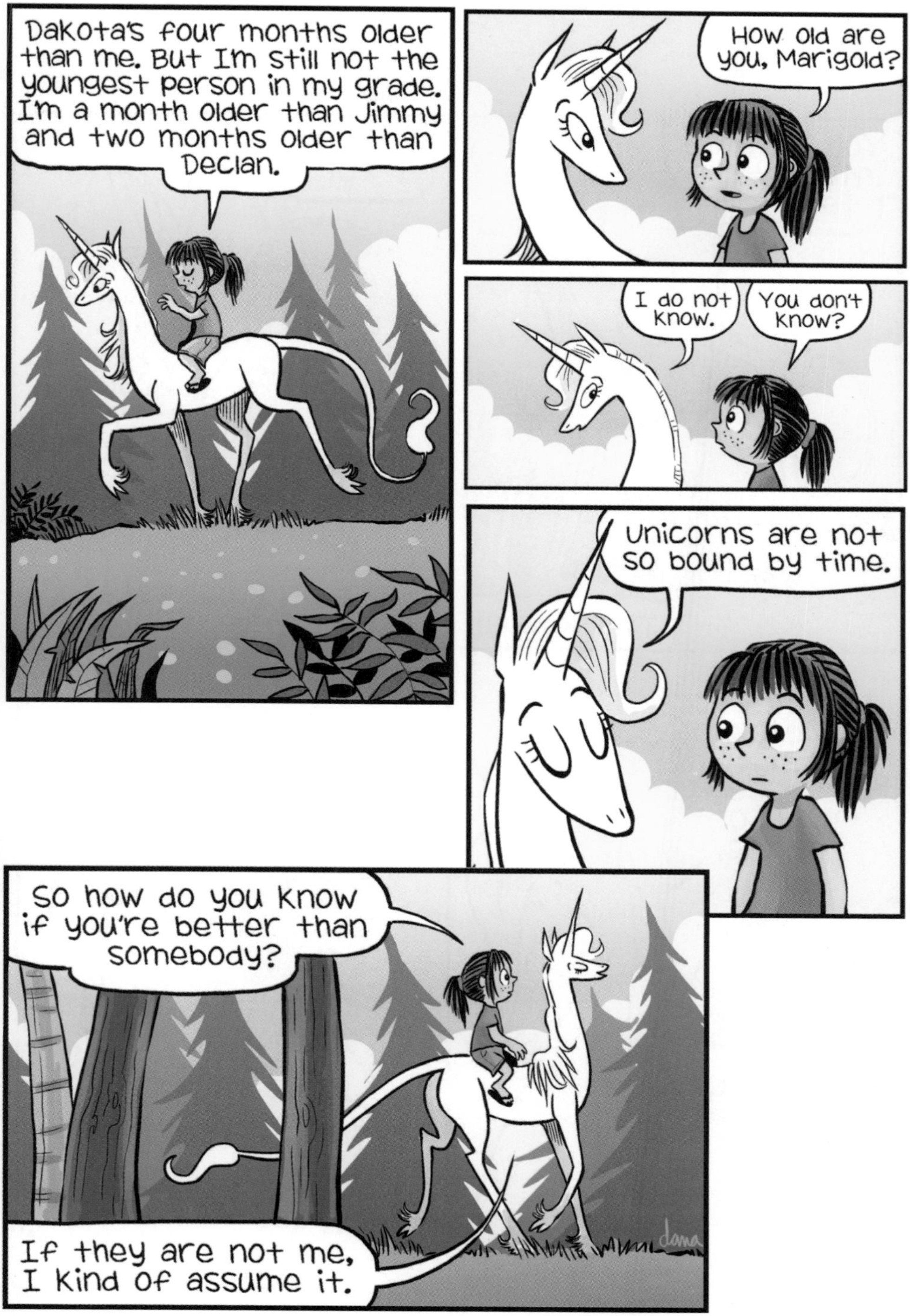
Dakota's four months older than me. But I'm still not the youngest person in my grade. I'm a month older than Jimmy and two months older than Declan.
How old are you, Marigold?
I do not know.
You don't know?
Unicorns are not so bound by time.
So how do you know if you're better than somebody?
If they are not me, I kind of assume it.
dana

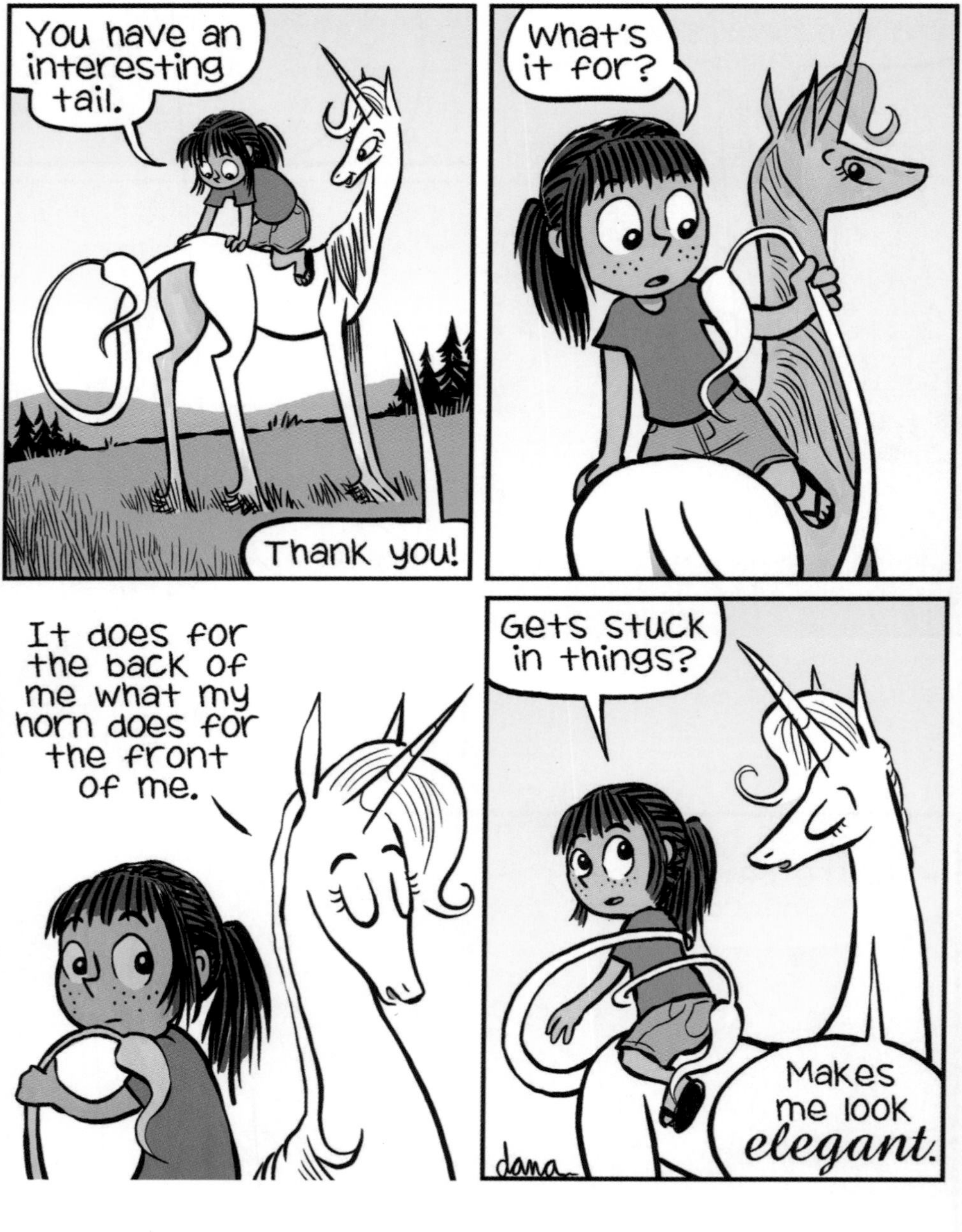
You have an interesting tail.
Thank you!
What's it for?
It does for the back of me what my horn does for the front of me.
Gets stuck in things?
Makes me look *elegant*.
dana

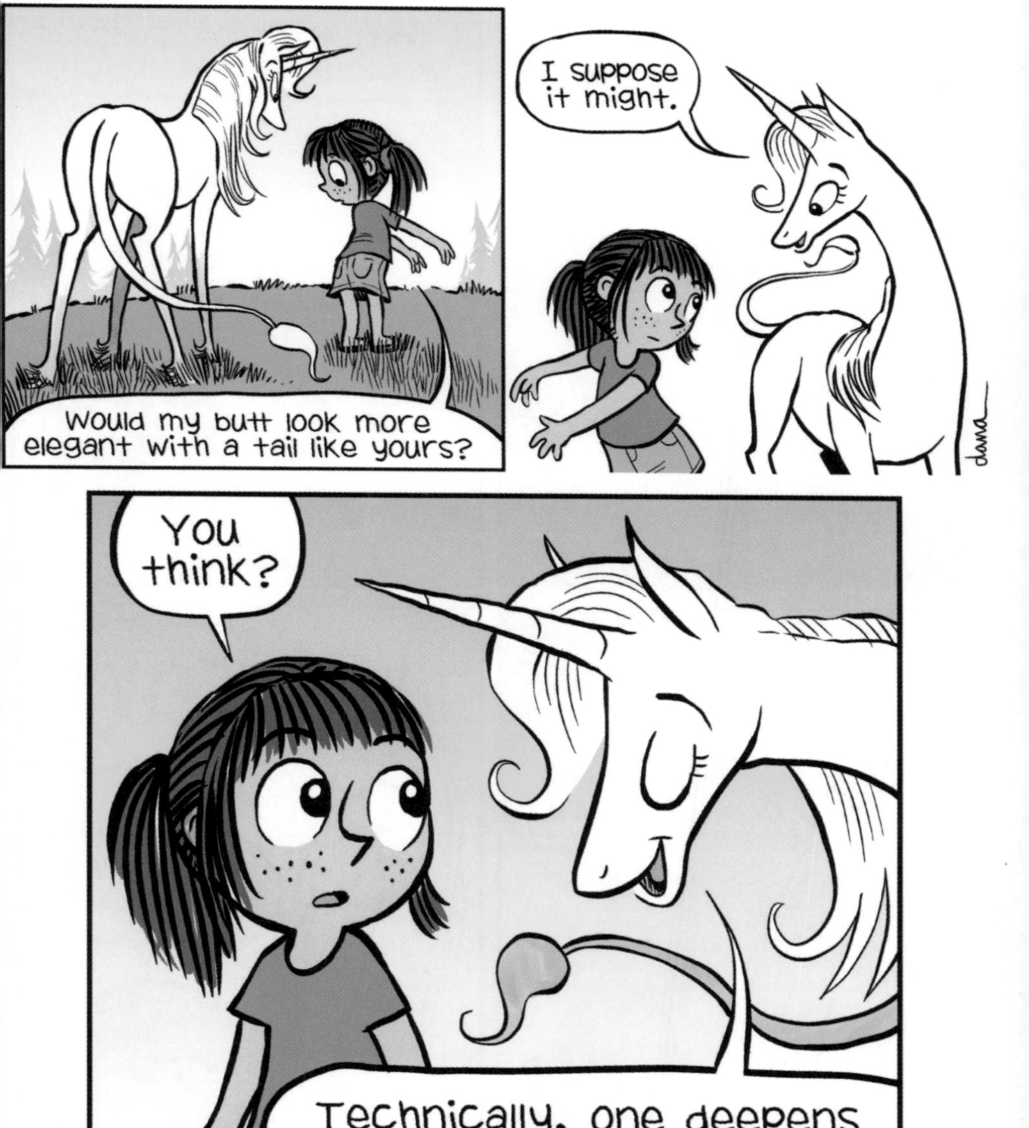
Would my butt look more elegant with a tail like yours?
I suppose it might.
dana
You think?
Technically, one deepens the ocean by spitting in it.

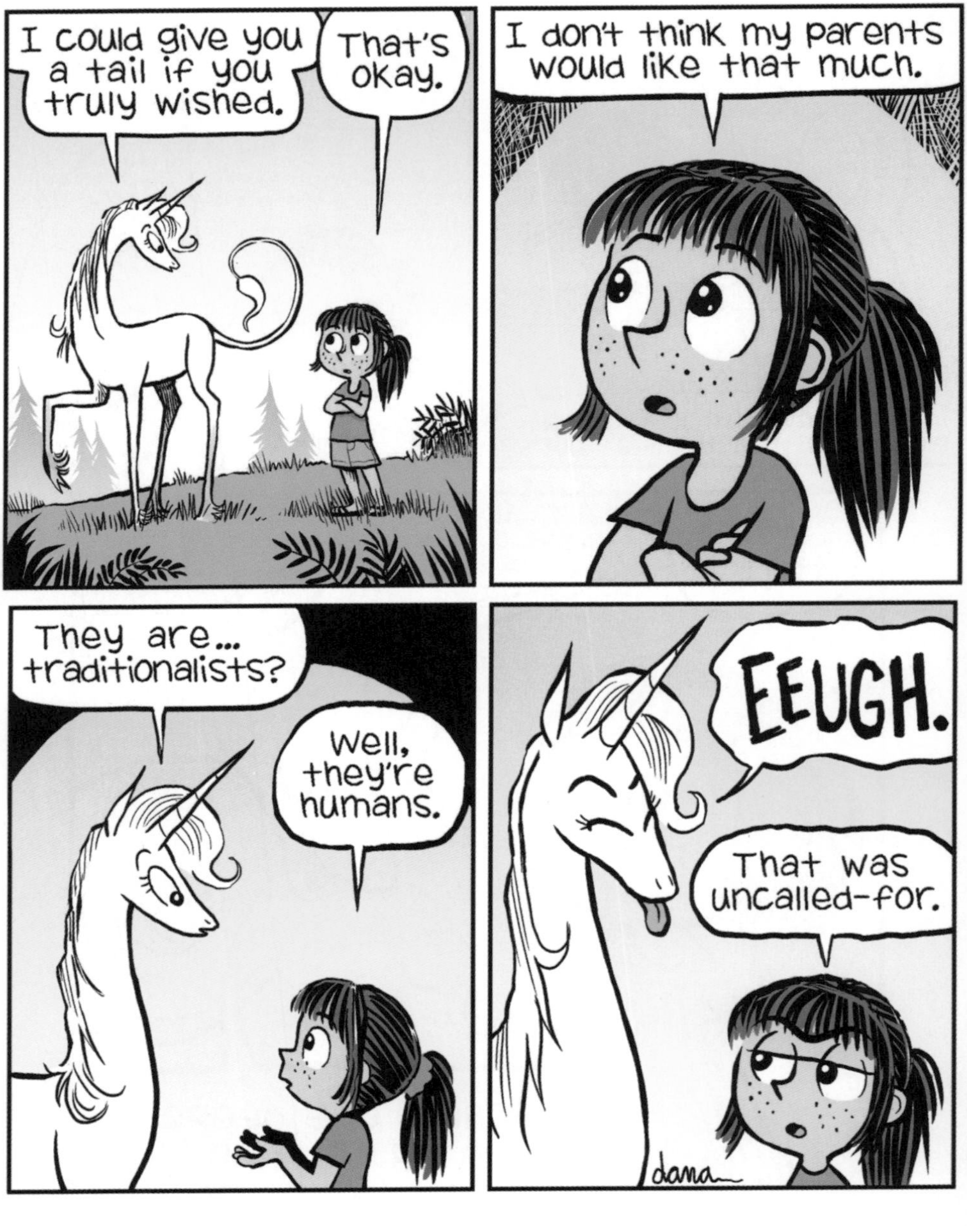
I could give you a tail if you truly wished.
That's okay.
I don't think my parents would like that much.
They are... traditionalists?
Well, they're humans.
EEUGH.
That was uncalled-for.
dana

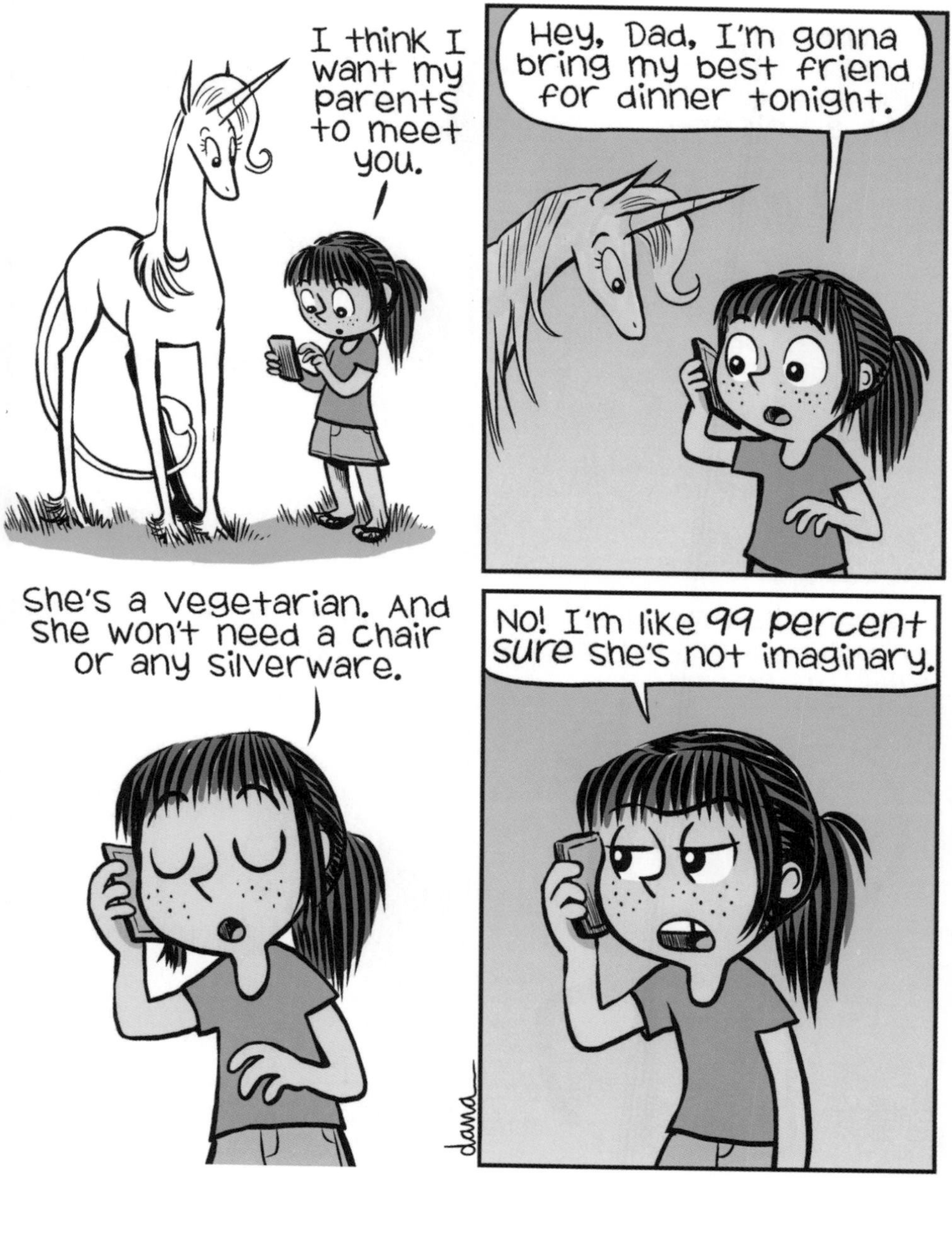
I think I want my parents to meet you.
Hey, Dad, I'm gonna bring my best friend for dinner tonight.
She's a vegetarian. And she won't need a chair or any silverware.
No! I'm like 99 percent sure she's not imaginary.
dana

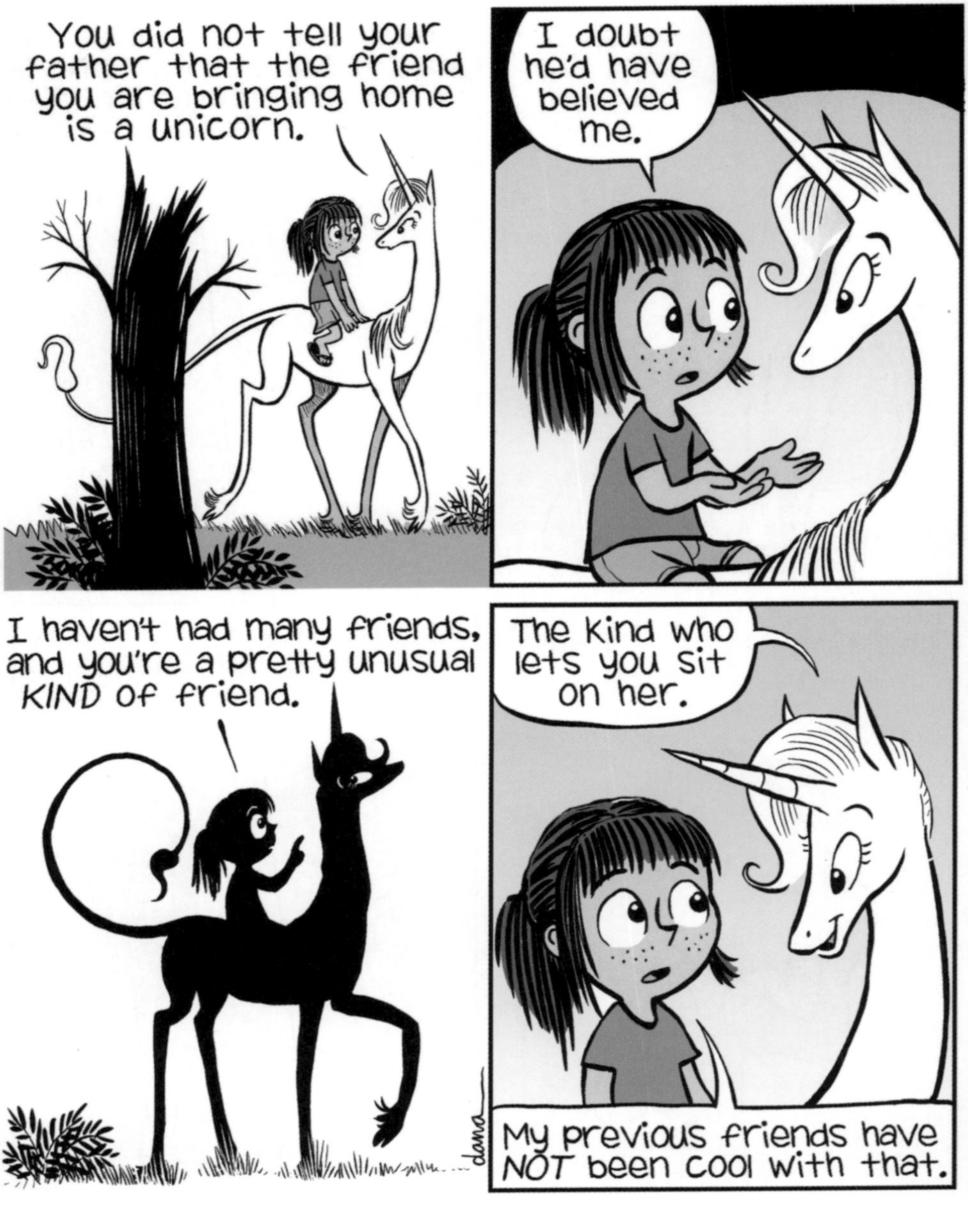
You did not tell your father that the friend you are bringing home is a unicorn.
I doubt he'd have believed me.
I haven't had many friends, and you're a pretty unusual *KIND* of friend.
The kind who lets you sit on her.
My previous friends have *NOT* been cool with that.
dana

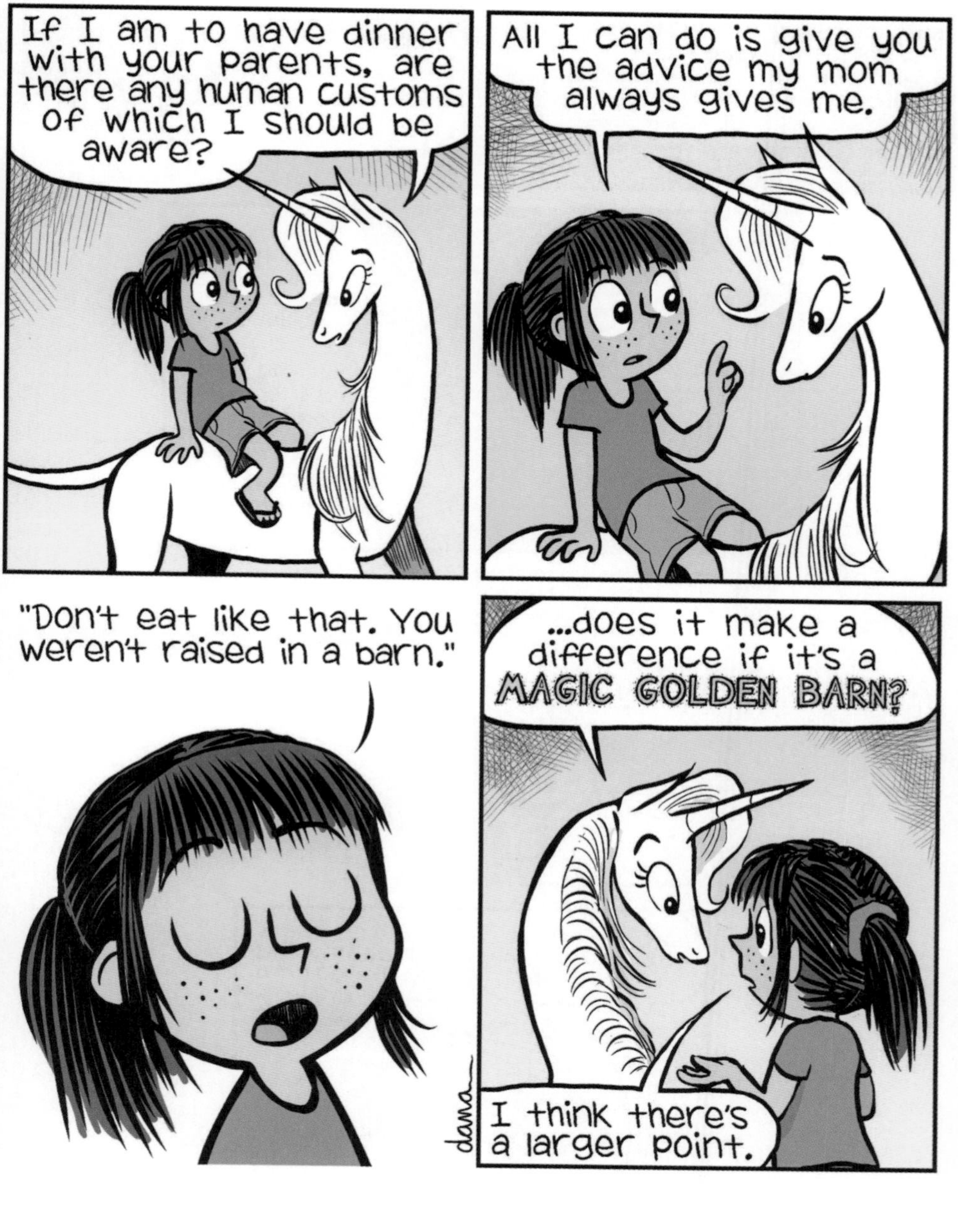
If I am to have dinner with your parents, are there any human customs of which I should be aware?
All I can do is give you the advice my mom always gives me.
"Don't eat like that. You weren't raised in a barn."
...does it make a difference if it's a MAGIC GOLDEN BARN?
I think there's a larger point.
dana

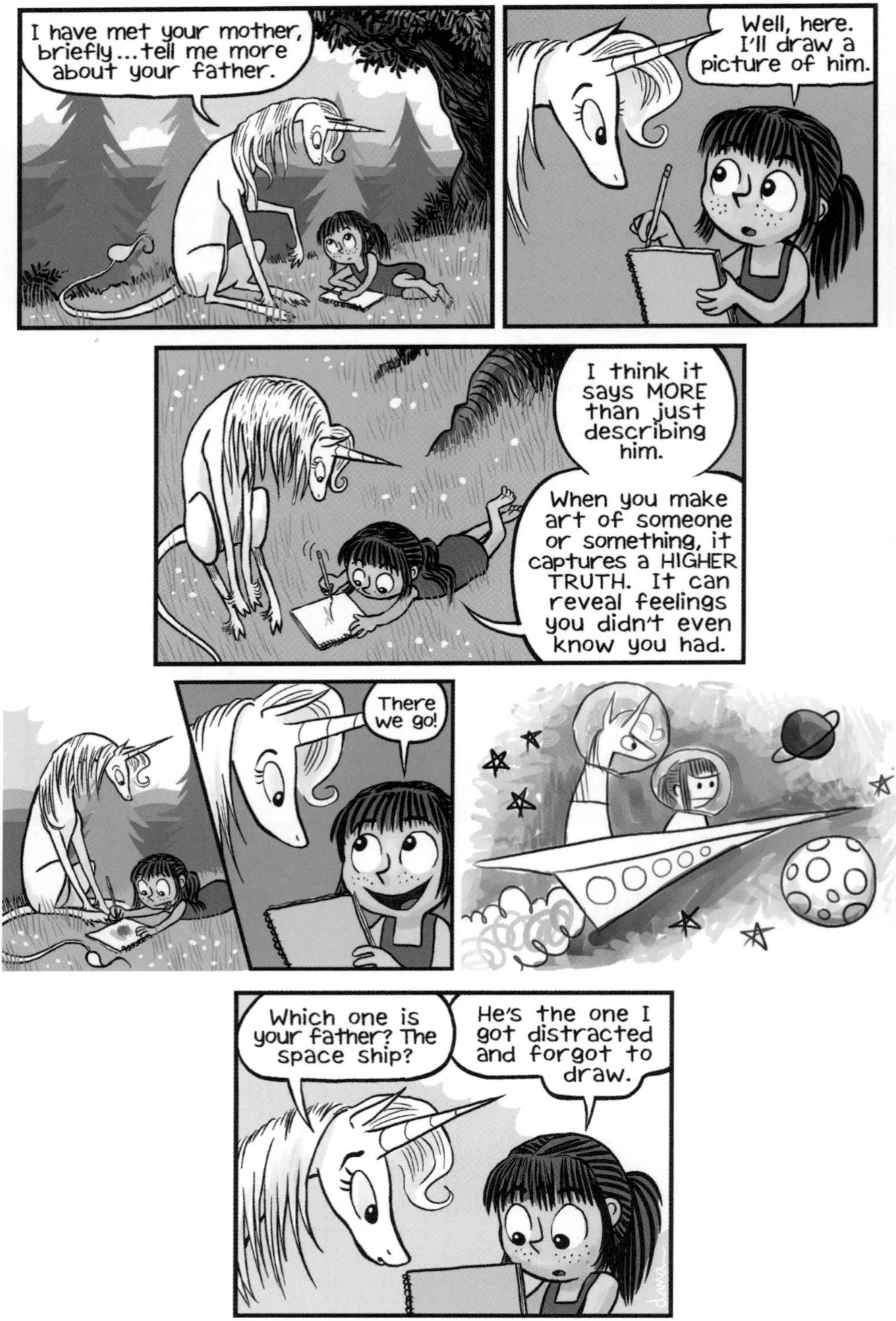
I have met your mother, briefly...tell me more about your father.
Well, here. I'll draw a picture of him.
I think it says MORE than just describing him.
When you make art of someone or something, it captures a HIGHER TRUTH. It can reveal feelings you didn't even know you had.
There we go!
Which one is your father? The space ship?
He's the one I got distracted and forgot to draw.

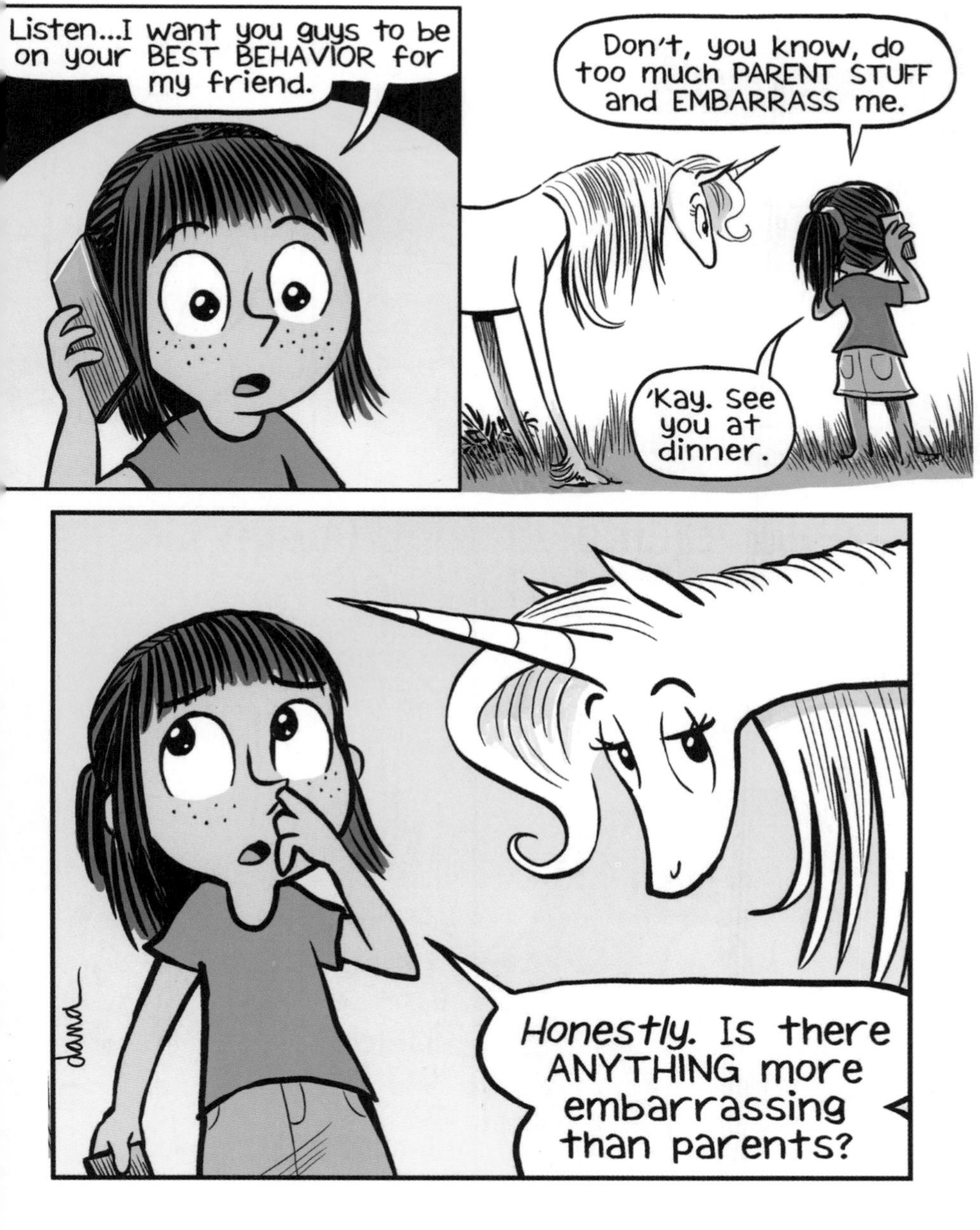
Listen...I want you guys to be on your BEST BEHAVIOR for my friend.
Don't, you know, do too much PARENT STUFF and EMBARRASS me.
'Kay. See you at dinner.
Honestly. Is there ANYTHING more embarrassing than parents?
dana

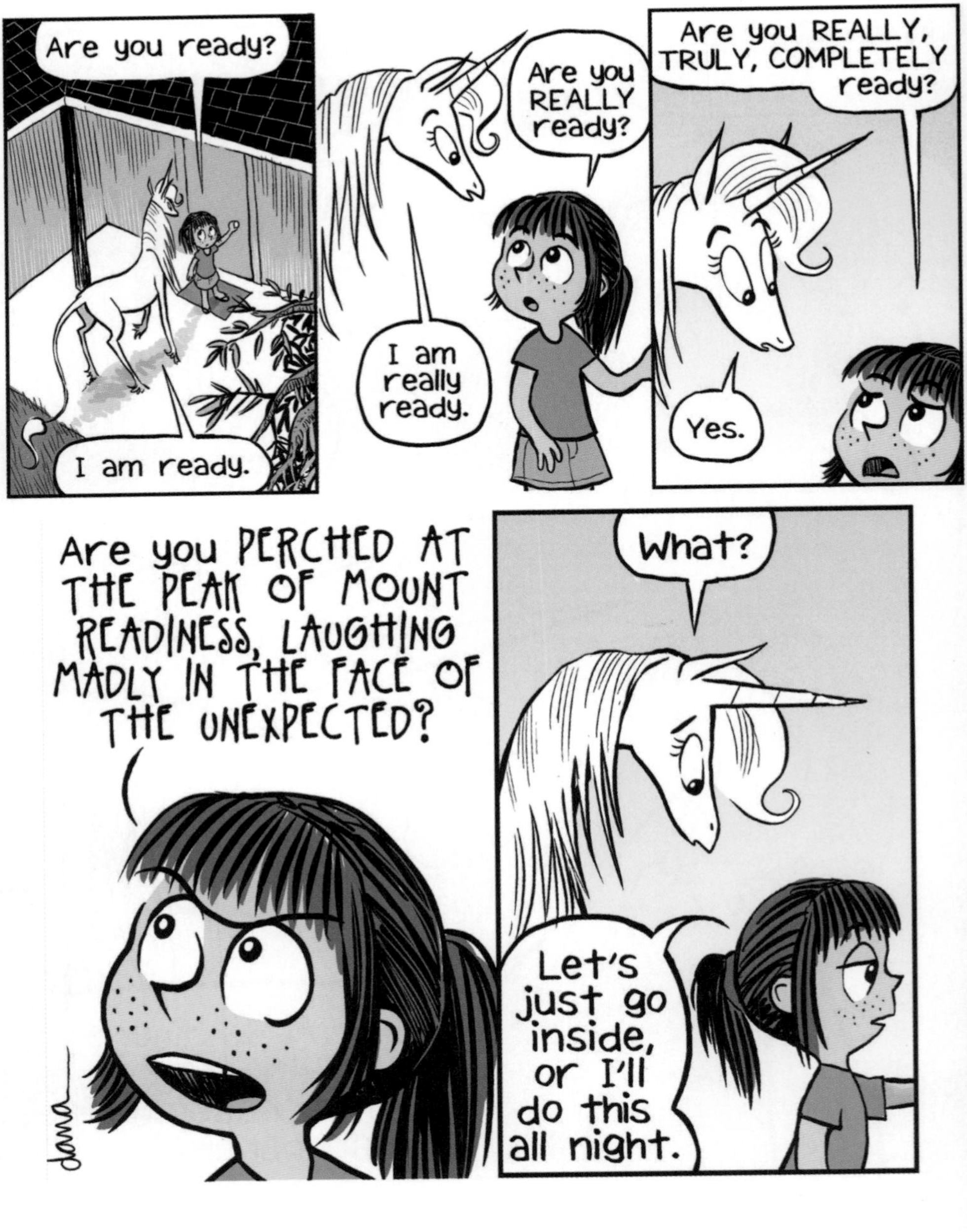
Are you ready?
I am ready.
Are you REALLY ready?
I am really ready.
Are you REALLY, TRULY, COMPLETELY ready?
Yes.
Are you PERCHED AT THE PEAK OF MOUNT READINESS, LAUGHING MADLY IN THE FACE OF THE UNEXPECTED?
What?
Let's just go inside, or I'll do this all night.
dana

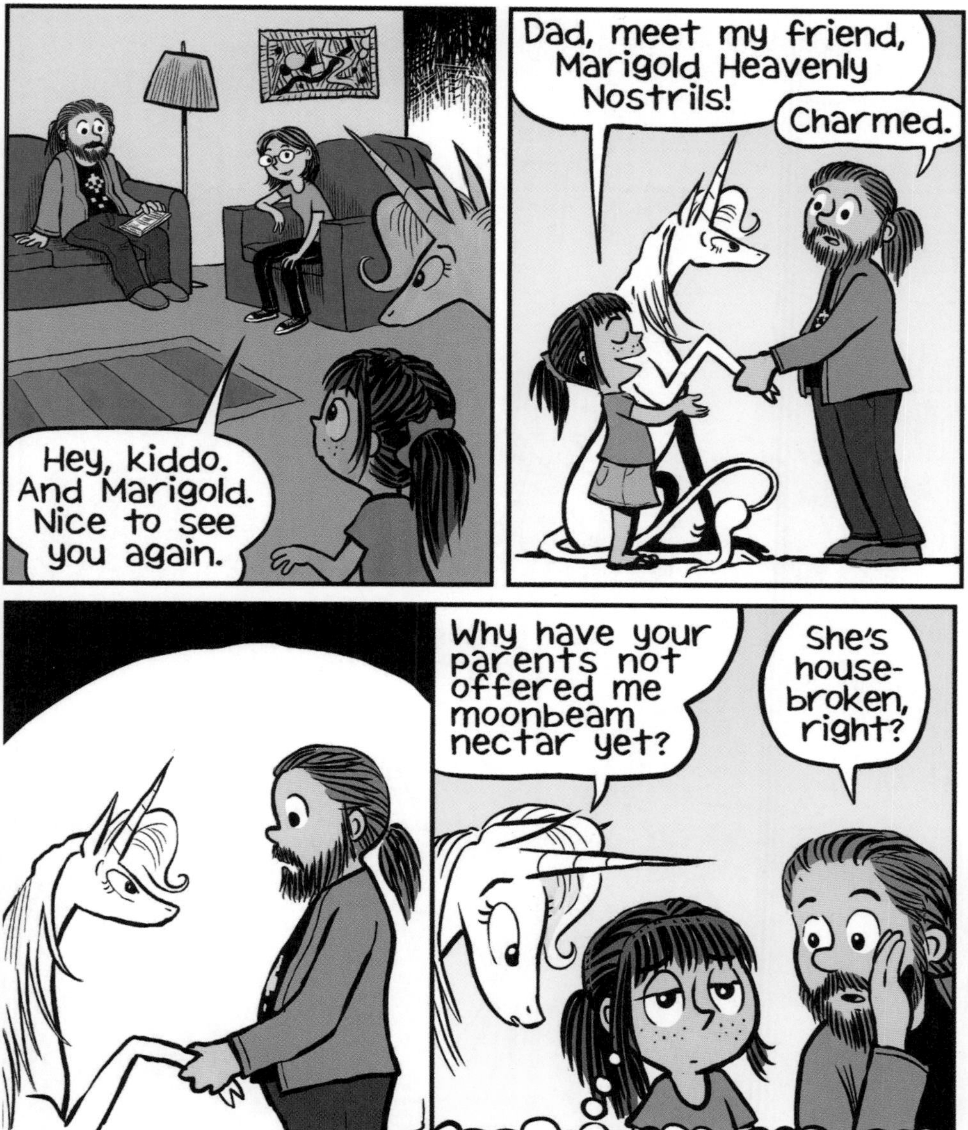
Hey, kiddo. And Marigold. Nice to see you again.
Dad, meet my friend, Marigold Heavenly Nostrils!
Charmed.
Why have your parents not offered me moonbeam nectar yet?
She's house-broken, right?
Yeah, this was a brilliant idea.
dana

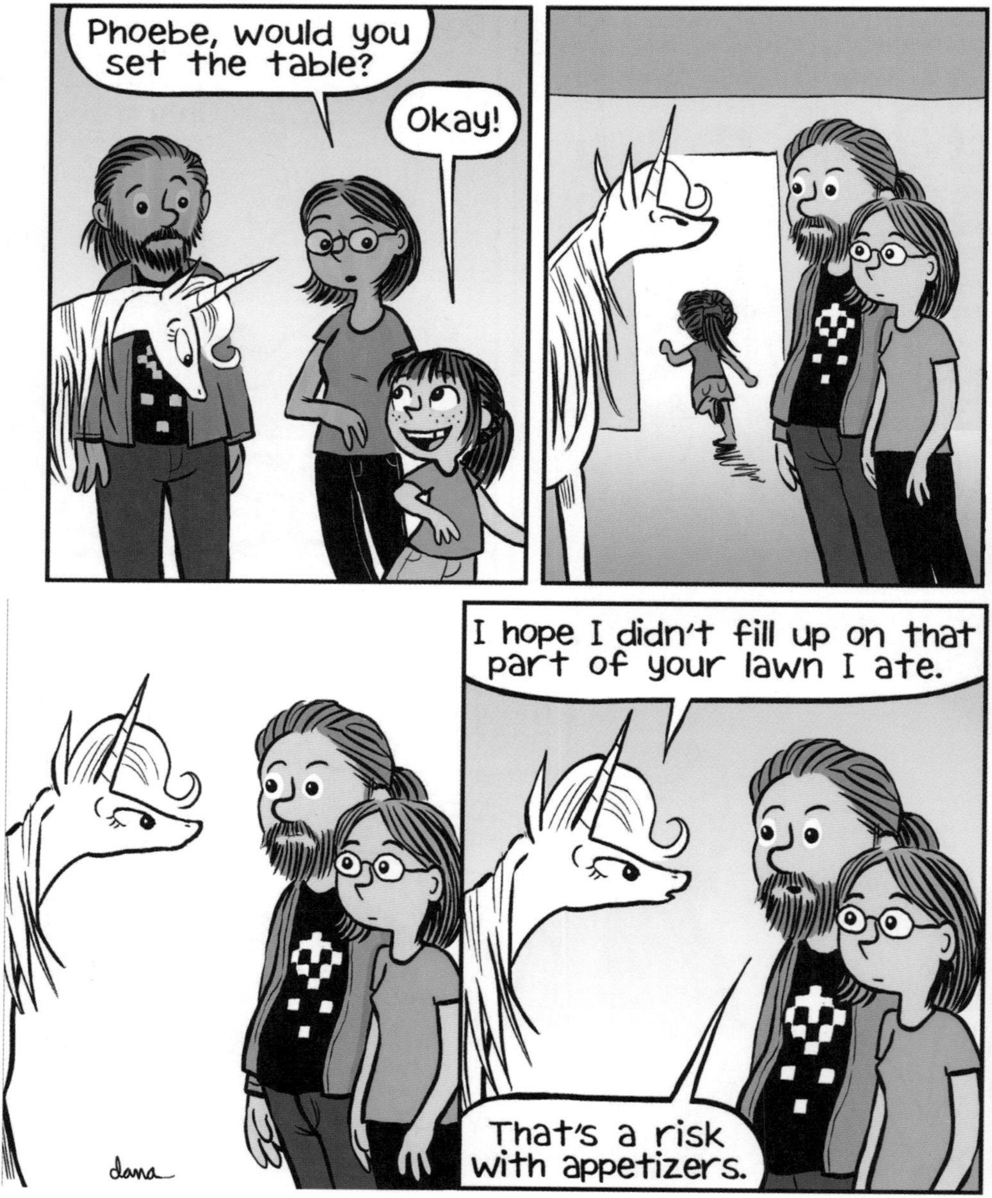
Phoebe, would you set the table?
Okay!
I hope I didn't fill up on that part of your lawn I ate.
That's a risk with appetizers.
dana

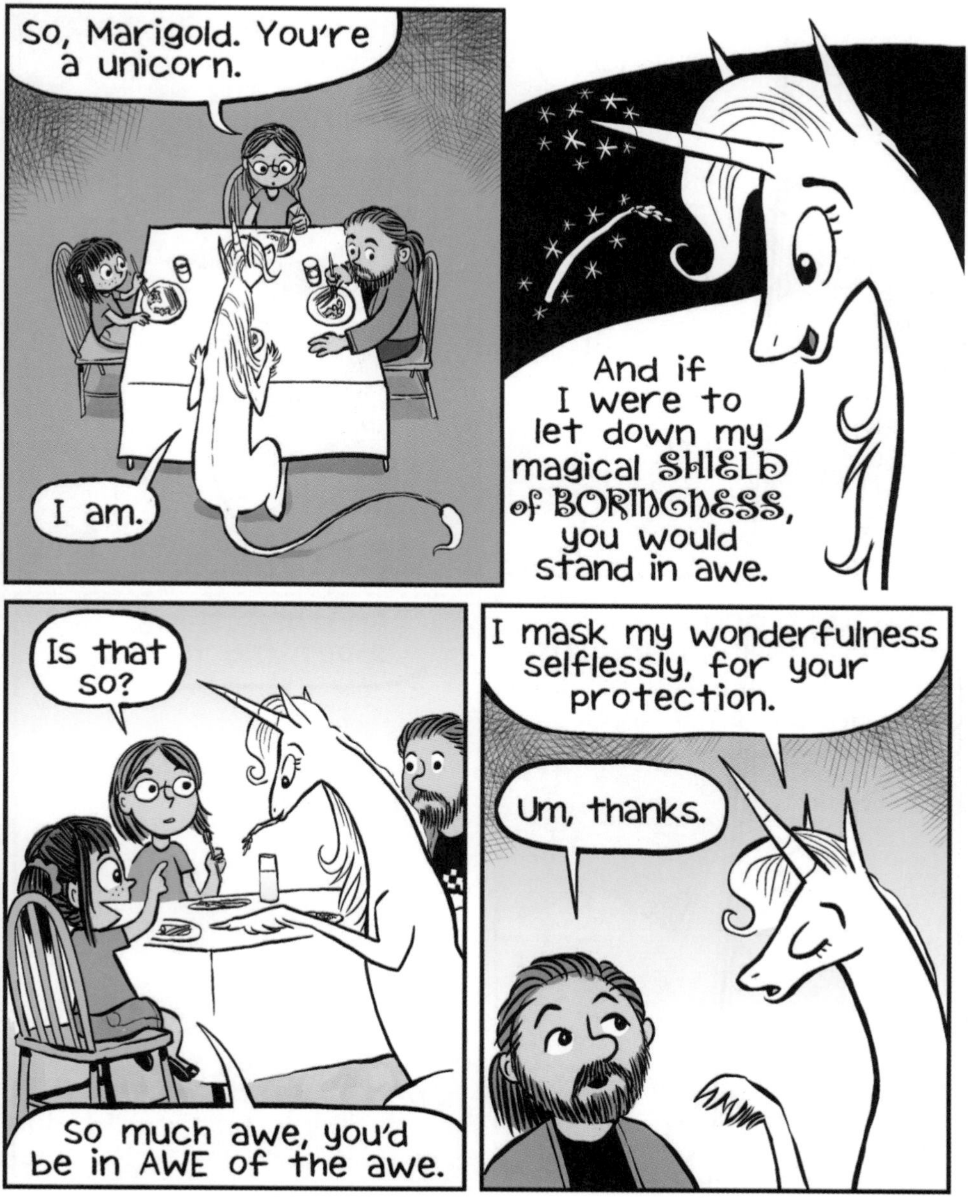
So, Marigold. You're a unicorn.
I am.
And if I were to let down my magical SHIELD of BORINGNESS, you would stand in awe.
Is that so?
So much awe, you'd be in AWE of the awe.
I mask my wonderfulness selflessly, for your protection.
Um, thanks.

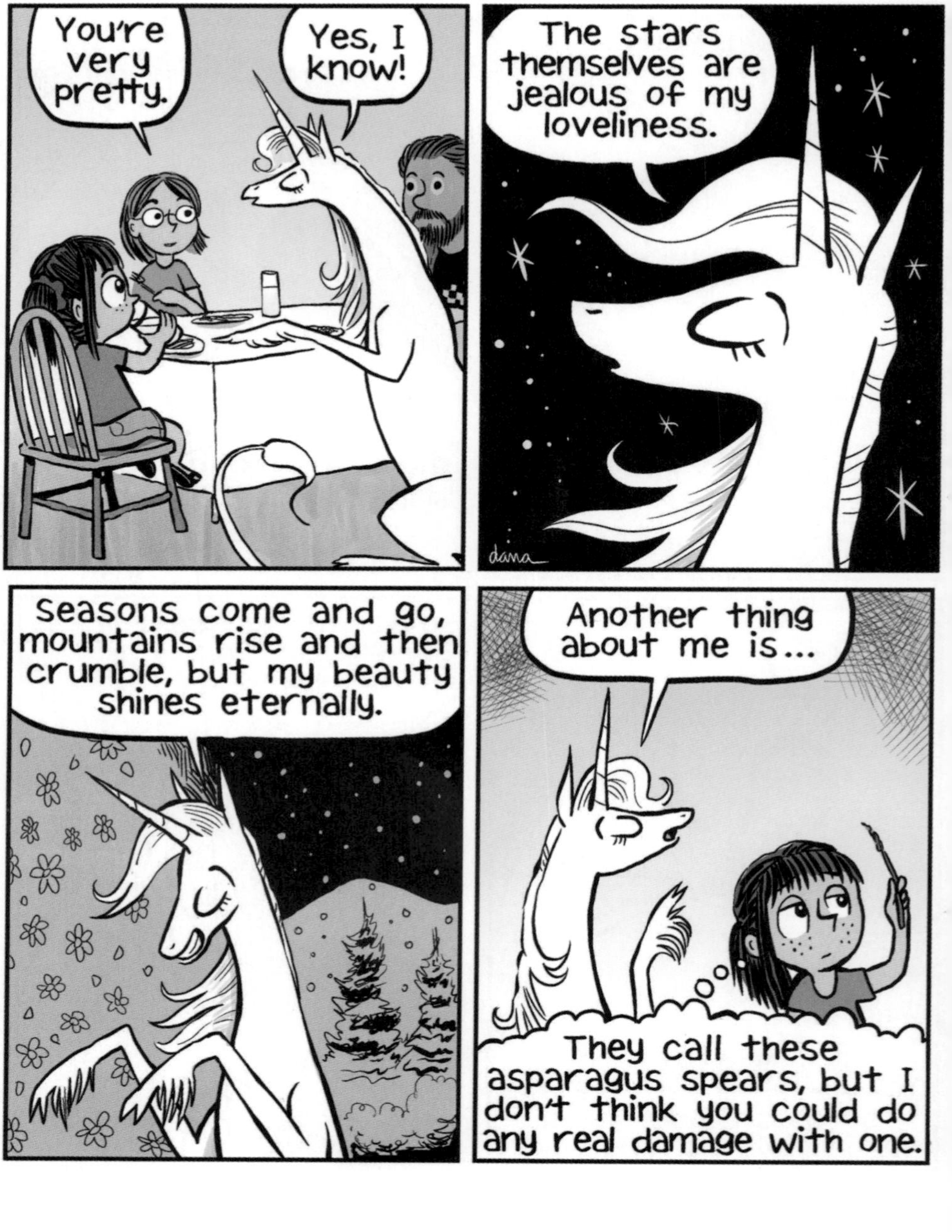
You're very pretty.
Yes, I know!
The stars themselves are jealous of my loveliness.
dana
Seasons come and go, mountains rise and then crumble, but my beauty shines eternally.
Another thing about me is...
They call these asparagus spears, but I don't think you could do any real damage with one.

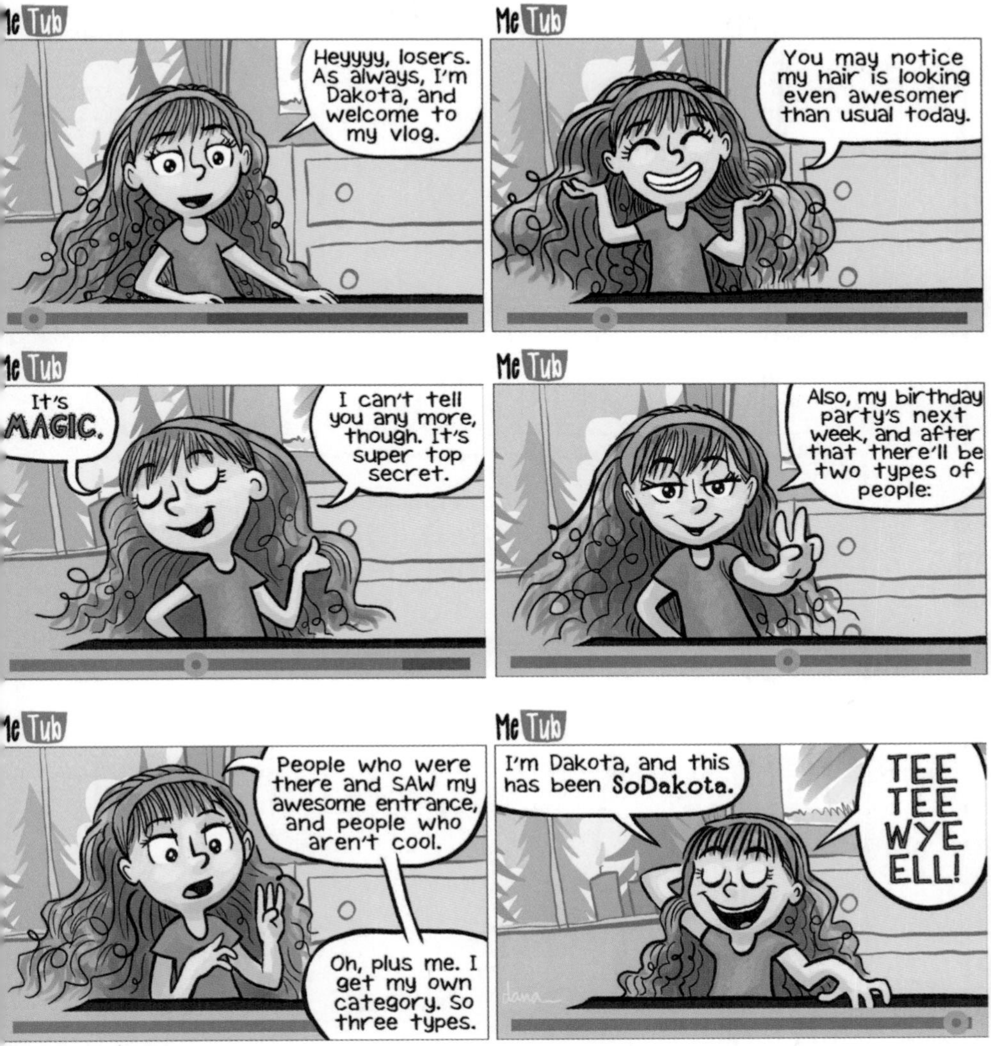
Me Tub
Heyyyy, losers. As always, I'm Dakota, and welcome to my vlog.
Me Tub
You may notice my hair is looking even awesomer than usual today.
Me Tub
It's MAGIC.
I can't tell you any more, though. It's super top secret.
Me Tub
Also, my birthday party's next week, and after that there'll be two types of people:
Me Tub
People who were there and SAW my awesome entrance, and people who aren't cool.
Oh, plus me. I get my own category. So three types.
Me Tub
I'm Dakota, and this has been SoDakota.
TEE TEE WYE ELL!
dana

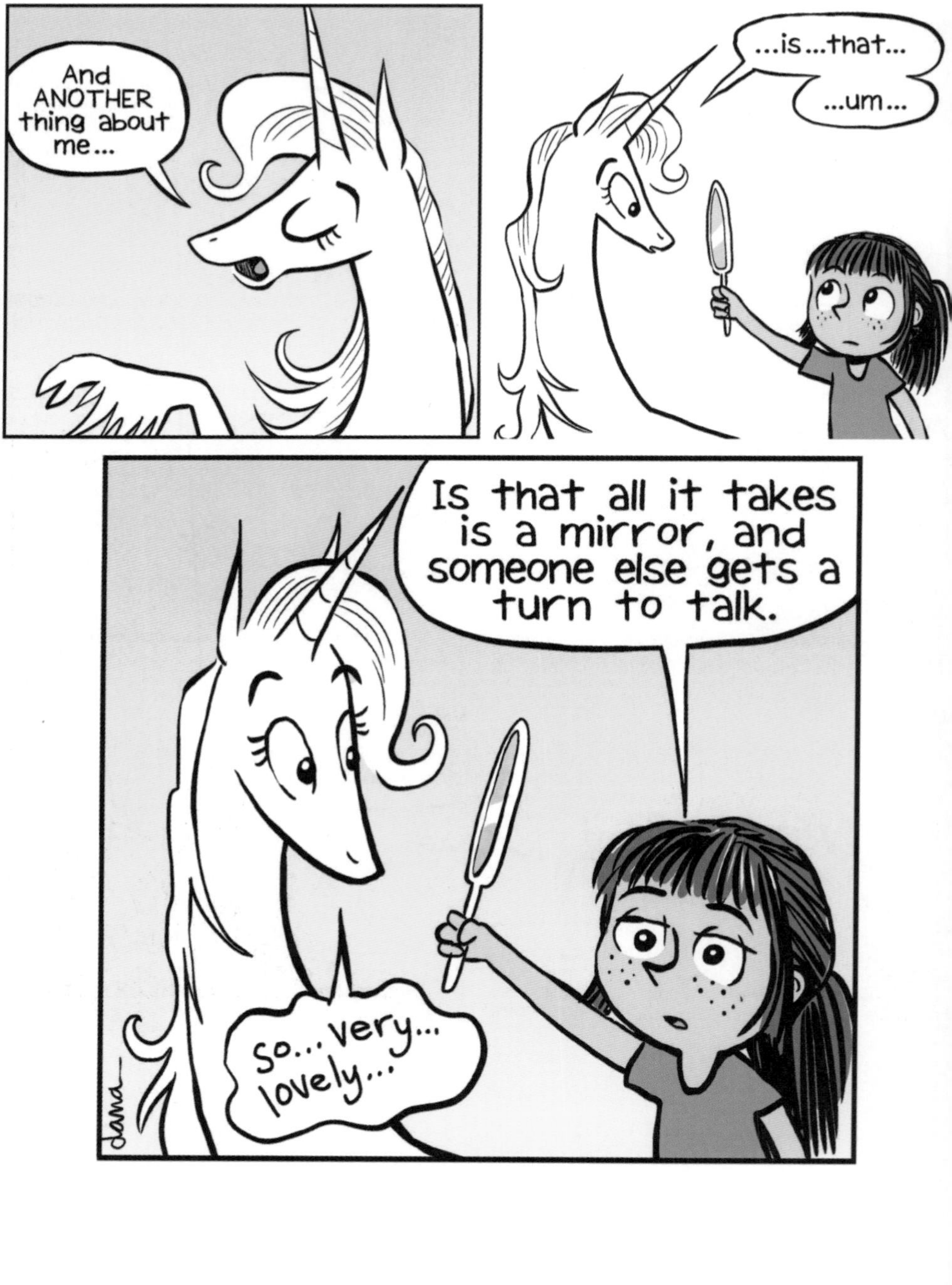
And ANOTHER thing about me...
...is...that...
...um...
Is that all it takes is a mirror, and someone else gets a turn to talk.
So... very... lovely...
dana

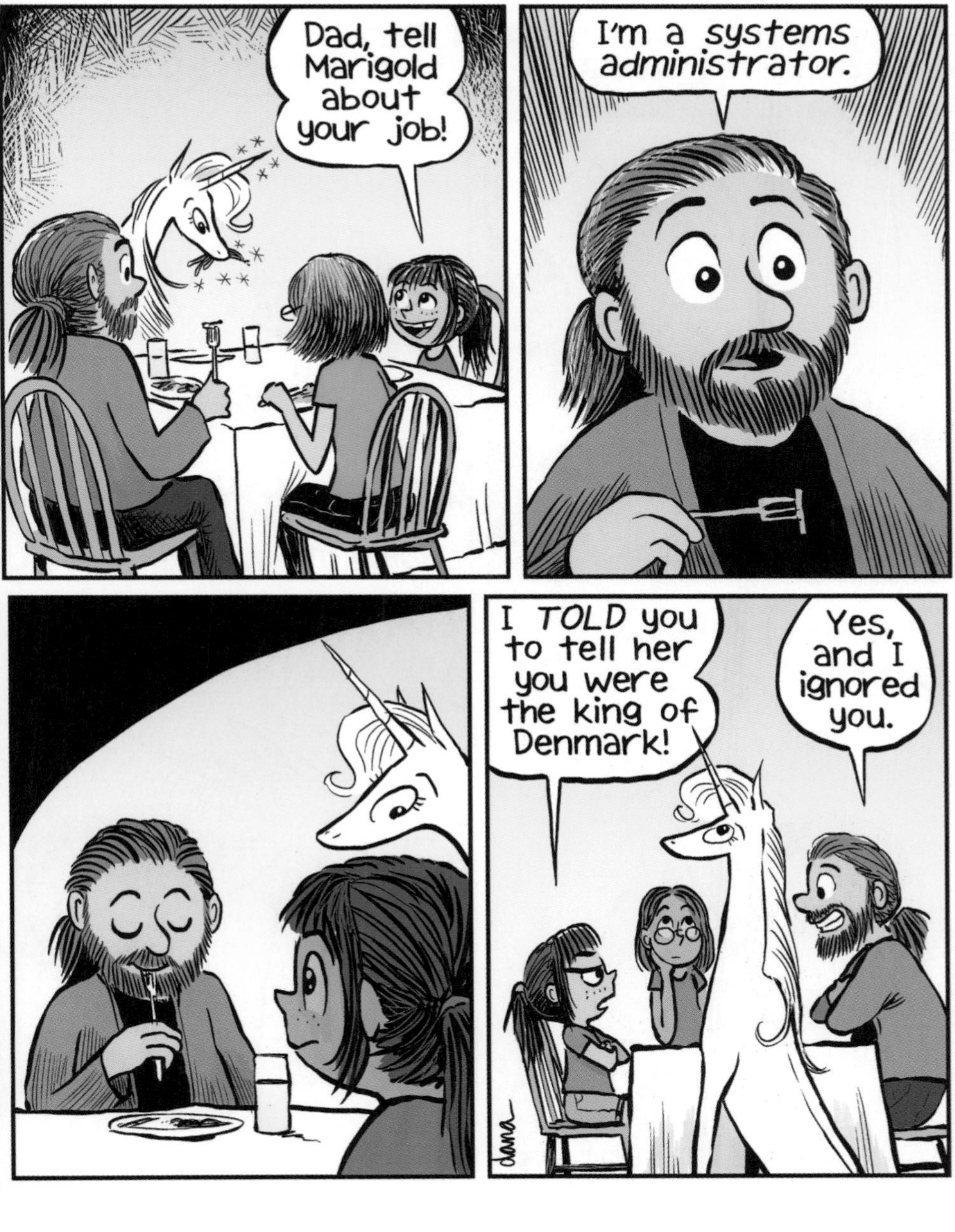
Dad, tell Marigold about your job!
I'm a *systems* administrator.
I *TOLD* you to tell her you were the king of Denmark!
Yes, and I ignored you.
dana

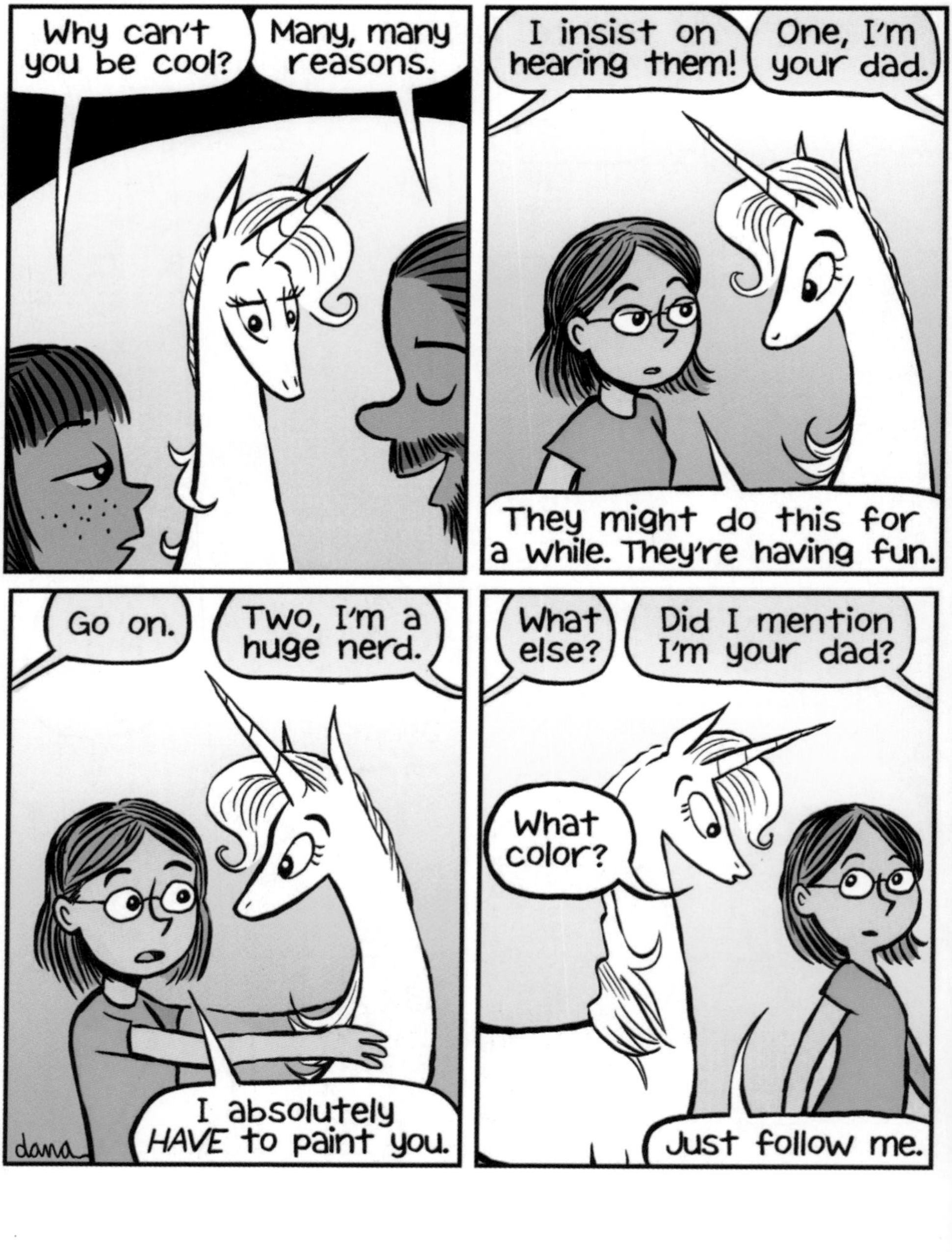
Why can't you be cool?
Many, many reasons.
I insist on hearing them!
One, I'm your dad.
They might do this for a while. They're having fun.
Go on.
Two, I'm a huge nerd.
I absolutely *HAVE* to paint you.
dana
What else?
Did I mention I'm your dad?
What color?
Just follow me.

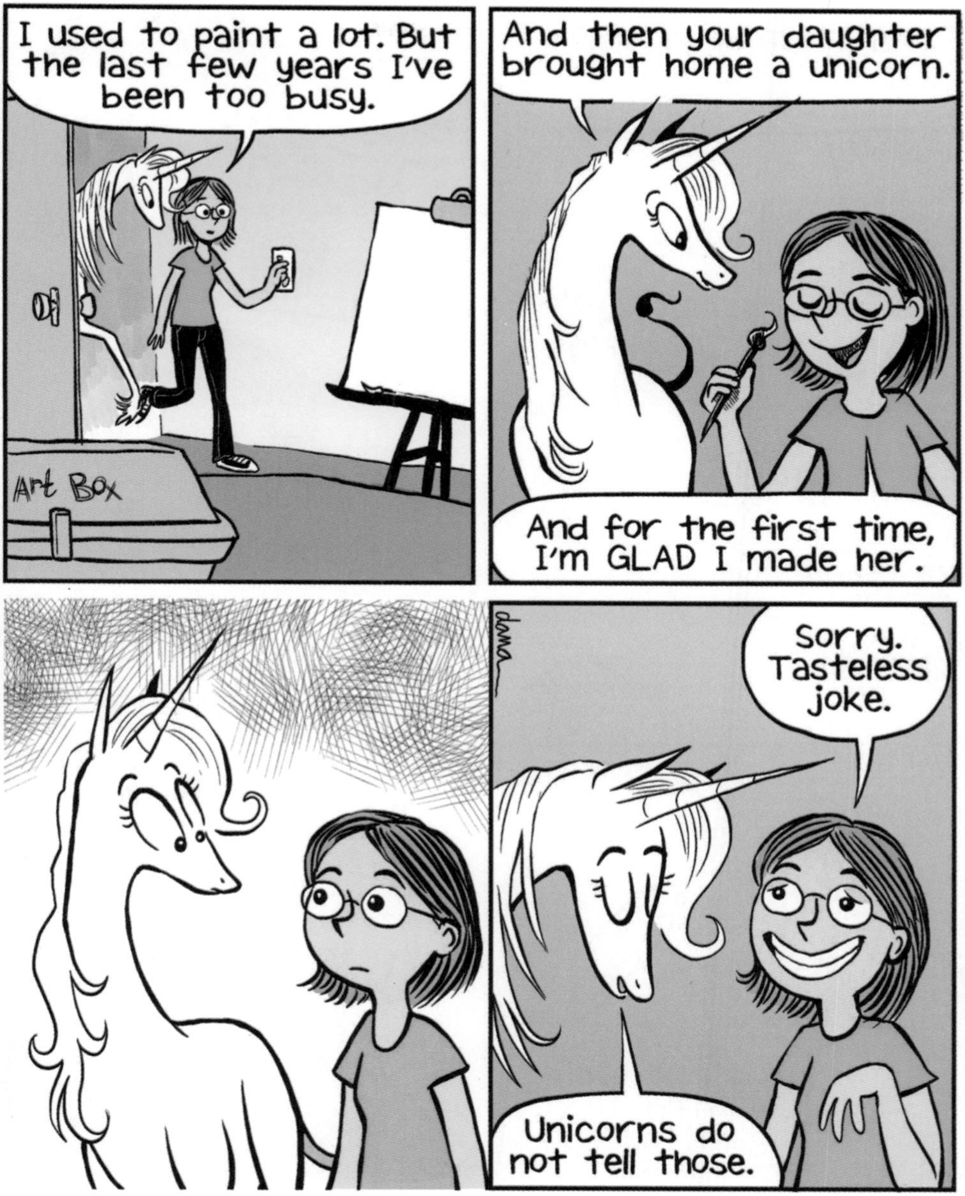
I used to paint a lot. But the last few years I've been too busy.
Art Box
And then your daughter brought home a unicorn.
And for the first time, I'm GLAD I made her.
dana
Sorry. Tasteless joke.
Unicorns do not tell those.

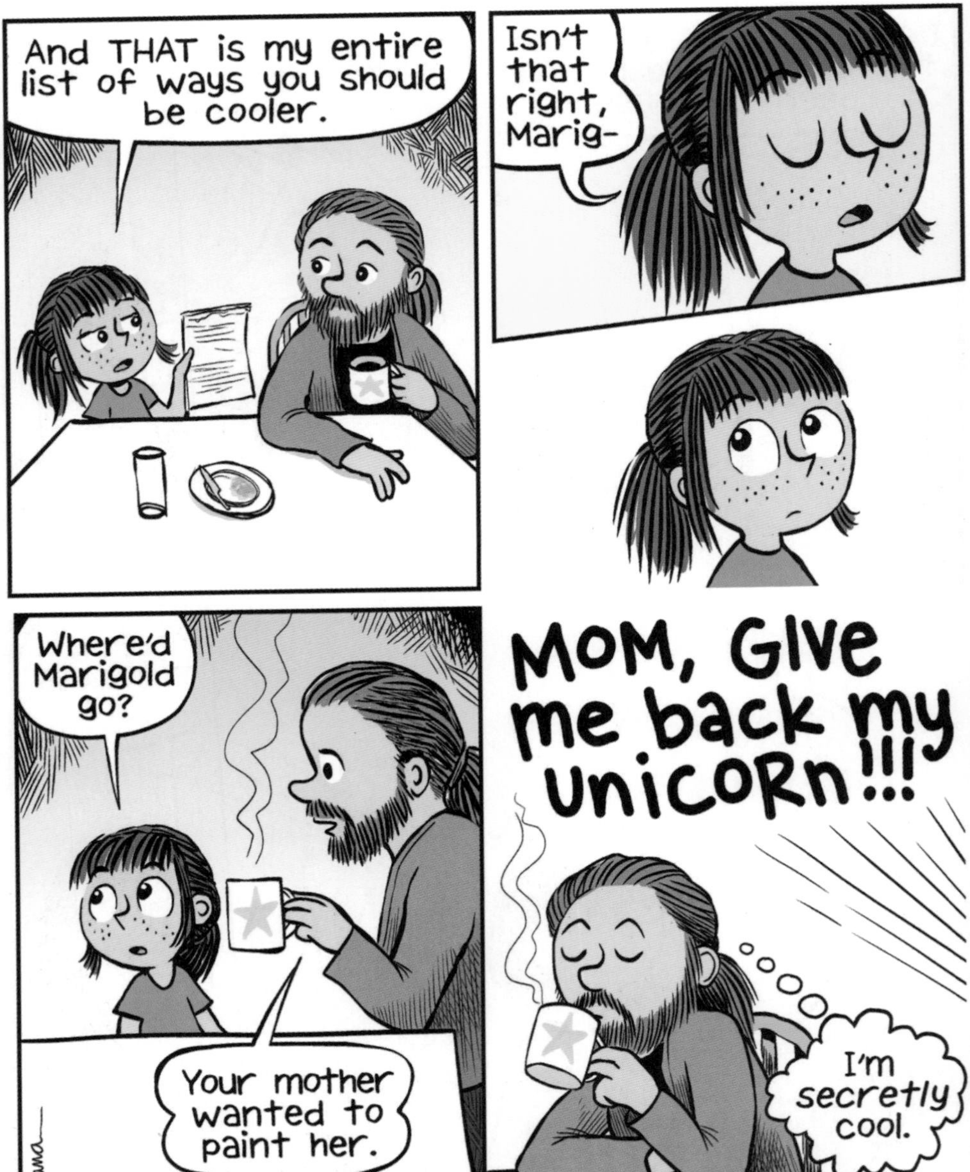
And THAT is my entire list of ways you should be cooler.
Isn't that right, Marig-
Where'd Marigold go?
Your mother wanted to paint her.
MOM, GIVE me back my UNICORN!!!
I'm secretly cool.
dana

Mom, you took my unicorn!
Oh, hello, Phoebe.
I *HAD* to paint her.
And I *HAD* to pose.
I have posed for innumerable grand tapestries.
I have always prided myself on my posing skills!
So you're saying you're a poser.
I am saying I am a **MAGNIFICENT** poser.
dana

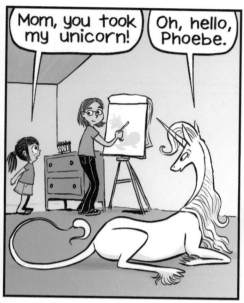

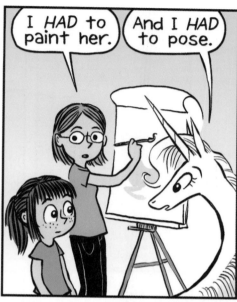

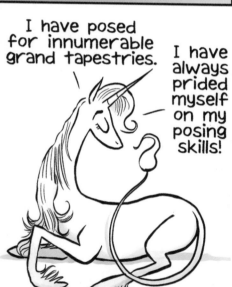

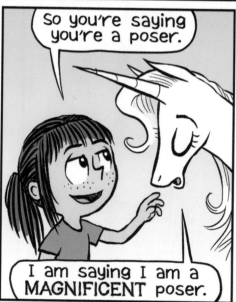

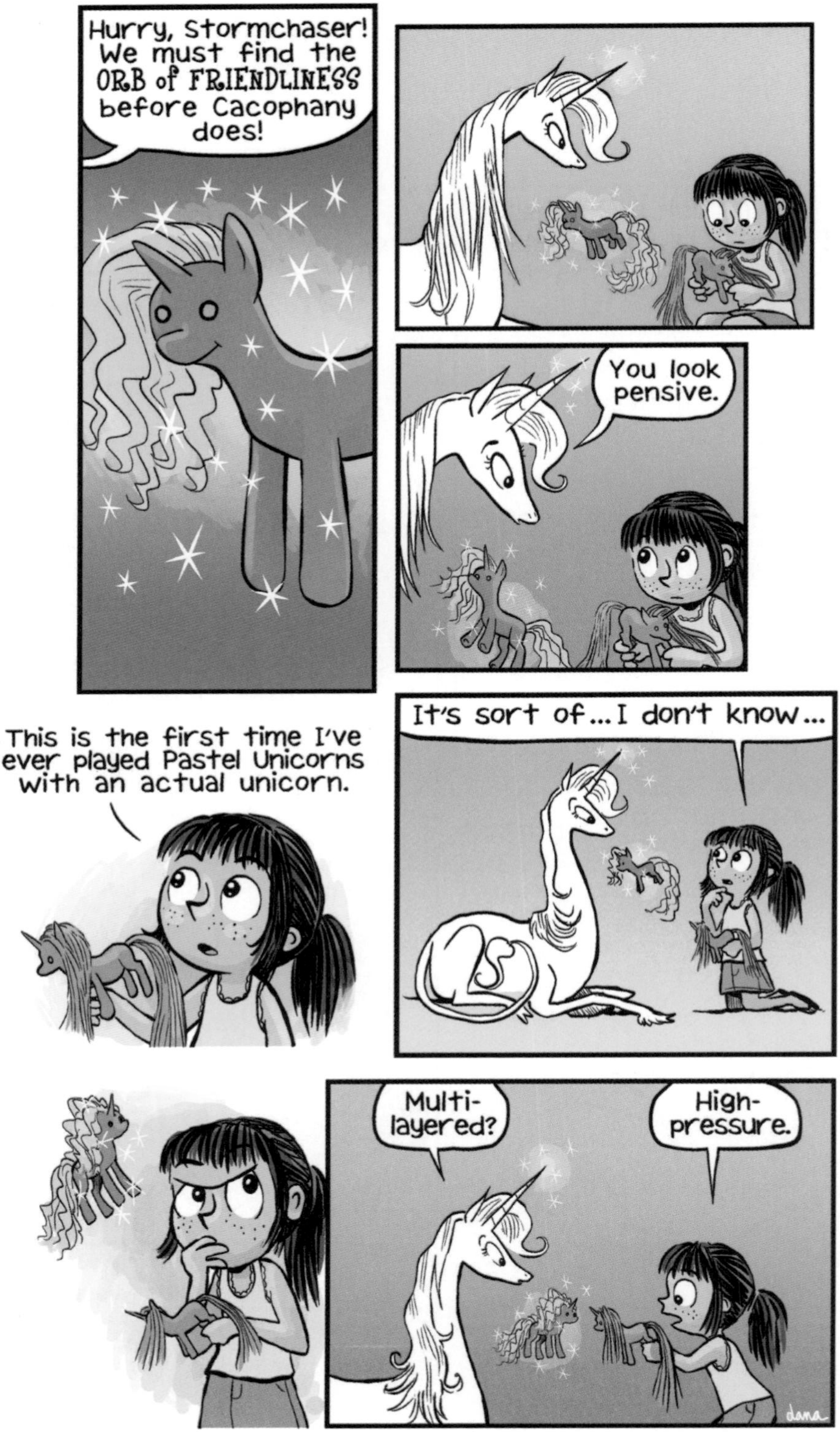
Hurry, Stormchaser! We must find the ORB of FRIENDLINESS before Cacophany does!
You look pensive.
This is the first time I've ever played Pastel Unicorns with an actual unicorn.
It's sort of... I don't know...
Multi-layered?
High-pressure.
dana

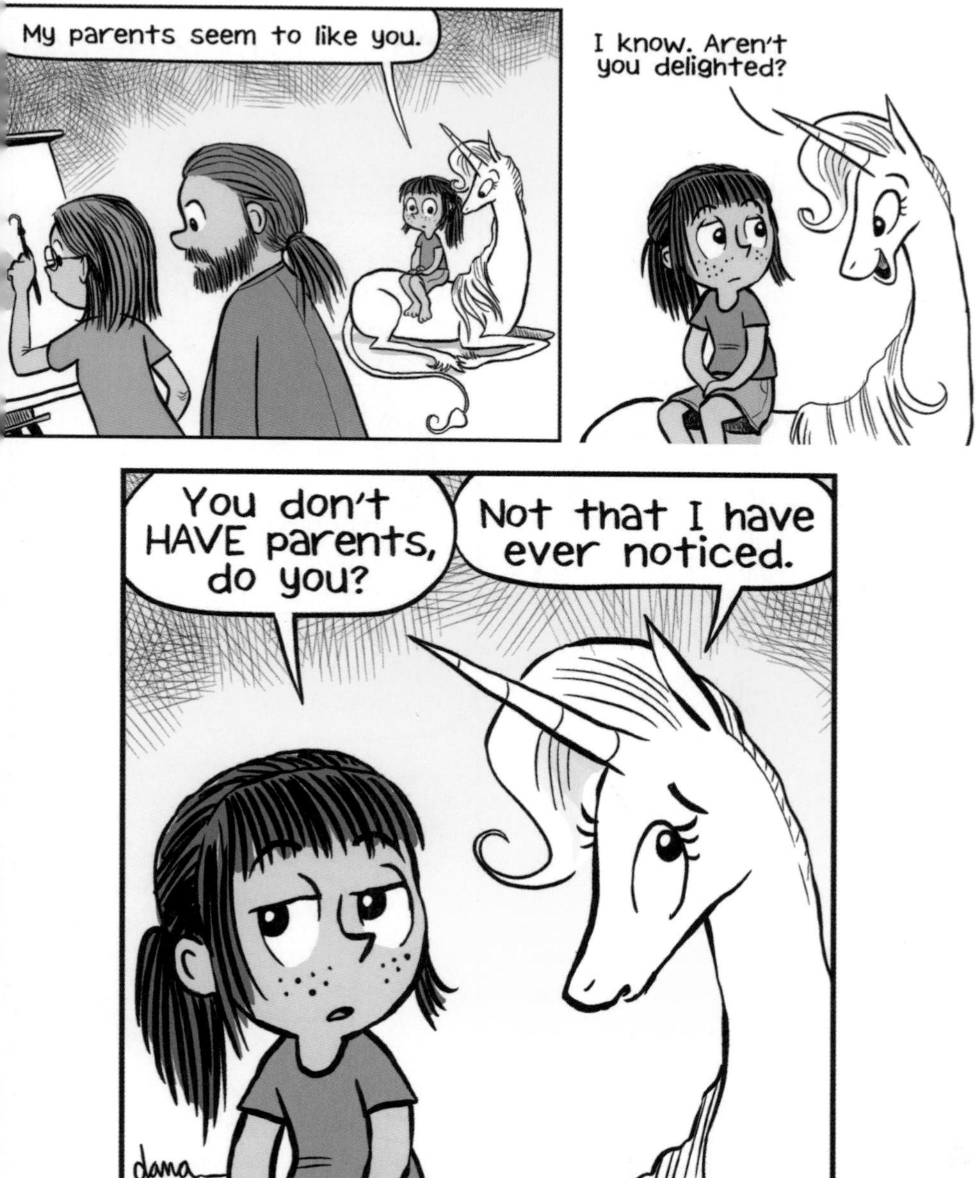
My parents seem to like you.
I know. Aren't you delighted?
You don't HAVE parents, do you?
Not that I have ever noticed.
dana

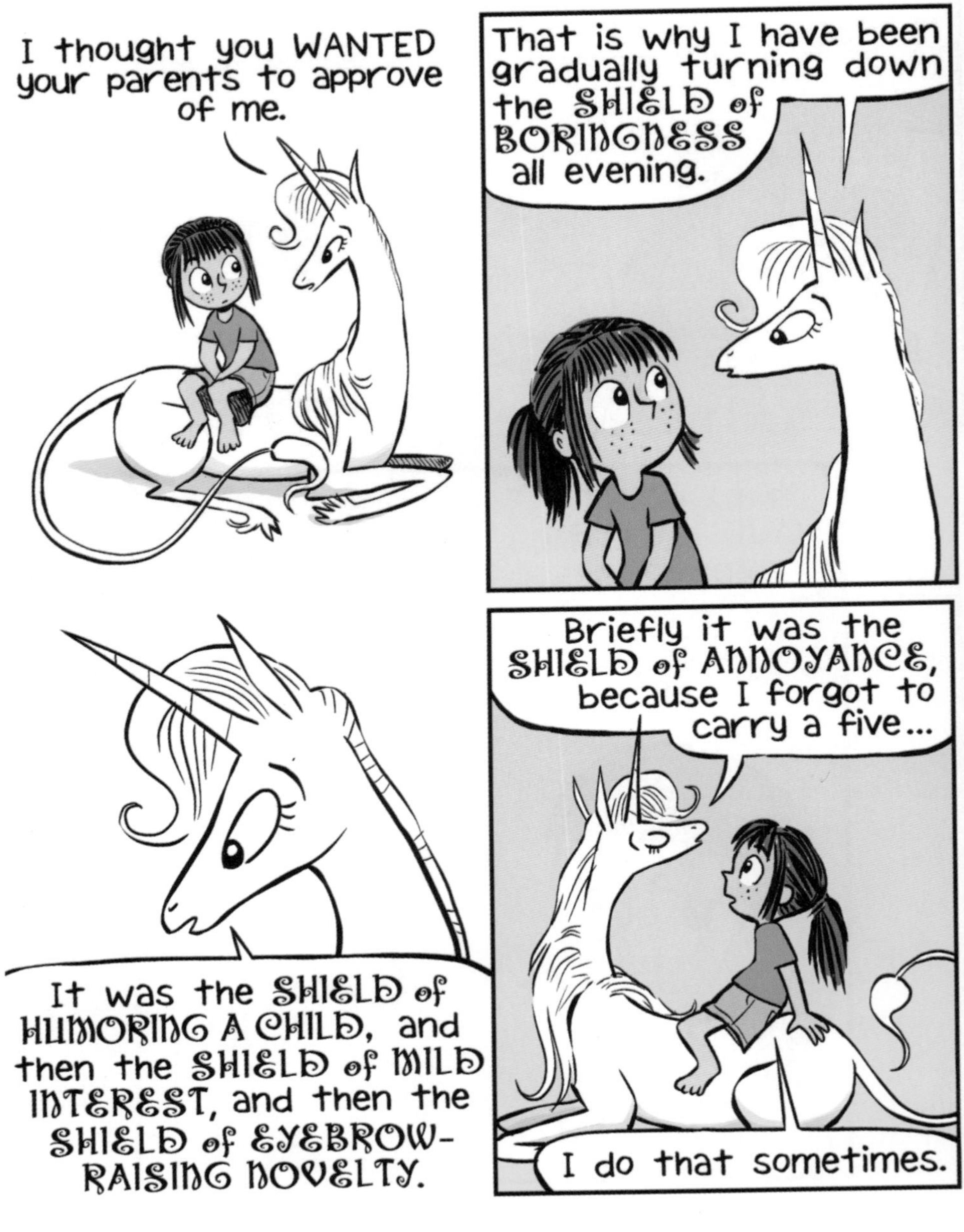
I thought you WANTED your parents to approve of me.
That is why I have been gradually turning down the SHIELD of BORINGNESS all evening.
It was the SHIELD of HUMORING A CHILD, and then the SHIELD of MILD INTEREST, and then the SHIELD of EYEBROW-RAISING NOVELTY.
Briefly it was the SHIELD of ANNOYANCE, because I forgot to carry a five...
I do that sometimes.

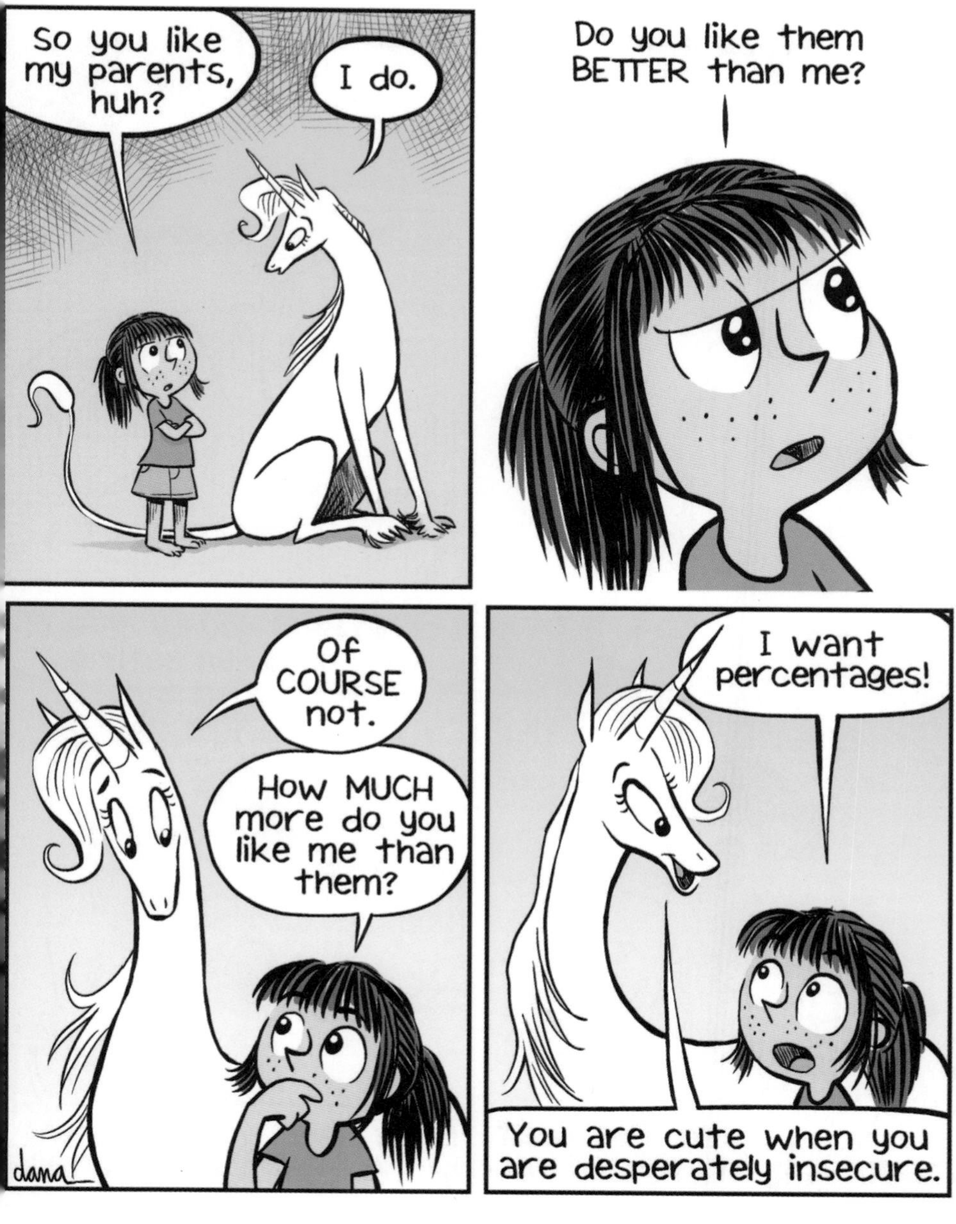
So you like my parents, huh?
I do.
Do you like them BETTER than me?
Of COURSE not.
How MUCH more do you like me than them?
I want percentages!
You are cute when you are desperately insecure.
dana

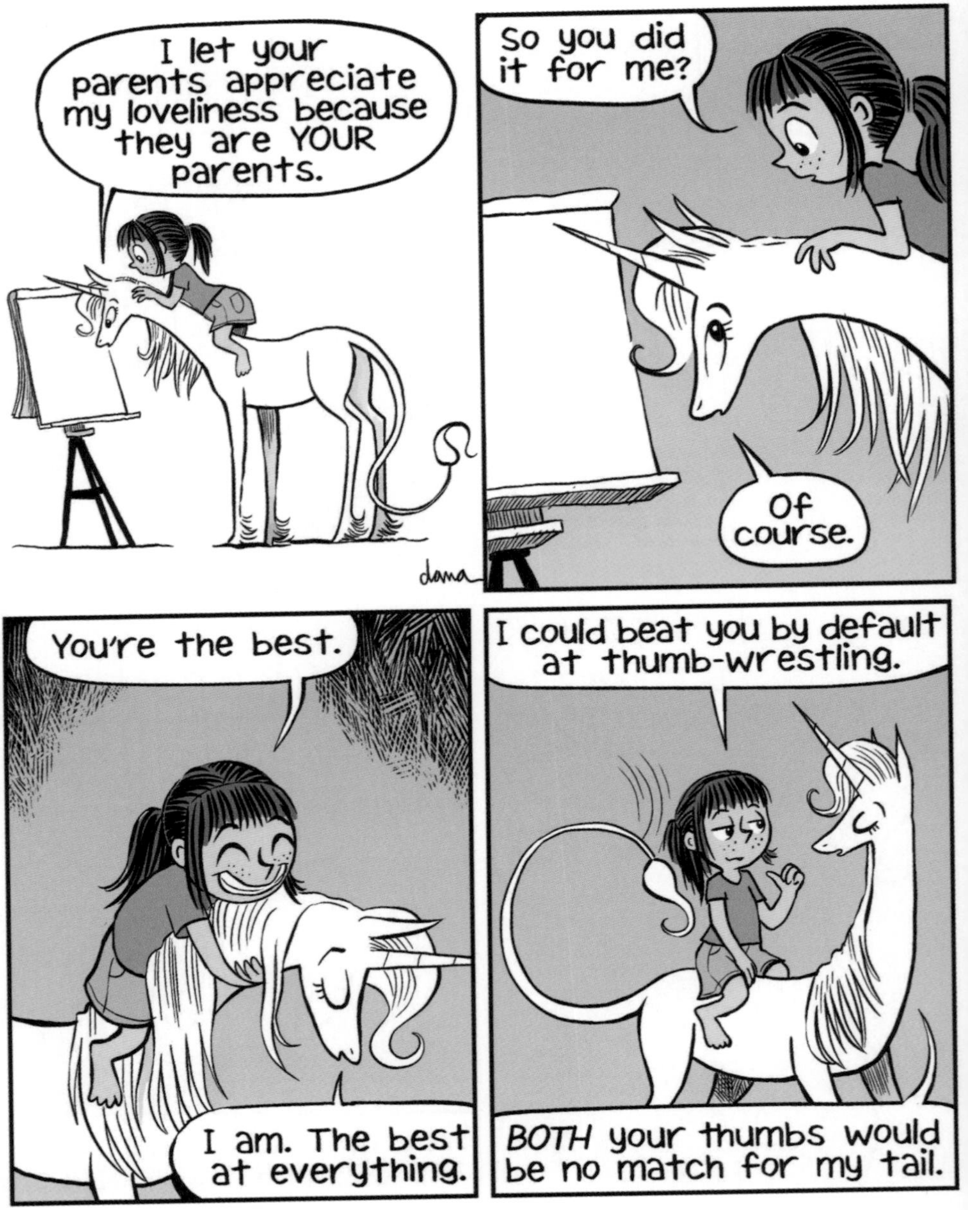
I let your parents appreciate my loveliness because they are YOUR parents.
dana
So you did it for me?
Of course.
You're the best.
I am. The best at everything.
I could beat you by default at thumb-wrestling.
BOTH your thumbs would be no match for my tail.

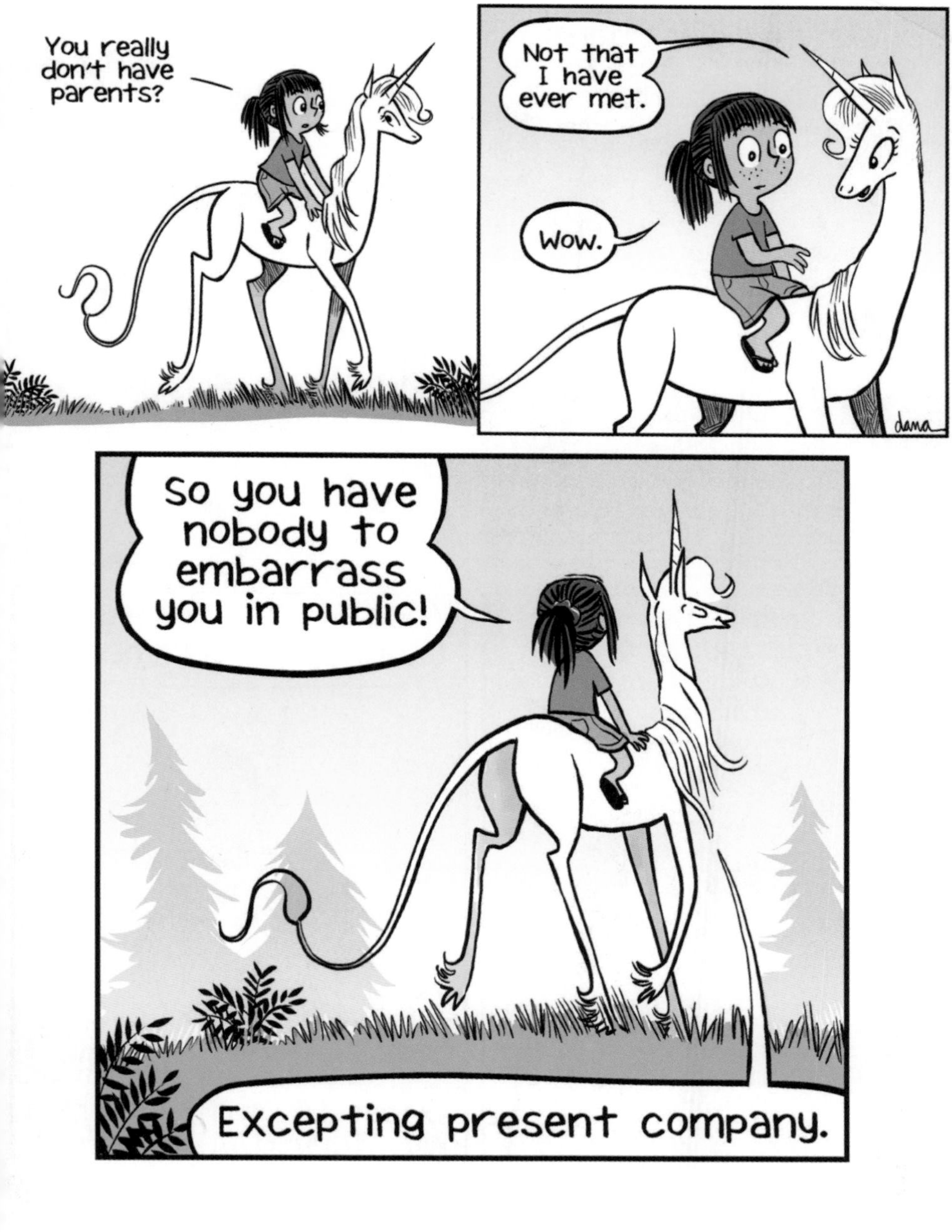
You really don't have parents?
Not that I have ever met.
Wow.
dana
So you have nobody to embarrass you in public!
Excepting present company.

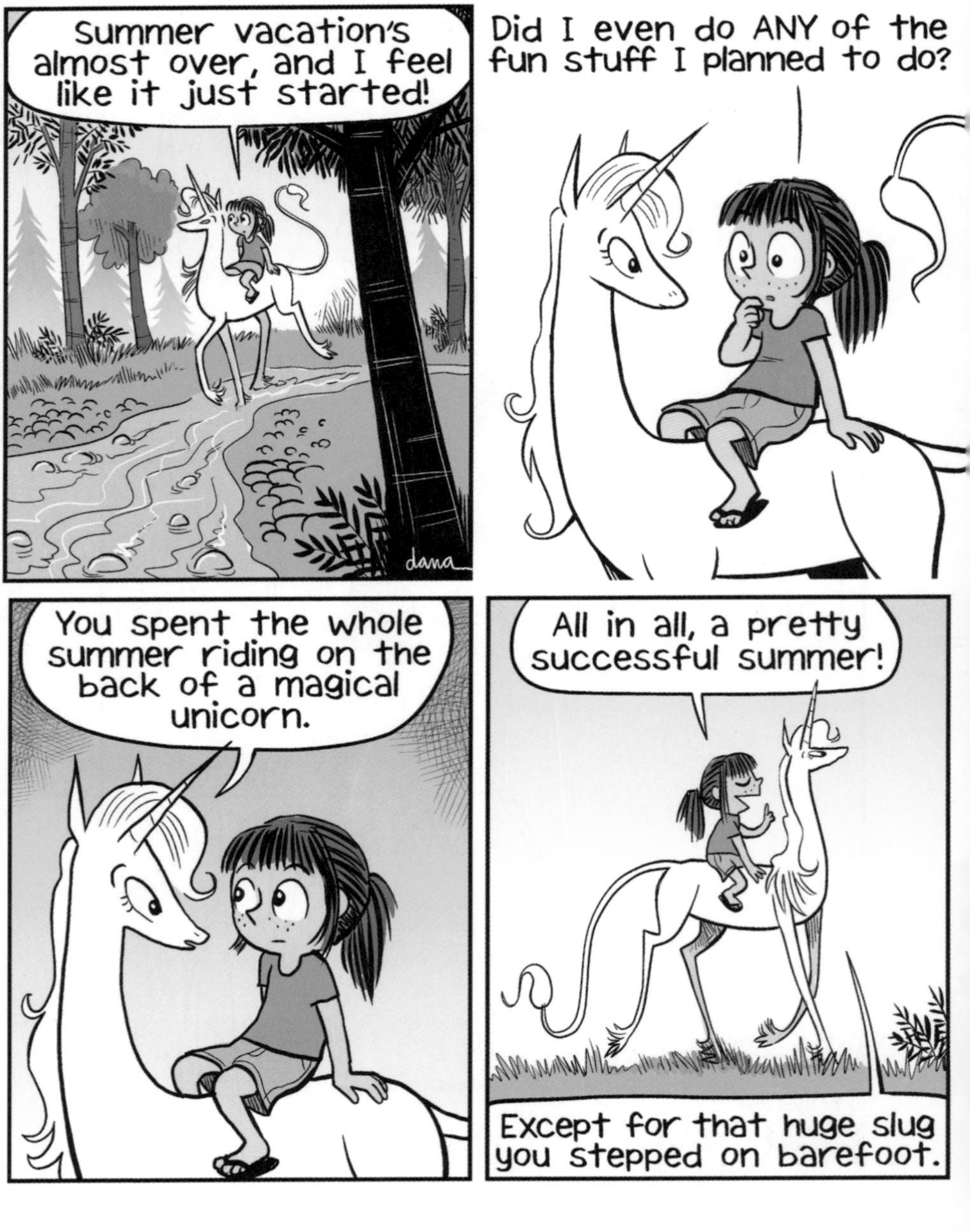
Summer vacation's almost over, and I feel like it just started!
dana
Did I even do ANY of the fun stuff I planned to do?
You spent the whole summer riding on the back of a magical unicorn.
All in all, a pretty successful summer!
Except for that huge slug you stepped on barefoot.

Dad, what was life like before the internet?

I knew this day would come.

That one day, you would ask about the **BEFORE TIMES.**

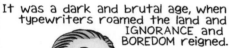

It was a dark and brutal age, when typewriters roamed the land and IGNORANCE and BOREDOM reigned.

It was VERY DIFFICULT to waste time watching videos of cats.

I'm going outside now.

Outside! I remember outside.

maow

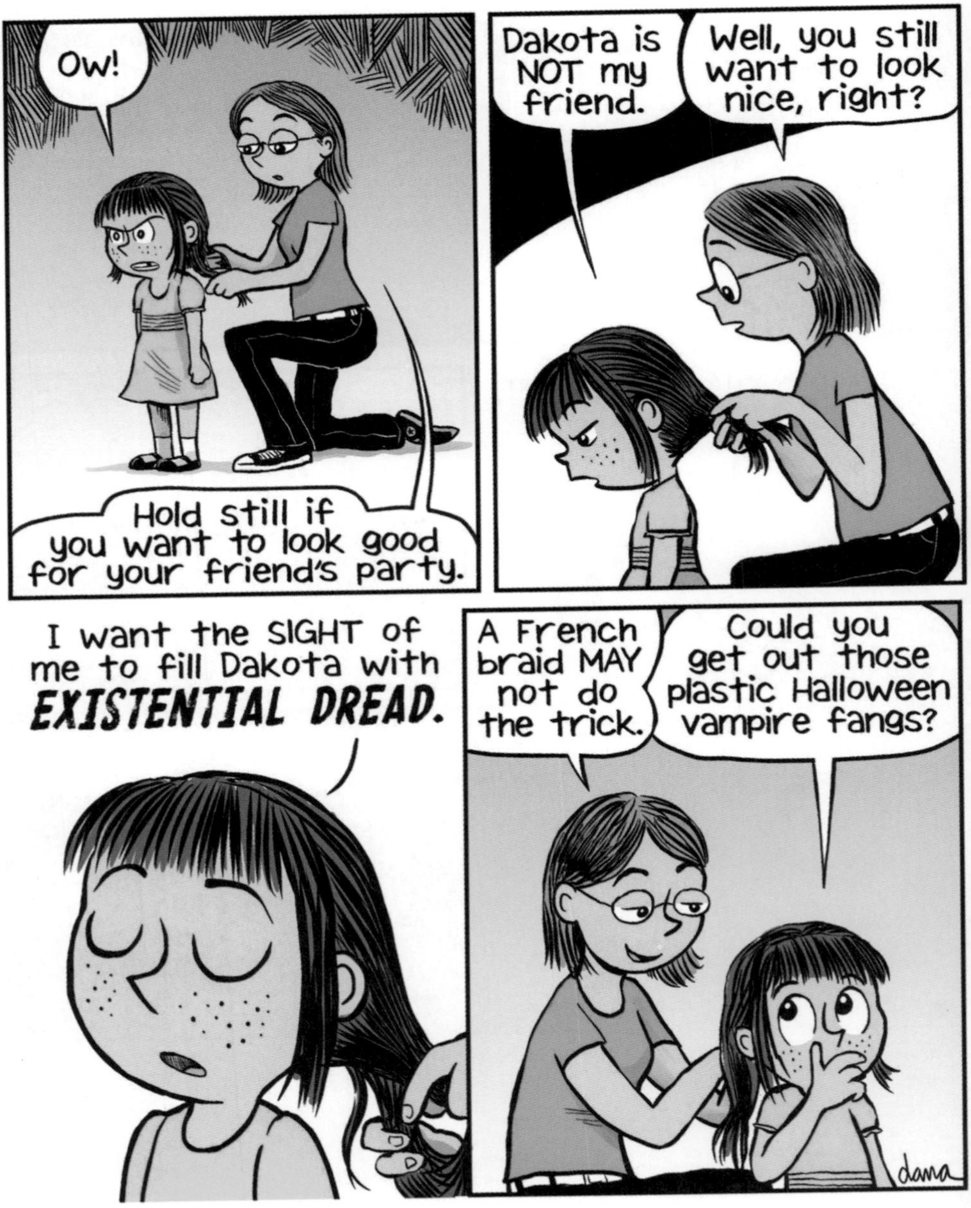
Ow!
Hold still if you want to look good for your friend's party.
Dakota is NOT my friend.
Well, you still want to look nice, right?
I want the SIGHT of me to fill Dakota with EXISTENTIAL DREAD.
A French braid MAY not do the trick.
Could you get out those plastic Halloween vampire fangs?
dana

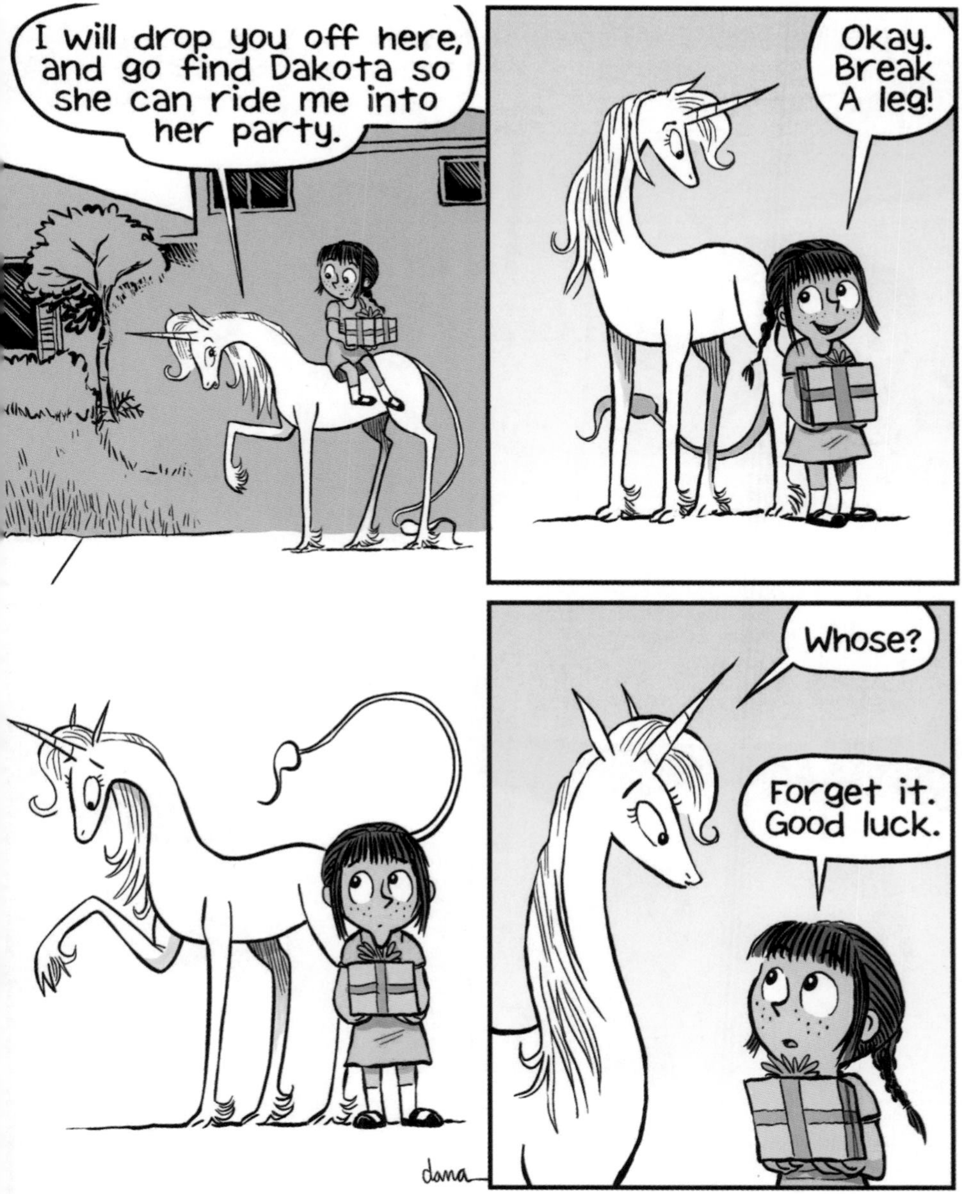
I will drop you off here, and go find Dakota so she can ride me into her party.
Okay. Break A leg!
Whose?
Forget it. Good luck.
dana

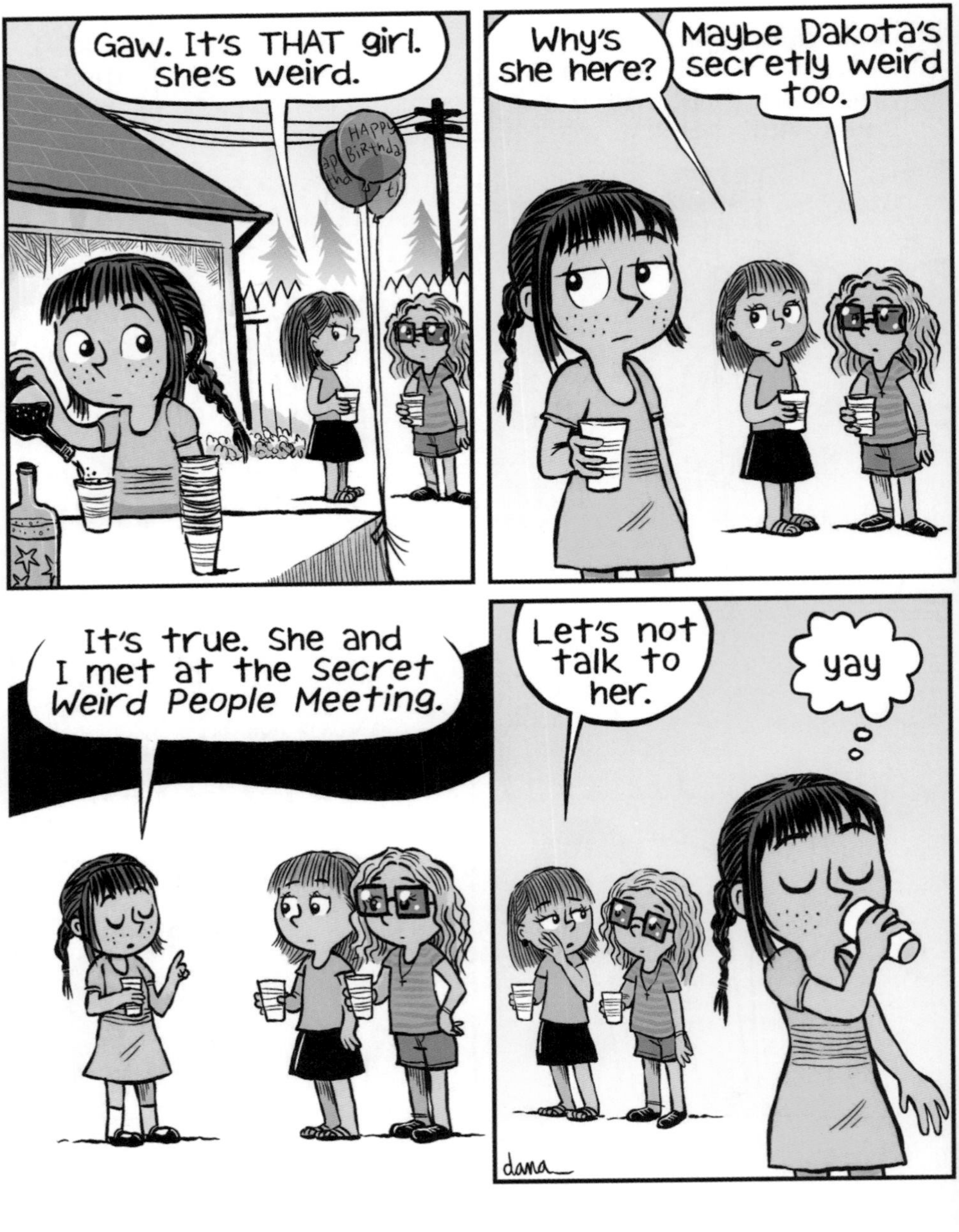
Gaw. It's THAT girl. she's weird.
HAPPY Birthday
Why's she here?
Maybe Dakota's secretly weird too.
It's true. She and I met at the Secret Weird People Meeting.
Let's not talk to her.
yay
dana

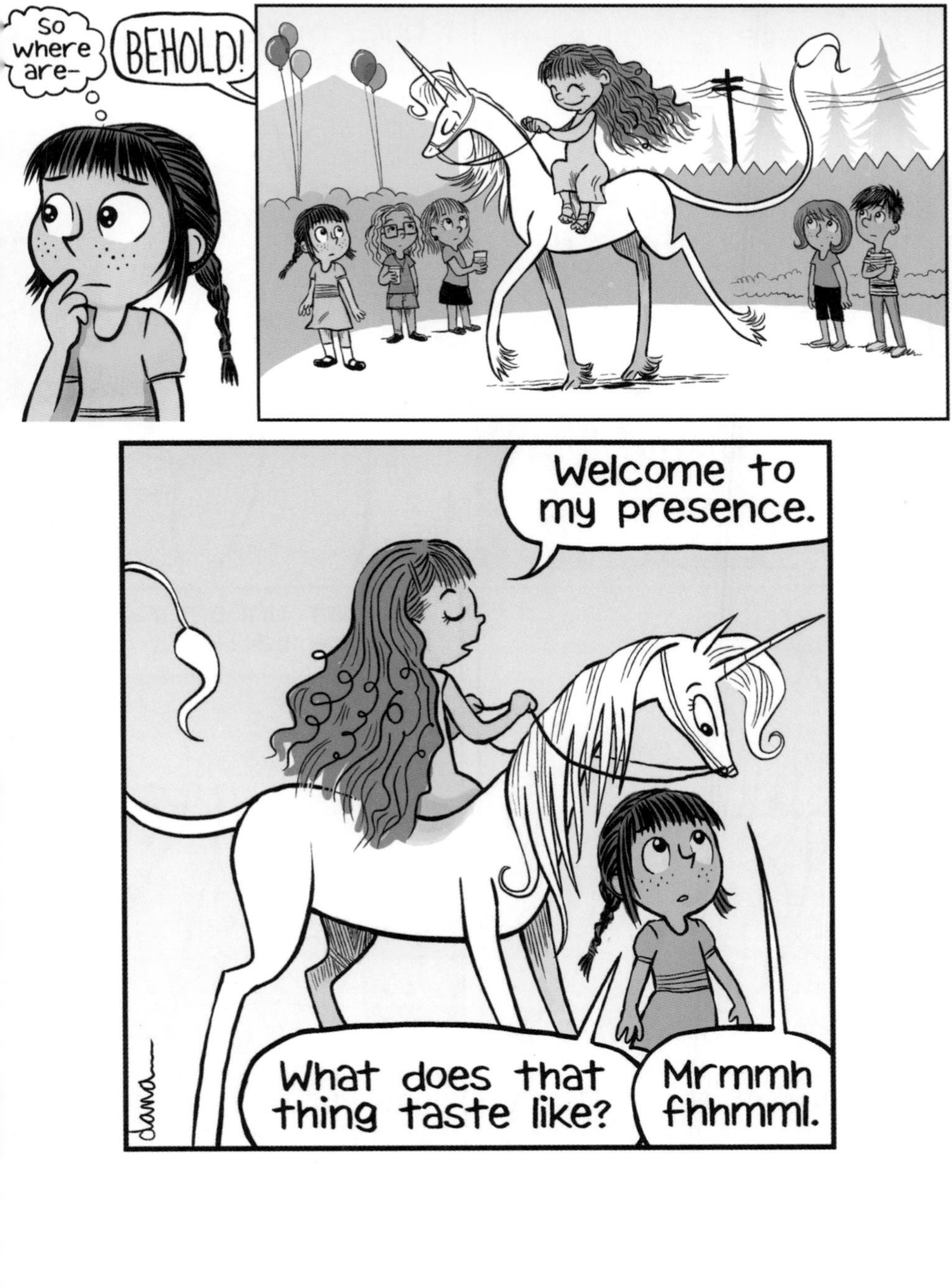
So where are-
BEHOLD!
Welcome to my presence.
What does that thing taste like?
Mrmmh fhhmml.
dana

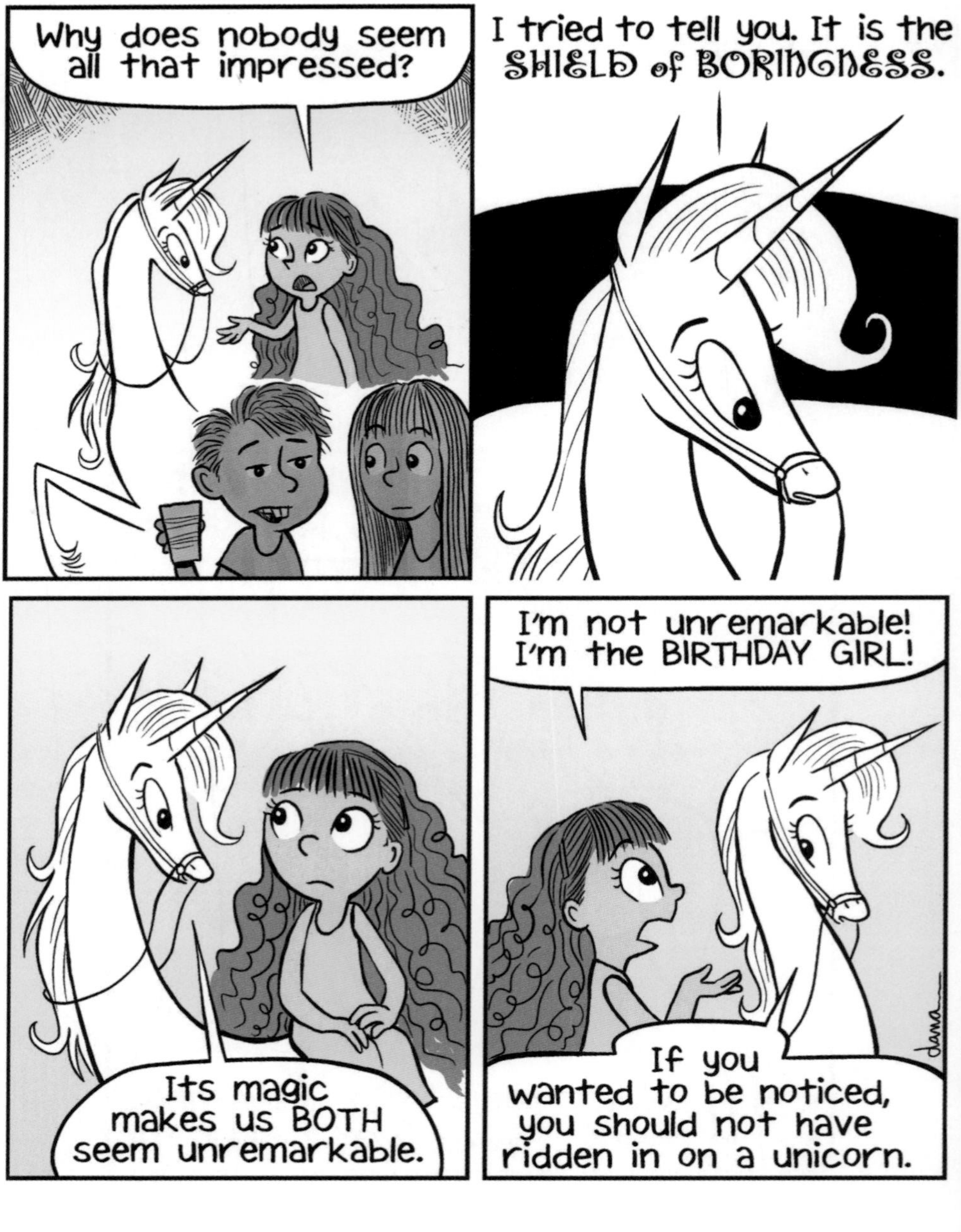
Why does nobody seem all that impressed?
I tried to tell you. It is the SHIELD of BORINGNESS.
Its magic makes us BOTH seem unremarkable.
I'm not unremarkable! I'm the BIRTHDAY GIRL!
If you wanted to be noticed, you should not have ridden in on a unicorn.
dana

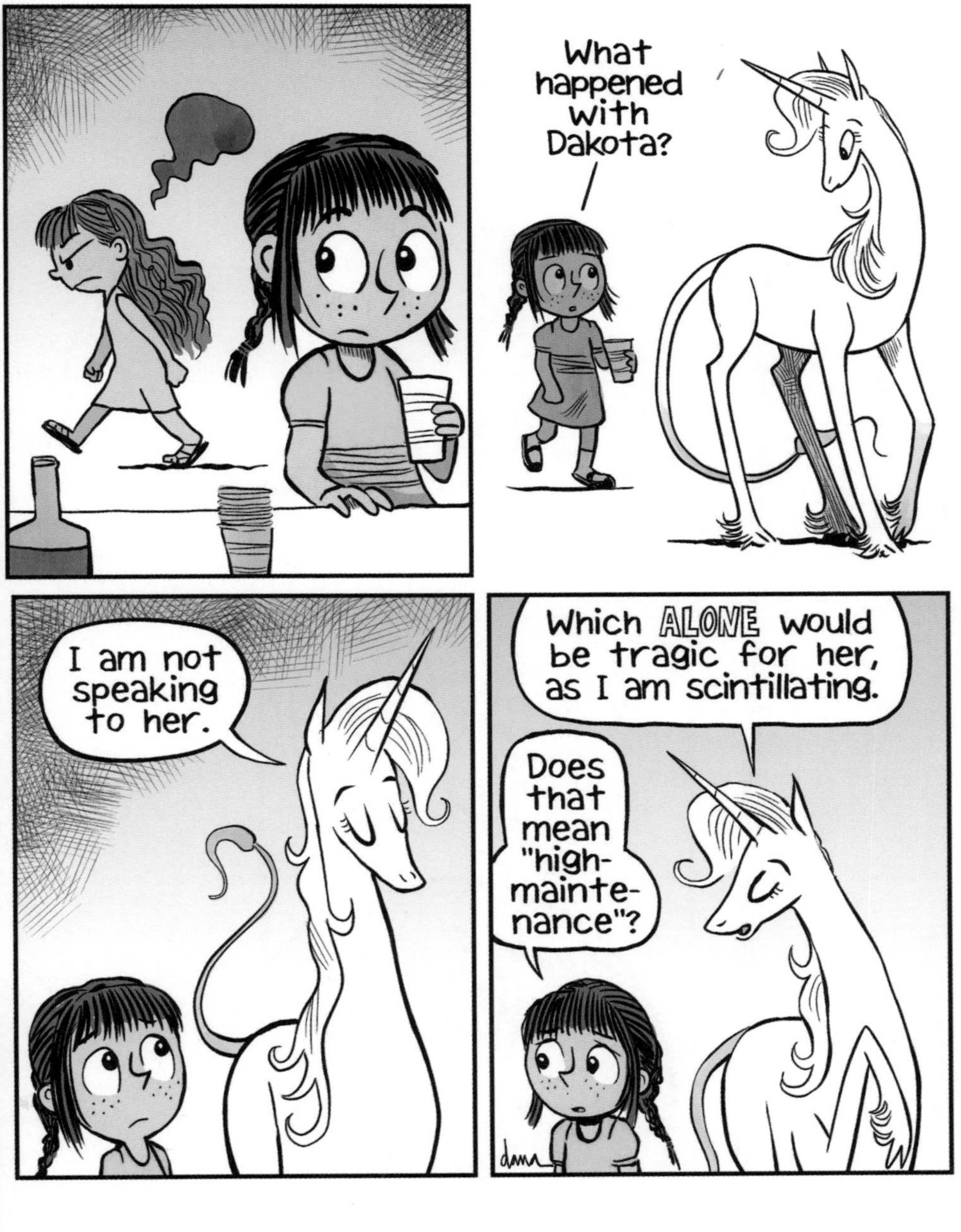
What happened with Dakota?
I am not speaking to her.
Which ALONE would be tragic for her, as I am scintillating.
Does that mean "high-maintenance"?
dana

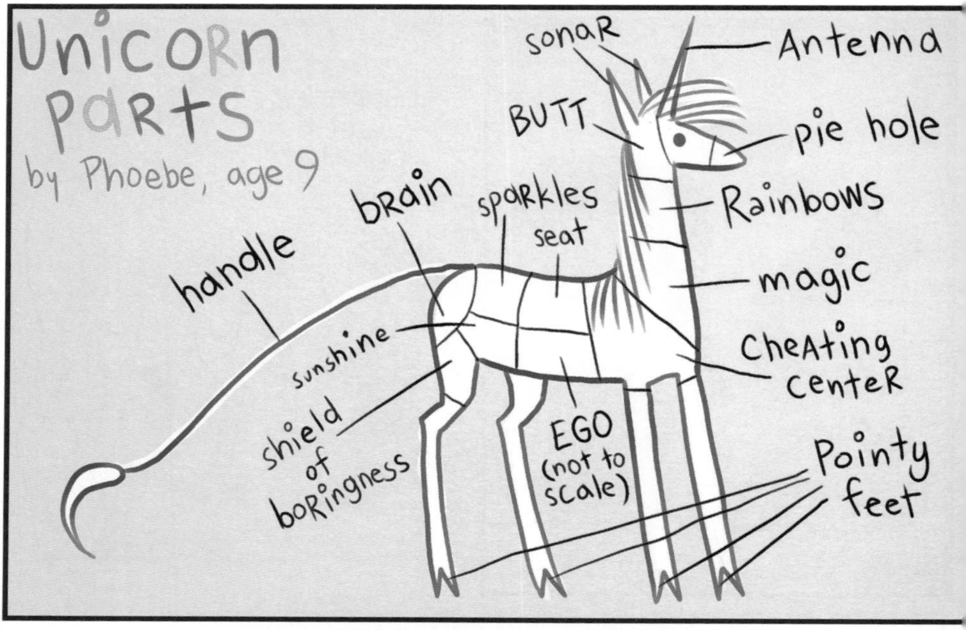
Unicorn parts
by Phoebe, age 9
sonaR
Antenna
BUTT
pie hole
brain
sparkles
seat
Rainbows
handle
magic
sunshine
Cheating center
shield of boringness
EGO (not to scale)
Pointy feet

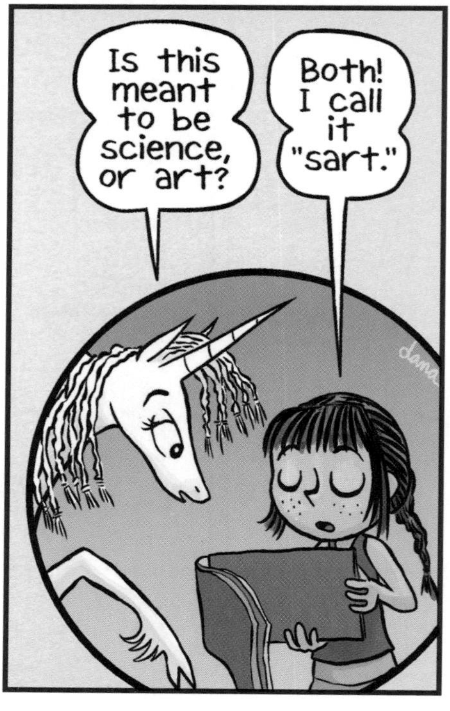
Is this meant to be science, or art?
Both! I call it "sart."

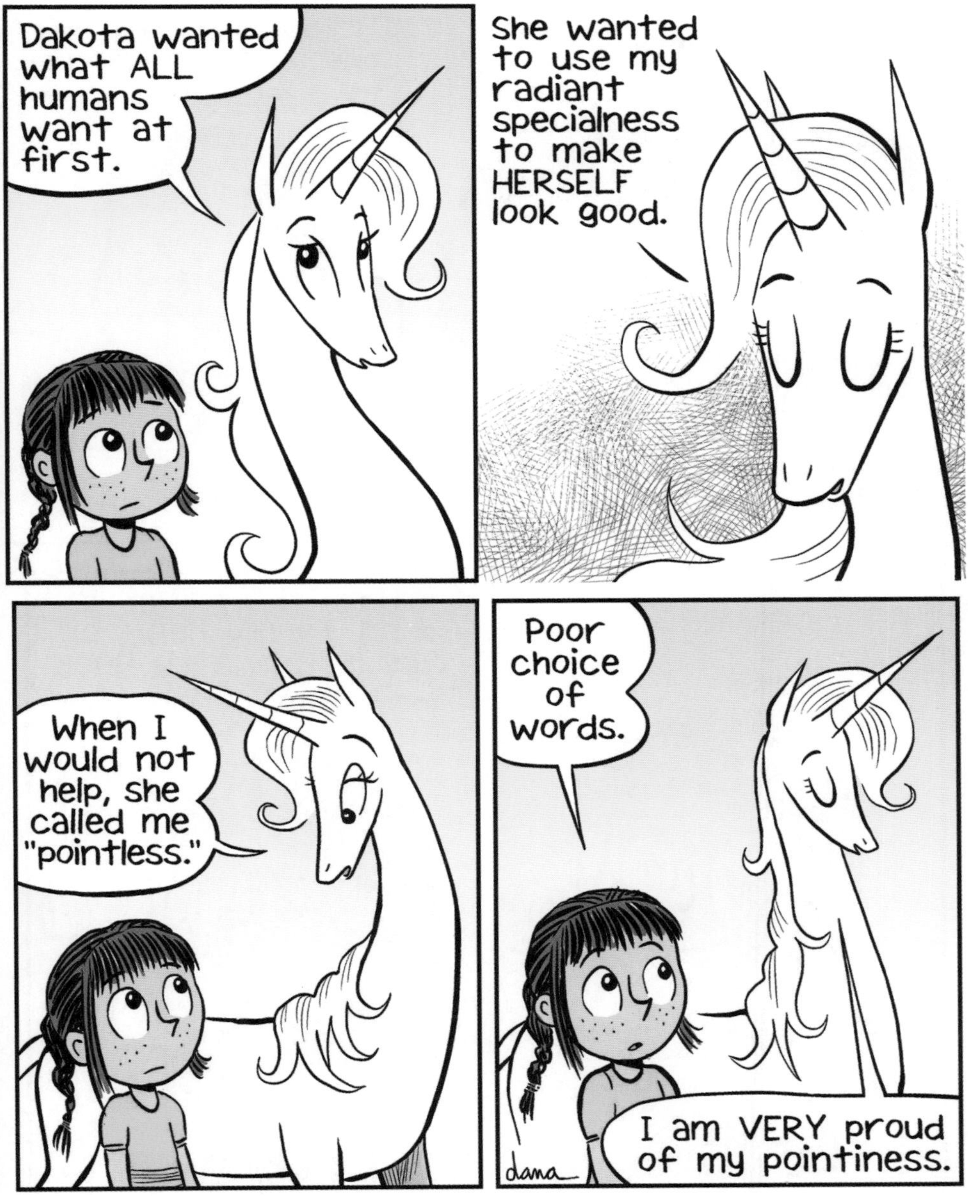
Dakota wanted what ALL humans want at first.
She wanted to use my radiant specialness to make HERSELF look good.
When I would not help, she called me "pointless."
Poor choice of words.
I am VERY proud of my pointiness.
dana

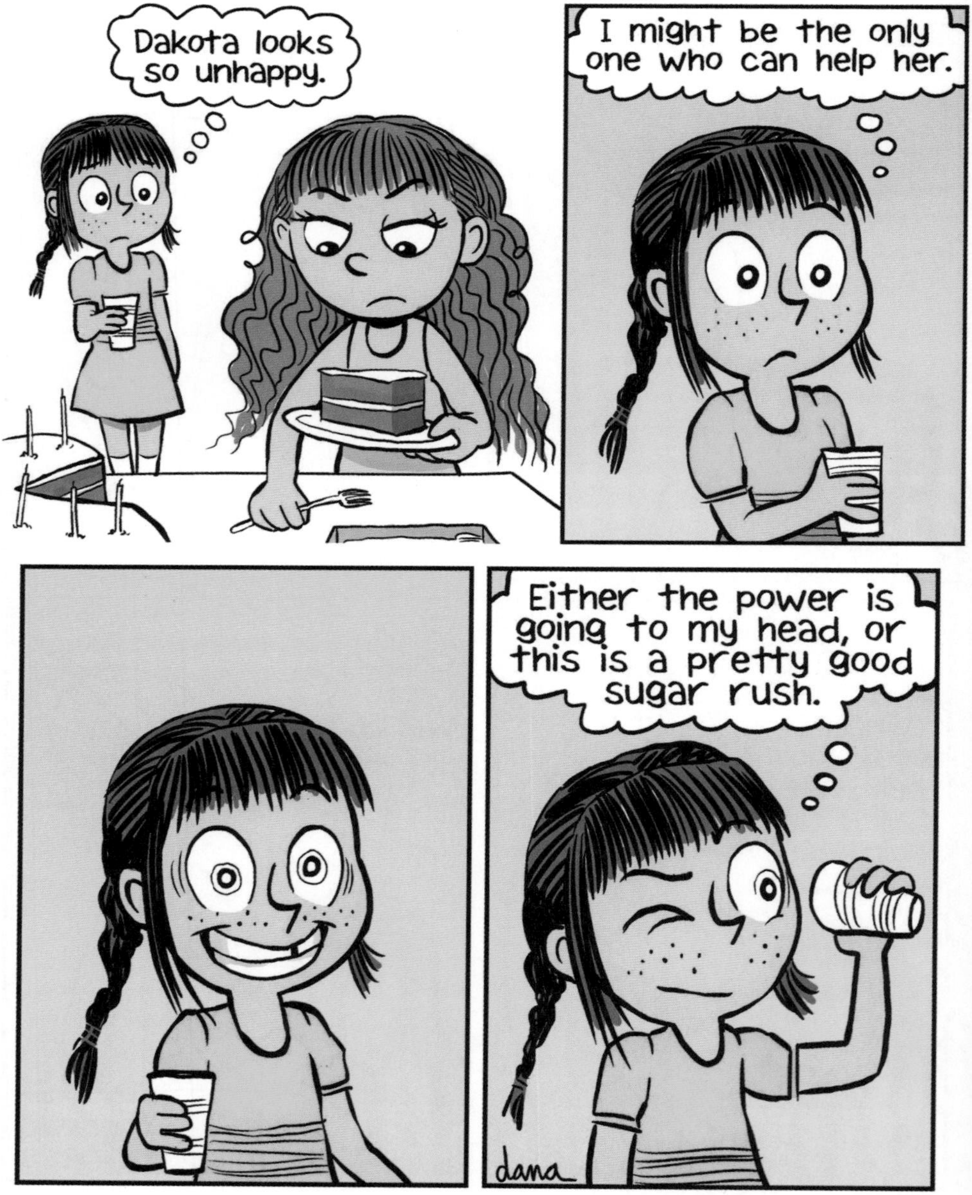
Dakota looks so unhappy.
I might be the only one who can help her.
Either the power is going to my head, or this is a pretty good sugar rush.
dana

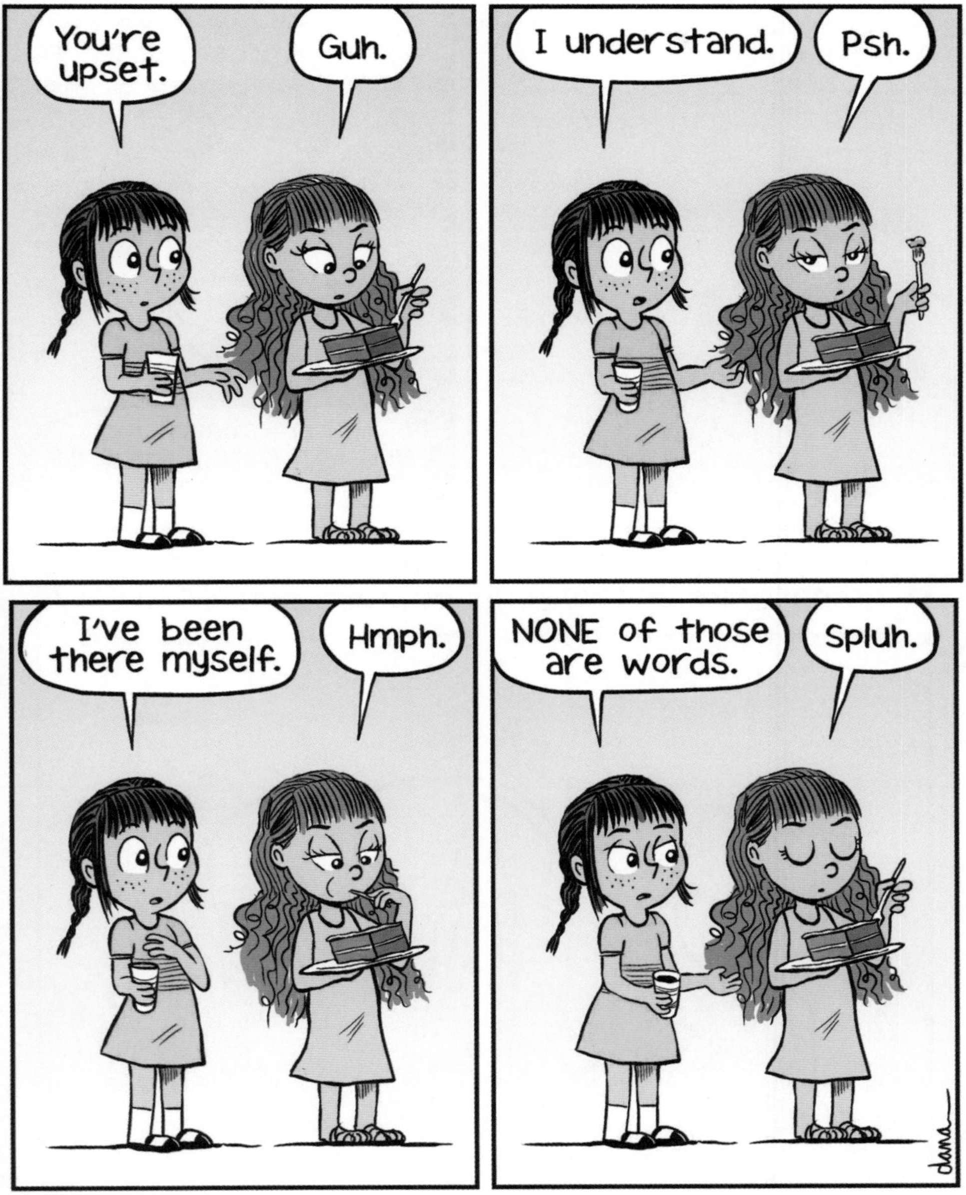
You're upset.
Guh.
I understand.
Psh.
I've been there myself.
Hmph.
NONE of those are words.
Spluh.
dana

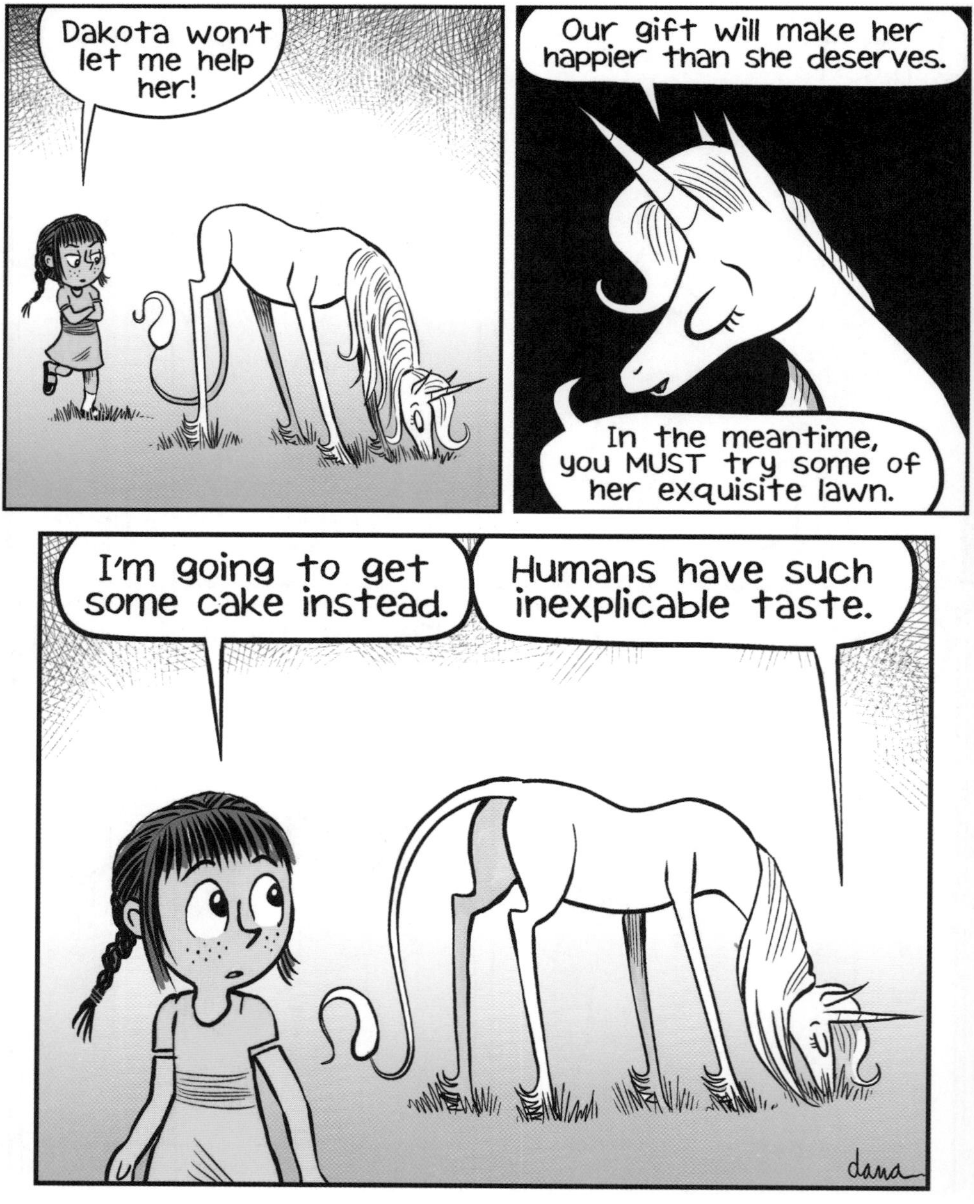
Dakota won't let me help her!
Our gift will make her happier than she deserves.
In the meantime, you MUST try some of her exquisite lawn.
I'm going to get some cake instead.
Humans have such inexplicable taste.
dana

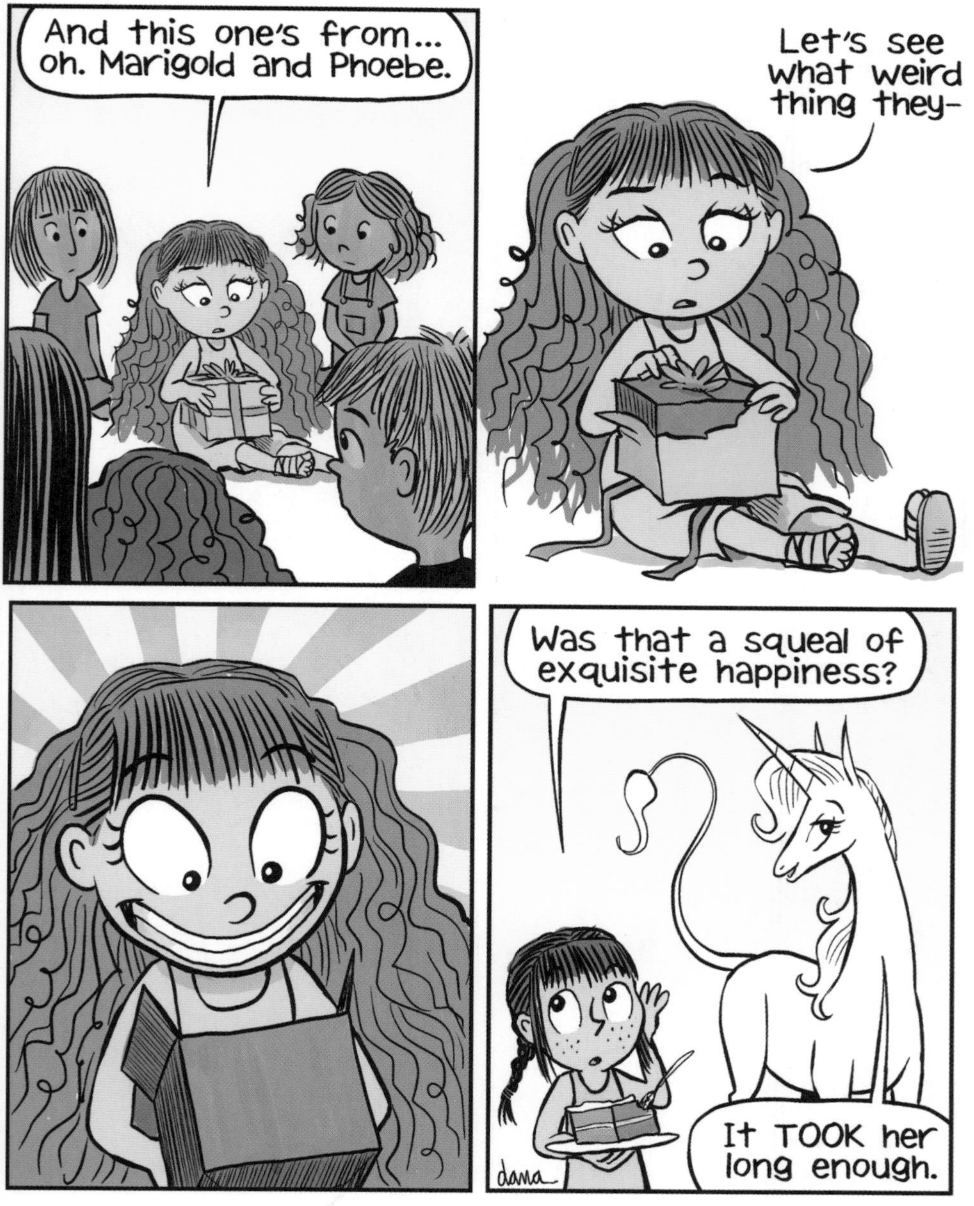
And this one's from... oh. Marigold and Phoebe.
Let's see what weird thing they-
Was that a squeal of exquisite happiness?
It TOOK her long enough.
dana

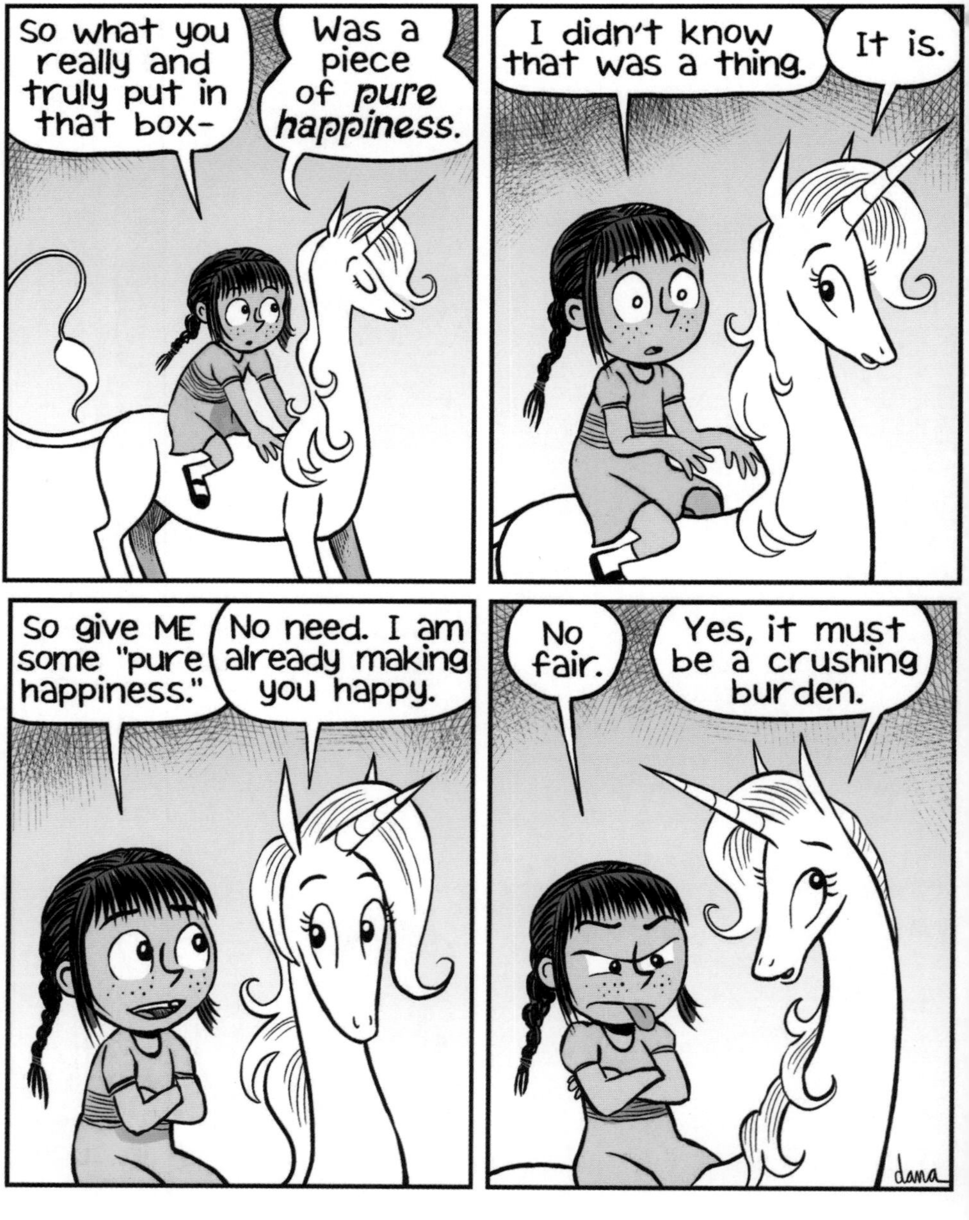
So what you really and truly put in that box-
Was a piece of *pure happiness.*
I didn't know that was a thing.
It is.
So give ME some "pure happiness."
No need. I am already making you happy.
No fair.
Yes, it must be a crushing burden.
dana

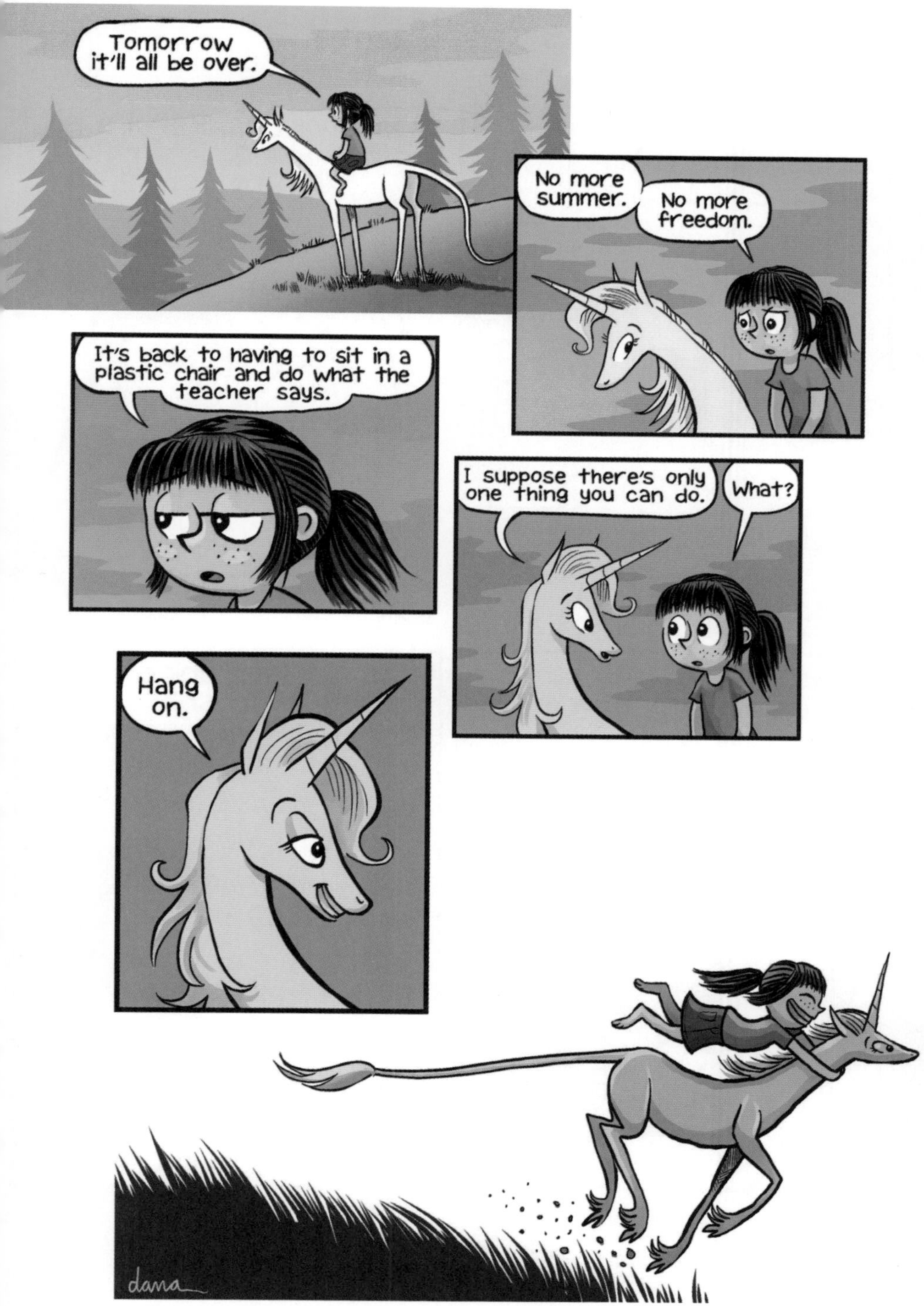
Tomorrow it'll all be over.
No more summer.
No more freedom.
It's back to having to sit in a plastic chair and do what the teacher says.
I suppose there's only one thing you can do.
What?
Hang on.
dana

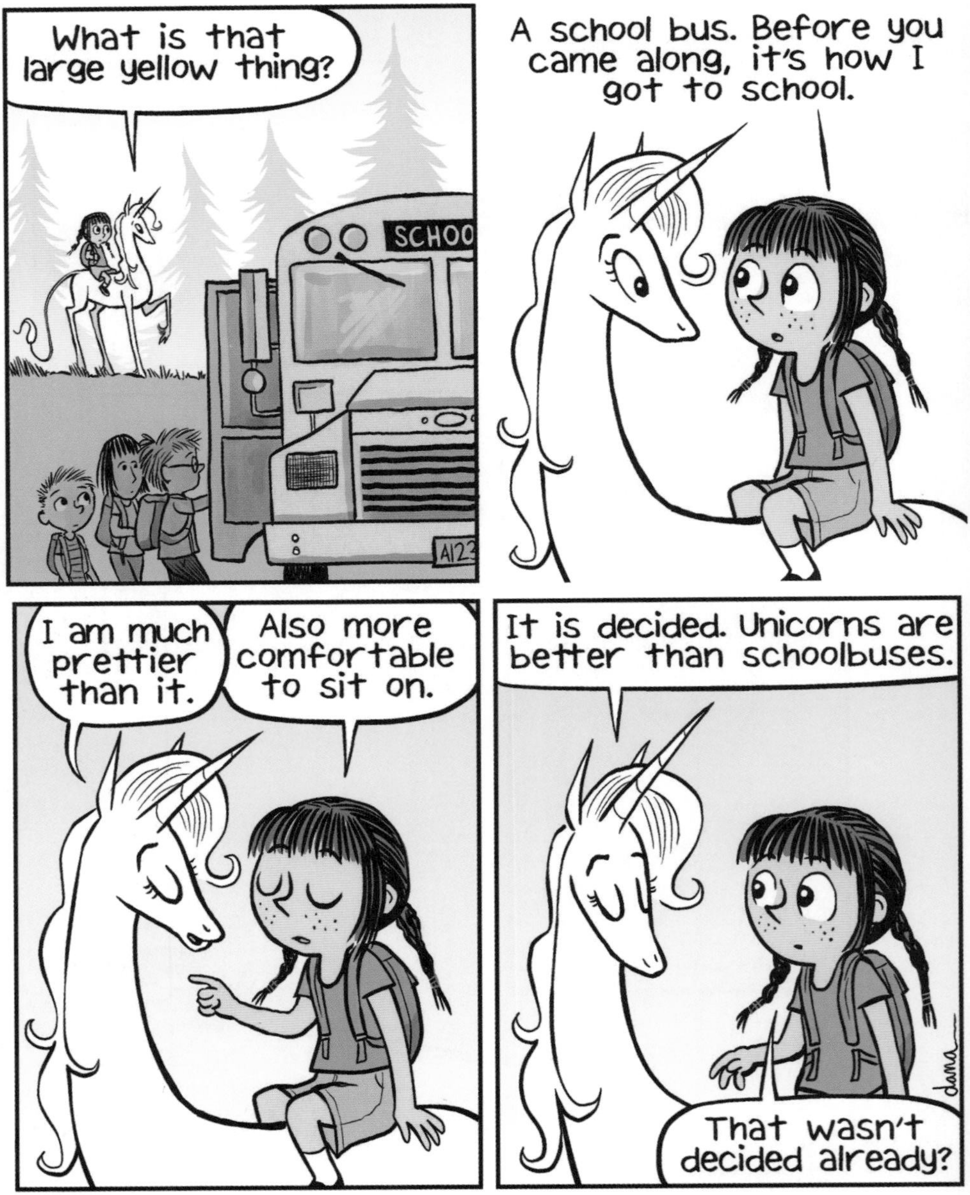
What is that large yellow thing?
SCHOO
A123
A school bus. Before you came along, it's how I got to school.
I am much prettier than it.
Also more comfortable to sit on.
It is decided. Unicorns are better than schoolbuses.
That wasn't decided already?
dana

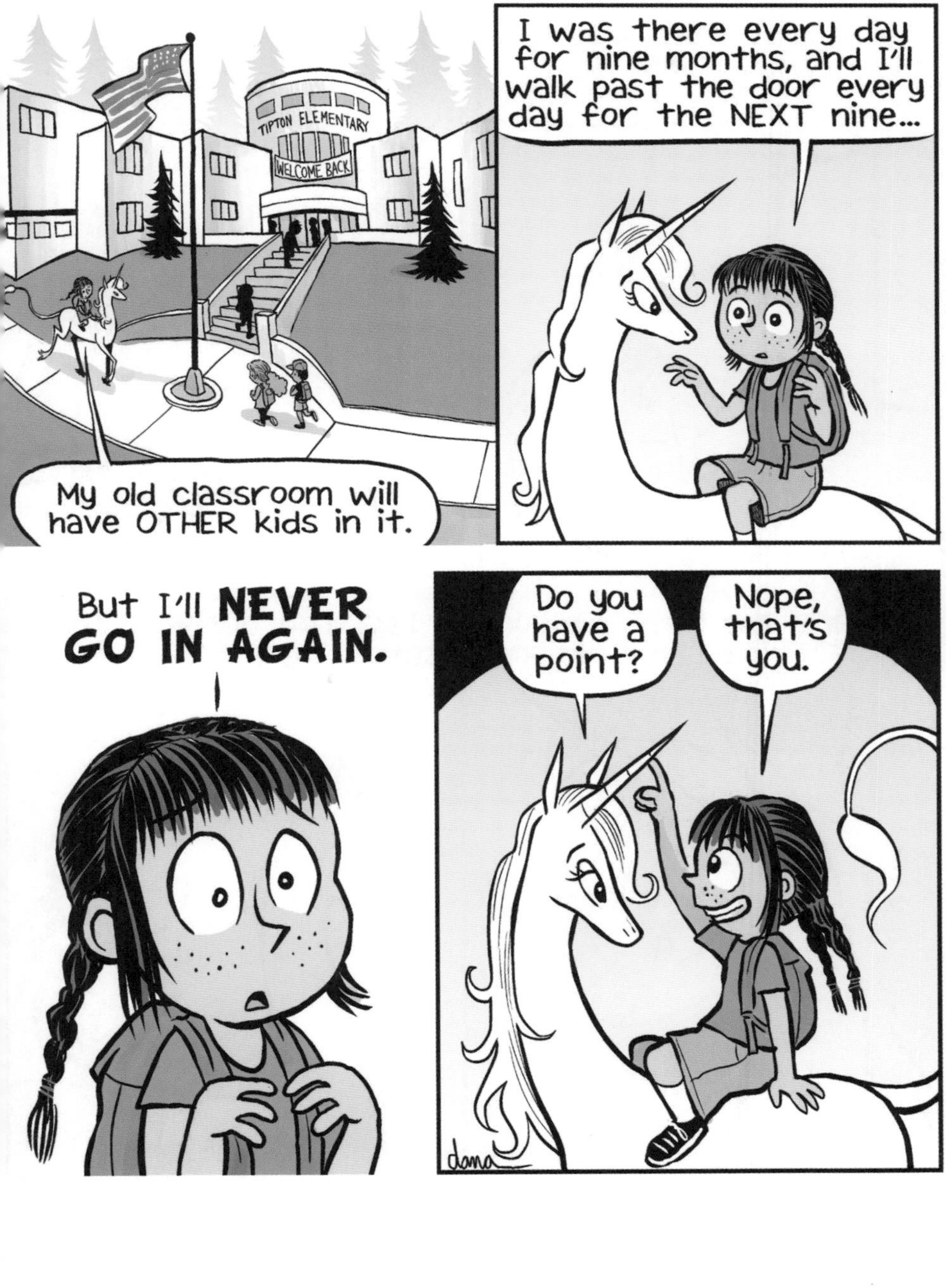
TIPTON ELEMENTARY
WELCOME BACK
My old classroom will have OTHER kids in it.
I was there every day for nine months, and I'll walk past the door every day for the NEXT nine...
But I'll **NEVER GO IN AGAIN.**
Do you have a point?
Nope, that's you.
dana

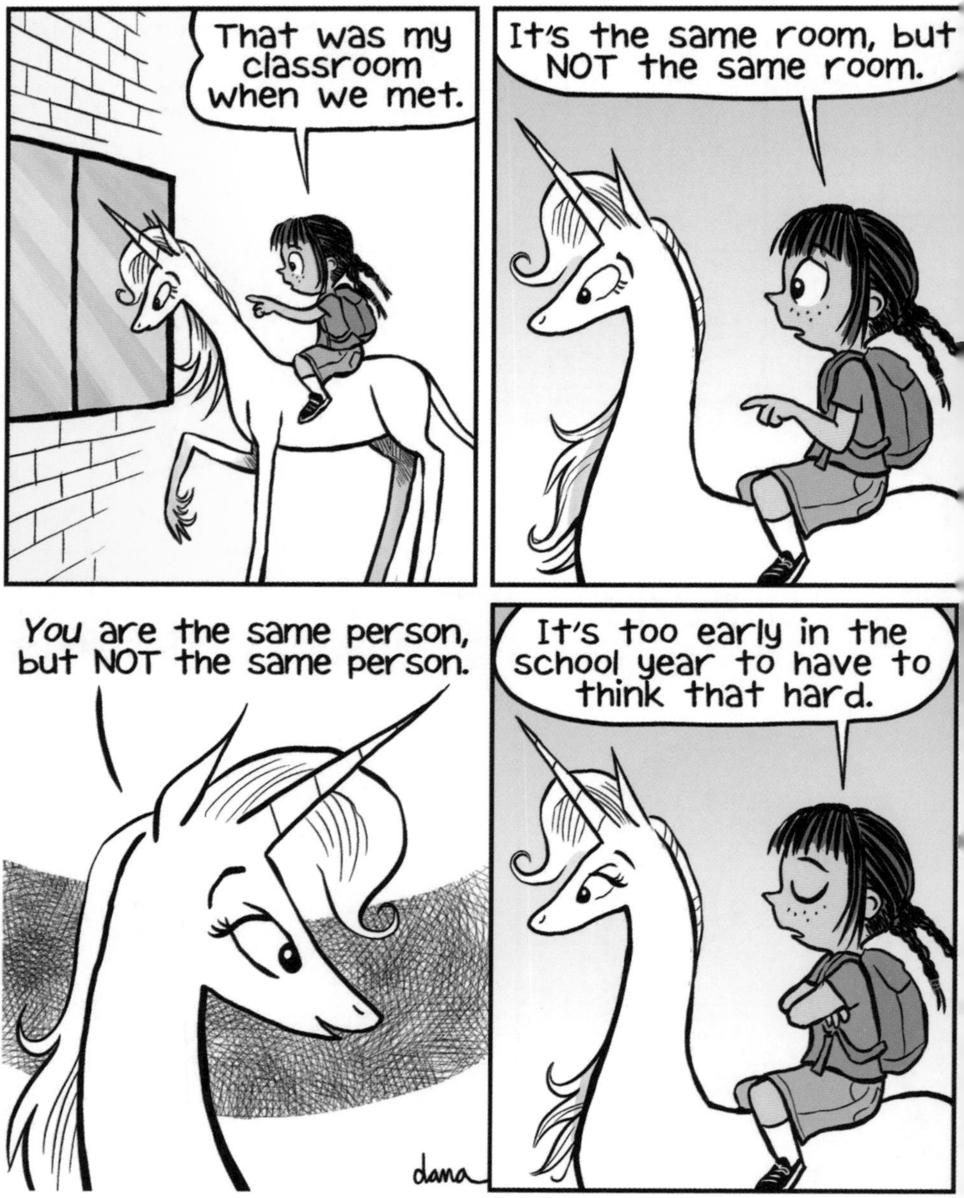
That was my classroom when we met.
It's the same room, but NOT the same room.
You are the same person, but NOT the same person.
It's too early in the school year to have to think that hard.
dana

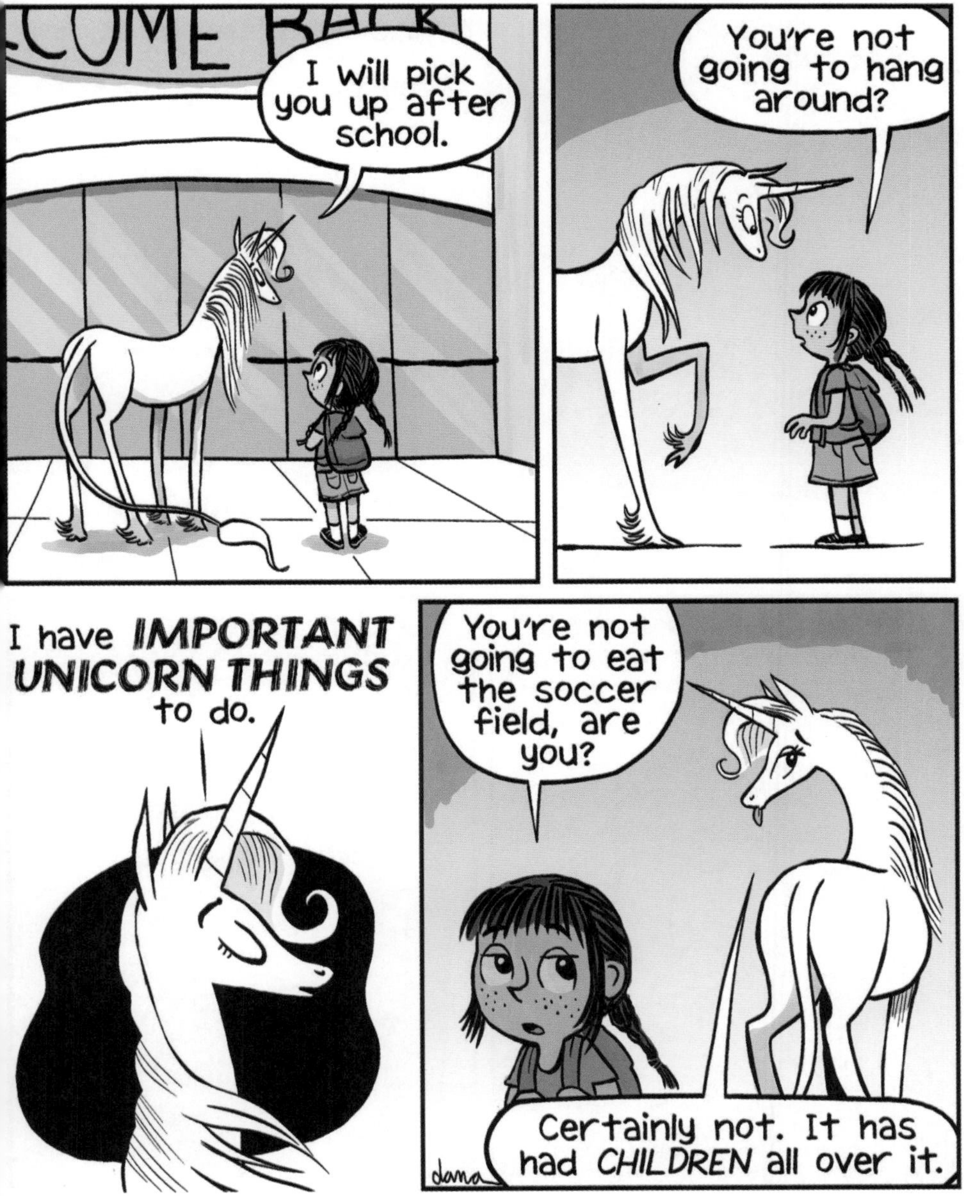

COME BACK
I will pick you up after school.
You're not going to hang around?
I have IMPORTANT UNICORN THINGS to do.
You're not going to eat the soccer field, are you?
Certainly not. It has had CHILDREN all over it.
dana

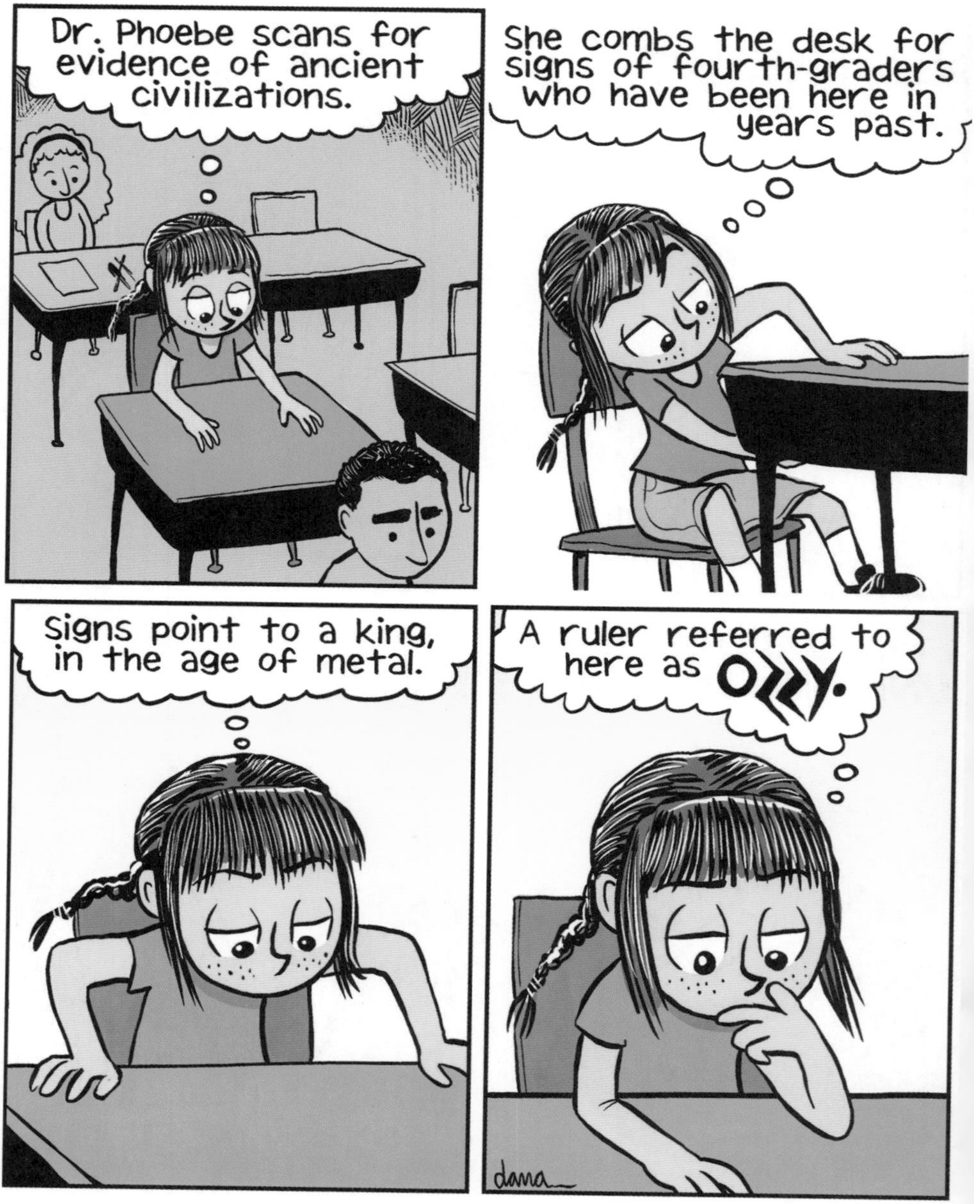
Dr. Phoebe scans for evidence of ancient civilizations.
She combs the desk for signs of fourth-graders who have been here in years past.
Signs point to a king, in the age of metal.
A ruler referred to here as OZZY.
dana

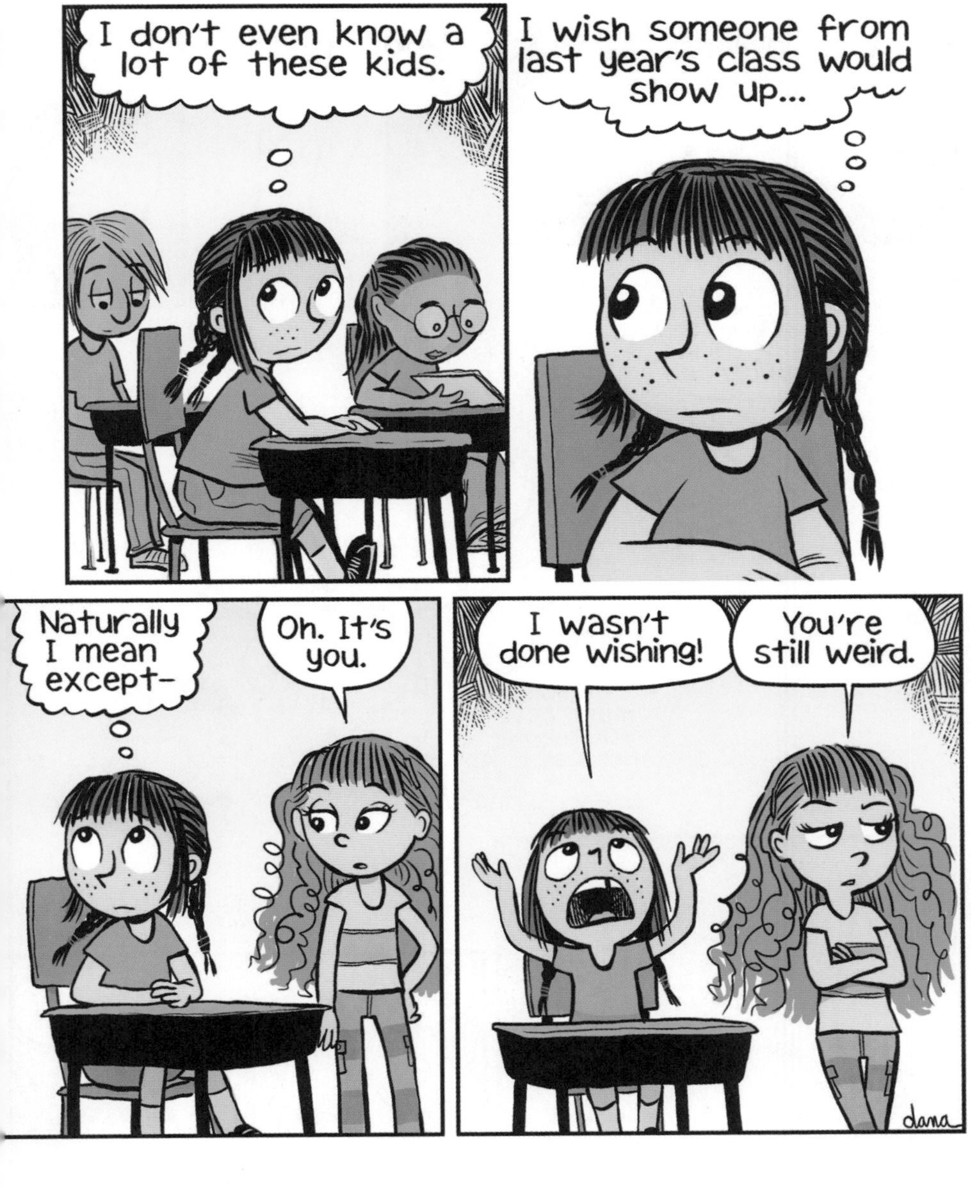
I don't even know a lot of these kids.
I wish someone from last year's class would show up...
Naturally I mean except-
Oh. It's you.
I wasn't done wishing!
You're still weird.
dana

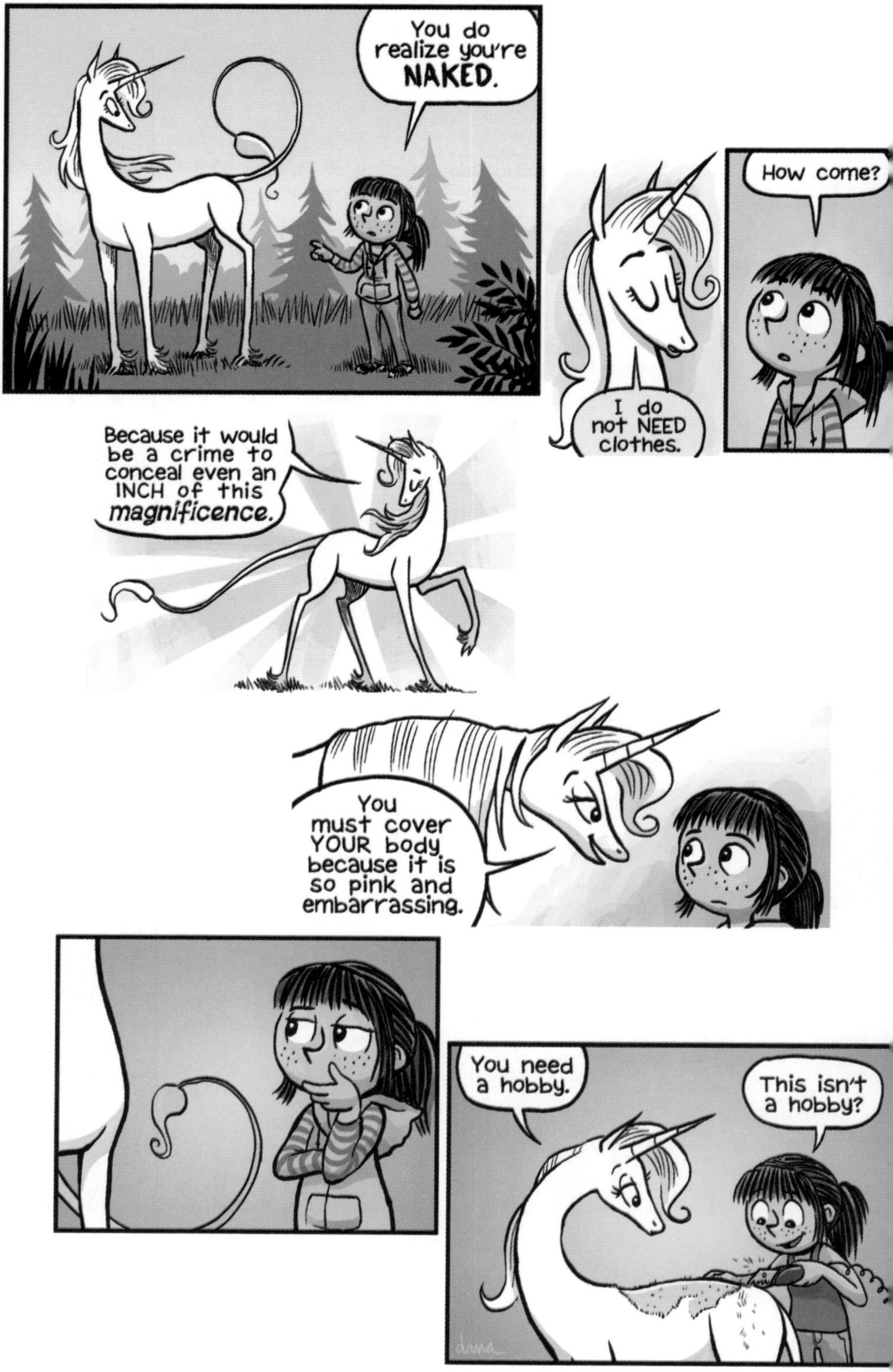
You do realize you're NAKED.
I do not NEED clothes.
How come?
Because it would be a crime to conceal even an INCH of this magnificence.
You must cover YOUR body because it is so pink and embarrassing.
You need a hobby.
This isn't a hobby?
dana

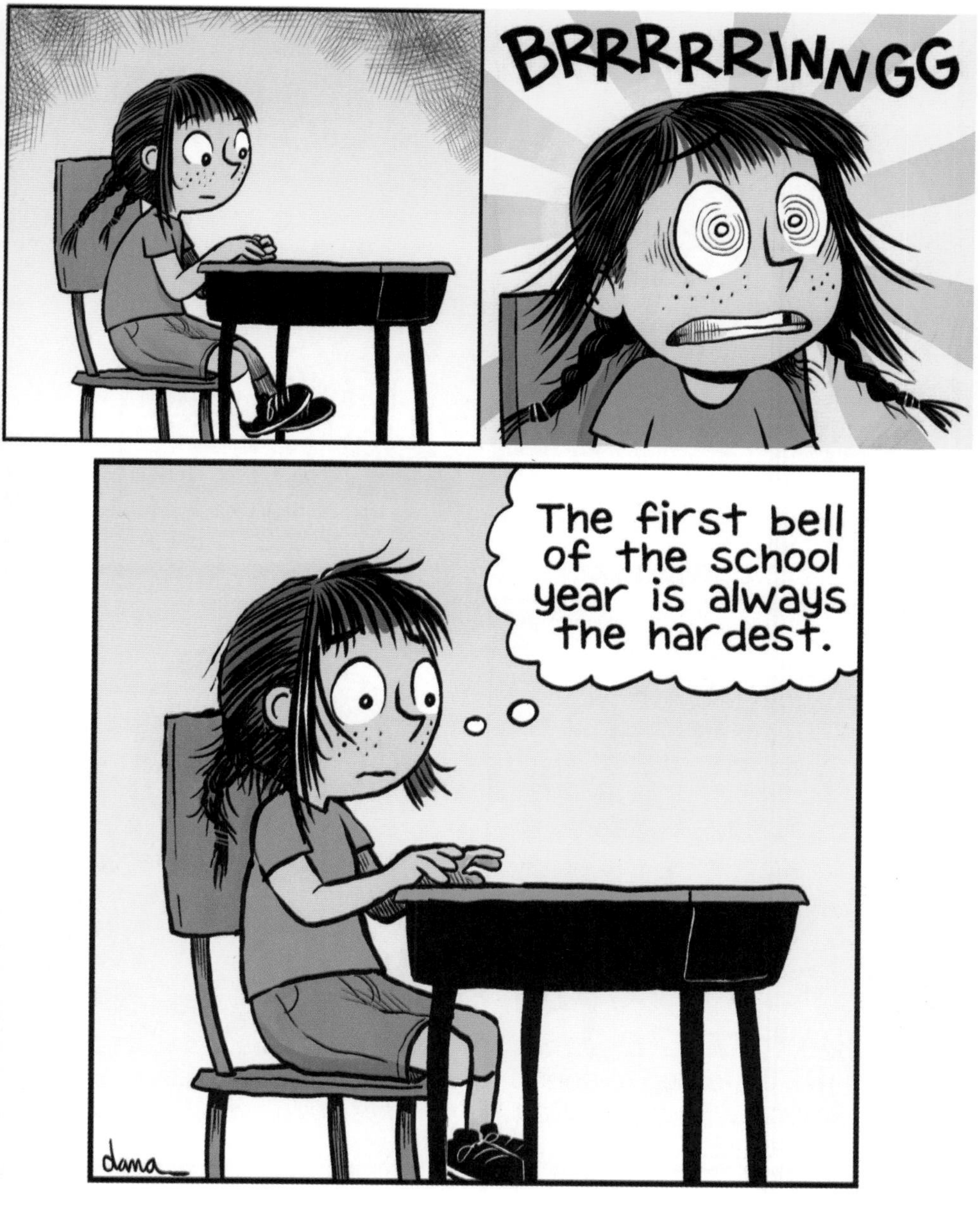
BRRRRRINNGG
The first bell of the school year is always the hardest.
dana

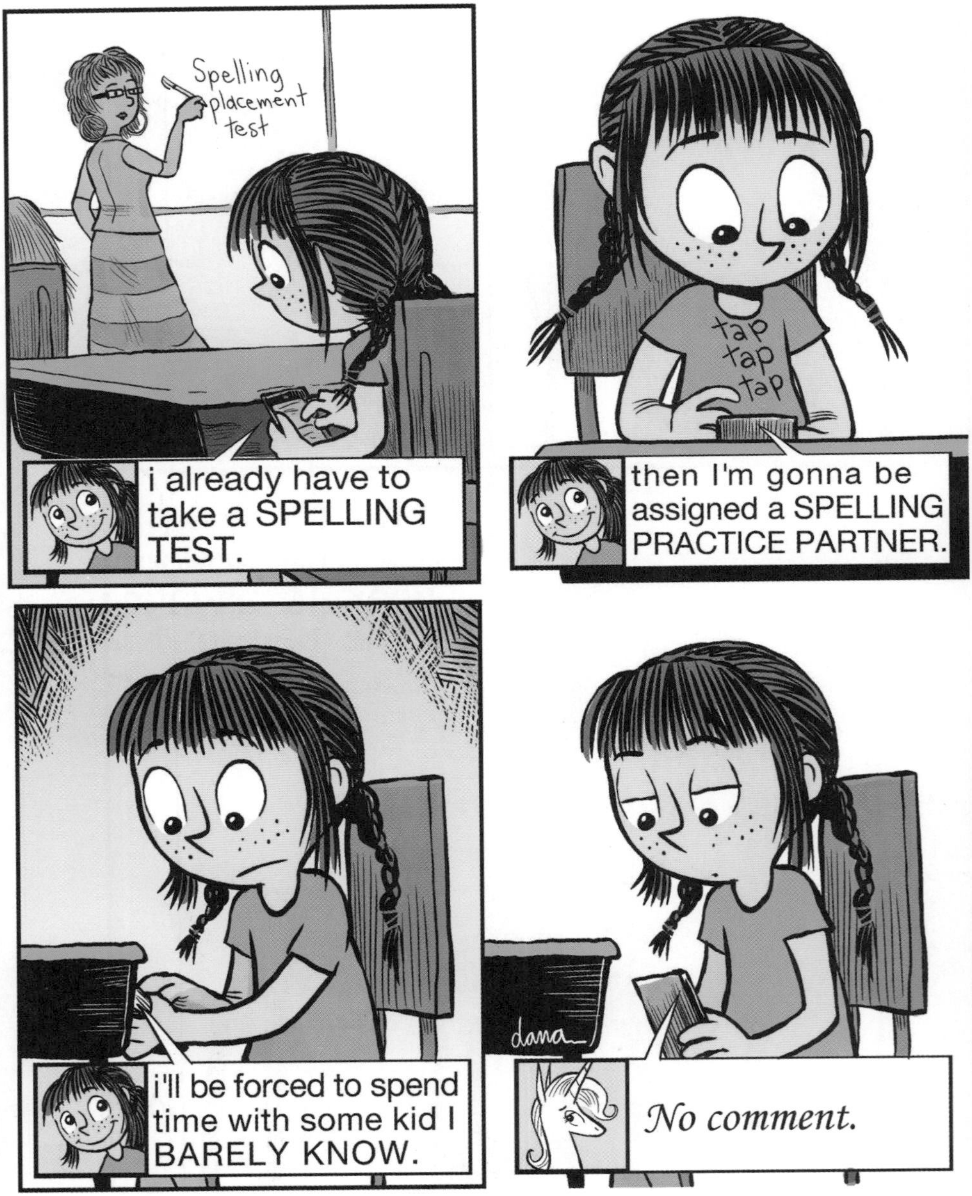
Spelling placement test
i already have to take a SPELLING TEST.
tap tap tap
then I'm gonna be assigned a SPELLING PRACTICE PARTNER.
i'll be forced to spend time with some kid I BARELY KNOW.
dana
No comment.

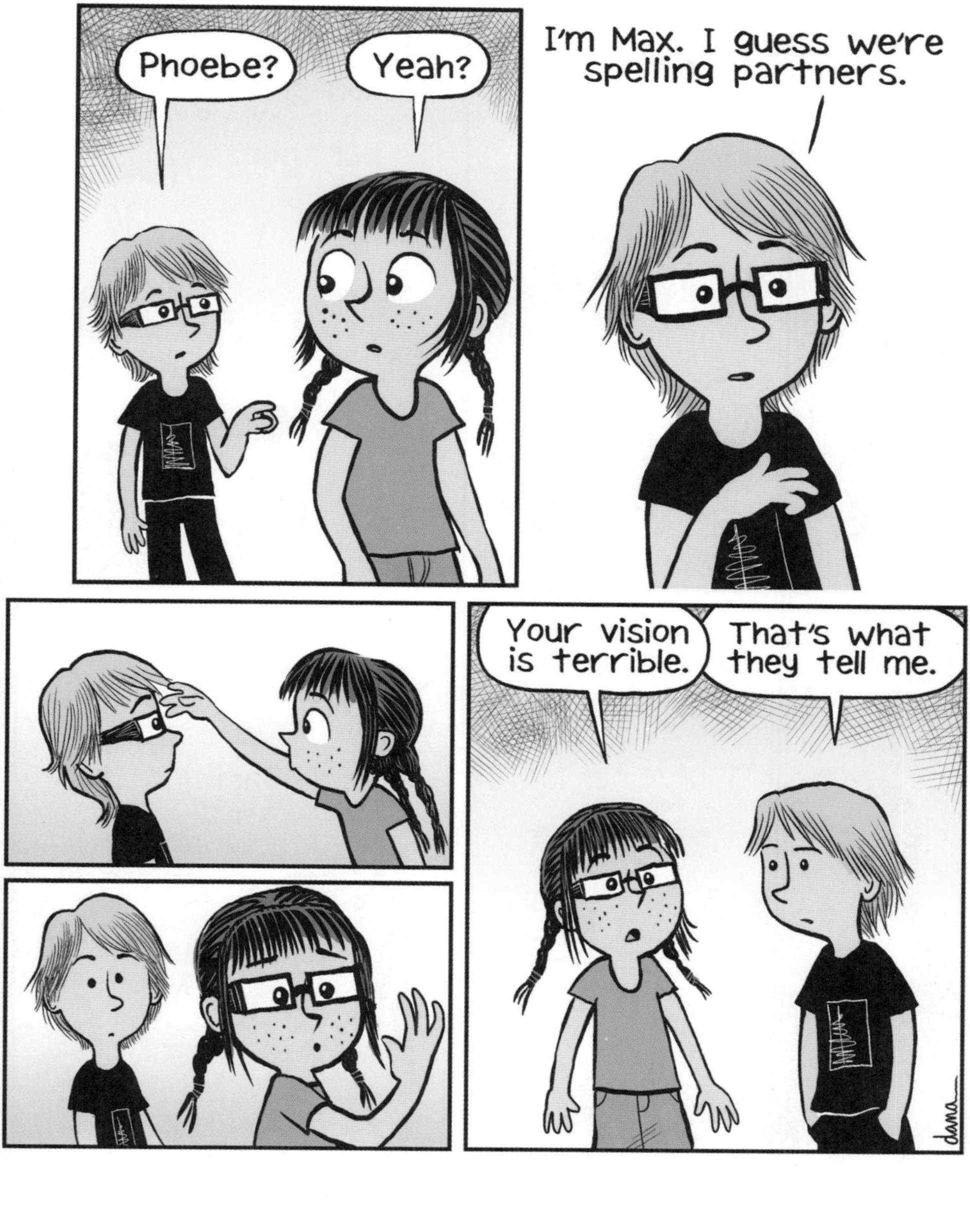
Phoebe?
Yeah?
I'm Max. I guess we're spelling partners.
Your vision is terrible.
That's what they tell me.
dana

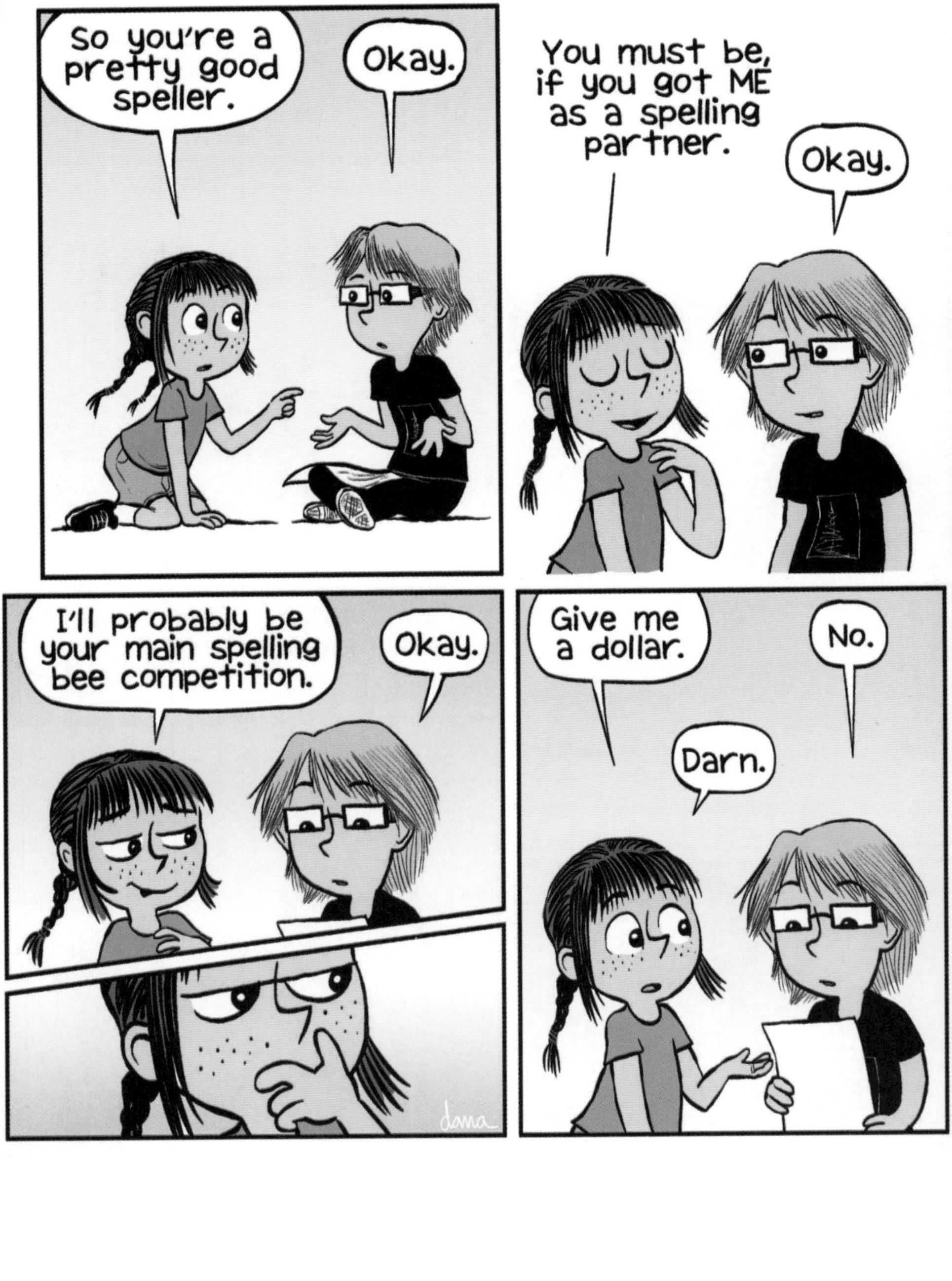
So you're a pretty good speller.
Okay.
You must be, if you got ME as a spelling partner.
Okay.
I'll probably be your main spelling bee competition.
Okay.
Give me a dollar.
No.
Darn.
dana

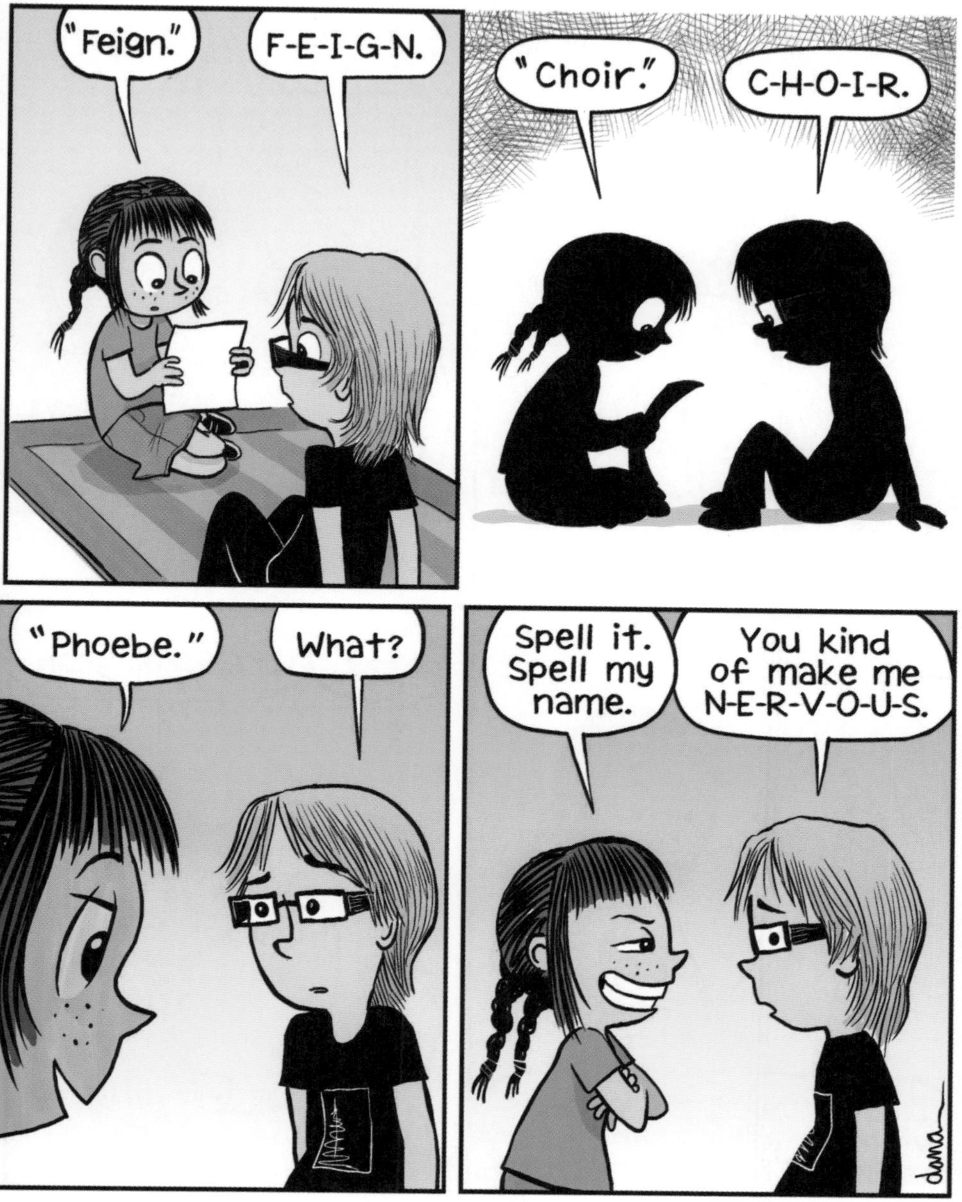
"Feign."
F-E-I-G-N.
"Choir."
C-H-O-I-R.
"Phoebe."
What?
Spell it. Spell my name.
You kind of make me N-E-R-V-O-U-S.
dana

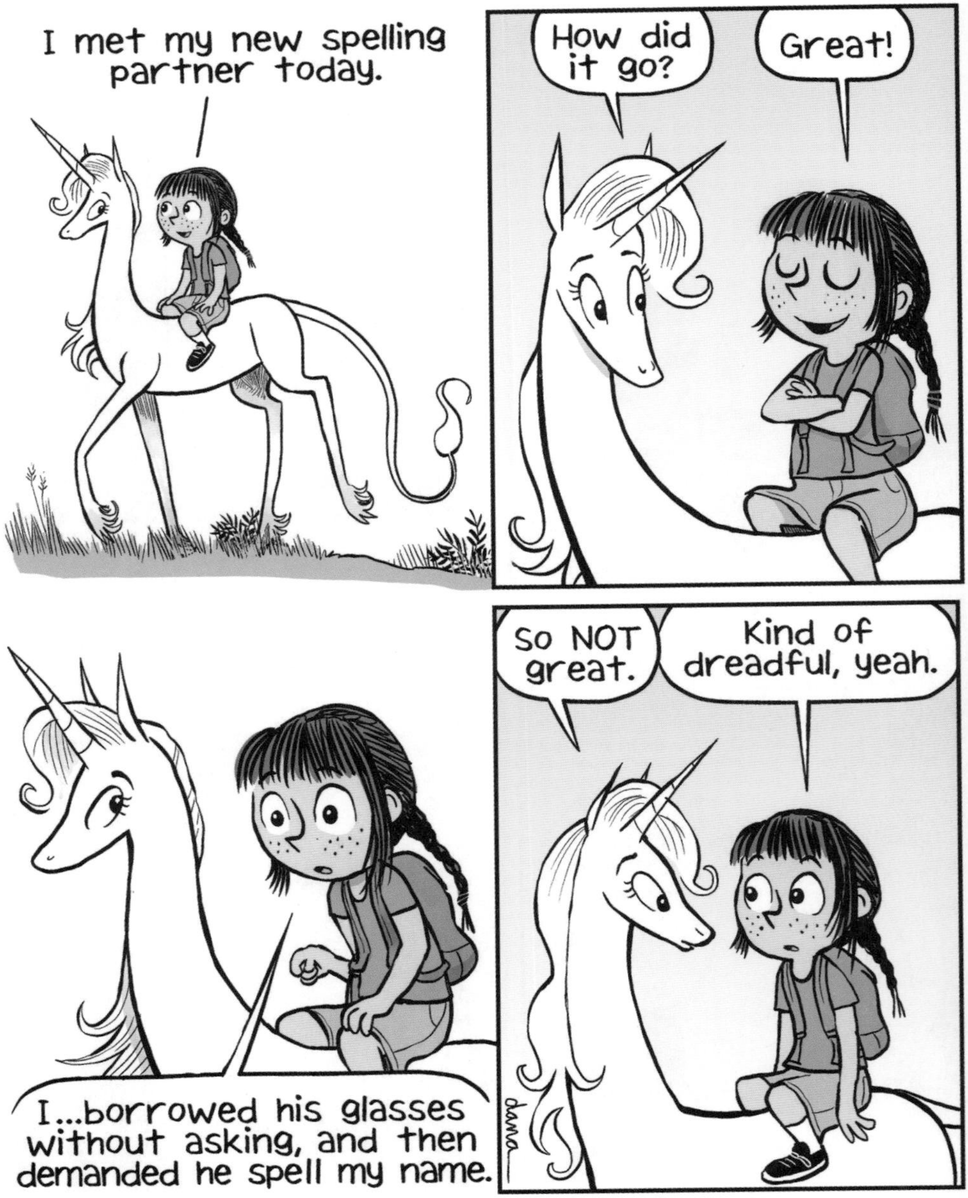
I met my new spelling partner today.
How did it go?
Great!
I...borrowed his glasses without asking, and then demanded he spell my name.
So NOT great.
Kind of dreadful, yeah.
dana

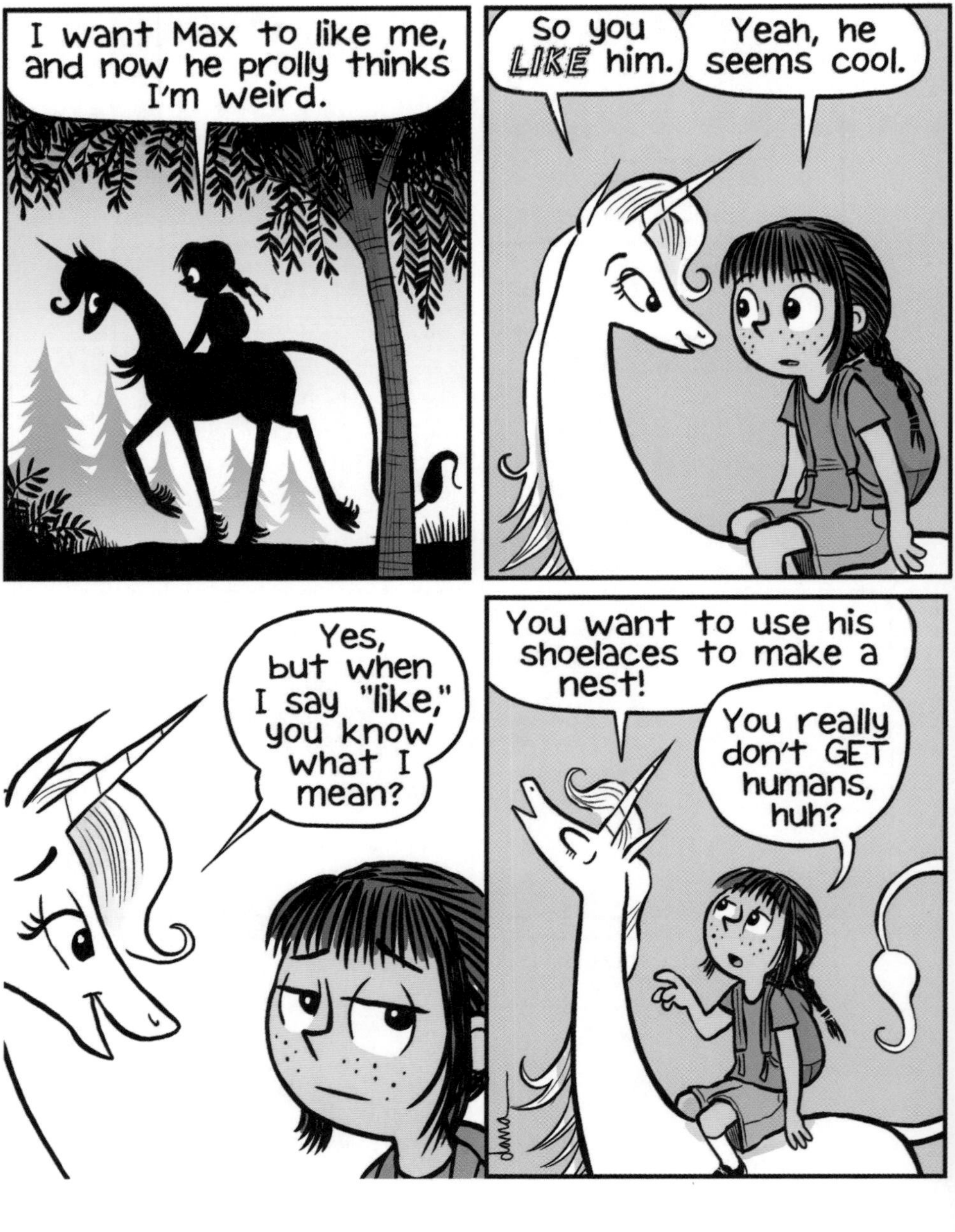

I want Max to like me, and now he prolly thinks I'm weird.
So you LIKE him.
Yeah, he seems cool.
Yes, but when I say "like," you know what I mean?
You want to use his shoelaces to make a nest!
You really don't GET humans, huh?

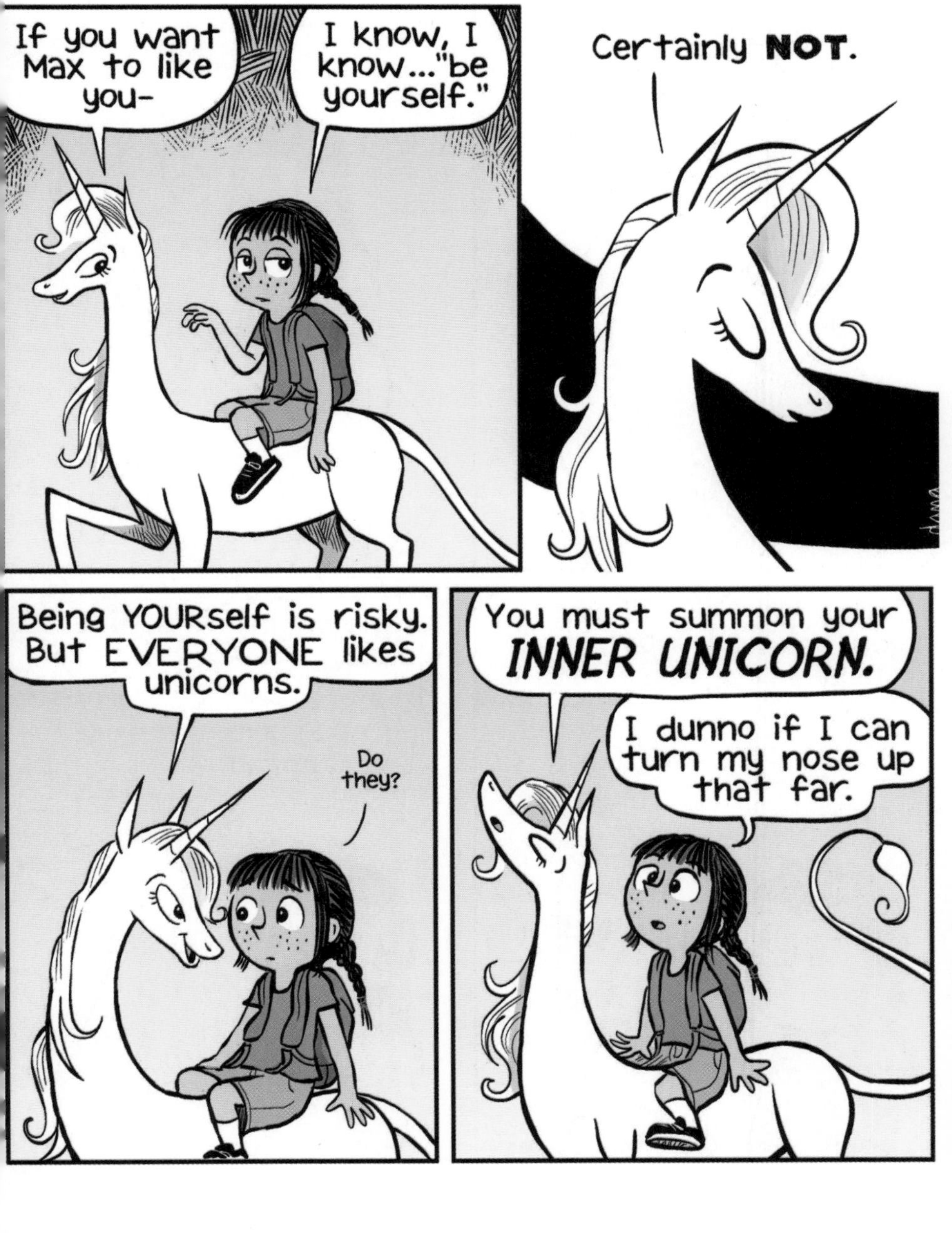
If you want Max to like you-
I know, I know..."be yourself."
Certainly **NOT**.
Being YOURself is risky. But EVERYONE likes unicorns.
Do they?
You must summon your *INNER UNICORN.*
I dunno if I can turn my nose up that far.

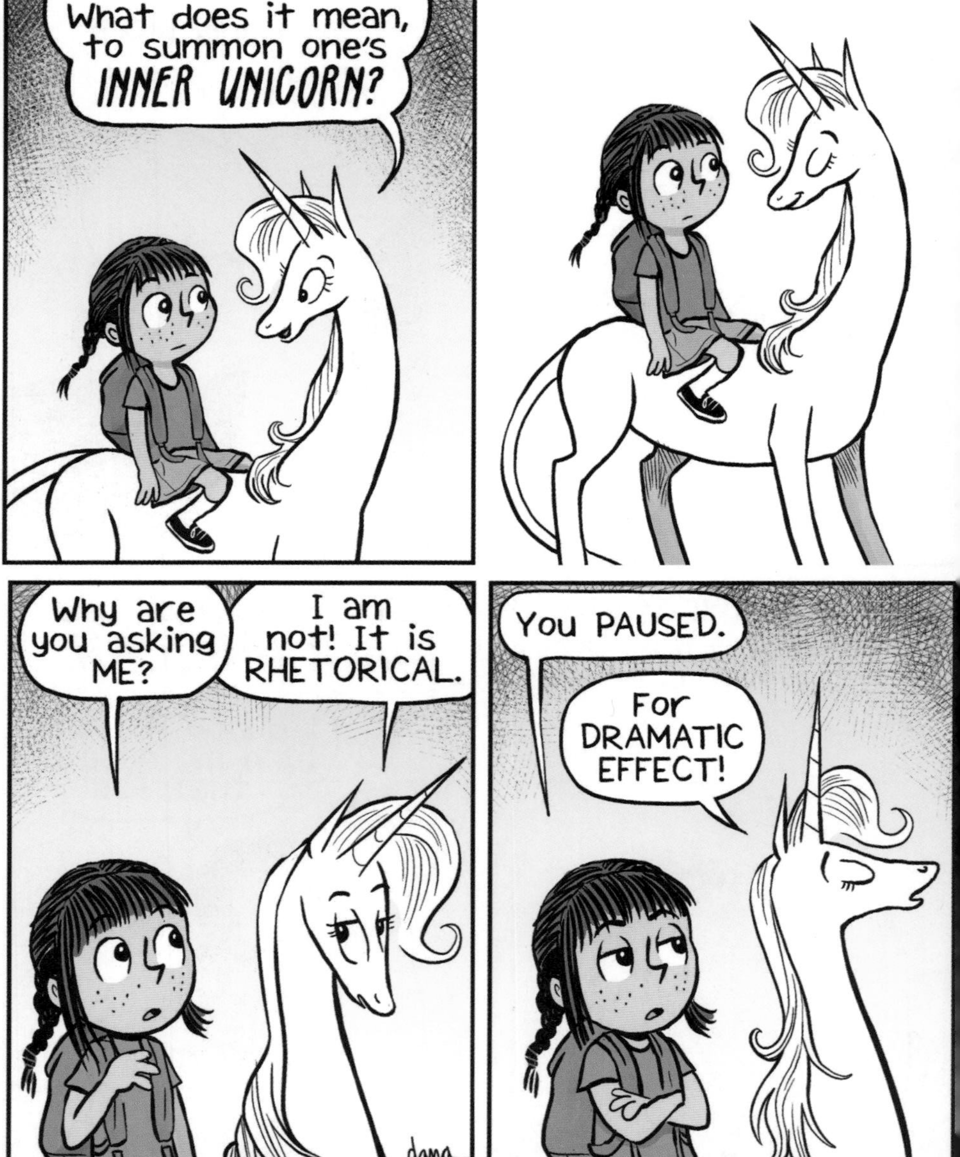
What does it mean, to summon one's INNER UNICORN?
Why are you asking ME?
I am not! It is RHETORICAL.
dana
You PAUSED.
For DRAMATIC EFFECT!

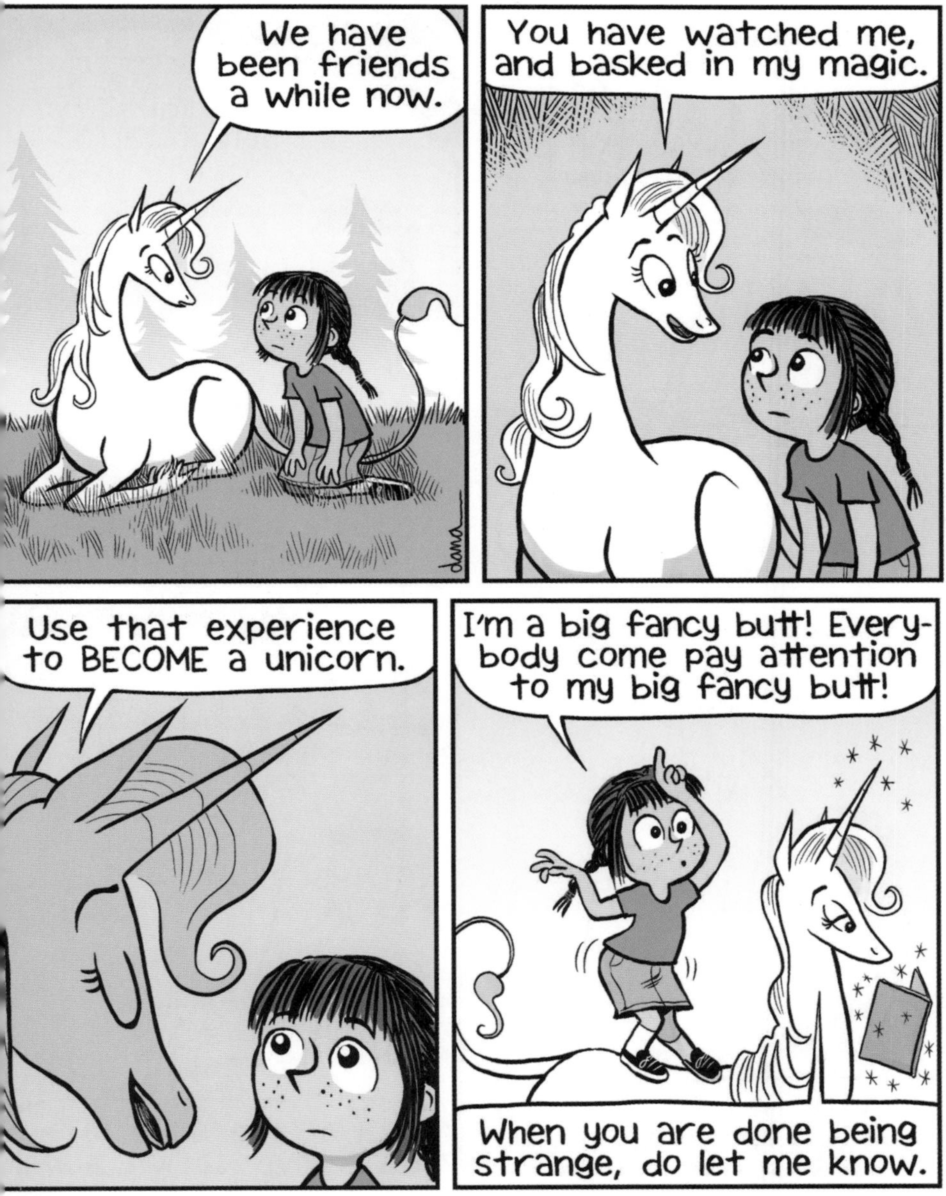
We have been friends a while now.
You have watched me, and basked in my magic.
Use that experience to BECOME a unicorn.
I'm a big fancy butt! Every-body come pay attention to my big fancy butt!
When you are done being strange, do let me know.

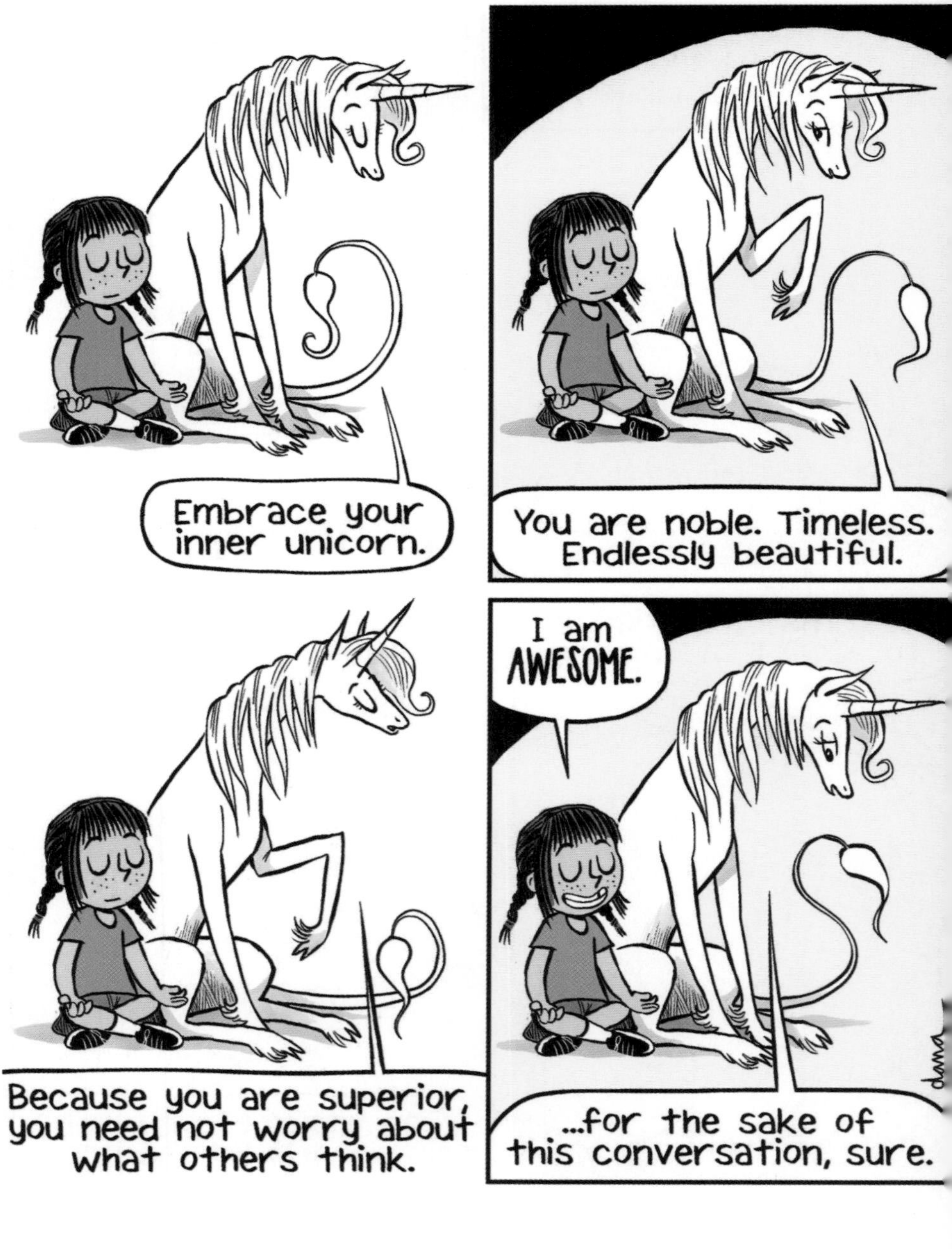
Embrace your inner unicorn.
You are noble. Timeless. Endlessly beautiful.
Because you are superior, you need not worry about what others think.
I am AWESOME.
...for the sake of this conversation, sure.
dana

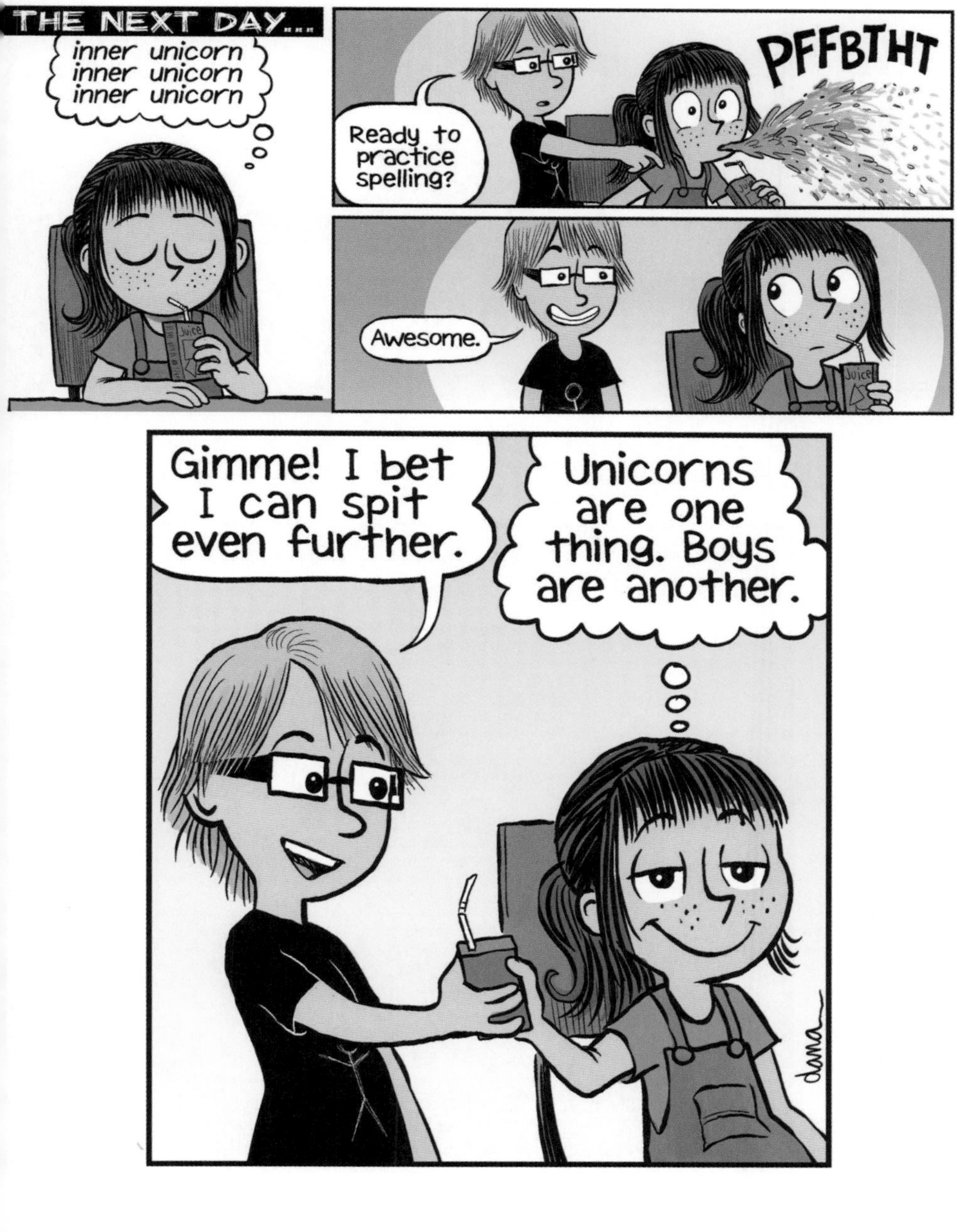
THE NEXT DAY...
inner unicorn inner unicorn inner unicorn
Ready to practice spelling?
PFFBTHT
Awesome.
Gimme! I bet I can spit even further.
Unicorns are one thing. Boys are another.
dana

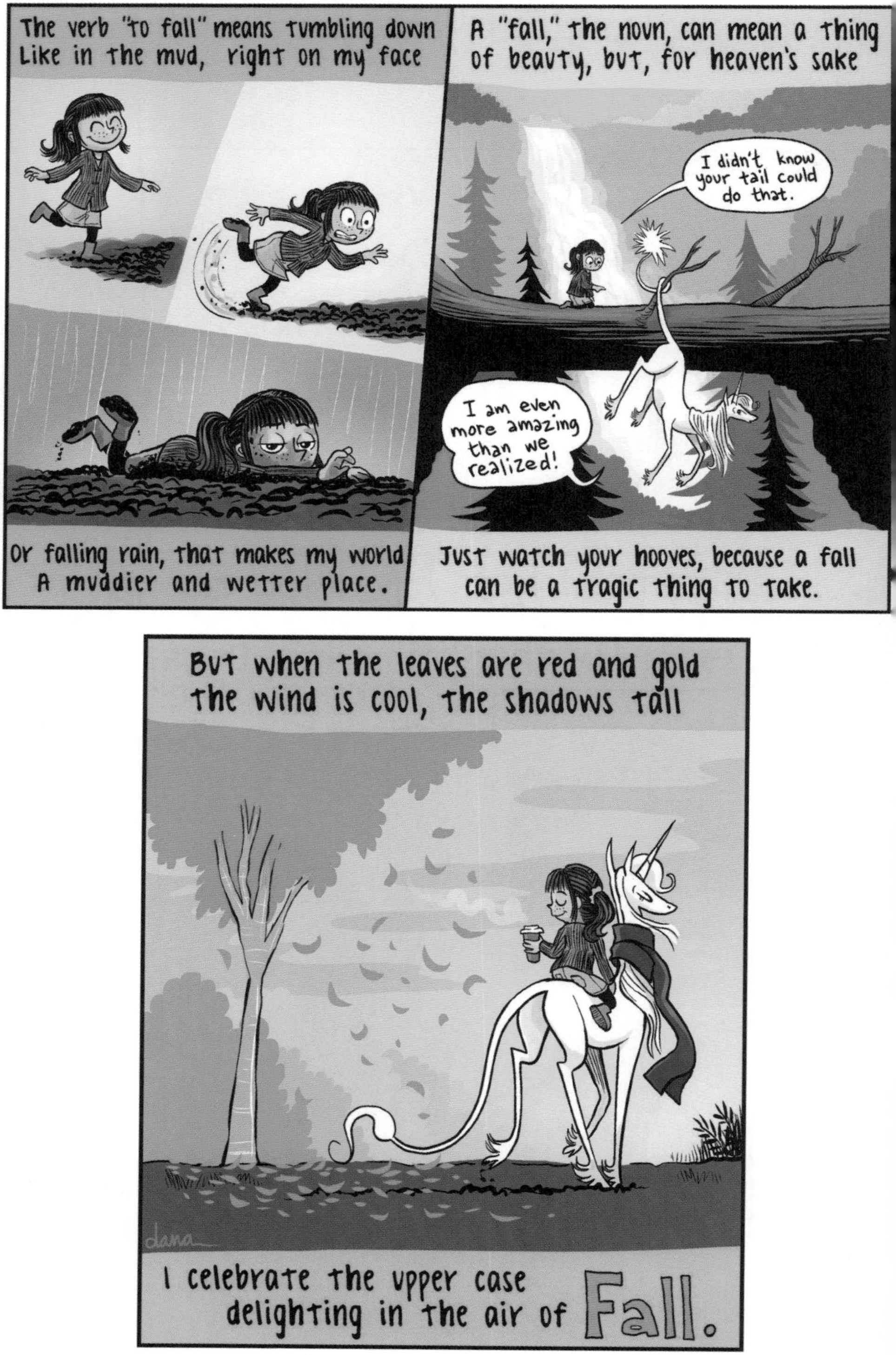
The verb "to fall" means tumbling down
Like in the mud, right on my face
Or falling rain, that makes my world
A muddier and wetter place.
A "fall," the noun, can mean a thing
of beauty, but, for heaven's sake
I didn't know your tail could do that.
I am even more amazing than we realized!
Just watch your hooves, because a fall
can be a tragic thing to take.
But when the leaves are red and gold
the wind is cool, the shadows tall
dana
I celebrate the upper case
delighting in the air of Fall.

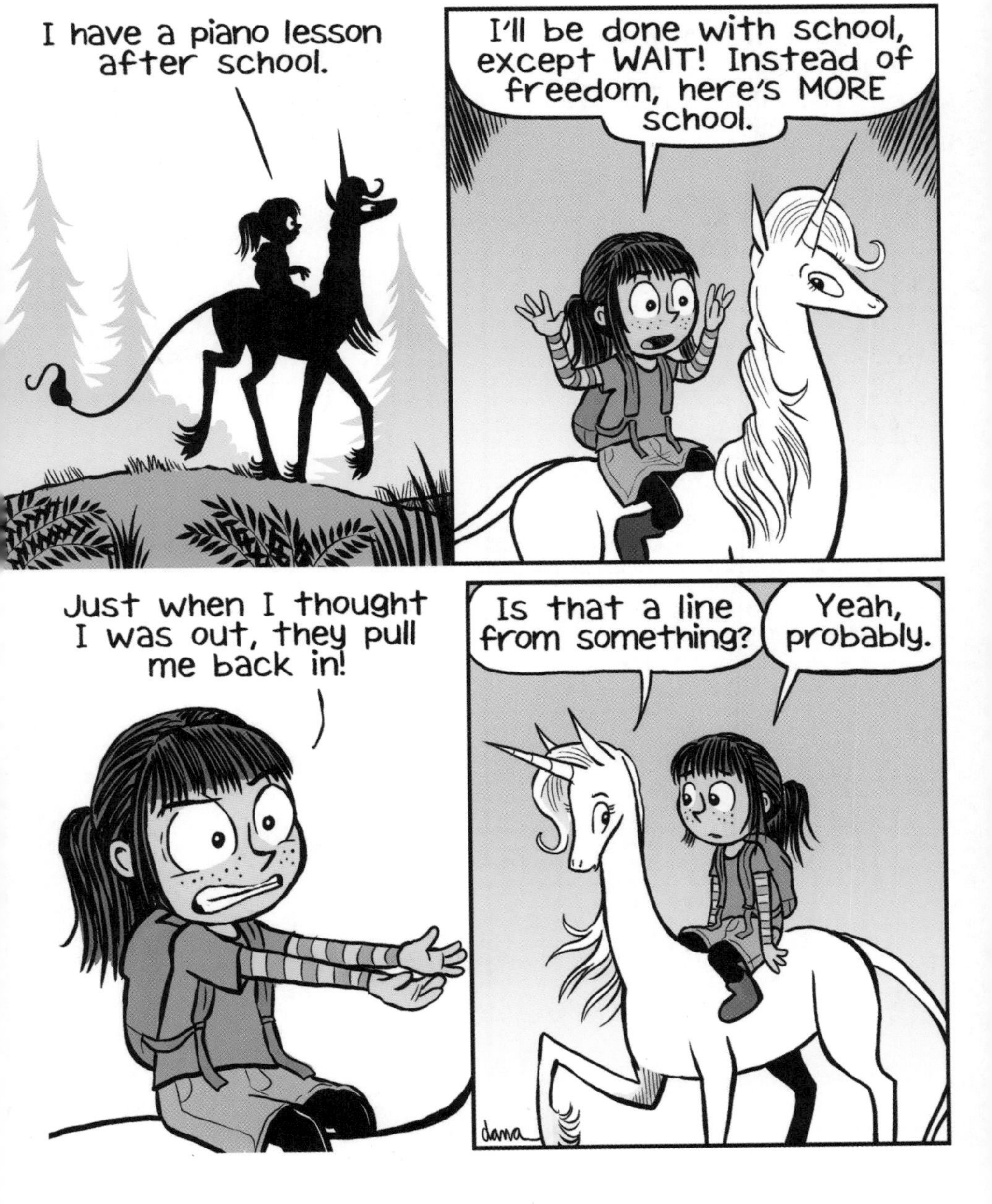
I have a piano lesson after school.
I'll be done with school, except WAIT! Instead of freedom, here's MORE school.
Just when I thought I was out, they pull me back in!
Is that a line from something?
Yeah, probably.
dana

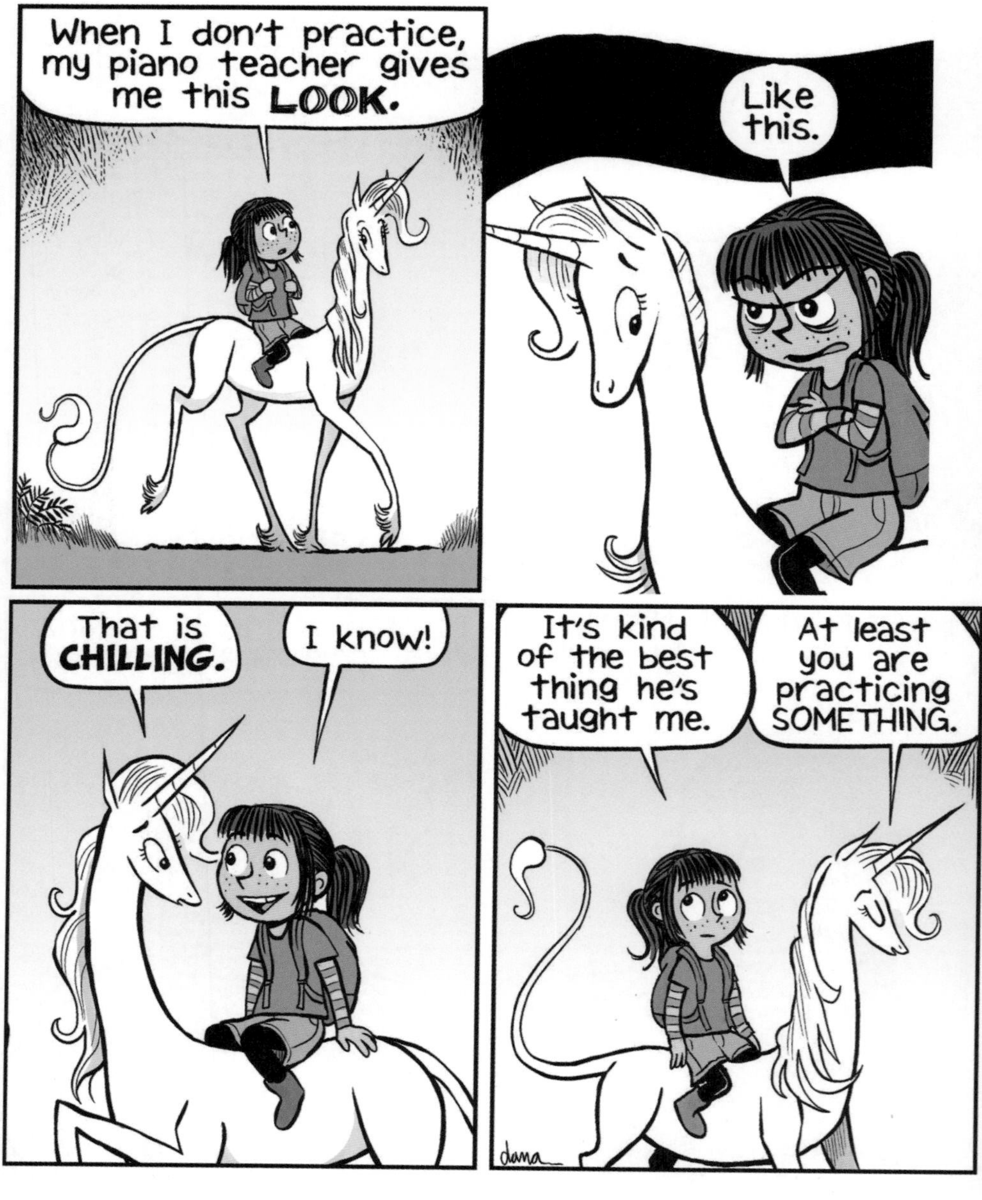
When I don't practice, my piano teacher gives me this LOOK.
Like this.
That is CHILLING.
I know!
It's kind of the best thing he's taught me.
At least you are practicing SOMETHING.
dana

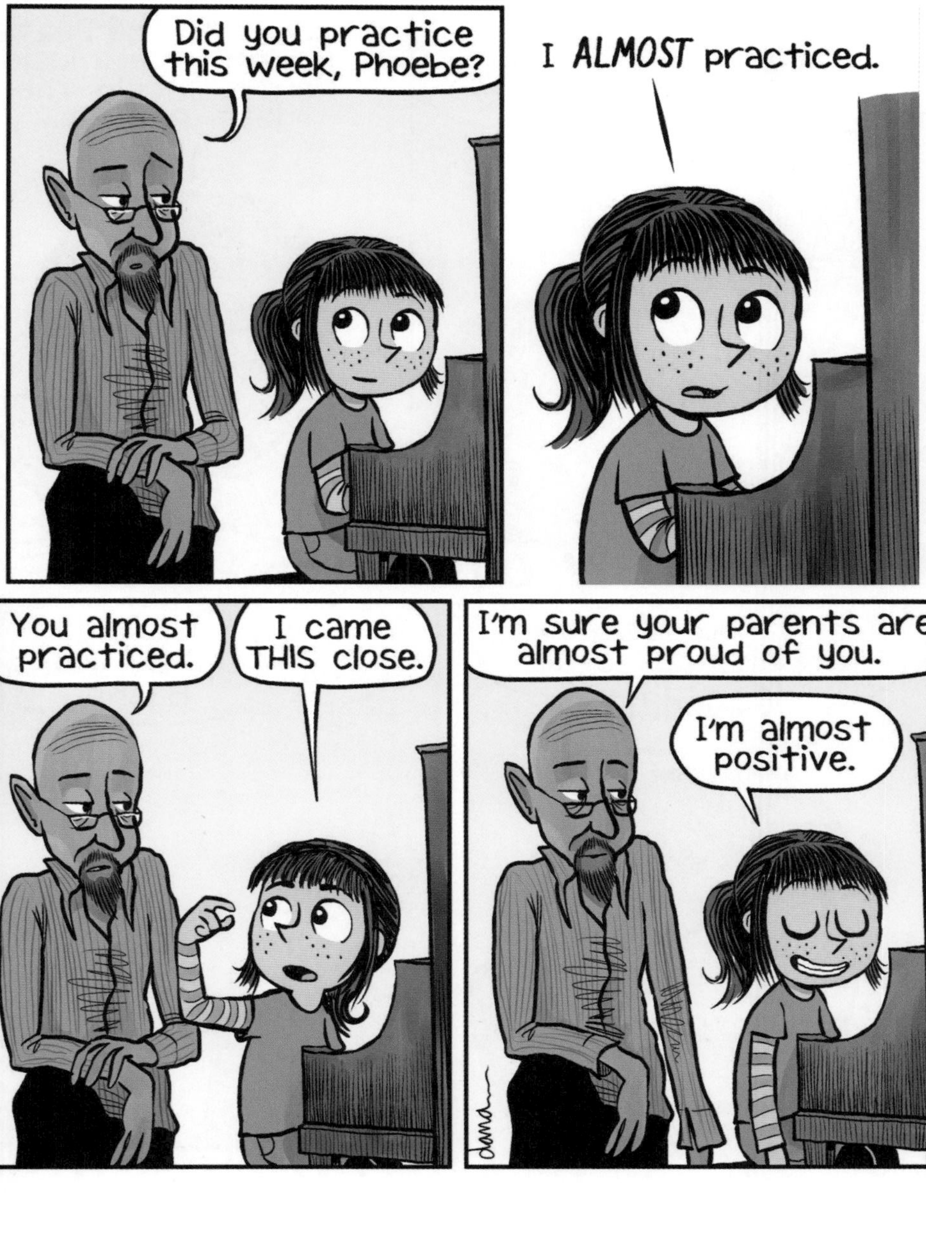
Did you practice this week, Phoebe?
I ALMOST practiced.
You almost practiced.
I came THIS close.
I'm sure your parents are almost proud of you.
I'm almost positive.
dana

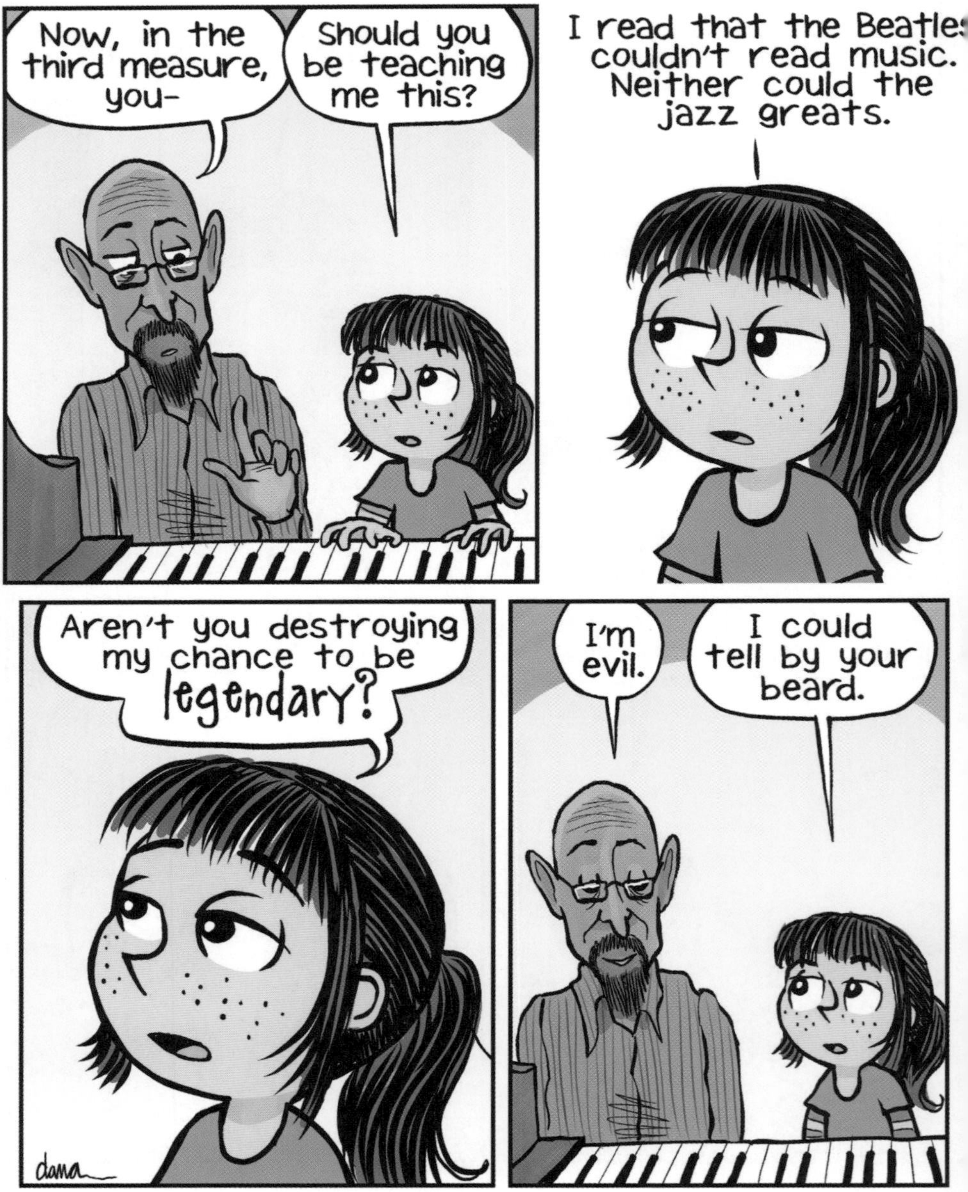
Now, in the third measure, you-
Should you be teaching me this?
I read that the Beatles couldn't read music. Neither could the jazz greats.
Aren't you destroying my chance to be legendary?
dana
I'm evil.
I could tell by your beard.

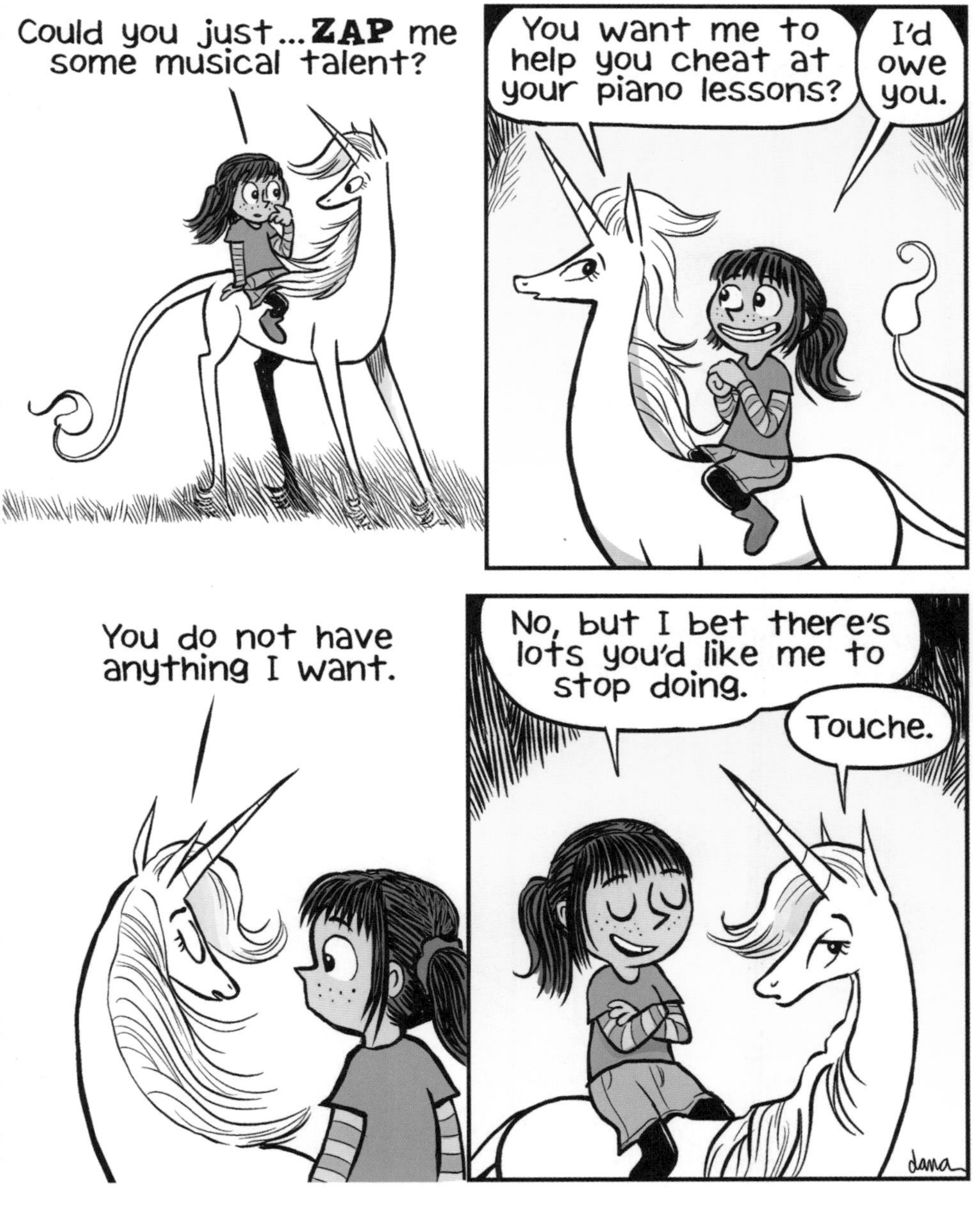
Could you just...ZAP me some musical talent?
You want me to help you cheat at your piano lessons?
I'd owe you.
You do not have anything I want.
No, but I bet there's lots you'd like me to stop doing.
Touche.
dana

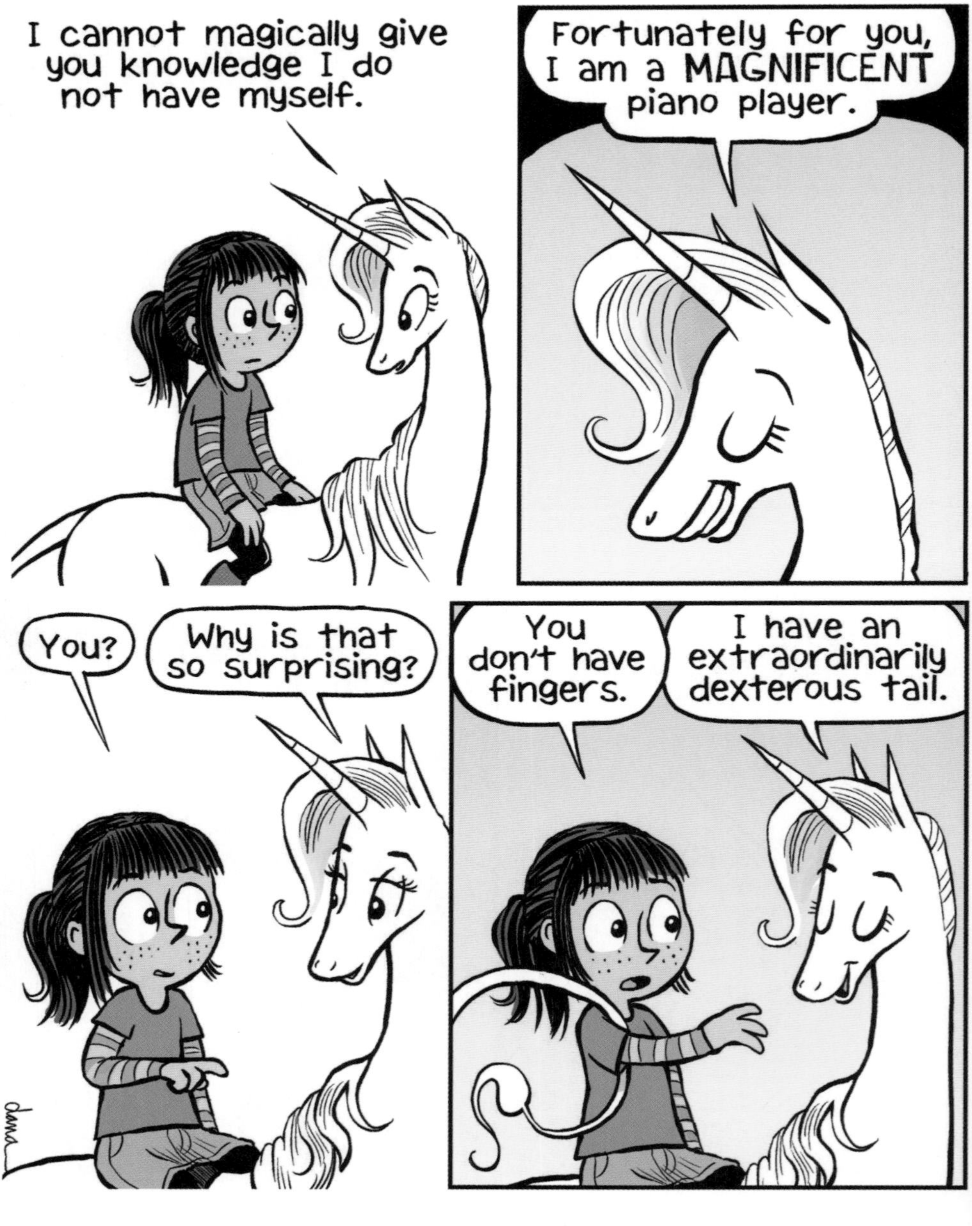
I cannot magically give you knowledge I do not have myself.
Fortunately for you, I am a MAGNIFICENT piano player.
You?
Why is that so surprising?
You don't have fingers.
I have an extraordinarily dexterous tail.
dana

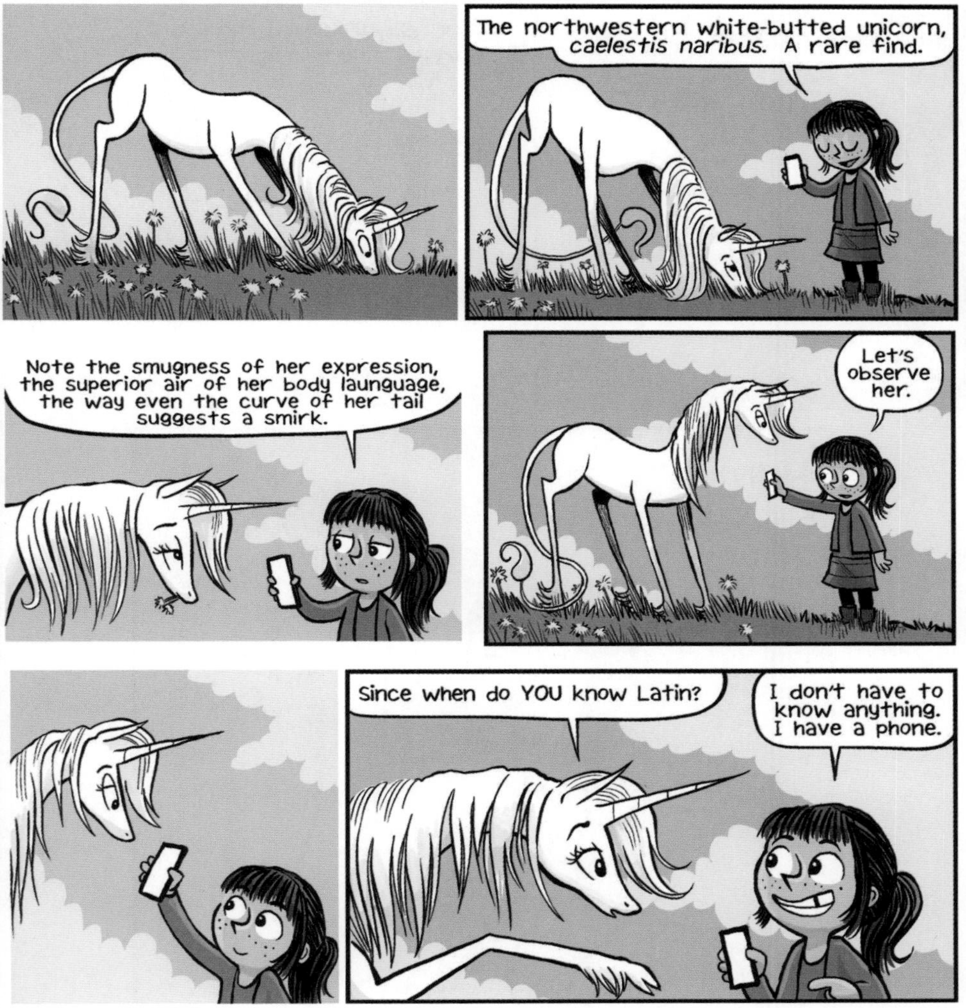
The northwestern white-butted unicorn, *caelestis naribus*. A rare find.
Note the smugness of her expression, the superior air of her body launguage, the way even the curve of her tail suggests a smirk.
Let's observe her.
Since when do YOU know Latin?
I don't have to know anything. I have a phone.

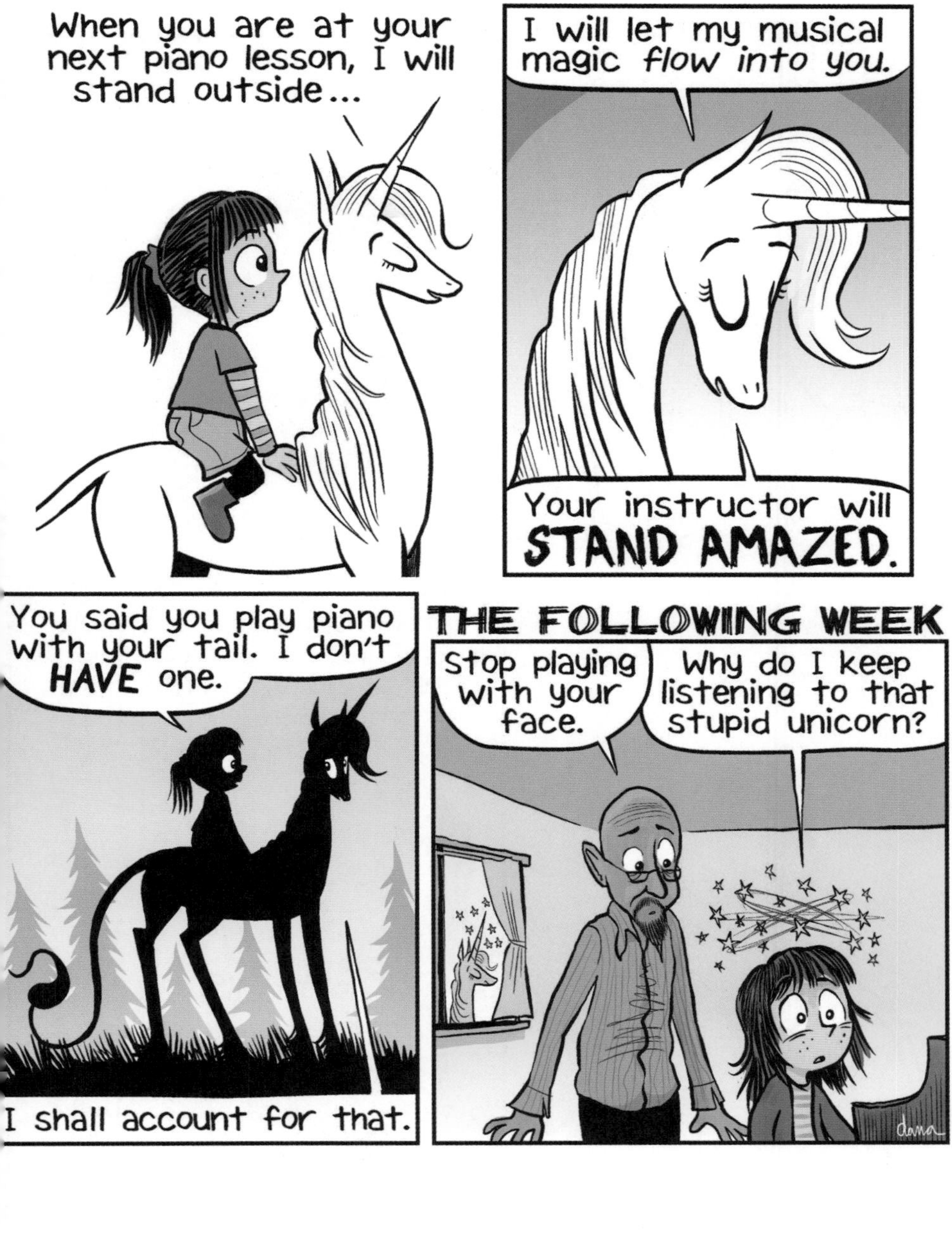
When you are at your next piano lesson, I will stand outside...
I will let my musical magic *flow into you.*
Your instructor will **STAND AMAZED.**
You said you play piano with your tail. I don't **HAVE** one.
I shall account for that.
THE FOLLOWING WEEK
Stop playing with your face.
Why do I keep listening to that stupid unicorn?
dana

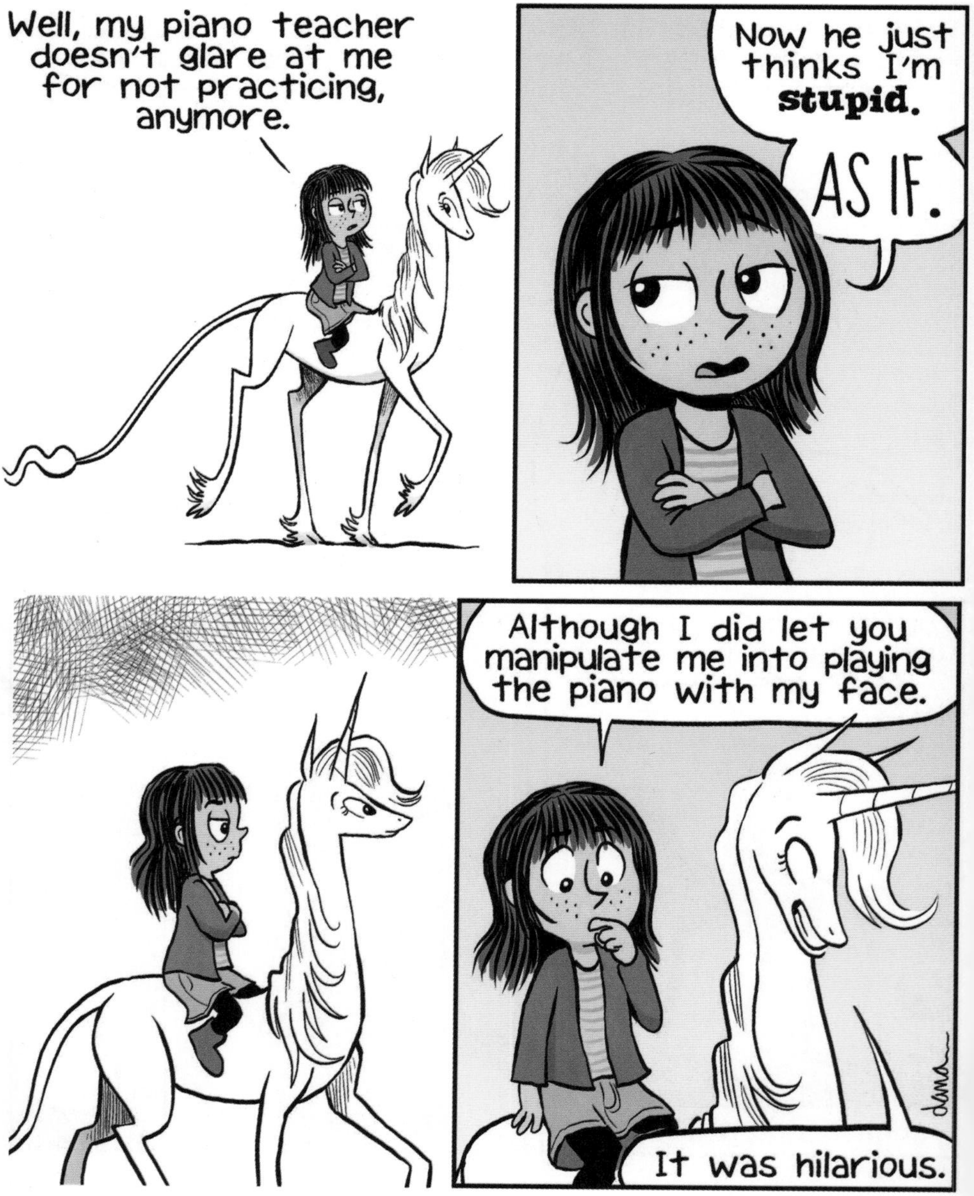
Well, my piano teacher doesn't glare at me for not practicing, anymore.
Now he just thinks I'm **stupid.**
AS IF.
Although I did let you manipulate me into playing the piano with my face.
It was hilarious.

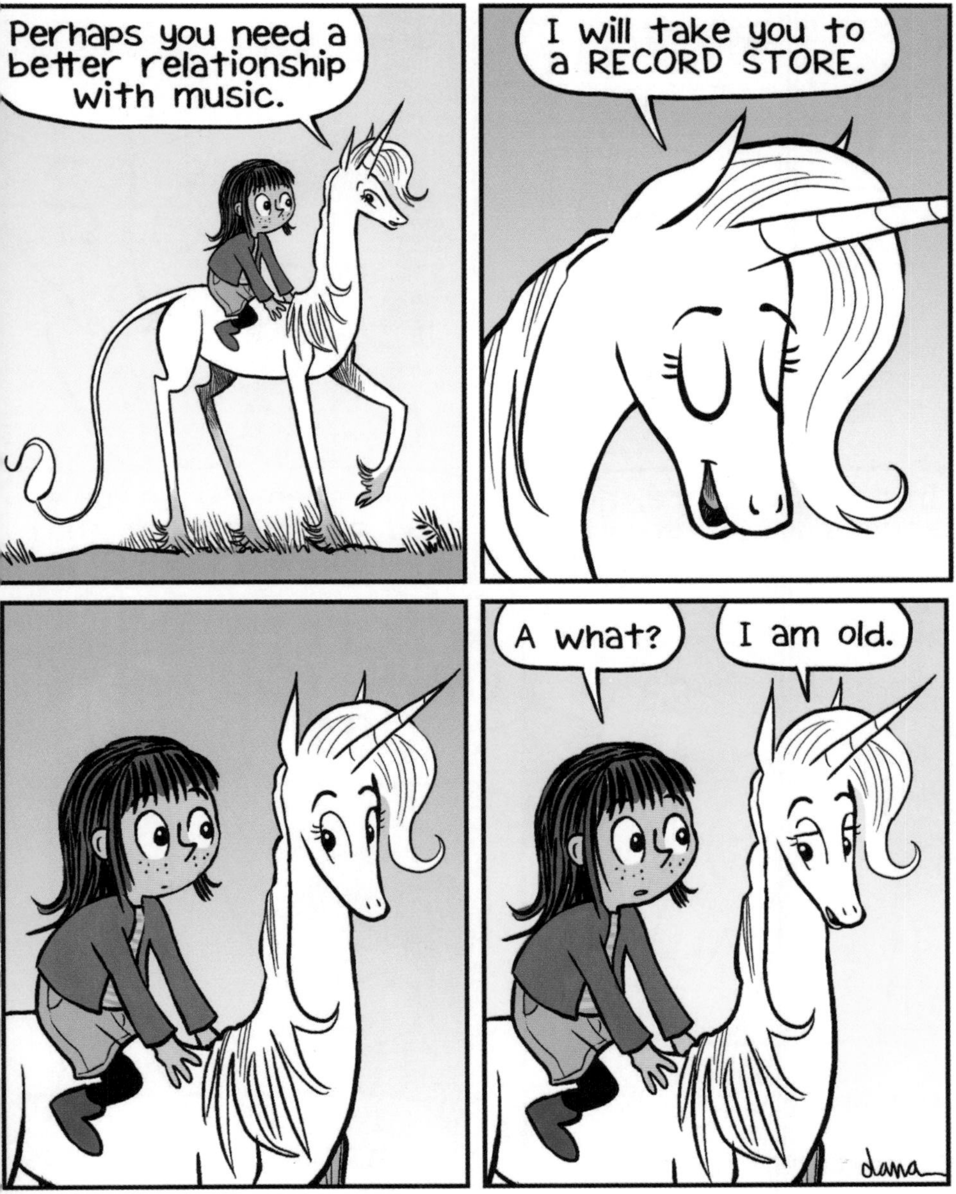
Perhaps you need a better relationship with music.
I will take you to a RECORD STORE.
A what?
I am old.
dana

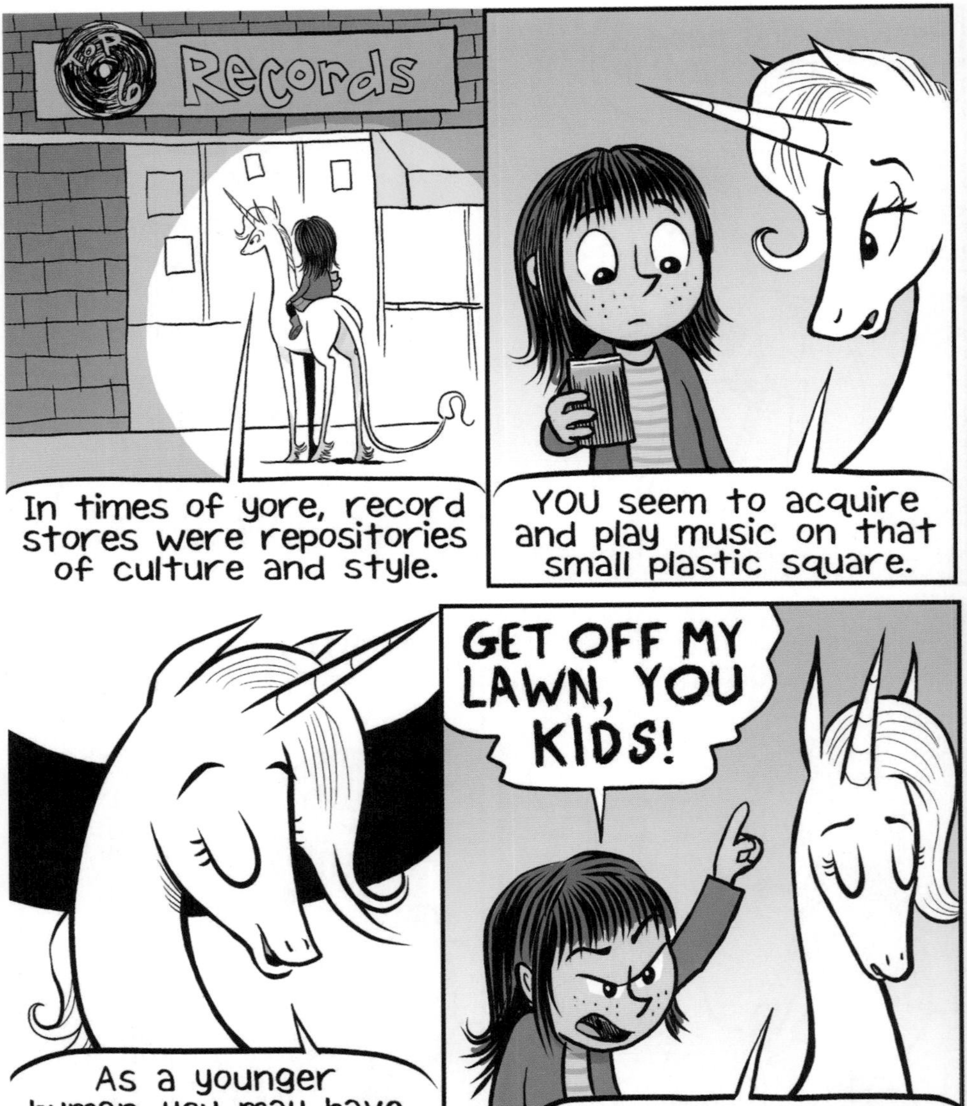
Records
In times of yore, record stores were repositories of culture and style.
YOU seem to acquire and play music on that small plastic square.
As a younger human, you may have trouble appreciating a record store properly.
GET OFF MY LAWN, YOU KIDS!
I happen to know **your** lawn is delicious.
dana

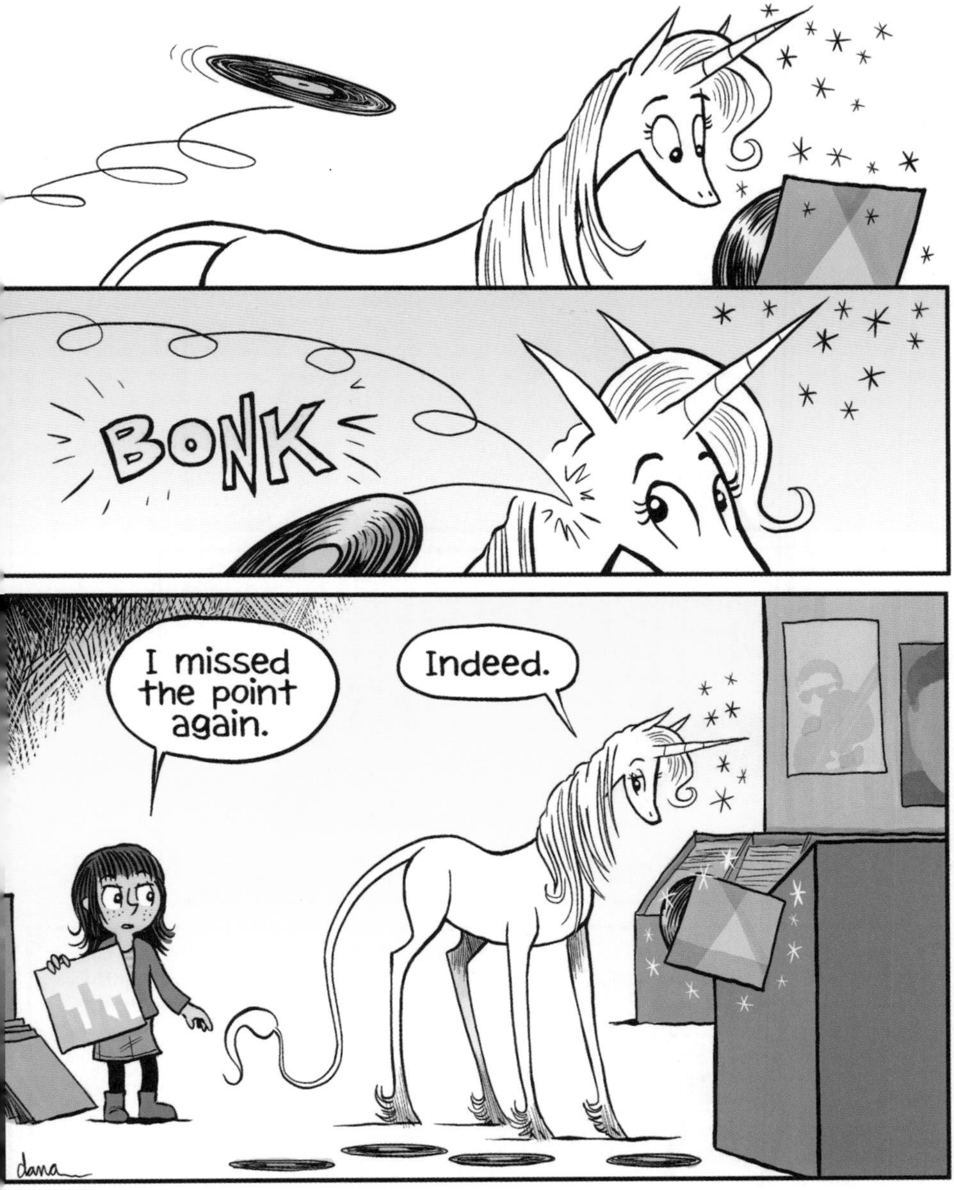
BONK
I missed the point again.
Indeed.
dana

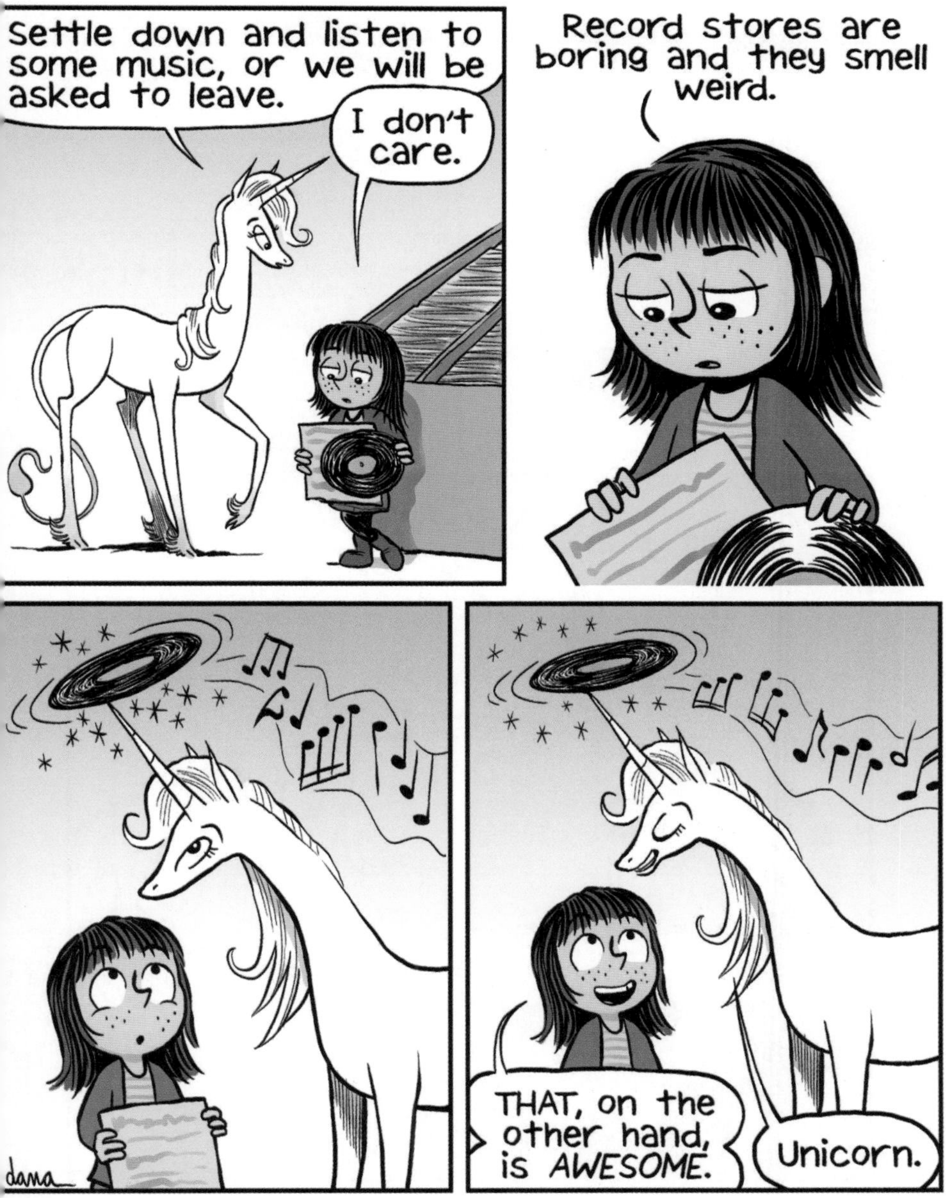
Settle down and listen to some music, or we will be asked to leave.
I don't care.
Record stores are boring and they smell weird.
THAT, on the other hand, is AWESOME.
Unicorn.
dana

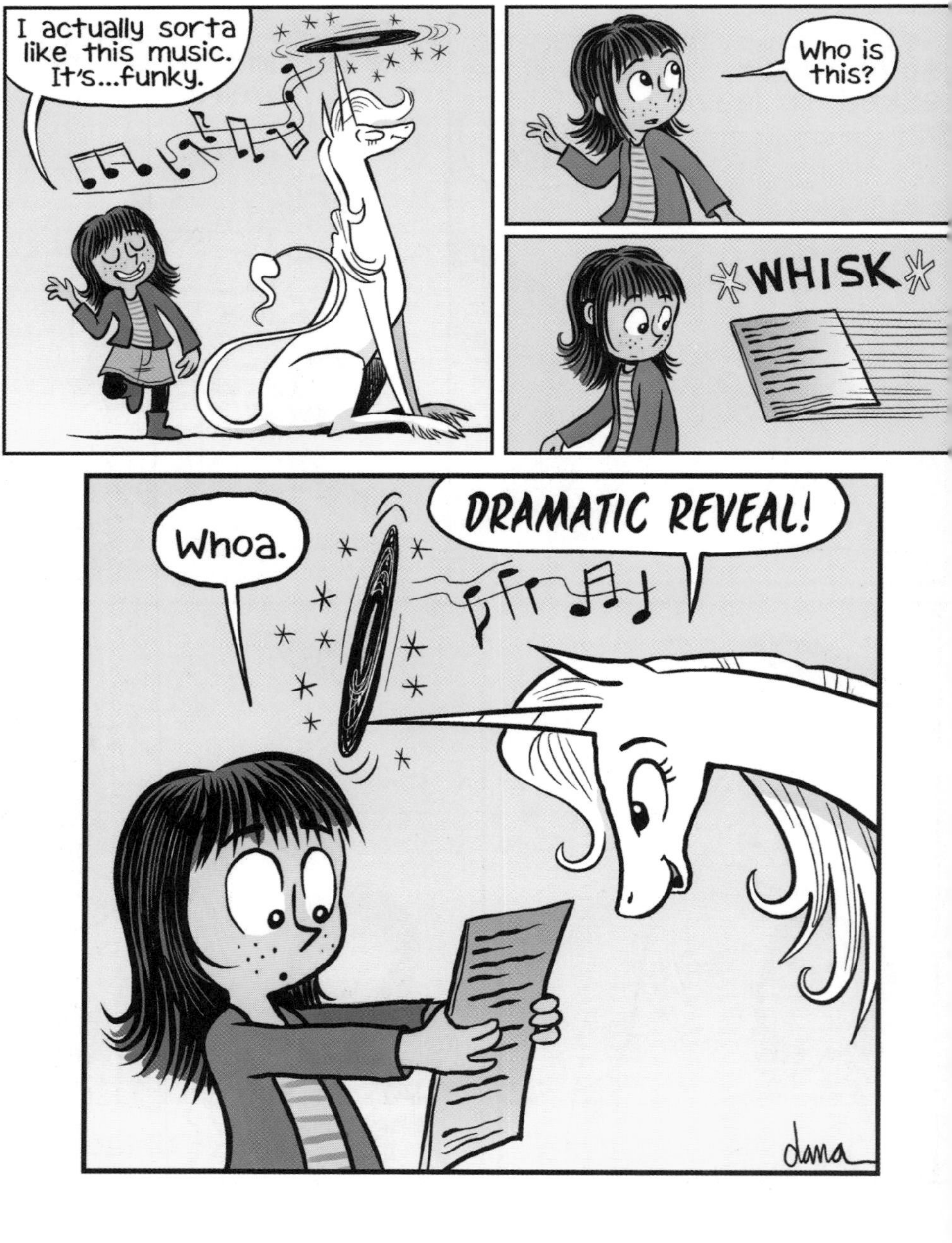
I actually sorta like this music. It's...funky.
Who is this?
WHISK
Whoa.
DRAMATIC REVEAL!
dana

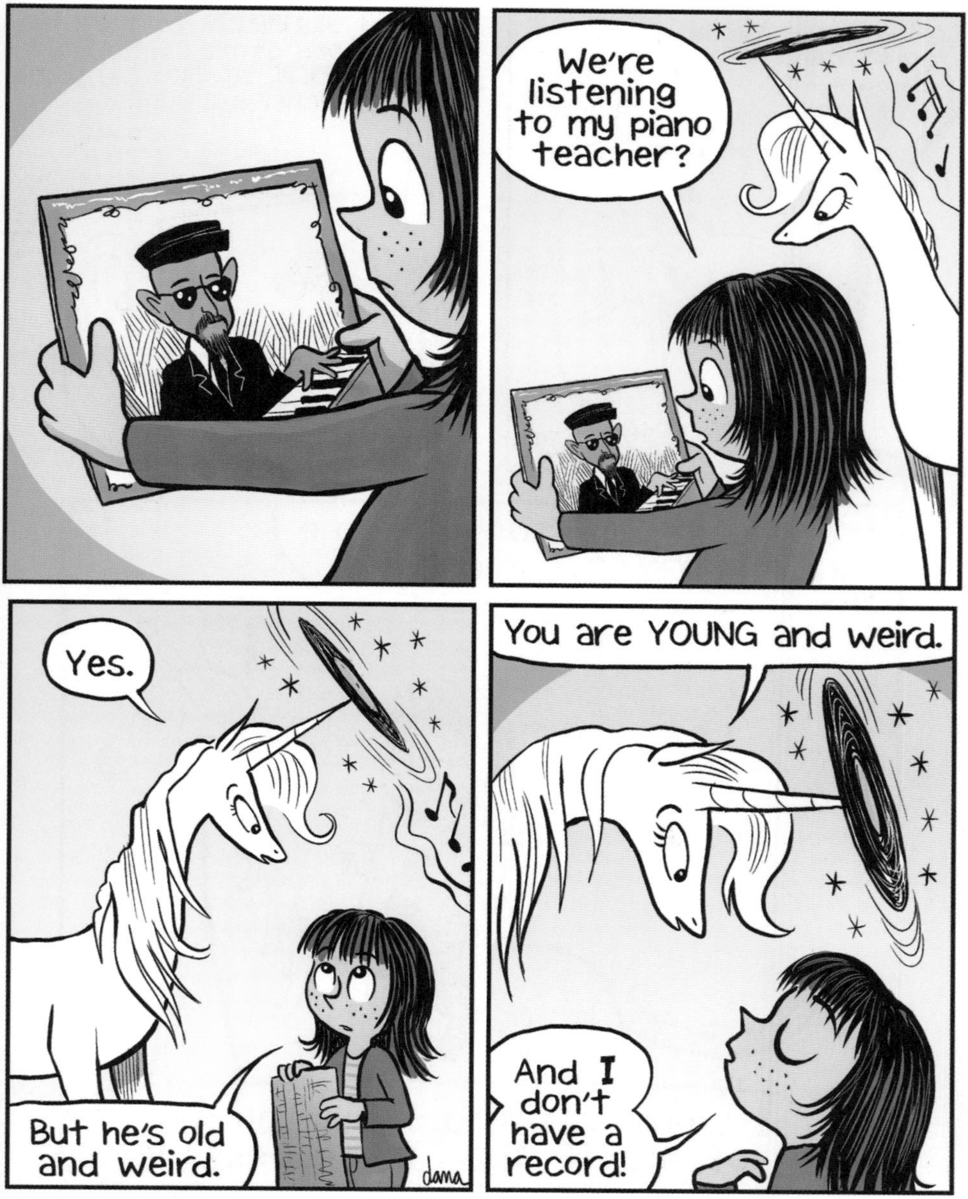
We're listening to my piano teacher?
Yes.
But he's old and weird.
You are YOUNG and weird.
And I don't have a record!
dana

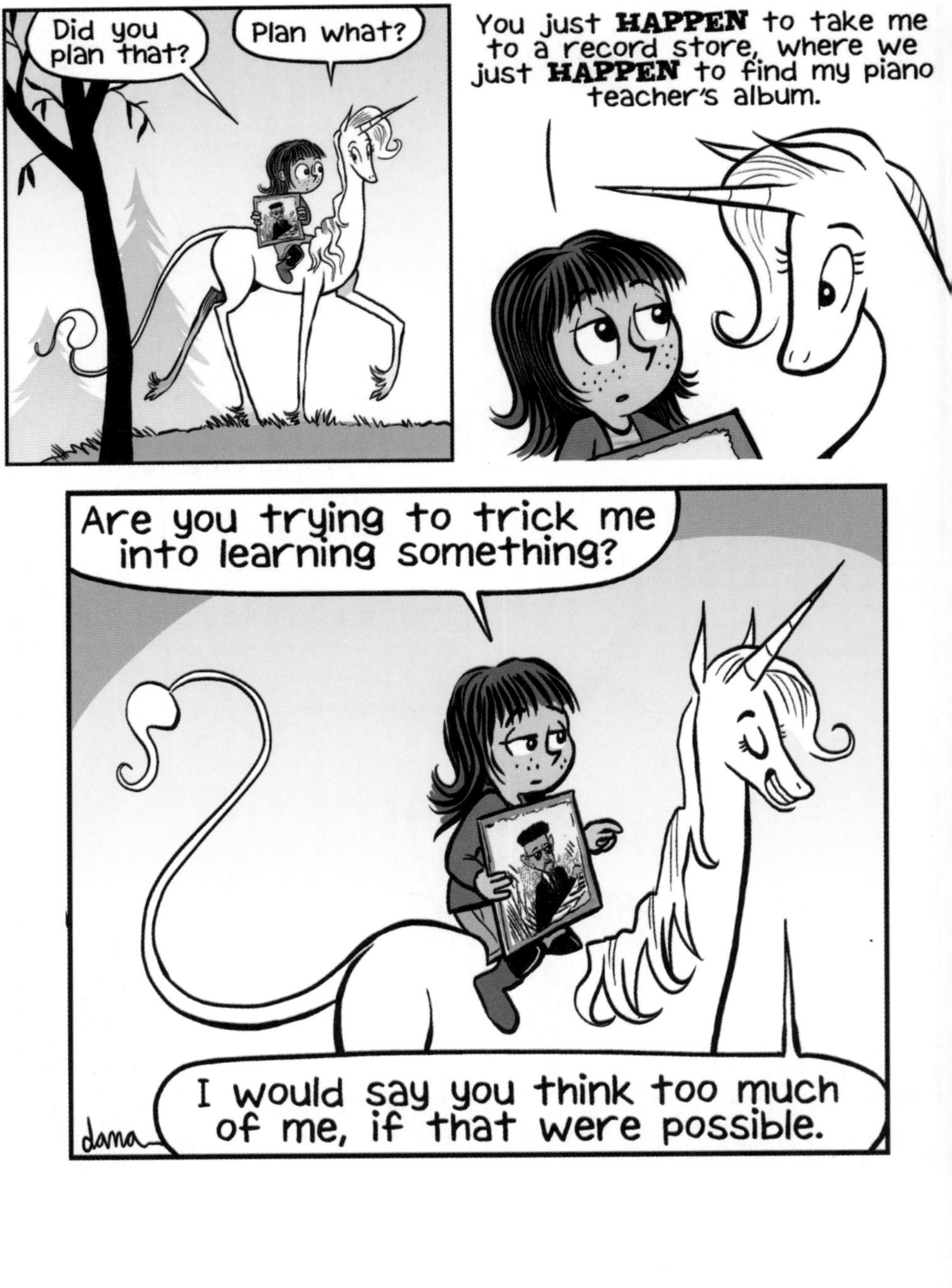
Did you plan that?
Plan what?
You just **HAPPEN** to take me to a record store, where we just **HAPPEN** to find my piano teacher's album.
Are you trying to trick me into learning something?
I would say you think too much of me, if that were possible.
dana

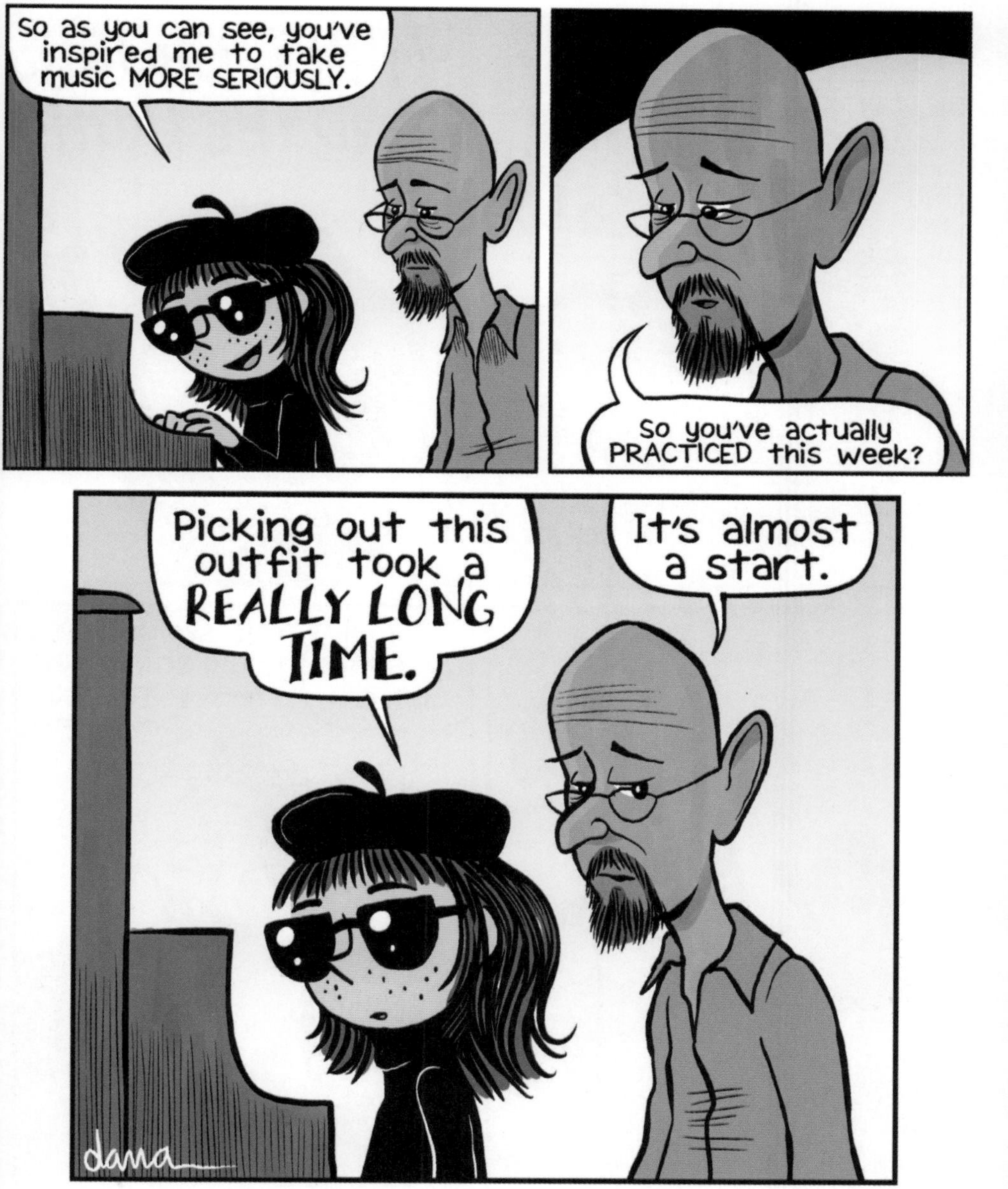
So as you can see, you've inspired me to take music MORE SERIOUSLY.
So you've actually PRACTICED this week?
Picking out this outfit took a REALLY LONG TIME.
It's almost a start.
dana

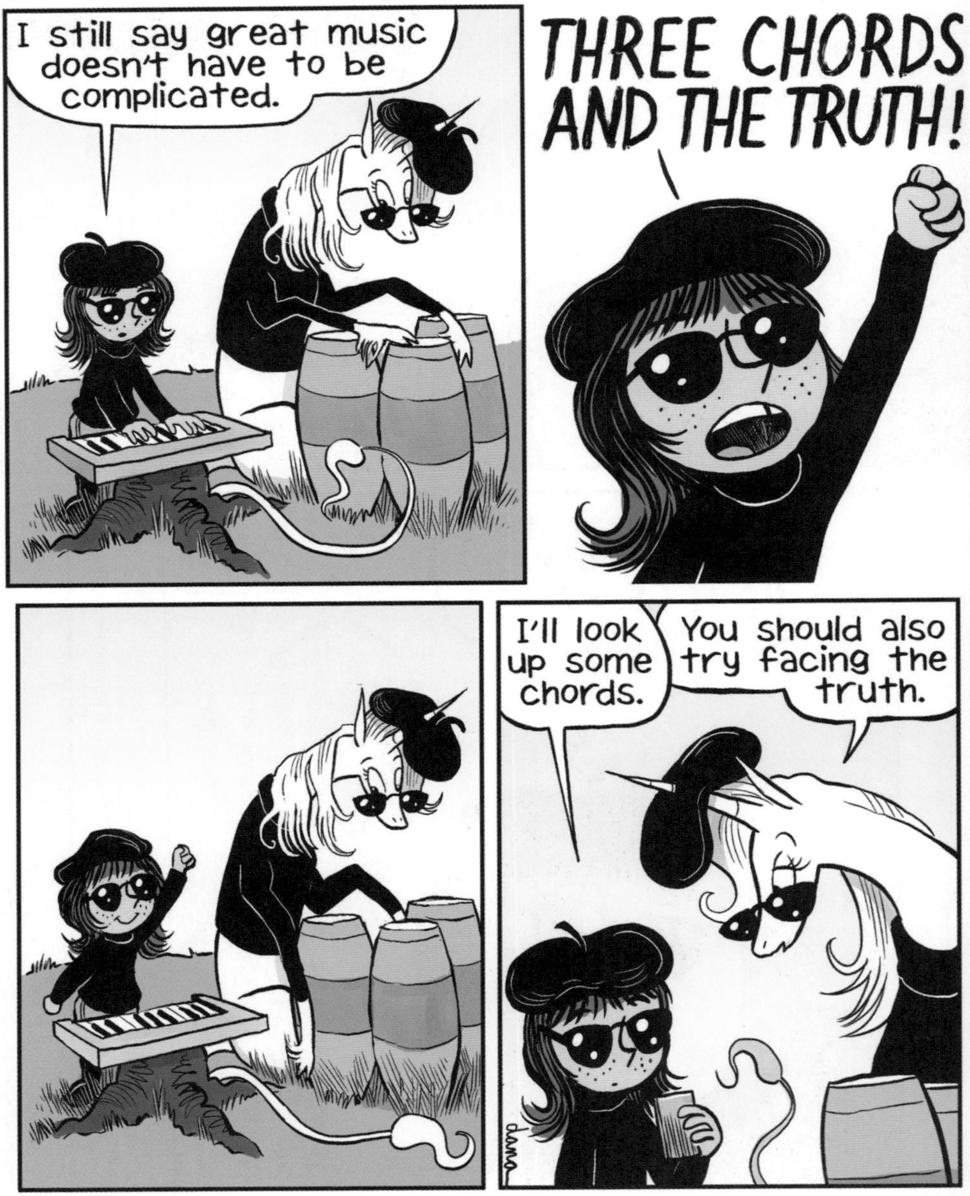
I still say great music doesn't have to be complicated.
THREE CHORDS AND THE TRUTH!
I'll look up some chords.
You should also try facing the truth.
dana

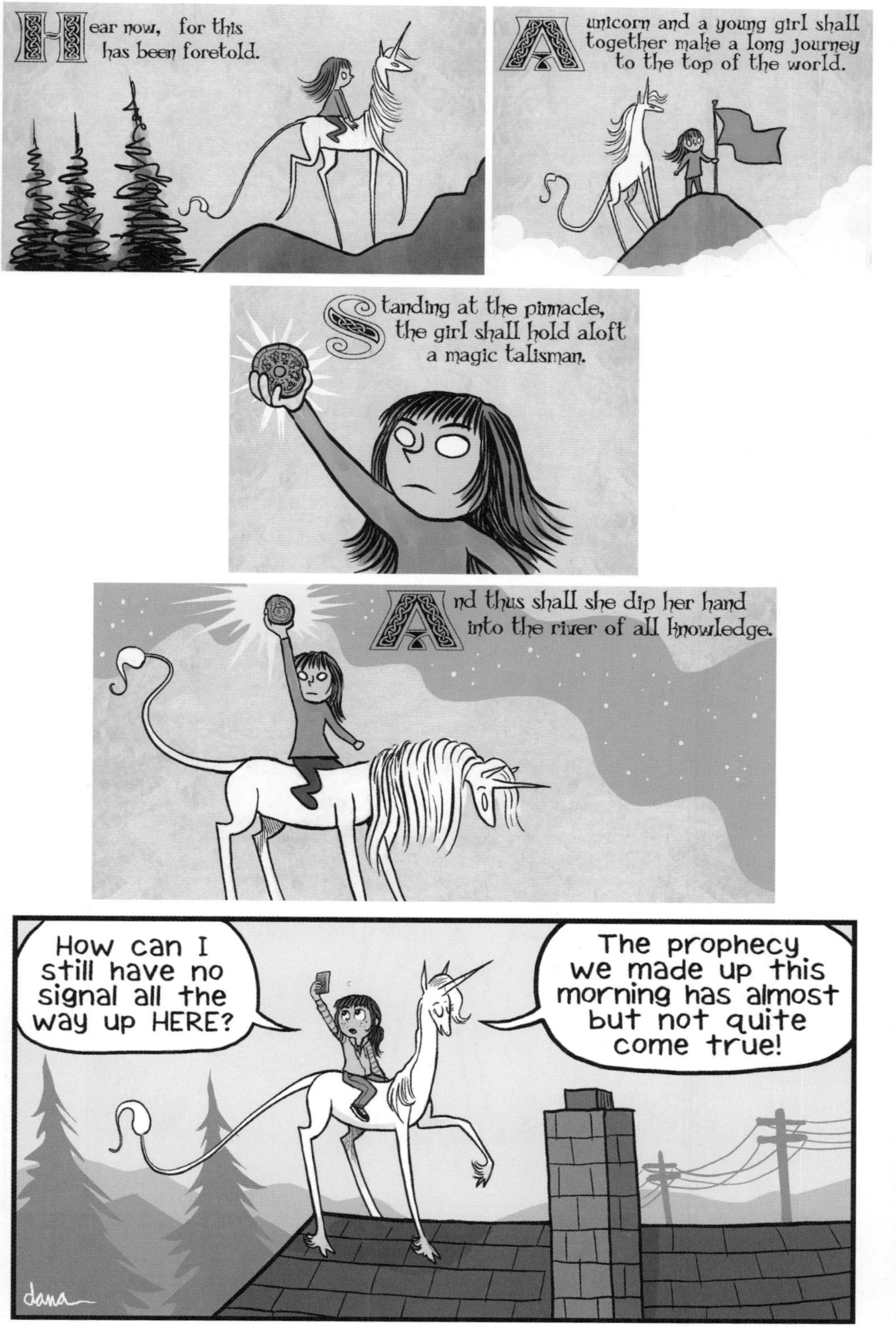
Hear now, for this has been foretold.
A unicorn and a young girl shall together make a long journey to the top of the world.
Standing at the pinnacle, the girl shall hold aloft a magic talisman.
And thus shall she dip her hand into the river of all knowledge.
How can I still have no signal all the way up HERE?
The prophecy we made up this morning has almost but not quite come true!
dana

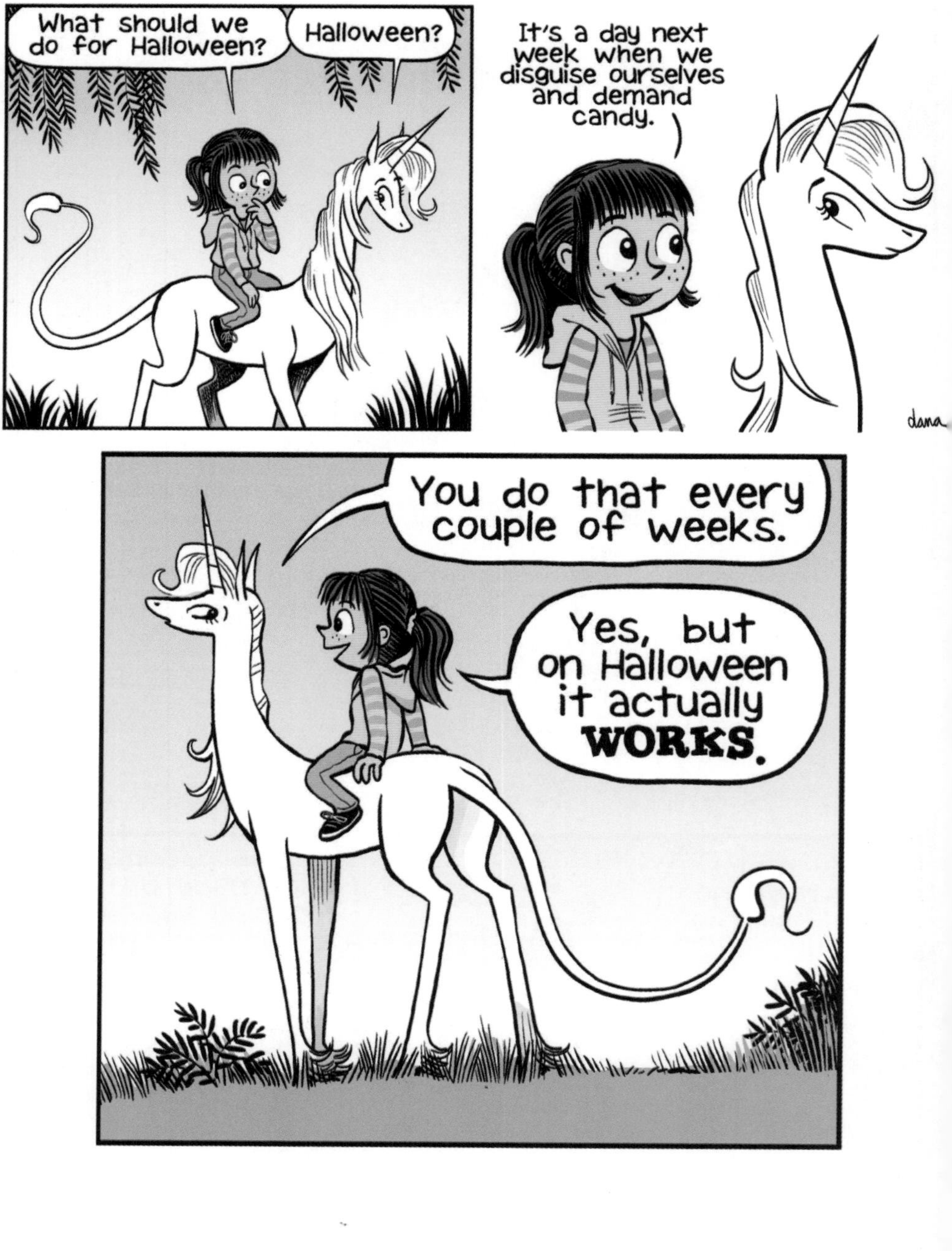
What should we do for Halloween?
Halloween?
It's a day next week when we disguise ourselves and demand candy.
dana
You do that every couple of weeks.
Yes, but on Halloween it actually **WORKS**.

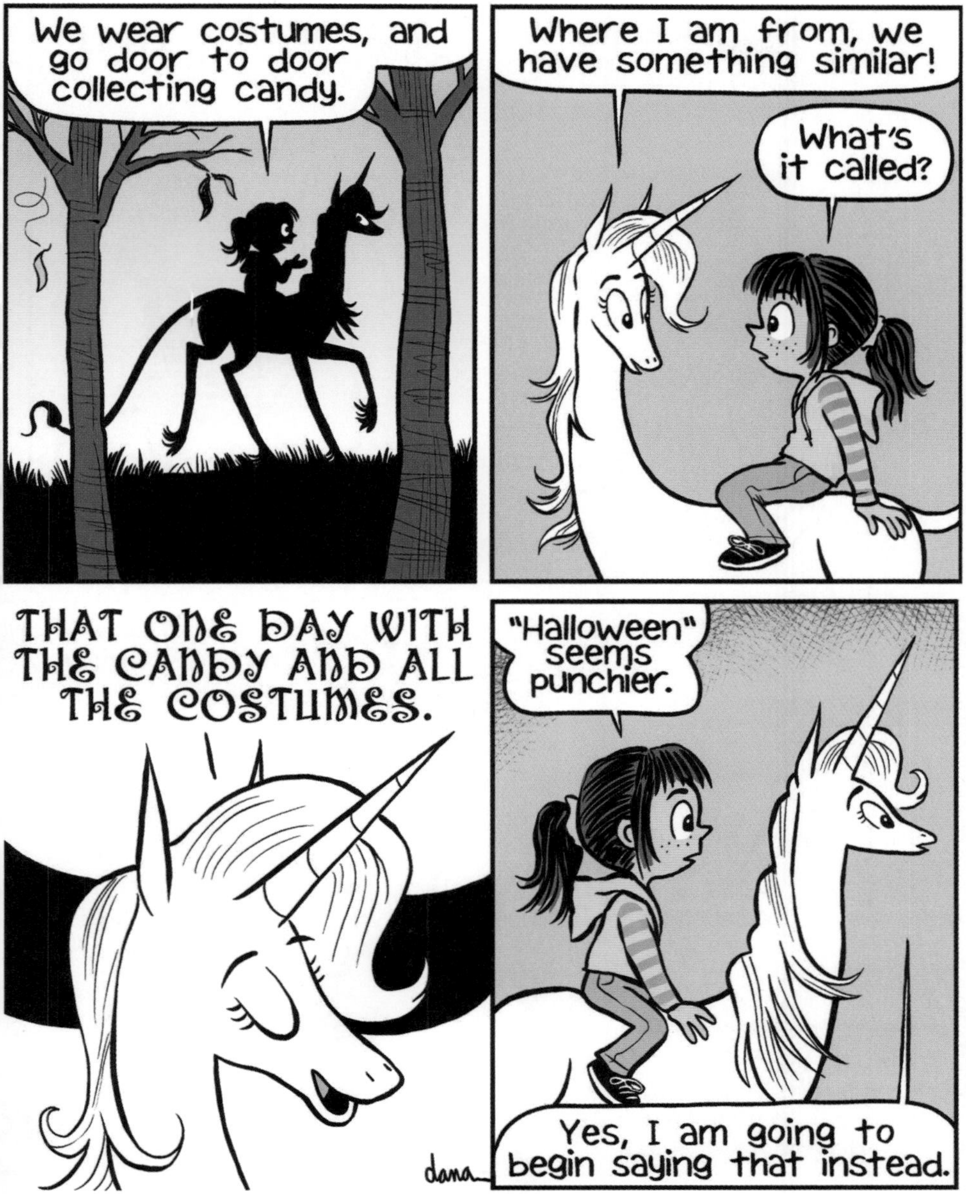
We wear costumes, and go door to door collecting candy.
Where I am from, we have something similar!
What's it called?
THAT ONE DAY WITH THE CANDY AND ALL THE COSTUMES.
"Halloween" seems punchier.
Yes, I am going to begin saying that instead.
dana

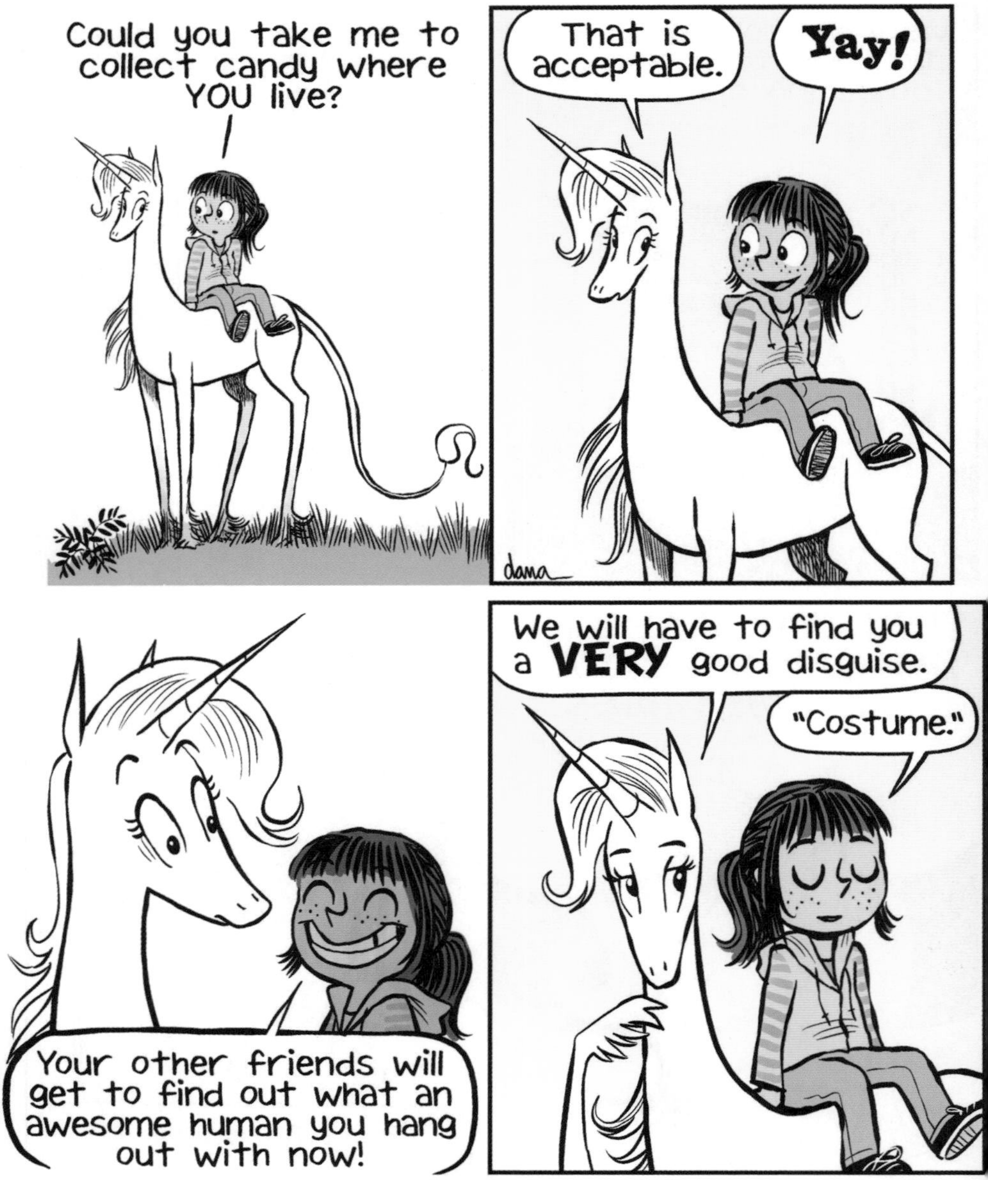

Could you take me to collect candy where YOU live?
That is acceptable.
Yay!
dana
Your other friends will get to find out what an awesome human you hang out with now!
We will have to find you a VERY good disguise.
"Costume."

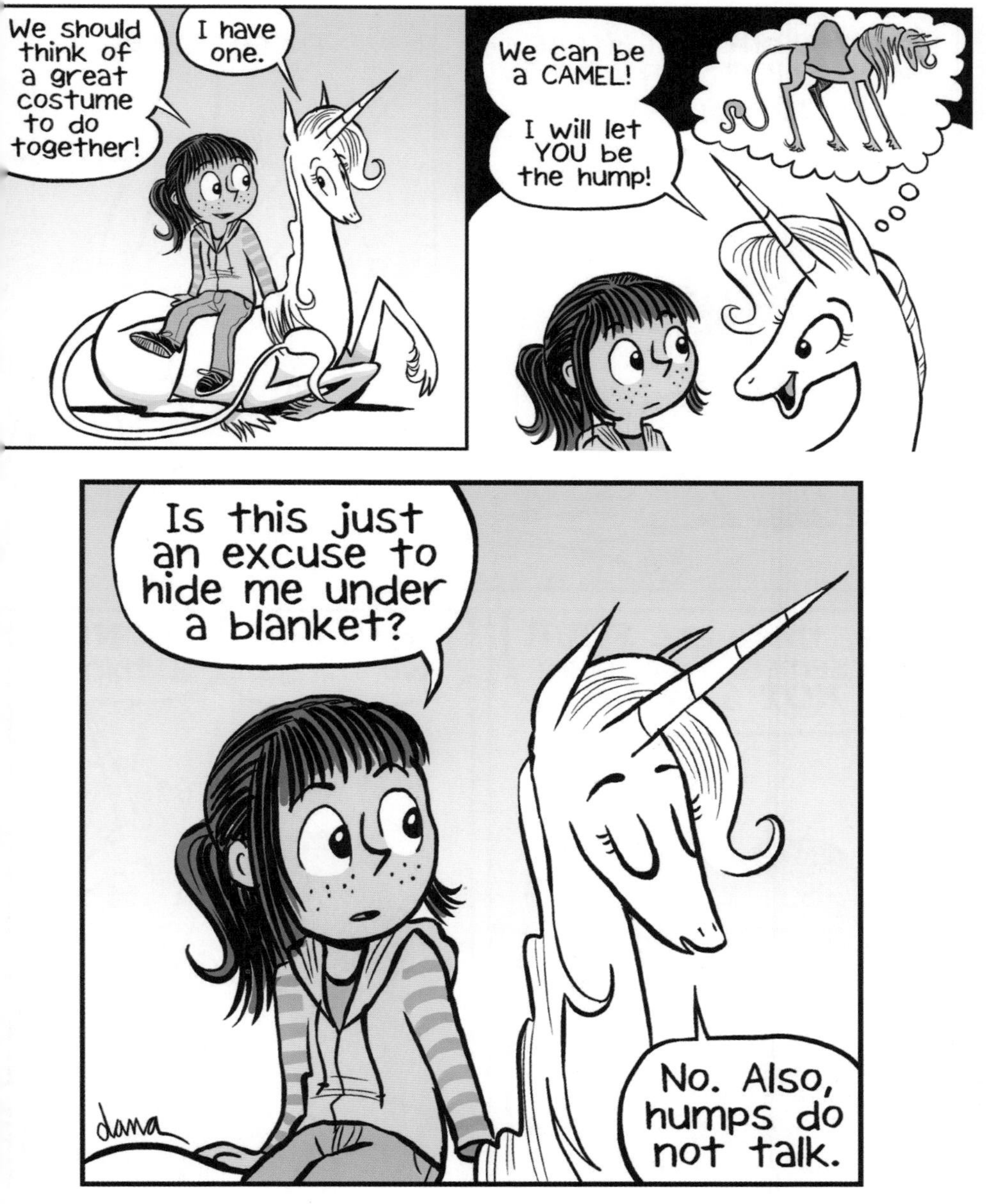

We should think of a great costume to do together!
I have one.
We can be a CAMEL!
I will let YOU be the hump!
Is this just an excuse to hide me under a blanket?
No. Also, humps do not talk.
dana

What about if I dress up as the **HORSEMAN OF THE APOCALYPSE?**

Three things.

One, there are **FOUR** horsemen. Two, I am **NOT** a horse.

That's only two things.

Is **"NO"** a thing?

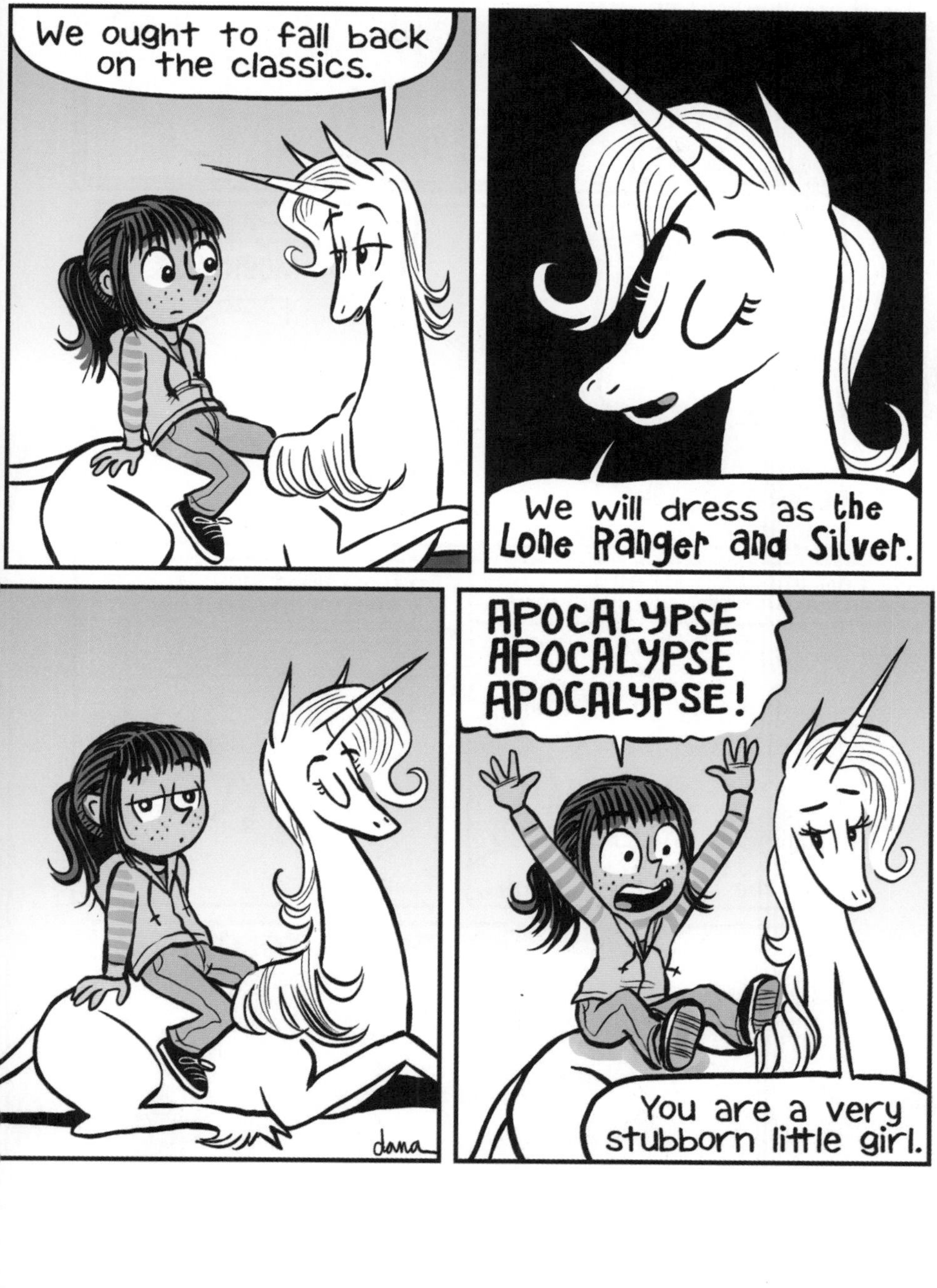
We ought to fall back on the classics.
We will dress as the Lone Ranger and Silver.
APOCALYPSE APOCALYPSE APOCALYPSE!
You are a very stubborn little girl.
dana

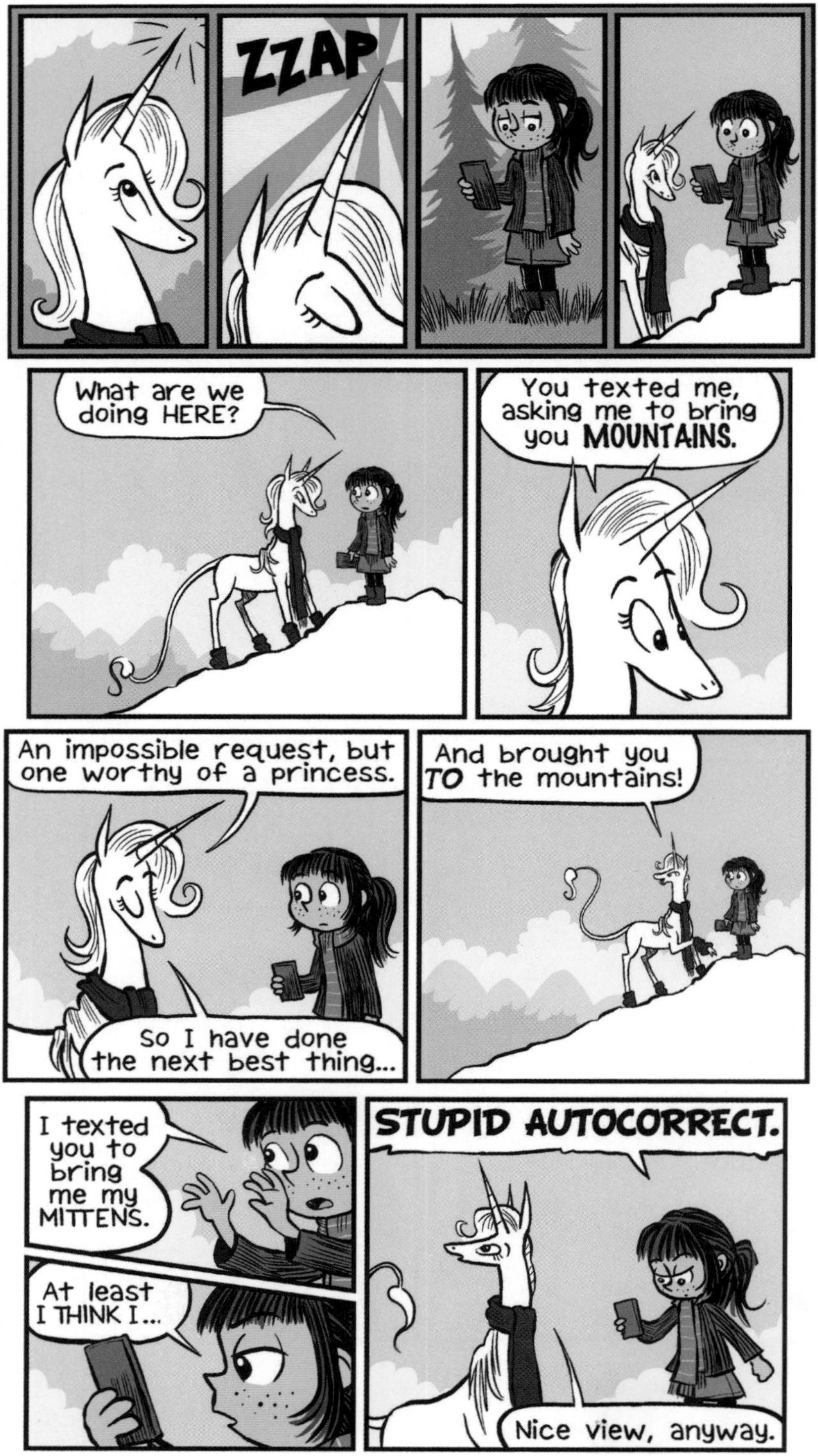
ZZAP
What are we doing HERE?
You texted me, asking me to bring you MOUNTAINS.
An impossible request, but one worthy of a princess.
So I have done the next best thing...
And brought you TO the mountains!
I texted you to bring me my MITTENS.
At least I THINK I...
STUPID AUTOCORRECT.
Nice view, anyway.

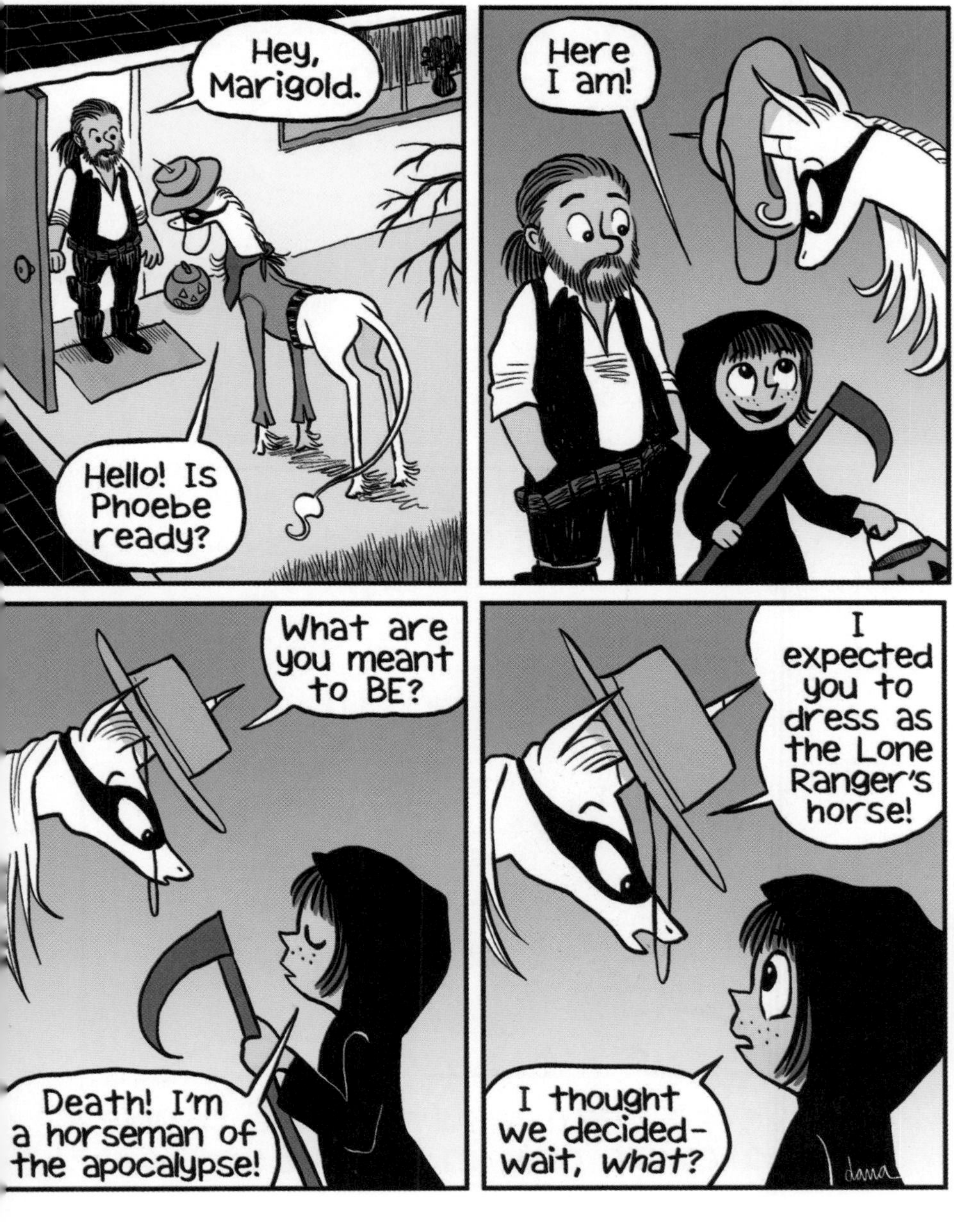

Hey, Marigold.
Hello! Is Phoebe ready?
Here I am!
What are you meant to BE?
Death! I'm a horseman of the apocalypse!
I expected you to dress as the Lone Ranger's horse!
I thought we decided- wait, what?
dana

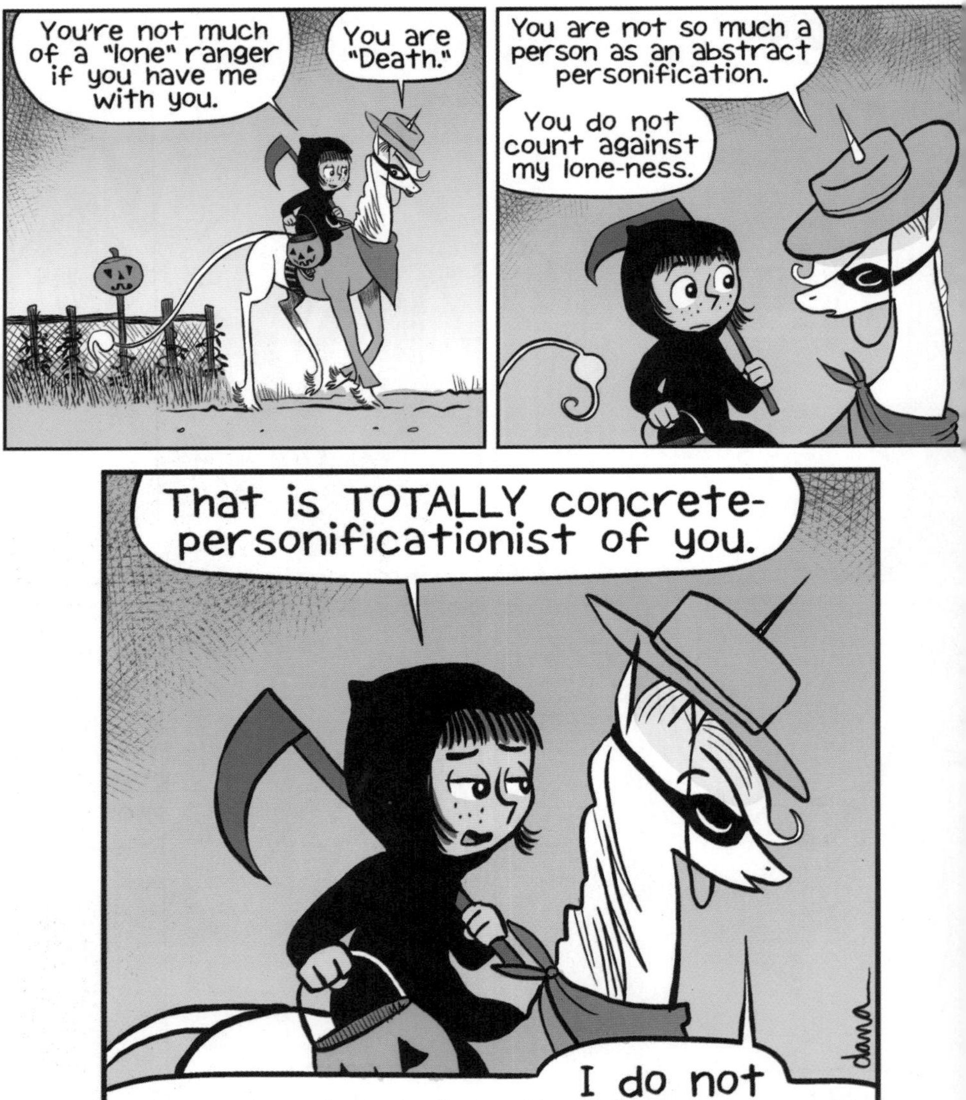
You're not much of a "lone" ranger if you have me with you.
You are "Death."
You are not so much a person as an abstract personification.
You do not count against my lone-ness.
That is TOTALLY concrete-personificationist of you.
I do not have to take insults from people who exist only in the abstract.
dana

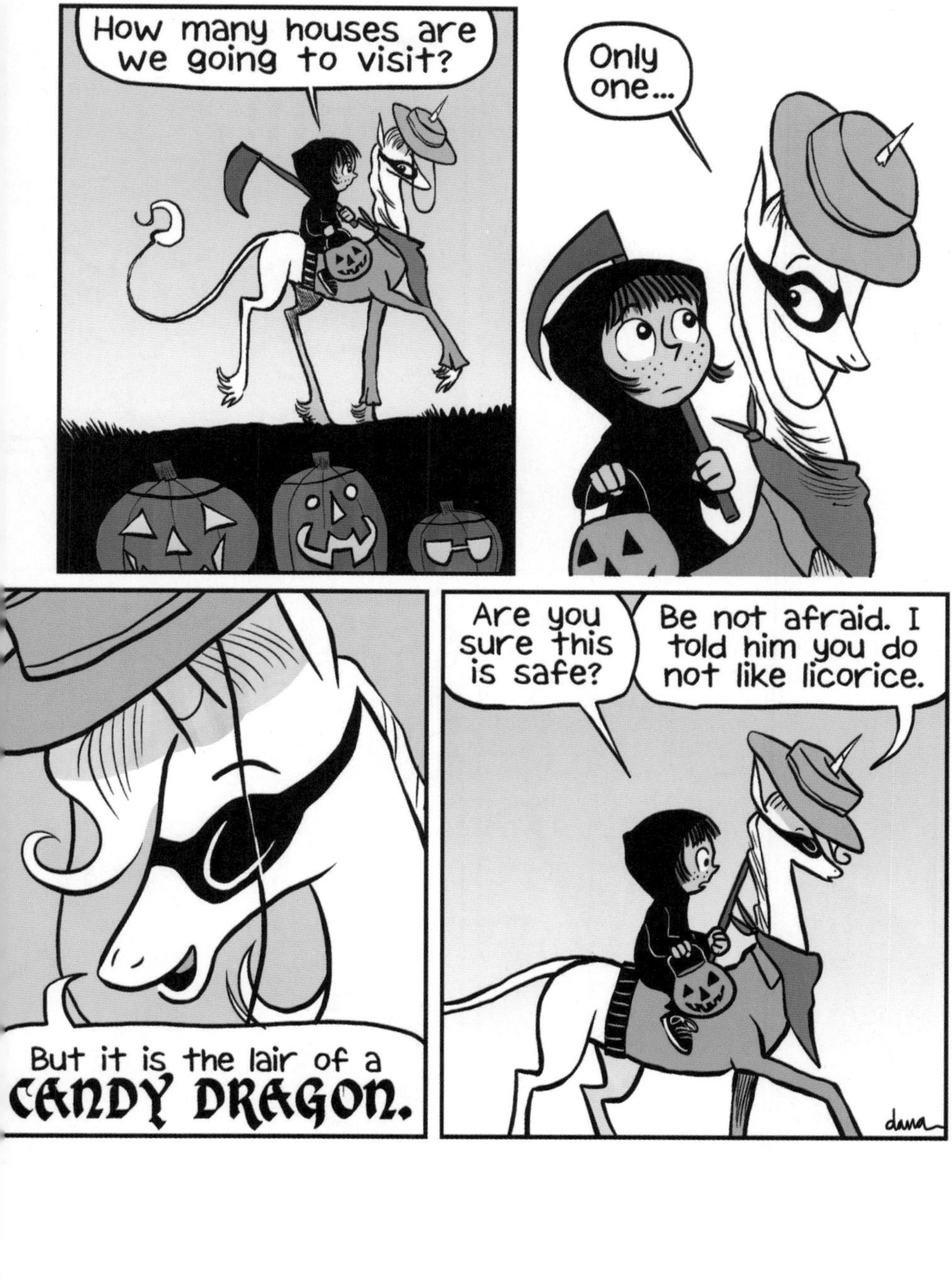
How many houses are we going to visit?
Only one...
But it is the lair of a CANDY DRAGON.
Are you sure this is safe?
Be not afraid. I told him you do not like licorice.
dana

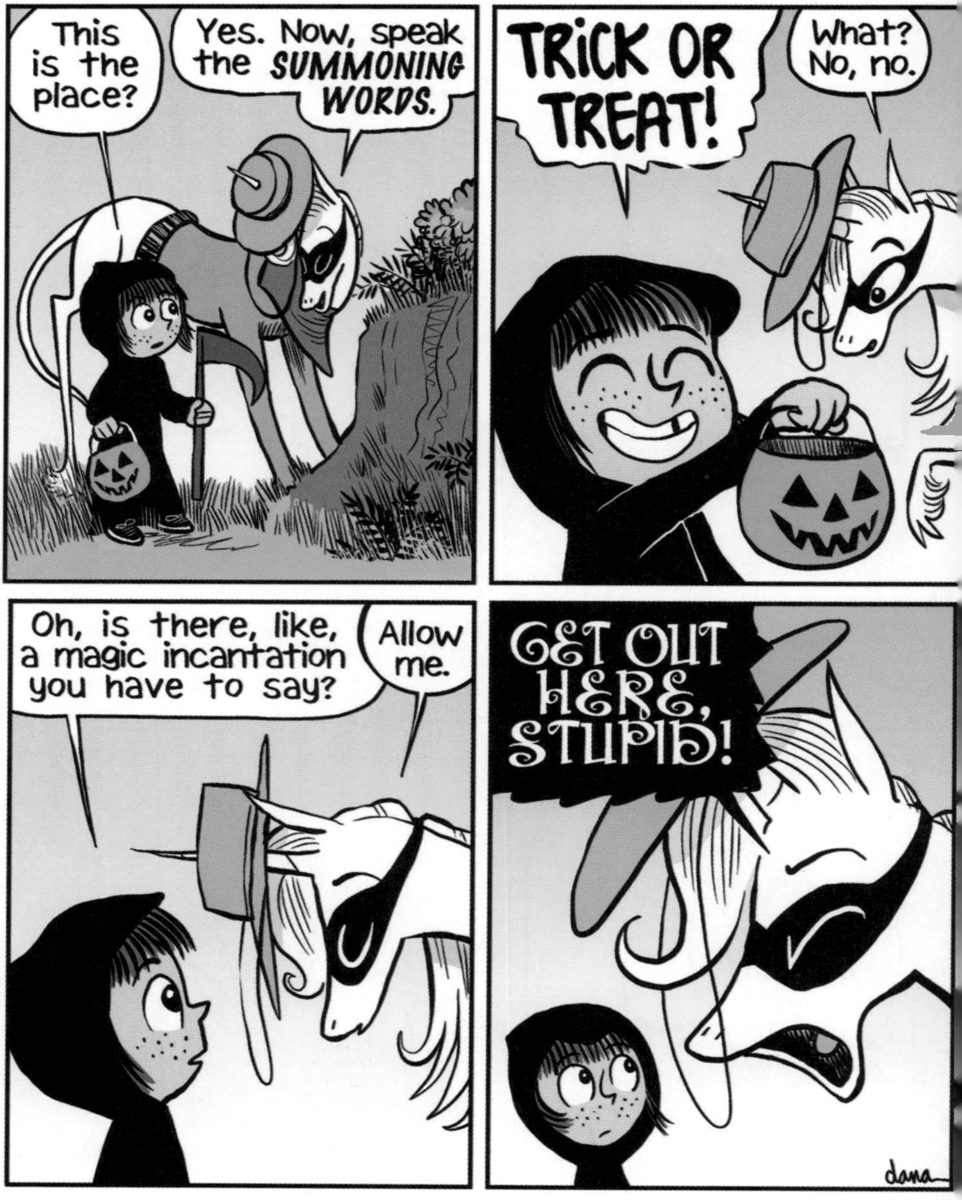
This is the place?
Yes. Now, speak the SUMMONING WORDS.
TRICK OR TREAT!
What? No, no.
Oh, is there, like, a magic incantation you have to say?
Allow me.
GET OUT HERE, STUPID!
dana

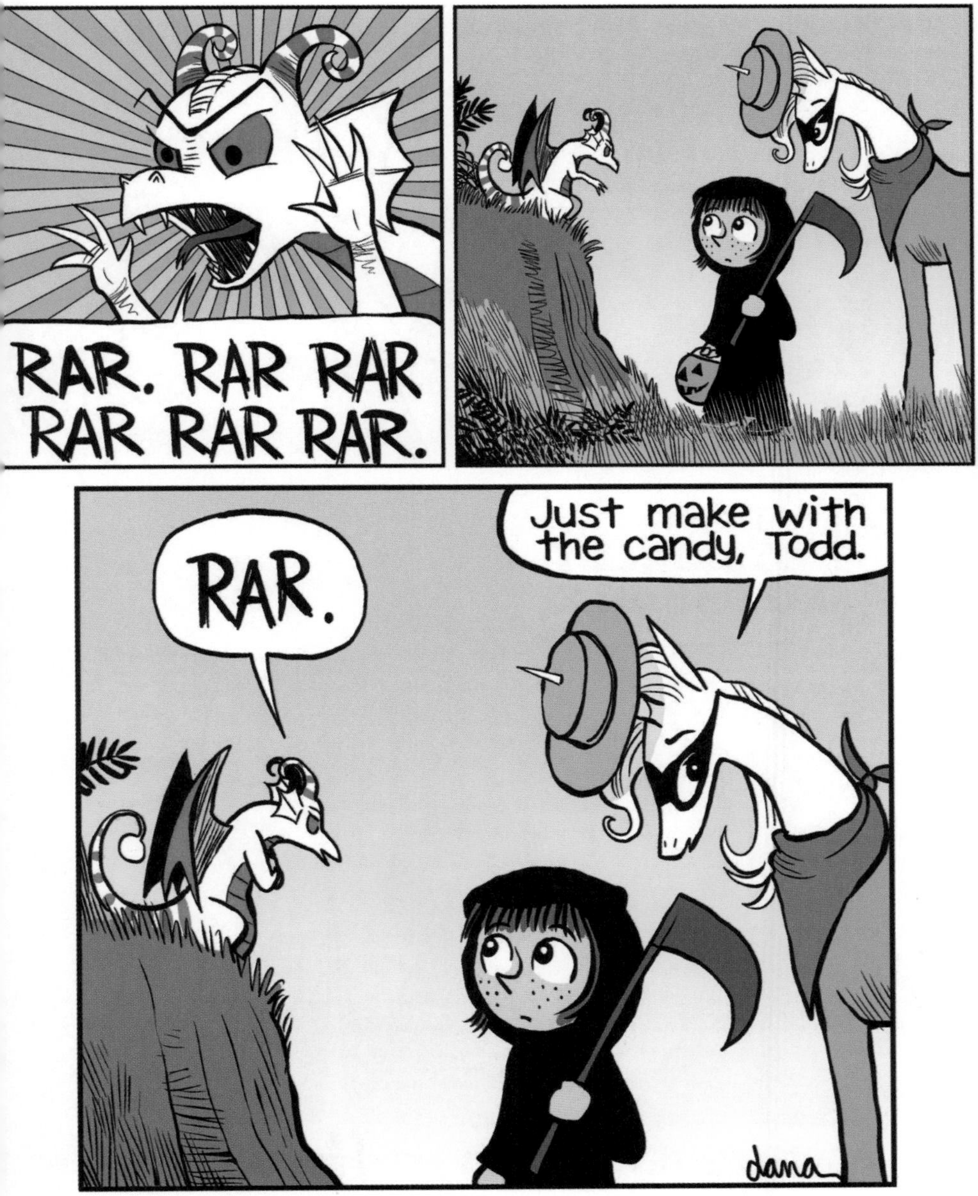
RAR. RAR RAR RAR RAR RAR.
RAR.
Just make with the candy, Todd.
dana

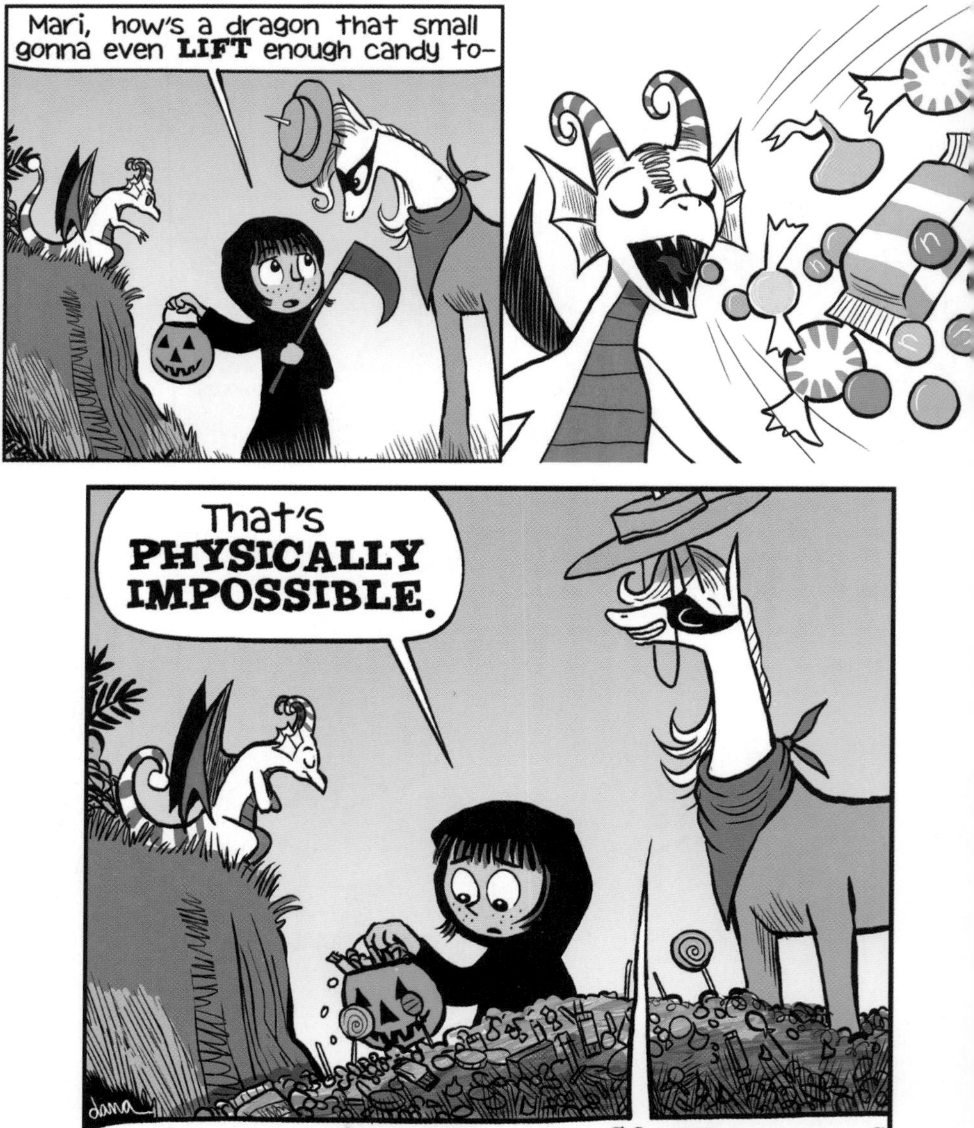
Mari, how's a dragon that small gonna even LIFT enough candy to-
That's PHYSICALLY IMPOSSIBLE.
Anything can happen on Halloween!
dana

Hey...

That's my spelling partner Max. He looks sad.

Hey, Max. What's wrong?

People don't believe me that I'm in costume.

That's stupid. You're **CLEARLY** Steve Jobs.

THANK you.

C'mon. I have enough candy that I can share.

People who DO get it think it's funny to give me apples.

SOMEbody ate all **MY** apples already.

What is this about someone back there having more apples?

201

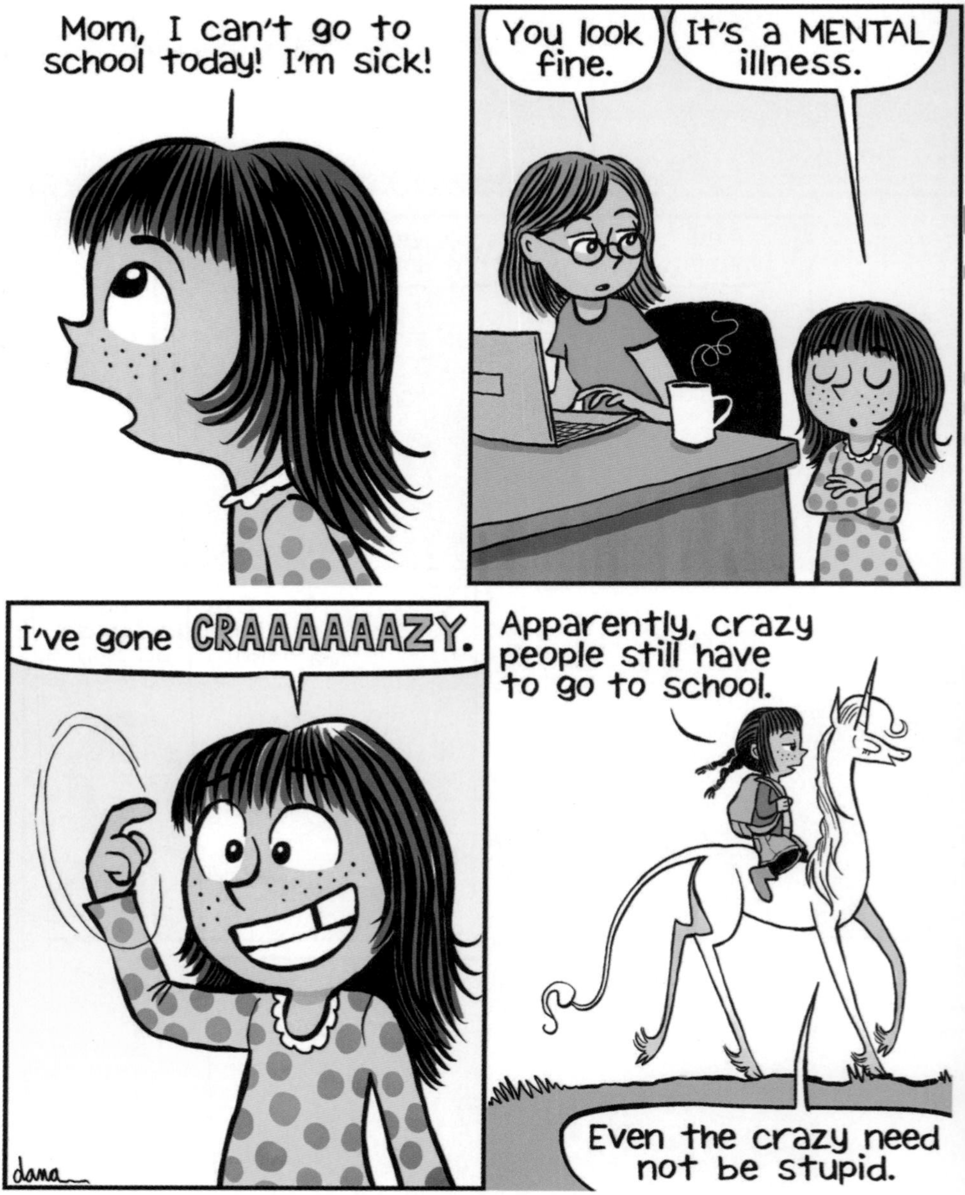
Mom, I can't go to school today! I'm sick!
You look fine.
It's a MENTAL illness.
I've gone CRAAAAAAAZY.
dana
Apparently, crazy people still have to go to school.
Even the crazy need not be stupid.

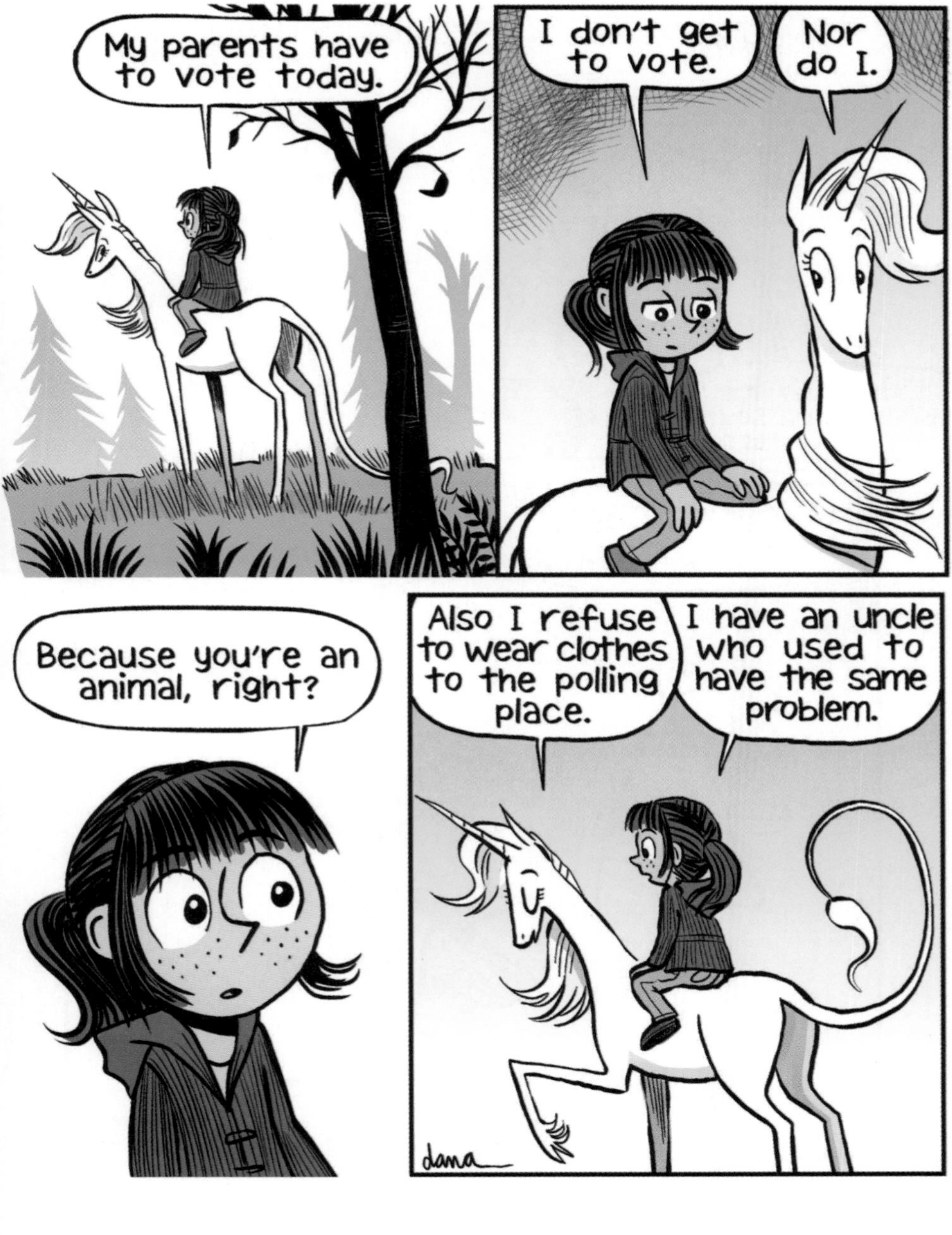
My parents have to vote today.
I don't get to vote.
Nor do I.
Because you're an animal, right?
Also I refuse to wear clothes to the polling place.
I have an uncle who used to have the same problem.
dana

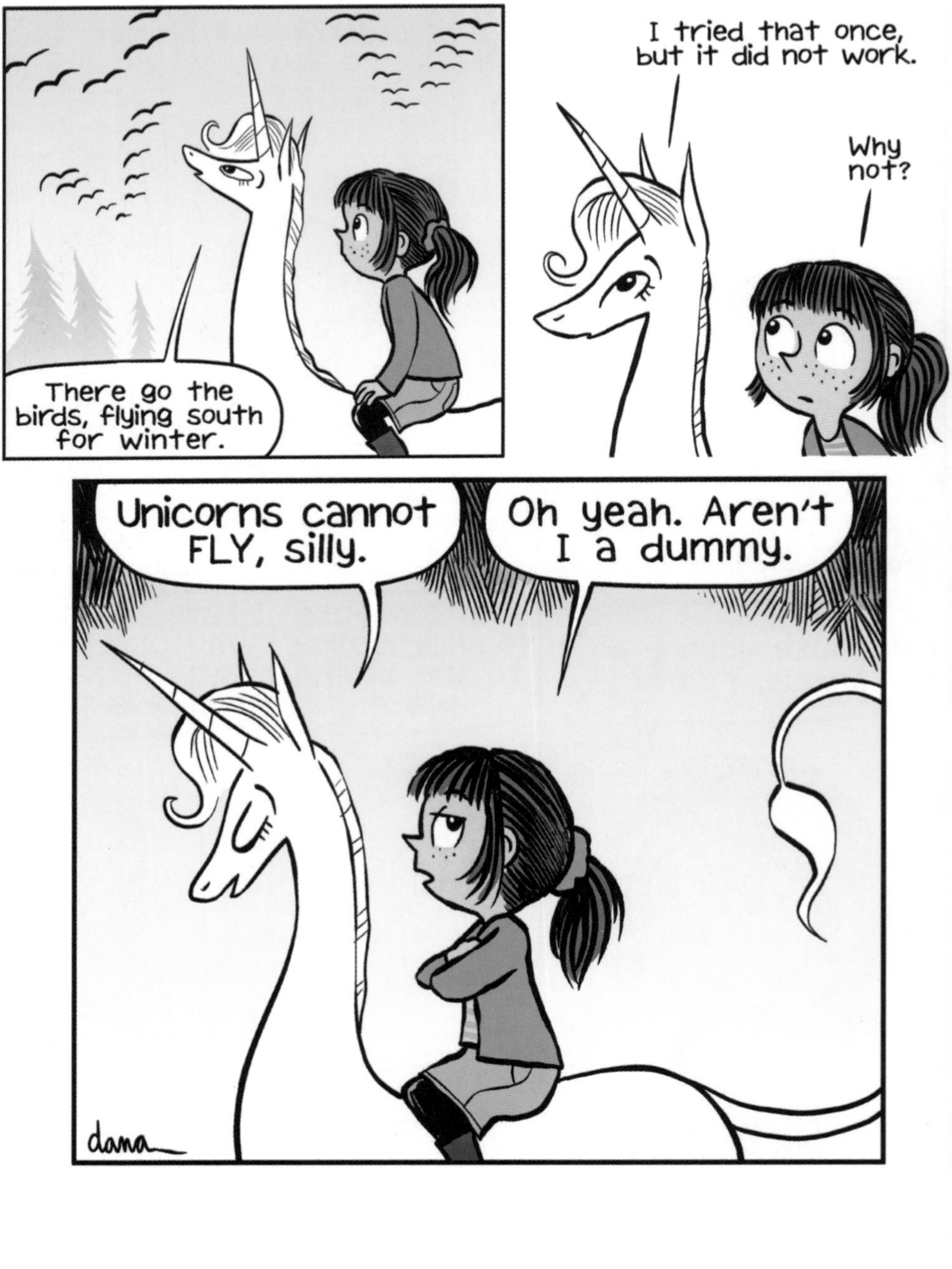
There go the birds, flying south for winter.
I tried that once, but it did not work.
Why not?
Unicorns cannot FLY, silly.
Oh yeah. Aren't I a dummy.
dana

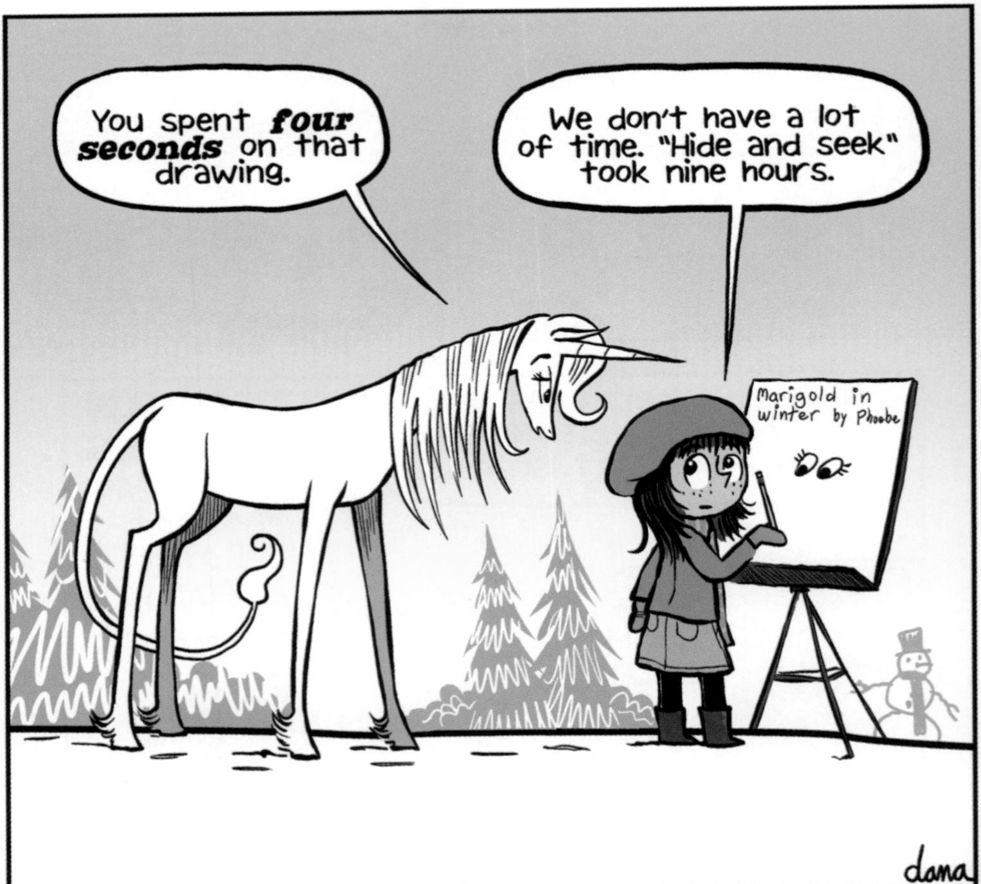
You spent **four seconds** on that drawing.
We don't have a lot of time. "Hide and seek" took nine hours.
Marigold in winter by Phoebe
dana

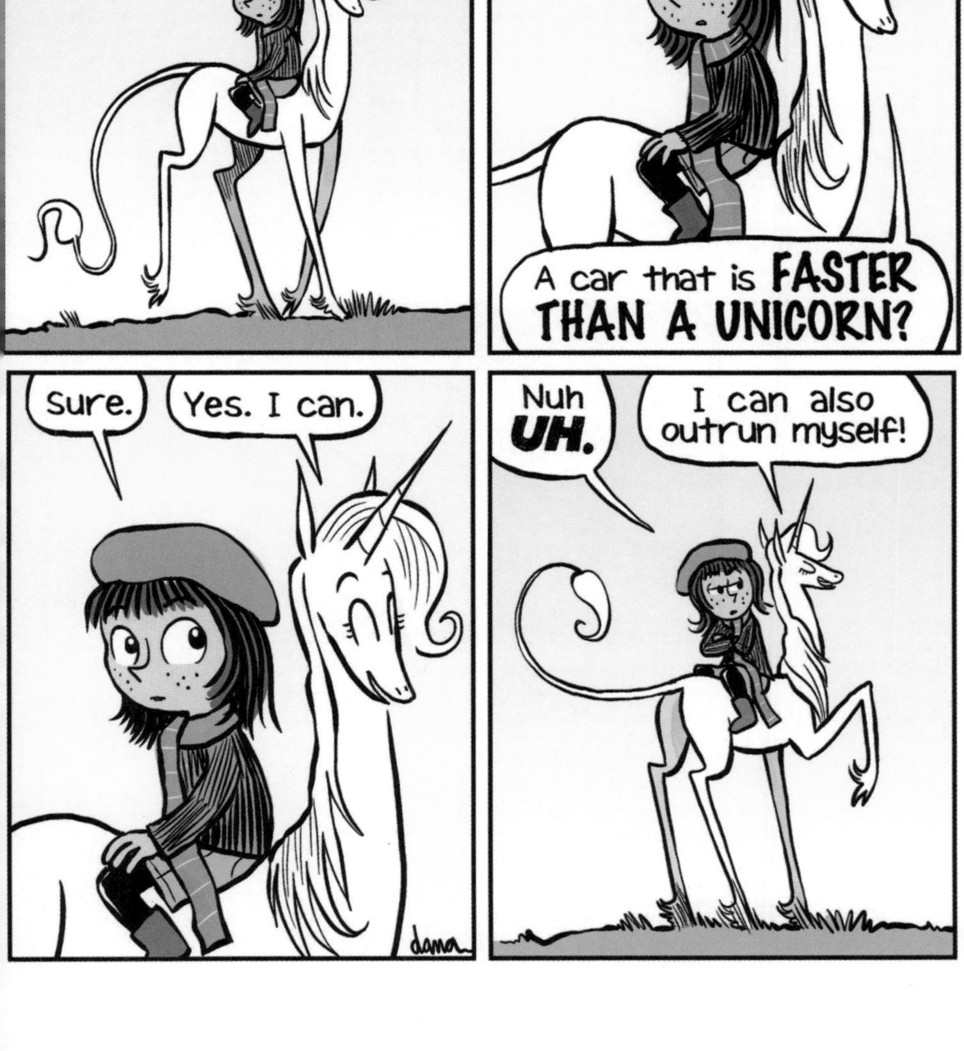
Marigold? Can you run faster than a car?
How fast a car?
I 'unno, just a car.
A car that is FASTER THAN A UNICORN?
Sure.
Yes. I can.
Nuh UH.
I can also outrun myself!
dana

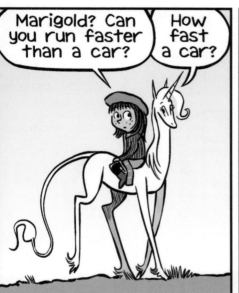

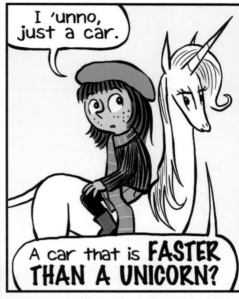

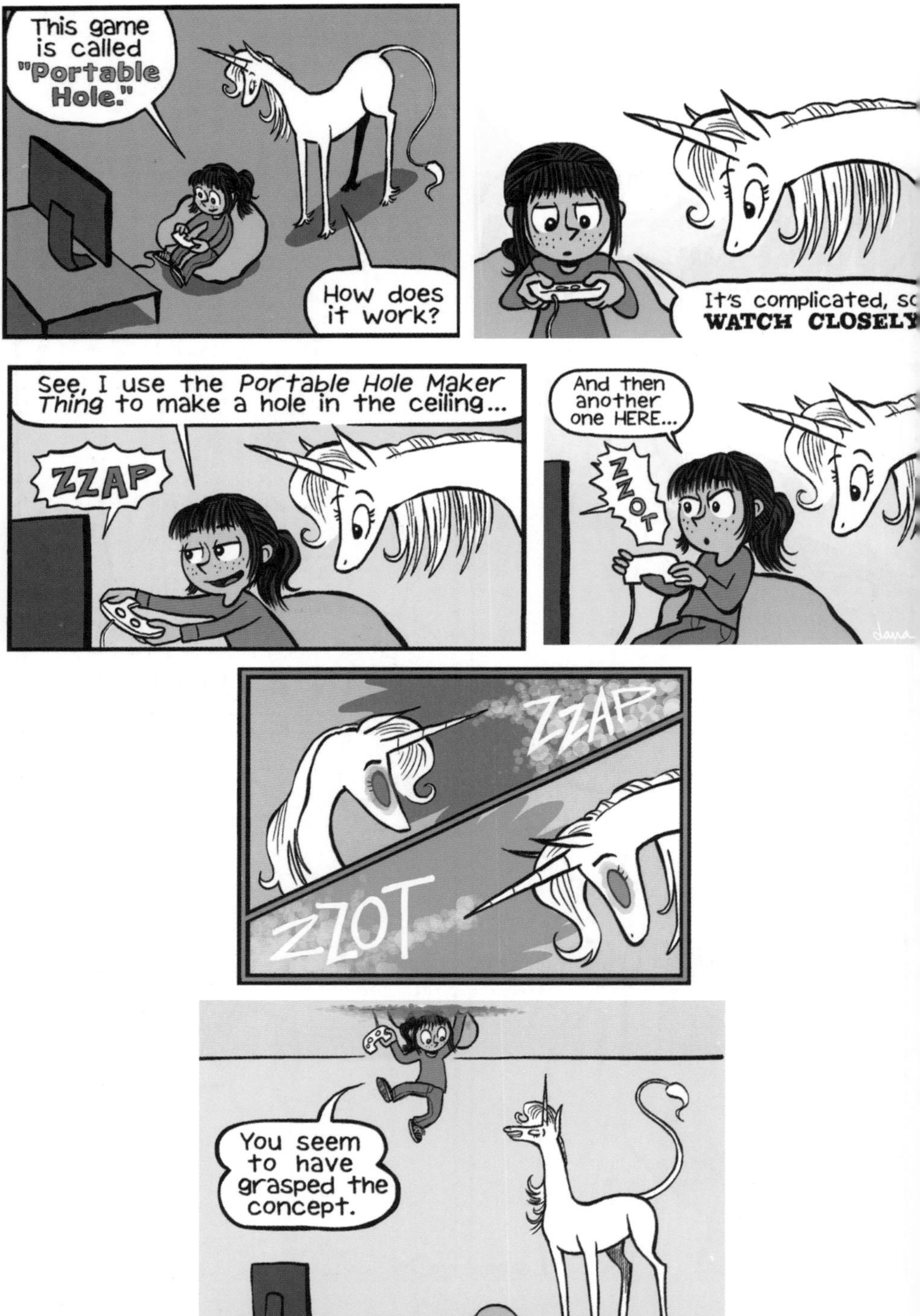
This game is called "Portable Hole."
How does it work?
It's complicated, sc
WATCH CLOSELY
See, I use the *Portable Hole Maker Thing* to make a hole in the ceiling...
ZZAP
And then another one HERE...
ZZOT
ZZAP
ZZOT
You seem to have grasped the concept.

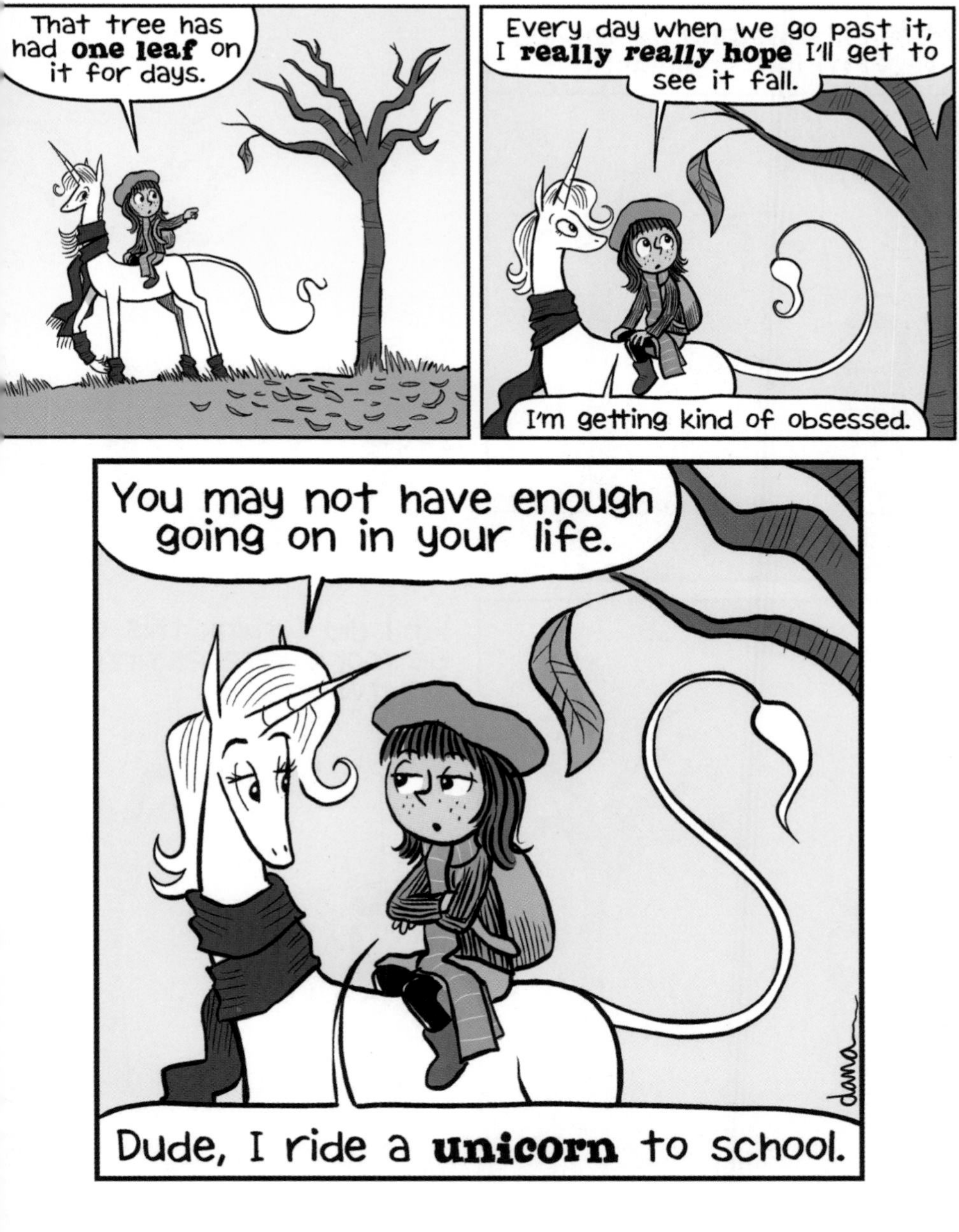
That tree has had **one leaf** on it for days.
Every day when we go past it, I **really** ***really*** **hope** I'll get to see it fall.
I'm getting kind of obsessed.
You may not have enough going on in your life.
Dude, I ride a **unicorn** to school.
dana

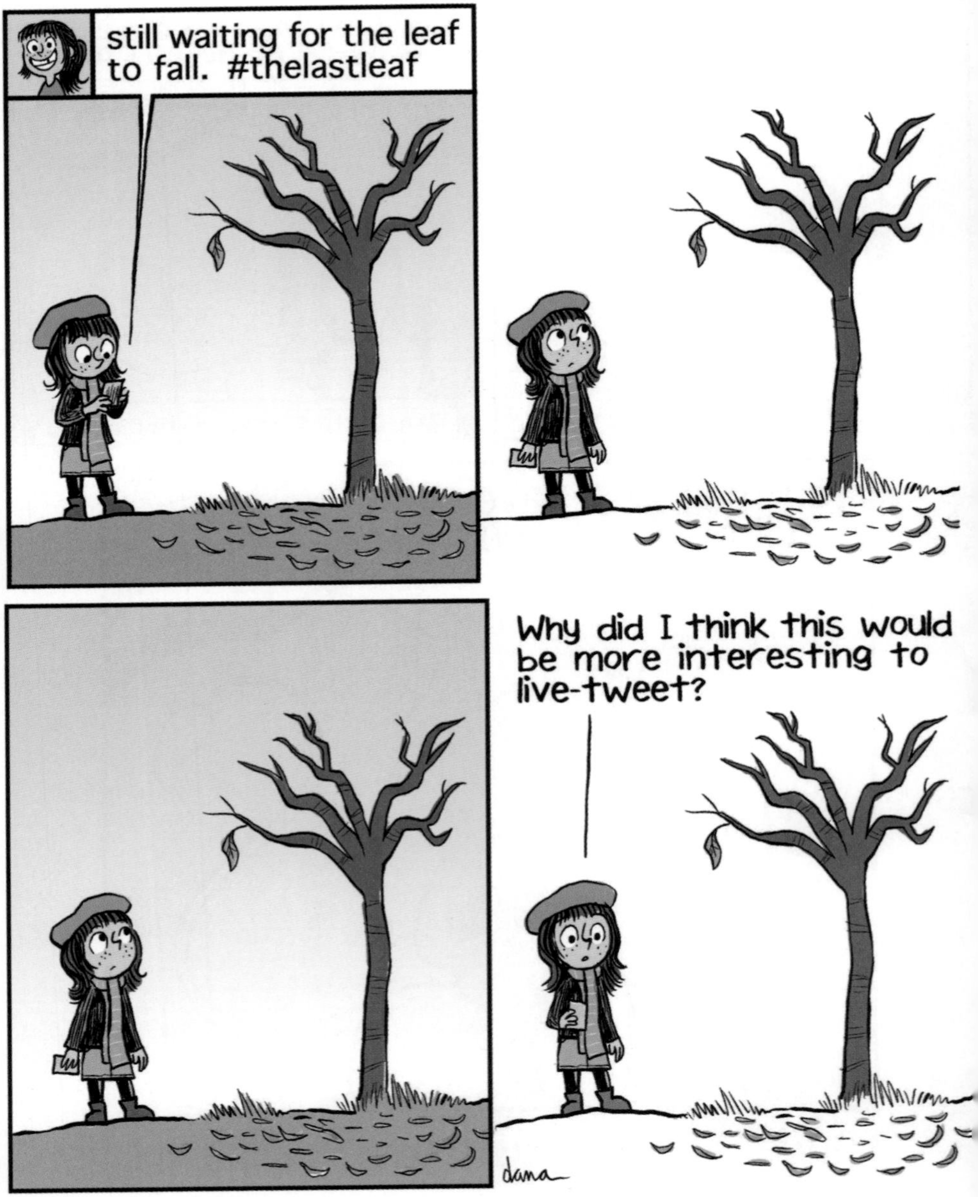
still waiting for the leaf to fall. #thelastleaf
Why did I think this would be more interesting to live-tweet?
dana

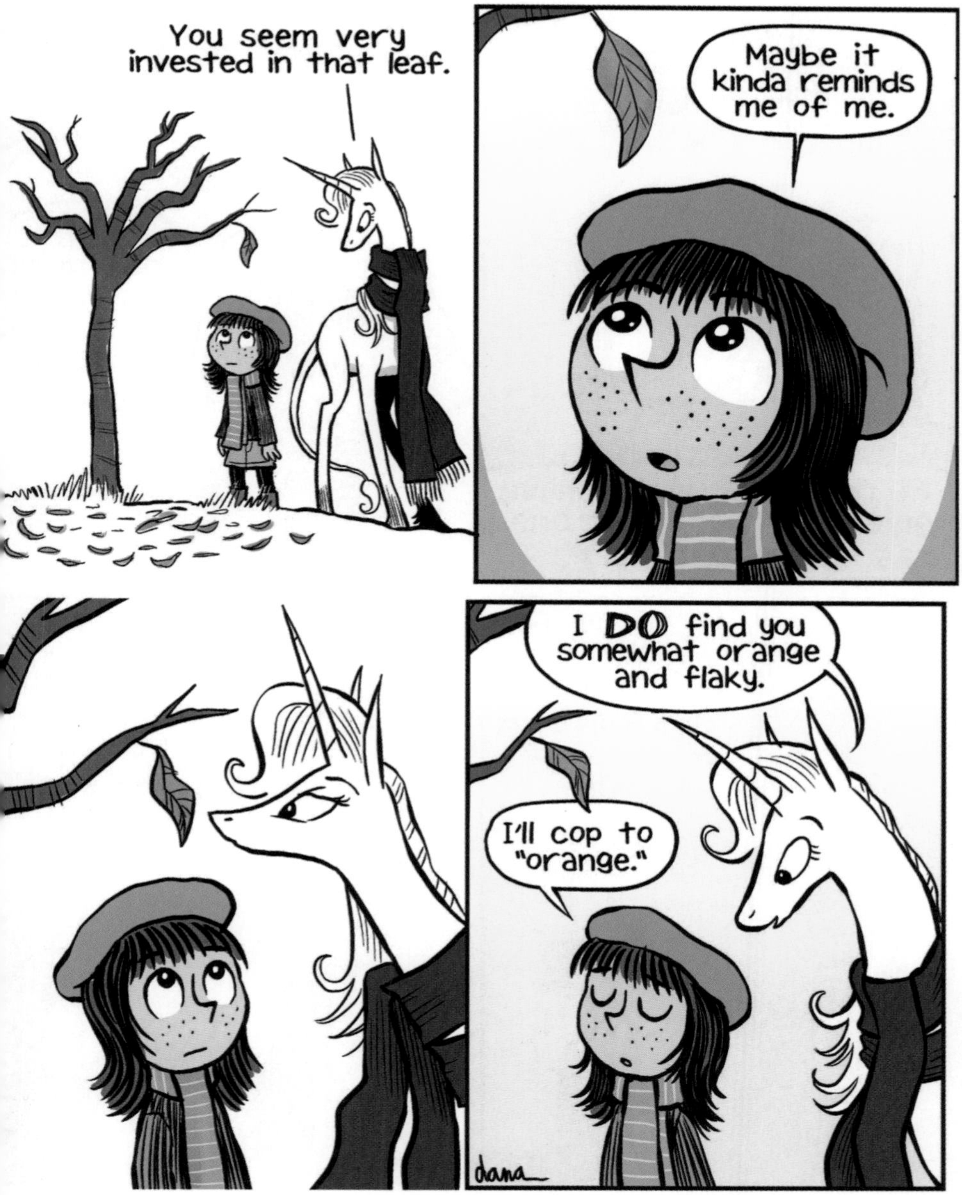
You seem very invested in that leaf.
Maybe it kinda reminds me of me.
I DO find you somewhat orange and flaky.
I'll cop to "orange."
dana

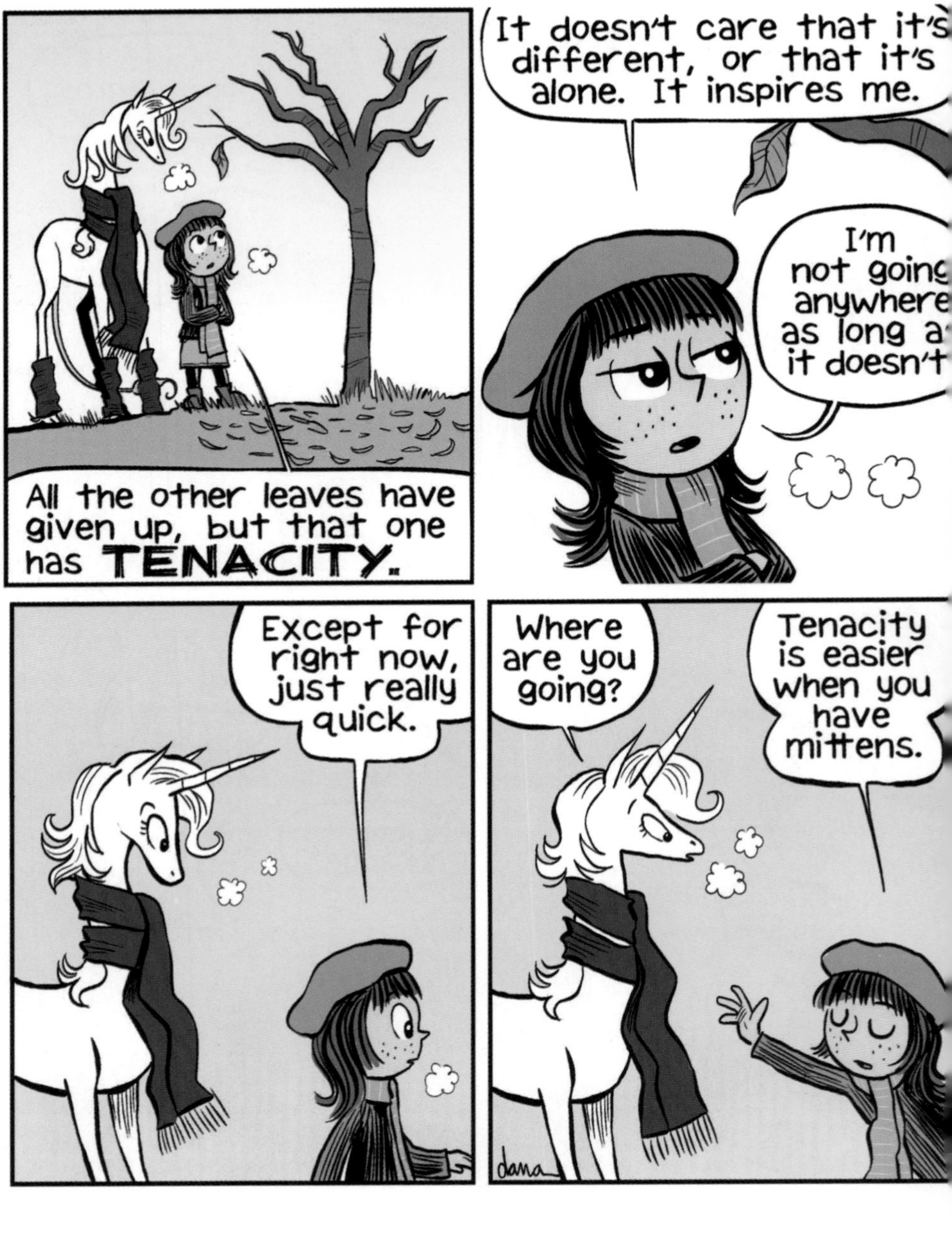

All the other leaves have given up, but that one has TENACITY.
It doesn't care that it's different, or that it's alone. It inspires me.
I'm not going anywhere as long a it doesn't
Except for right now, just really quick.
Where are you going?
Tenacity is easier when you have mittens.
dana

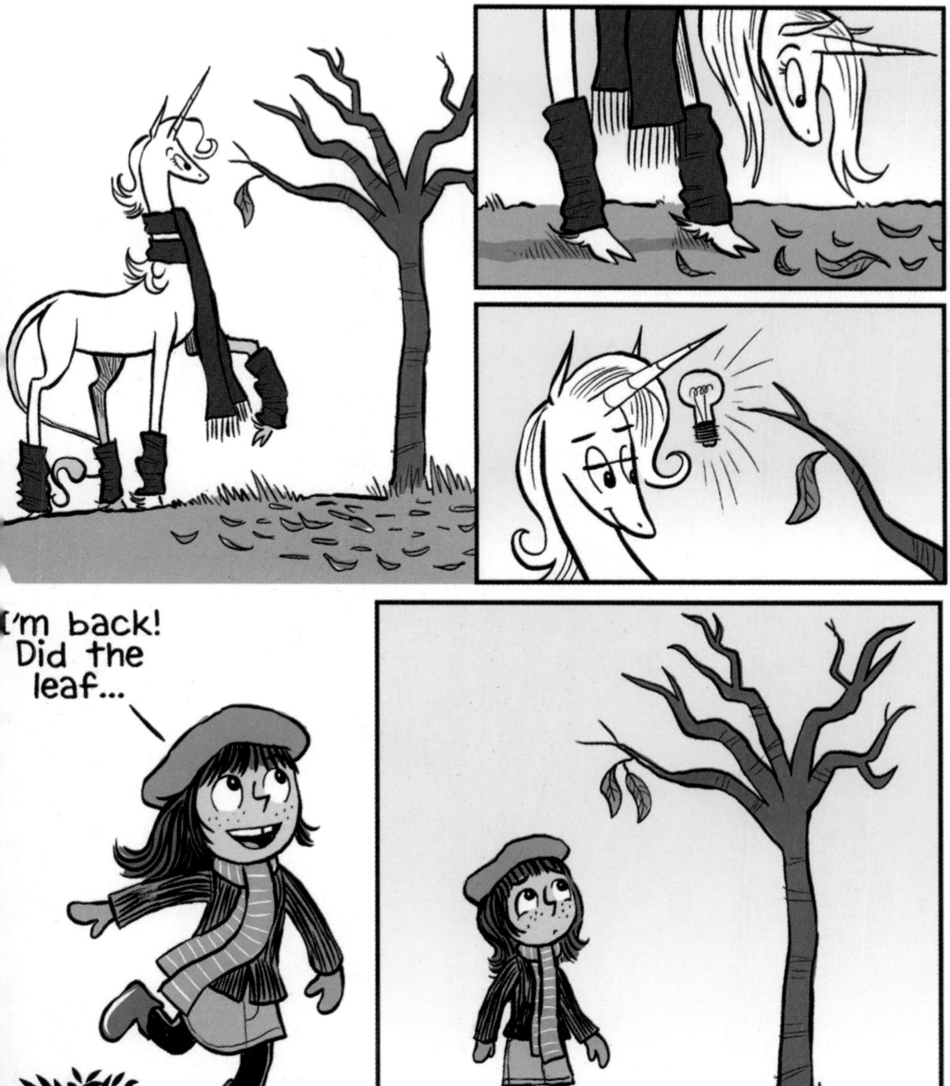
I'm back! Did the leaf...
dana

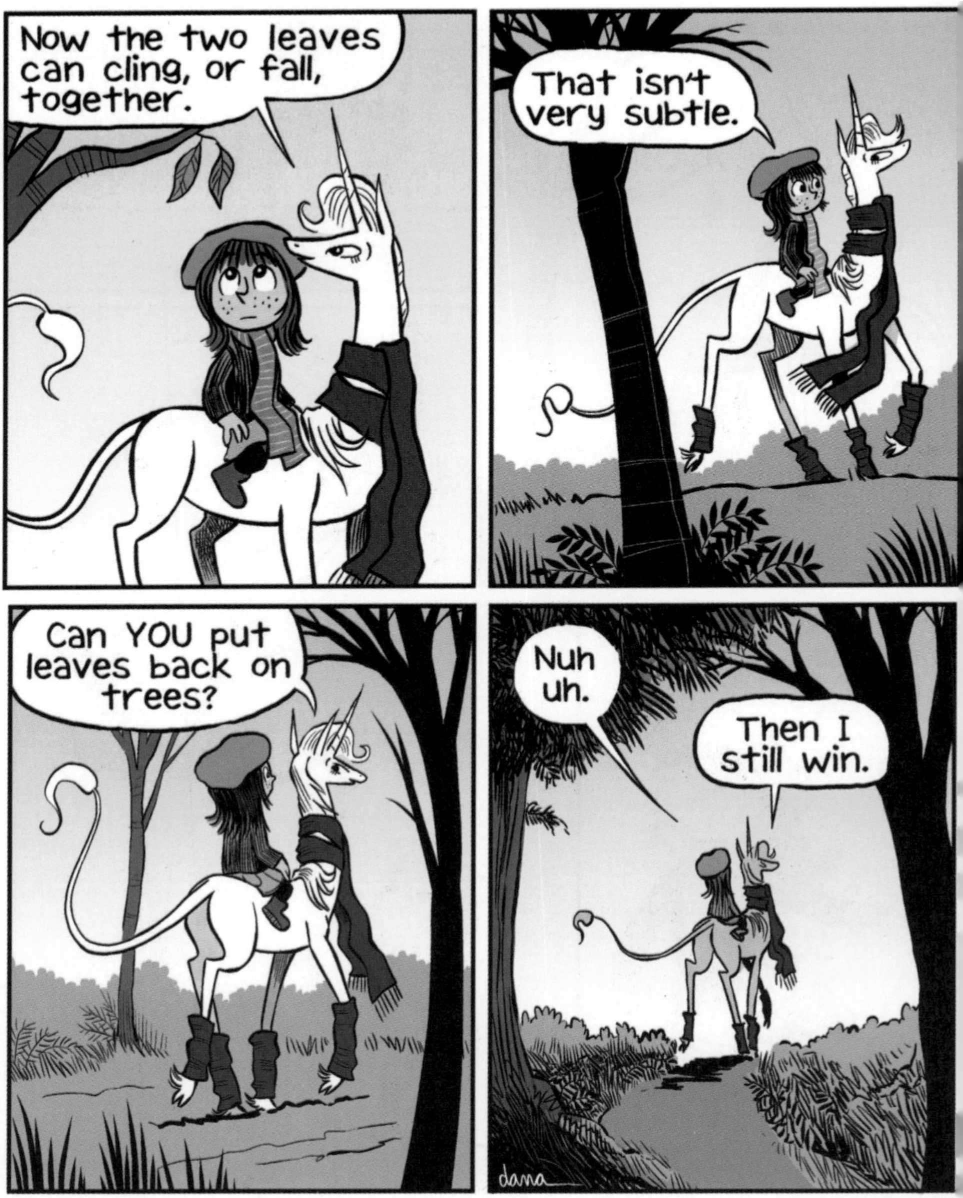
Now the two leaves can cling, or fall, together.
That isn't very subtle.
Can YOU put leaves back on trees?
Nuh uh.
Then I still win.
dana

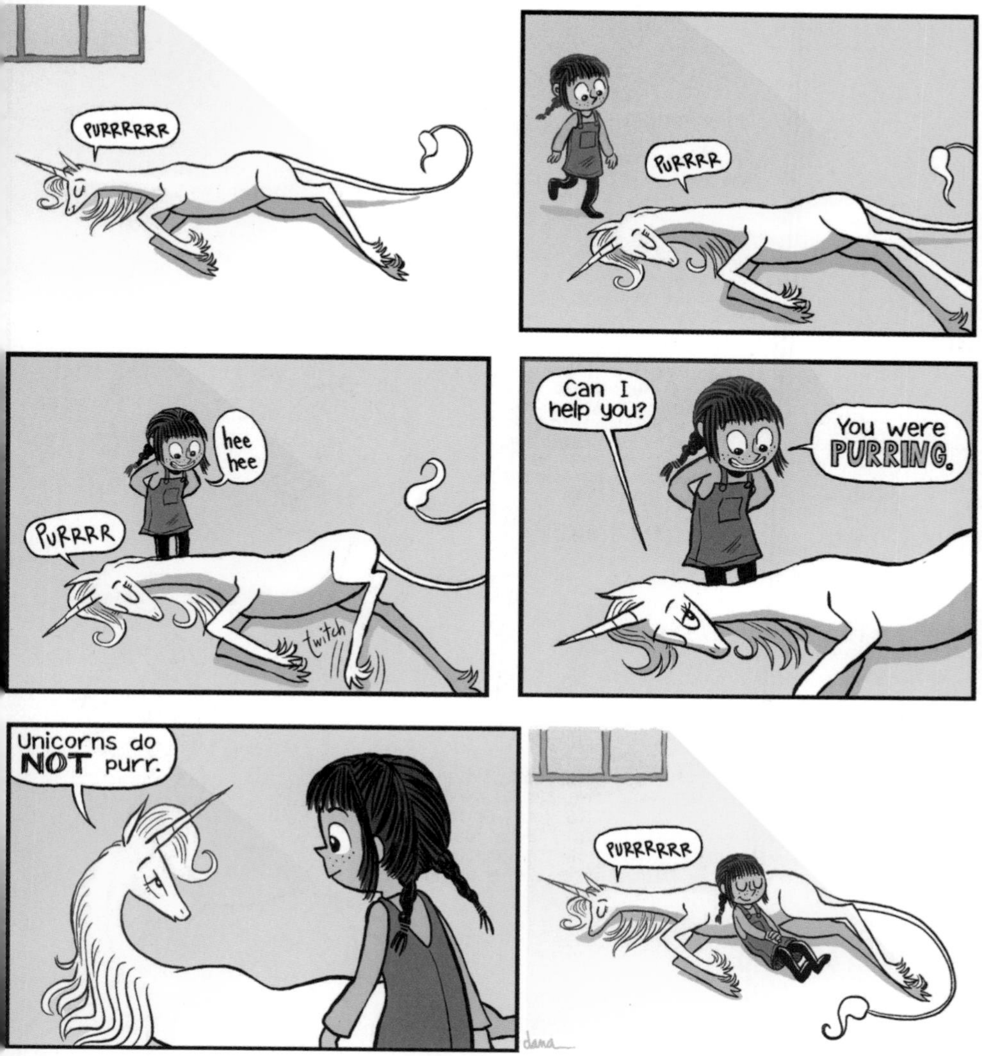
PURRRRRR
PURRRR
hee hee
PURRRR
twitch
Can I help you?
You were PURRING.
Unicorns do NOT purr.
PURRRRRR
dana

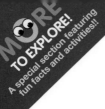

How to Draw Marigold

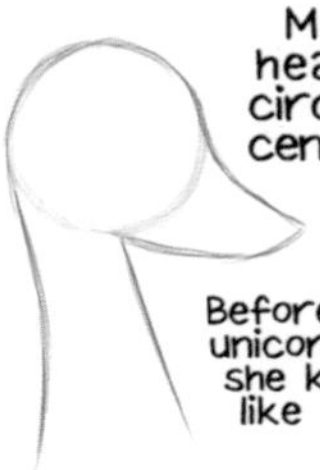

Marigold's head has a circle at the center of it.

Before I draw her unicorny features, she kind of looks like a dinosaur.

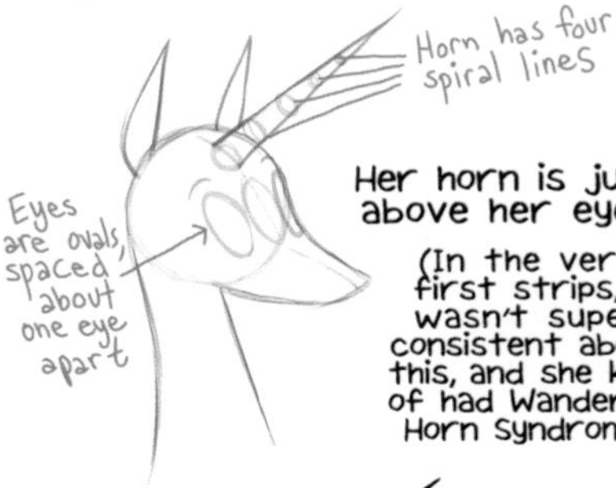
Horn has four spiral lines
Eyes are ovals, spaced about one eye apart

Her horn is just above her eyes.

(In the very first strips, I wasn't super consistent about this, and she kind of had Wandering Horn Syndrome.)

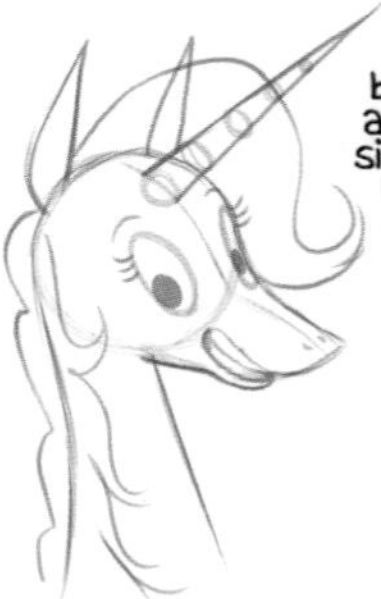

The front part of her mane is basically a swoop, and is on the far side of her head and horn no matter which way she's facing.

(It's magic.)

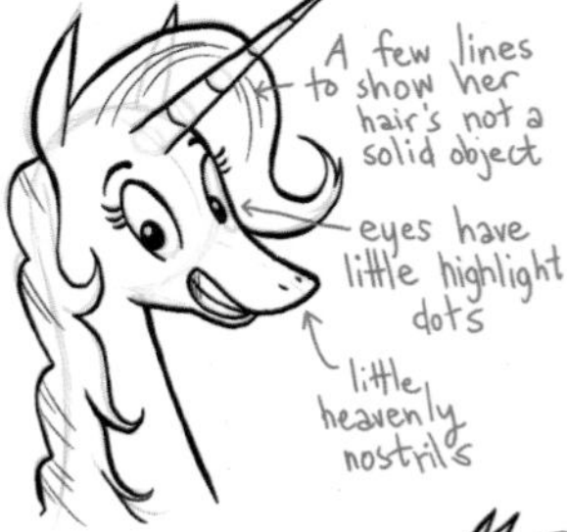
A few lines to show her hair's not a solid object
eyes have little highlight dots
little heavenly nostrils

Marigold is kind of swan-shaped, with a long slender neck.

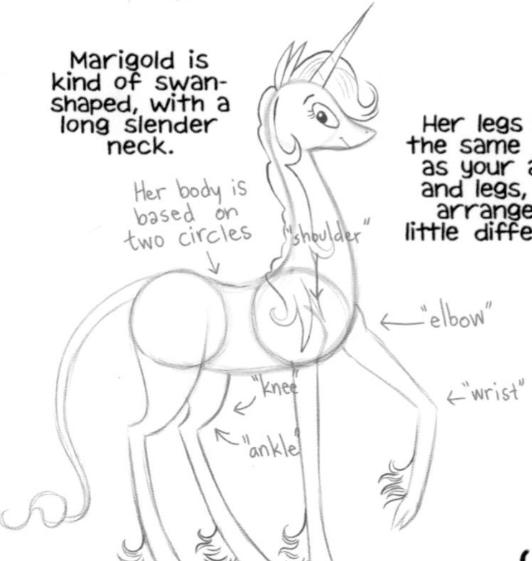
Her body is based on two circles
"shoulder"
"elbow"
"wrist"
"knee"
"ankle"

Her legs have the same joints as your arms and legs, just arranged a little differently.

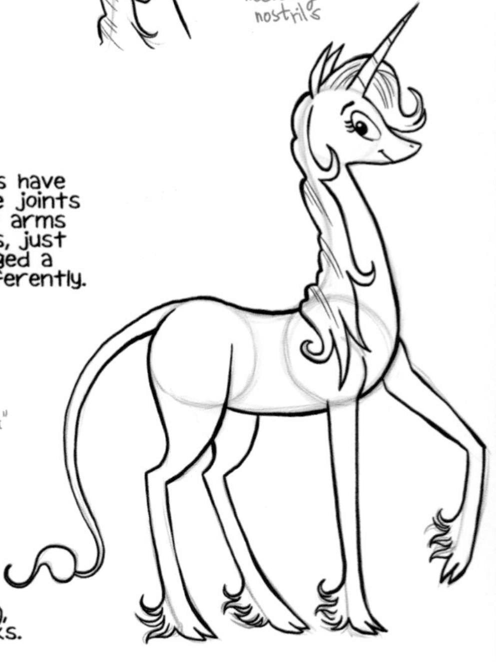

Her hooves are cloven (two-pointed), like a deer's. Also she has fluffy fetlocks.

How to Draw
Phoebe

Phoebe's head
is very round.

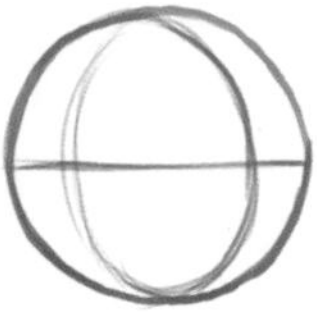

She has oval eyes
and a little point
for a nose.

Her hair has a
lot of lines in it.

She usually,
but not always,
wears a ponytail.

Eyes have
little highlight
dots

Freckles!

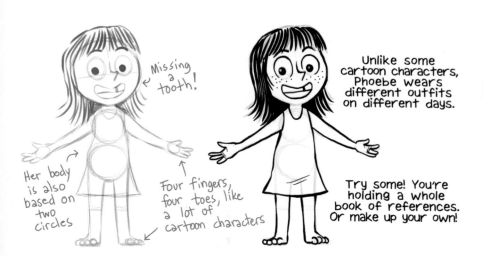

Missing
a
tooth!

Her body
is also
based on
two
circles

Four fingers,
four toes, like
a lot of
cartoon characters

Unlike some
cartoon characters,
Phoebe wears
different outfits
on different days.

Try some! You're
holding a whole
book of references.
Or make up your own!

Make a Marigold Heavenly Nostrils Stick Puppet

MATERIALS: white cardboard or white paper plate; scissors; pencil; large craft stick; markers; glue; tape; yarn

INSTRUCTIONS:

 Photocopy or trace the picture of Marigold, below.

 Color the picture with markers.

 Cut out the picture and glue it on the cardboard or paper plate.

 Cut the cardboard or paper plate around the picture.

 Tape the picture to the craft stick.

 Glue yarn for mane.

Make an Animated Flip Book

Cartoonists create stories in cartoon panels. Often cartoonists are also animators. An animator must capture a broad range of movements in order for a cartoon to look continuous. Animation is possible because of a phenomenon called "persistence of vision," when a sequence of images moves past the eye fast enough, the brain fills in the missing parts so the subject appears to be moving.

MATERIALS: paper, index cards, or sticky notes; stapler and staples, paper clips, or brads; pencil or marker

INSTRUCTIONS:

 Cut at least 20 strips of paper to be the exact same size, or use alternative materials, such as index cards or sticky notes.

 Fasten the pages together with a staple, brad, or paperclip.

 Pick a subject—anything from a bouncing ball to a running Marigold or a shooting star.

 Draw three key images first: the first on page one, the last on page twenty, and the middle on page ten, then fill in the pages between the key images.

Make Unicorn Slumber Party Snack Mix

Marigold's favorite food might be luscious, tender grass, but snack mix is required at a slumber party! This is a yummy, easy-to-make treat.

INGREDIENTS: 1 bag Bugles (they look just like unicorn horns!), 1 bag cheddar fish crackers, 1 bag round pretzels, 1 cup nuts (either cashews or peanuts), 1 package ranch salad dressing mix, ½ cup vegetable oil

INSTRUCTIONS:

 1 Mix the vegetable oil with the dressing mix in a small bowl.

 2 Put the Bugles, crackers, pretzels, and nuts in a large bowl.

 3 Add the dressing mixture to the large bowl and mix.

 4 Store in airtight container or storage bags.

Fun Things to Know About Unicorns

Even though the unicorn is a fictitious animal, it is one of the official animals of Scotland and was used on the royal coat of arms of Scotland in medieval times. (The red lion shown in the shield on the crest is the other official animal.)

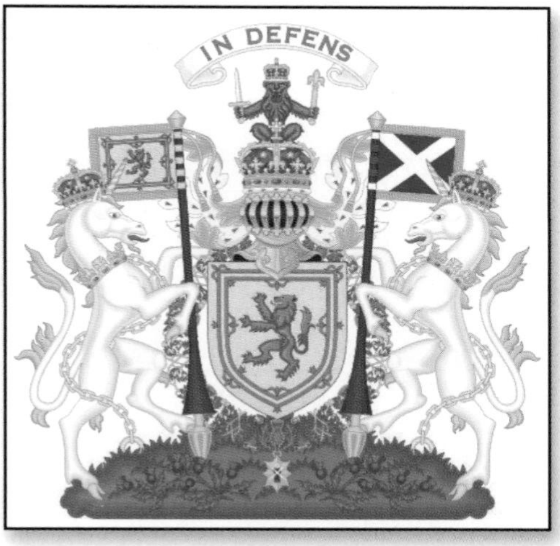
IN DEFENS

Lake Superior State University (through its Department of Natural Unicorns of the Unicorn Hunters) issues Questing Unicorn Licenses. Check it out at: www.lssu.edu/banished/uh_license.php.

Unicorns have appeared in folklore and art since ancient times in such different places as China, Greece, and France. One of the most famous depictions of unicorns is the *The Hunt of the Unicorn*, a series of seven tapestries that is in The Cloisters, which is part of The Metropolitan Museum of Art in New York. You can see them and learn more about them at: www.metmuseum.org/collections/search-the-collections/467642.

Create Your Own Cartoon Strip

The comic strip *Phoebe and Her Unicorn* began when Phoebe met Marigold and they became friends. Think about how you met one of your favorite friends and draw a comic strip about it.

MATERIALS: blank piece of paper, pencil, markers, or colored pencils

INSTRUCTIONS:

 Make three blank cartoon panels.

 Look at the example above to see how Dana Simpson set the stage for the meeting and ended with the punch line.

 Once you have decided on the story you want to tell, draw it in three panels. Remember, it should have a beginning, a middle, and an end.

 In the first panel, give your comic strip a name.

"We'll be friends forever, won't we, Pooh?" asked Piglet. "Even longer," Pooh answered.
—Winnie the Pooh

Andrews McMeel Publishing
a division of Andrews McMeel Universal
1130 Walnut Street, Kansas City, Missouri 64106

www.andrewsmcmeel.com

17 18 19 20 21 SDB 15 14 13 12 11

ISBN: 978-1-4494-4620-8

Library of Congress Control Number: 2013957200

Made by:
Shenzhen Donnelley Printing Company Ltd.
Address and location of manufacturer:
No. 47, Wuhe Nan Road, Bantian Ind. Zone,
Shenzhen China, 518129
11th Printing—11/13/17

ATTENTION: SCHOOLS AND BUSINESSES

Andrews McMeel books are available at quantity discounts with bulk purchase for educational, business, or sales promotional use. For information, please e-mail the Andrews McMeel Publishing Special Sales Department: specialsales@amuniversal.com.

Check out more *Phoebe and Her Unicorn*

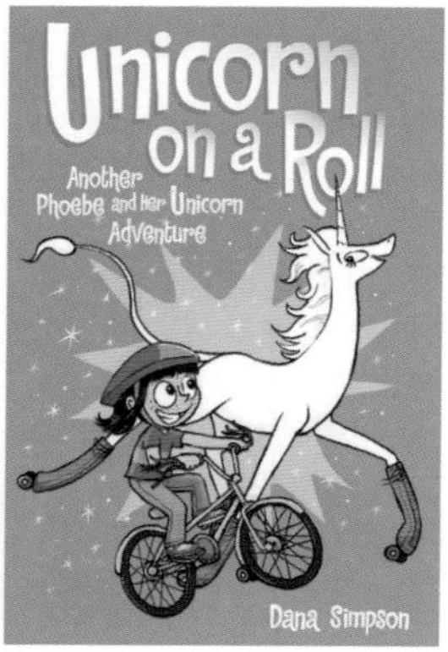
Unicorn on a Roll
Another Phoebe and Her Unicorn Adventure
Dana Simpson

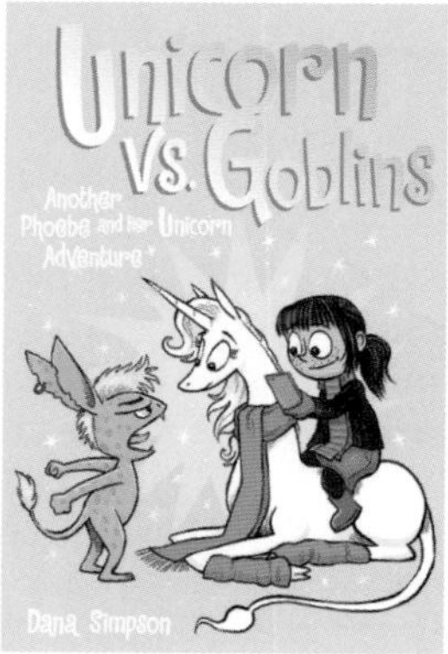
Unicorn vs. Goblins
Another Phoebe and Her Unicorn Adventure
Dana Simpson

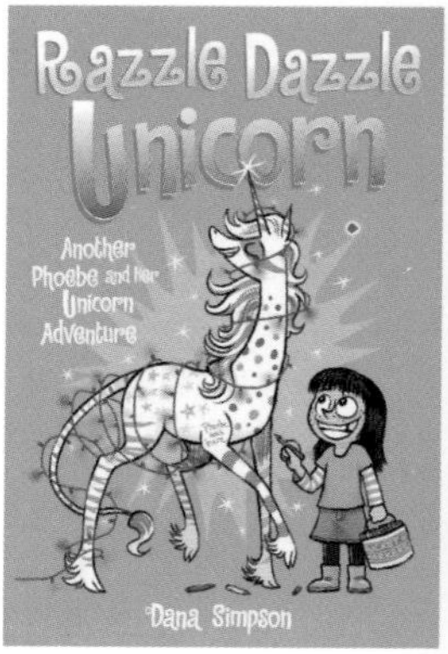
Razzle Dazzle Unicorn
Another Phoebe and Her Unicorn Adventure
Dana Simpson

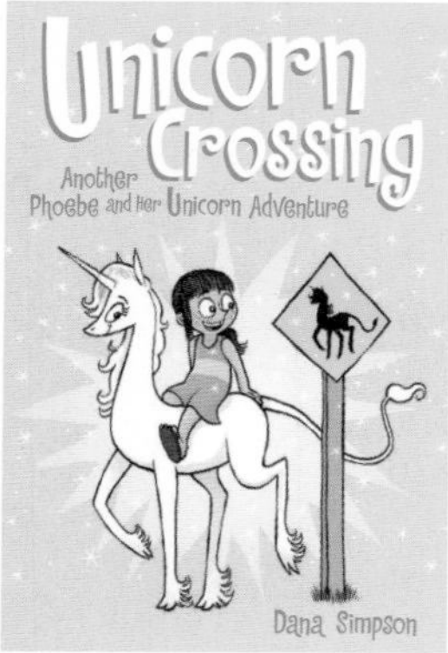
Unicorn Crossing
Another Phoebe and Her Unicorn Adventure
Dana Simpson

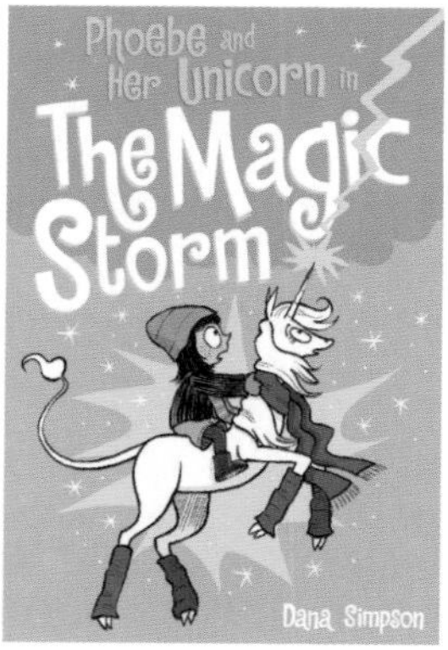
Phoebe and Her Unicorn in
The Magic Storm
Dana Simpson

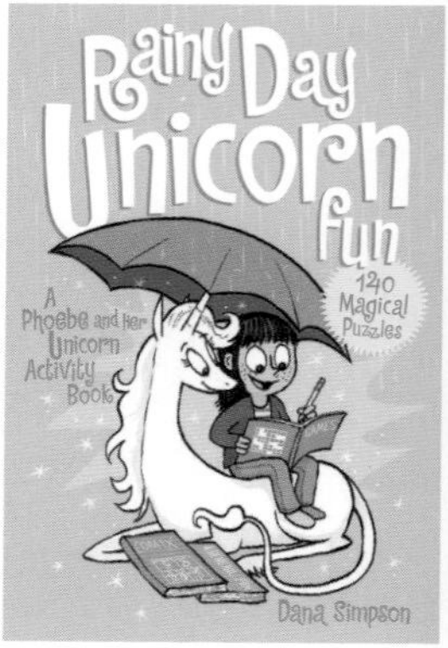
Rainy Day Unicorn Fun
140 Magical Puzzles
A Phoebe and Her Unicorn Activity Book
Dana Simpson

If you like Phoebe, look for these books!

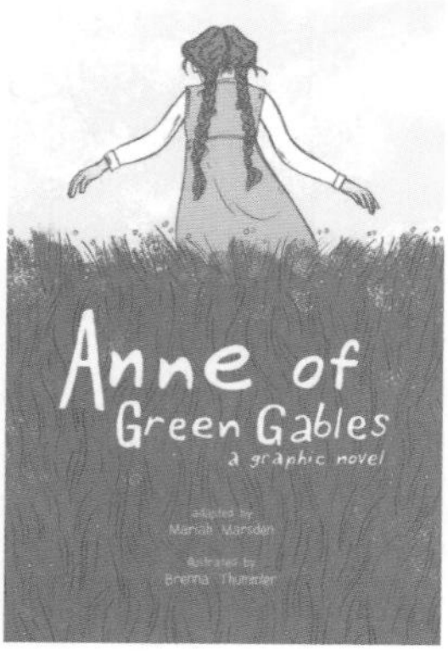
Anne of Green Gables
a graphic novel
adapted by Mariah Marsden
illustrated by Brenna Thummler

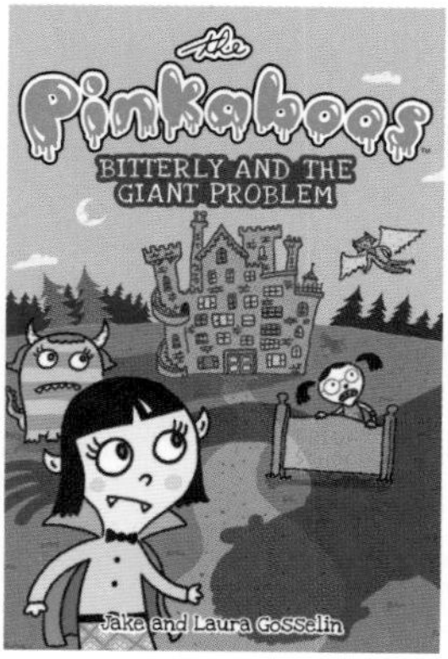
the Pinkaboos
Bitterly and the Giant Problem
Jake and Laura Gosselin

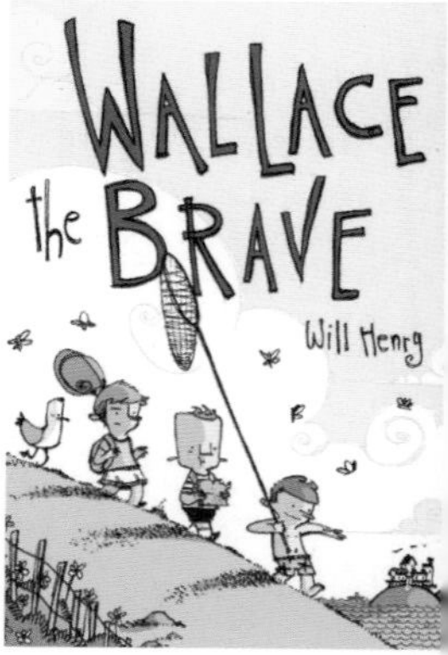
Wallace the Brave
Will Henry